CW00484737

COVERING SHAKESPEARE

David Weston

COVERING SHAKESPEARE

An Actor's Saga of Near Misses and Dogged Endurance

OBERON BOOKS
LONDON

WWW.OBERONBOOKS.COM

First published in 2014 by Oberon Books Ltd
521 Caledonian Road, London N7 9RH
Tel: +44 (0) 20 7607 3637 / Fax: +44 (0) 20 7607 3629
e-mail: info@oberonbooks.com
www.oberonbooks.com

A catalogue record for this book is available from the British Library.

HB ISBN: 978-1-78319-064-5
E ISBN: 978-1-78319-563-3

Cover design by James Illman

Printed and bound by Replika Press Pvt. Ltd., India.

For Michael Croft, who made it all happen
(for me and so many others)

My deepest thanks go to Steve Marians, who first put the idea of this book into my head, and to David Beresford and Michael Butcher for their perceptive advice and editing.

I am also indebted to Dame Diana Rigg's hilarious *No Stone Unturned*, Lord Olivier's *Confessions of an Actor*, *Small-Screen Shakespeare* by Peter Cochran, the writings of Kenneth Tynan, and a host of theatrical books too numerous to mention. I thank David Warner, John Fraser, Geoffrey Bayldon, Gerry O'Hara, Brian Croft and Robert Hardy for giving me their personal reminiscences, and to all those actors and actresses, past and present, who have exchanged stories with me in dressing room or pub.

'Actors live from hand to mouth; they plunge from want to luxury; they have no means of making money breed. Uncertain of the future, they make sure of the present moment. Chilled in poverty, steeped in contempt, they sometimes pass into the sunshine of fortune, and are lifted to the very pinnacle of public favour, but even there cannot calculate on the continuance of success, but are, "like the giddy sailor on the mast, ready with every blast to topple down into the fatal bowels of the deep."'

William Hazlitt, 30 November 1816.

Contents

Foreword

I found myself at a complete loss when I tried to find an adjective to define David Weston's *Covering McKellen*, his book about what happened behind the scenes when he understudied the great Sir Ian on a tour of *King Lear*. Yes, it was fascinating, often hilarious and fully deserved the Theatre Book Prize it went on to win. But how to evoke its mix of the rueful, the jokey, the exasperated, the wistful, the salty, the enthusiastic, the gossipy, and plenty more, including the earnestness of Weston's obsession with Chelsea Football Club? I fell back on quirky, 'wonderfully quirky', feeling and still feeling that my description was inadequate.

Well, I'll have to be almost more inadequate about Weston's *Covering Shakespeare*. It's quirky in form as well as style. In the vast forest of Shakespeare Studies, with still more trees chopped down every day to provide yet more forgettable critical tomes and boring PhD theses, is there a book quite like it? It mixes 'tattle', which is Weston's word for stage history and theatrical anecdote, with personal memoir. As such, it somehow reconciles scholarship with entertainment and entertainment with the kind of observation that can only come from the shop floor. It lets you see each of the thirty-seven plays from the point of view of an actor as well as a lover of Shakespeare – and always in that idiosyncratic and, yes, quirky way.

Doing this, Weston draws on experience and more experience. As we discover, his sixty-year career began at Alleyn's School in Dulwich, where an inspirational and theatrically important figure, the late Michael Croft, happened to be a teacher. Croft directed school plays before going on to found the National Youth Theatre, casting Weston in leading roles, among them Mark Antony in a critically acclaimed *Julius Caesar* on Shaftesbury Avenue. Indeed, one of the pleasures of *Covering Shakespeare* is that it celebrates figures Weston remembers well but are now in danger of being forgotten: not just Croft but David Scase, a pioneer of regional rep who launched the careers of Robert Stephens, Patrick Stewart and many others, and Anthony Quayle, who turned down a Hollywood career in order to transform Stratford's Shakespeare Memorial Theatre into a centre of excellence, a magnet for major actors, and, as a result, a more than suitable home for the RSC when Peter Hall formed it in 1961.

But then Weston has worked for or with important and exciting figures galore, making a journey through his book a journey through modern theatrical and sometimes cinematic history. He's played Richard Burton's acolyte, Brother John, in the film of *Becket* and Willoughby to Kevin Spacey's stage *Richard II*. He's been directed by Zeffirelli and Trevor Nunn – in his view a refreshingly passionate exception to the Oxbridge-educated directors he finds too cerebral – and has himself directed Colin Firth as Mustard Seed in *A Midsummer Night's Dream* at the Roundhouse. He's played Falstaff in a touring *Henry IV* that co-opted a 'little bright-eyed boy called Ben Kingsley as a non-speaking soldier', been Paul Scofield's dresser, played Laertes to Richard Chamberlain's Hamlet, supped with Simone Signoret, played a racist mechanic in an improvised play directed by a fellow RSC member called Mike Leigh, spent a 'very rumbustious night with a purple-faced Trevor Howard' and had an affably patronizing John Gielgud in the back of the minicab he was then driving.

That last moment occurred during a particularly low period in a career that, as Weston confessed in *Covering McKellen* and repeats in *Covering Shakespeare*, hasn't lived up to his original expectations. After all, he won a scholarship to RADA and then its prestigious Silver Medal. But there came a point when, despite encouragement from men in high places, he realized 'I was never going to make it big'. Hence the subtitle to *Covering Shakespeare*, *'An Actor's Saga of Near Misses and Dogged Endurance'*. But does he really need to describe himself in the book itself as an 'old fart' and an 'old ham'? Here's my one quarrel with a fine book. Hams are not often as acute as Weston and, candid and sometimes sharp though he also is, seldom as generous to other actors' good work. To read him on Henry Goodman in *The Merchant of Venice* – 'a heart-wrenching Shylock, which I think will never be bettered' – is to encounter a man who loves Shakespeare, the theatre and the craft of acting with a disinterested passion rare in so competitive a profession.

And farts of any age are never as mentally lively and responsive as Weston. How many have launched on a second career in their seventies, writing not just the *Covering* books but a wonderfully readable novel about the further adventures of Dickens's Artful Dodger, *Dodger Down Under*? And what radiates from his latest book is an inquiring mind, an infectious curiosity that extends way beyond the obvious questions about the Bard and the theatre. How many old farts would ask why so many men called Antonio in Shakespeare seem to be gay? Or wonder if Adrian Lester, 'excellent' as Henry V, won't be the first black actor to be knighted? Or point out what, while Shakespearean characters sometimes belch, he seldom if ever mentions, er, farting?

Quirky, yes. Unpredictable, certainly. Amusing and instructive too.

Benedict Nightingale, 2014

'It is the habitual tendency of old men to bore their juniors with reminiscences and old-world sentiments.'

Why have I put together this mishmash of facts and reminiscences? Why should anyone be interested in my memories and opinions when the shelves are bursting with biographies of far more illustrious thespians and the studious works of acclaimed scholars? I have watched and acted Shakespeare for over sixty years, appearing in twenty-nine of his thirty-seven plays, many of them several times. Whenever I see current productions my mind is filled with half-forgotten images and voices long silent. Though I have had a varied career, including leading or featured roles in more than twenty films, a fair share of television from classic series and soaps to *Doctor Who* and *Basil Brush*, and have acted Shaw, Stoppard, Ayckbourn, Pinter, Congreve, Chekhov and all the other usual suspects, Shakespeare's plays have been with me at the crucial points in my life. I have played the major roles as well as the minor, on stage, film, radio and television, from the National Theatre to the outmost limits of Fringe, from Hollywood to Hong Kong. I have worked with the greats, the mediocre and the forgotten. In the following pages I have 'covered' the plays in their most likely chronological order with several diversions, discussions and diatribes along the way, adding a little theatrical tattle, noting the more intriguing triumphs and disasters. I've also added an appendix in which I have set down the basic plots, for those 'old men who forget', and skated over the well-trod tracks of Shakespeare's life and times. This all may seem like an old thespian blundering between too many pieces of furniture, but I believe it may interest the general theatre-goer as well as being a cautionary tale to the aspiring young actor and actress.

My previous book, '*Covering McKellen*,' was described as 'salty' and 'splendidly indiscreet' – I hope these latest 'untutored lines' may be thought worthy of some acceptance.

School Plays

I was a tubby thirteen year-old in 1952, not very good at anything, when my father died at the tragically early age of forty-eight. He owned a fish and chip shop in Brixton Market as my grandfather had before him, and I suppose I would have followed if it hadn't been for Michael Croft. He was my form master at Alleyn's, which was then a direct grant Grammar School. Croft had been born illegitimate, a terrible social stigma in pre-war Britain, and had been brought up by a series of foster parents without ever having had a proper home. Perhaps, because he had never known a father himself, he felt a special compassion for me and suggested that I apply for a part in *Hamlet,* which he was about to put on as the school play. I had no particular interest in drama, but I dutifully stayed behind after school one dark, foggy, wintry afternoon and sat at the back of a classroom, I think I was the only third-former there, whilst boys from the upper echelons of the school read for the leading parts. Everyone expected Julian Glover, who had already established a reputation for being an outstanding actor, to be cast as Hamlet. They read slowly through the first act. I began to wonder what I was doing there as boys stumbled and droned through unintelligible lines, when suddenly a voice rang out, clear and resonant. The words, magnificent, poetic words were full of meaning, passion and pain – I listened and understood. I felt Hamlet's anguish and grief for his father, especially; '*But two months dead – nay, not so much, not two…*' – my mother was already seeing the man who would eventually become my stepfather. I knew at that moment I wanted to be able to express feelings and speak like that. I couldn't score goals at football or make runs at cricket, but I might just possibly be able to do that. I raised my eyes from the text of my ink-stained school edition and looked towards the desk where the voice was coming from, anticipating the blonde head of Julian Glover, but saw instead the untidy locks of a rough fifth-former called John Stride. Julian suffered one of the few setbacks of his extremely successful career and ended up as Laertes, whilst John became the first of

Michael Croft's long line of protégés or 'golden lads'. I was given the four lines of the sailor that delivers Hamlet's letter to Horatio and endeavoured to make the very most of them. And that was how it all began.

South London was gloomy and dreary in 1952. Meat and bacon were still rationed; bomb sites were still all over the place. Some of my school-fellows lived in prefabs; the poorer ones had gas-light in their homes. We had thick smogs throughout the winter; the trees were all sooty and brown. There were hardly any restaurants – Indian and Chinese establishments were only to be found in way-off, exotic places in the East End. The highlight of the week was a visit to the cinema – and cinemas really were picture palaces then, not poky multi-screens. Brixton boasted the Astoria, where you watched the screen amid an enchanting Mediterranean landscape, and the baroque, marble-fronted, Palladium, complete with dome. We went every week no matter what was playing, and watched entranced through the thick fug of cigarettes. Only seven years after the defeat of Hitler and the Cold War was at its height. The nuclear threat seemed very real, we were well within the range of Russian rockets and could still remember the sound the German ones had made. Boys left school, were called up for their two years of National Service, and in a few months could find themselves fighting in Korea or the Malayan jungle. Every Friday afternoon was dedicated to compulsory training in the CCF (Combined Cadet Force); we went to school that day in Army uniform with brasses polished and belts blancoed. We sat each morning for assembly in the Great Hall and gazed at the hundreds of names on the War Memorial and wondered where they would find space for us. But rehearsing Shakespeare with Croft made me aware of another world, the vast and entrancing world of literature and drama that existed beyond the bounds of Brixton. I loved the security of going into the rehearsal after school and entering the enclosed realm of the play – I still do over sixty years later – but it all started with Croft. Nearly every actor I know tells of a great teacher at school who inspired him, but Michael Croft was really something different. My dear, departed friend, Simon Ward, described it best: 'There is a sort of torpor of adolescence: you do not know quite where you are going so it's best not to go anywhere, and a thin layer of ice forms above the surface of ambition and hopes – if you pop your head up through the ice who knows what's going to happen? So you just lie there and wait under the ice. Croft went round with a bloody great axe and SMACK! He pulled you out from underneath it.'

He certainly pulled me out – I'd be frying chips to this day if it hadn't been for him. Michael was a tough northerner who'd served as an Able Seaman throughout the war before going to Oxford in the vintage post-war intake on an ex-serviceman scholarship. Though his ambition was to become a writer, he had become deeply involved in the University theatrical scene and had briefly, but unsuccessfully, tried his hand at professional acting. He'd applied for the teaching job at Alleyn's to further his literary ambitions because the novelist, Edward Upward, friend and associate of Christopher Isherwood and W.H. Auden, was head of English; but Michael Croft only found his true calling when he began directing boys in Shakespeare. Following that *Hamlet,* every year throughout my adolescence he put on another play – *Macbeth, Antony & Cleopatra, Henry V* and *Henry IV Part Two*. The productions became more and more ambitious and successful. Croft would rehearse us late into the night with hardly any thought of tomorrow's school, keeping us going on bottled beer. Often my stepfather, with an eye on the takings, would bring left-over fish and chips from the shop in Brixton and sell them, at knock-down rates, to the famished boys and Croft – who was never known to refuse food or drink.

Croft was a dab hand at publicity; we received glowing notices from leading critics in the national press, including W.A. Darlington of the *Daily Telegraph* and the *News Chronicle's* Alan Dent, acolyte to the legendary James Agate, both of whom were adequately supplied with gin and sherry in the headmaster's study. Other schools, including establishments for the education of girls, for us a very rare and desirable commodity, began to send parties from all over London. Our urinals were modestly boarded up for their convenience. Instead of the one or two performances of the usual school play, we ended up doing weekly runs; by the time Croft finished at Alleyn's well over a hundred pupils were involved in the various facets of the production. Those boys I grew up with would eventually become the nucleus of the National Youth Theatre. They were not effete types, as most actors were before the explosion of *Look Back in Anger* in 1956, but sturdy athletes and footballers – Croft also coached the Under-Sixteen Soccer team. Julian Glover, who was never really one of us, soon left for the Royal Academy of Dramatic Art (RADA), to be followed by a few terms later by John Stride, but Ken Farrington, Richard Hampton, Col Farrell, Simon Ward, myself and a host of others stayed with Croft for years. Not just actors. Brian Croft (no relation) was the Stage Manager. He would go on to be Production Manager for The Rolling Stones, Stage Manager for Live Aid and, ironically for a life-long leftie, to design the lighting for the Queen's Golden Jubilee Concert at Buckingham Palace. Brian Eatwell, a very pretty boy who sometimes played female roles (although a multitude of South London girls could confirm that he was one hundred-per-cent heterosexual) helped with the scenery. He ended up as an award-winning set designer in Hollywood. Michael Hastings, whose ambition was to become an athletics coach, left school early to become a tailor, but rapidly transmogrified into one of the original Angry Young Men at the Royal Court.

Michael Croft opened the eyes of so many of us, as we sat drinking beer out of quart-sized, screw-top brown bottles (whatever happened to them?) in his poky bedsit in Lordship Lane, Dulwich. My stepfather often voiced his suspicions, homosexuality was still a criminal offence, but it never occurred to us that Croft was 'queer' – gay meant something different then. He was tough, addicted to sports and Frank Sinatra, and as far as I know never laid a finger on one of us. I've read somewhere that Ian McKellen claimed he only became an actor because of the boys. If I'm really honest, pulling girls had quite a bit to do with my theatrical ambitions. John Stride and Richard Hampton, in their heroic roles, had plenty of admirers at Lewisham High and Mary Datchelor's, but the parts I played, especially Pistol and Falstaff, failed to arouse any female excitement. I did attain a certain status among my fellow pupils, but even then I was definitely a second-class citizen compared with the least accomplished member of the First Eleven.

There was some live theatre in our manor before mass television arrived with ITV in September 1955. The art deco Empress at Brixton was home to the last days of music hall. One of their advertising boards was outside our fish shop and we received complimentary tickets each week. I saw Frankie Howerd, Ted Ray, the young Bruce Forsyth (even Brucie was young once), Jimmy Wheeler, Two-Ton Tessie O'Shea, Alma Cogan, and, not least, Laurel and Hardy on their farewell tour. Their dresser even got them cod and chips, wrapped in newspaper, from our shop, which was just across the road from the stage door. I always found them funnier than

Chaplin, who was supposed to have been a customer in my grandfather's time. Streatham Hill Theatre, now a bingo hall, had pre- and post-West End plays; I can just remember seeing Bela Lugosi as Dracula and being very disappointed. There was even a tatty repertory company 'The Court Players' at the Palace Theatre by Camberwell Green. I never saw the rep but I did catch one of the 'girlie' shows that took over for a year or two before it was demolished. In those days of the Lord Chamberlain, the girls were not allowed to move, and one morning at school we read with great excitement in *The Daily Mirror* that the extremely well-endowed Peaches Page had run across the stage naked at the sight of a mouse. My close friend, the highly-sexed P.R.R. Jackson, a hefty shot-putter trained by Michael Hastings, persuaded me to accompany him to Camberwell that very night. Feeling extremely guilty, with our school caps thrust deep into our pockets, we obtained entry claiming to be eighteen, and sat among heavily breathing rain-coated men in the faded gilt of the once splendid theatre. But alas, the mouse did not make a re-appearance. Neither did Peaches – we learnt to our mortification that she had been sacked. There were girls aplenty but not one of them so much as flicked a nipple – I know, my eyes were fixed on them throughout. Even so, both of us found the evening truly erotic. We dreamt about it for weeks. It was the rarity of the occasion. The crude porn now available on tap on the internet and digital television was beyond our wildest comprehension.

And, of course, the most famous theatre in England was only a tram ride away. Croft's adherents became regulars in the gallery of the Old Vic. I think we got in for one and six. Anyway it was even cheaper than Travelex at the Olivier. We were doubly fortunate to see the plays in lavish but straightforward productions. Take a look at the photographs and you will see what I mean. So many modern directors and designers forget that the majority of their audience are seeing the plays for the first time and mangle the plots, working against basic sense, trying to demonstrate how clever and inventive they are. The anonymous critic of *The Morning Herald* got it right in 1814: 'This, in the saucy jargon of the day, may be called "a new reading", but it is a proceeding that is deeply injurious to common sense.' In recent years there have been *Tempests* set in the Arctic, *Macbeths* in kitchens and *Merchants of Venice* in Las Vegas. The Hamlet of that superb actor Martin Sheen seemed to be located in a mental home. On top of that Horatio and Osric were played by the same woman. How on earth can kids be expected to understand what Shakespeare wrote? I am not against modern dress but I believe it should only be used if it helps to illuminate the play. As I write, a production of *Macbeth* is currently playing at the Whitehall Theatre with a lavatory prominently positioned on stage. Pathetic! *'This castle hath a pleasant seat,'* has been a schoolboy joke for generations – not to mention '*rhubarb, senna and purgative drugs*'. Throughout the sixties I heard smart young directors from the universities speak in a derogatory manner of the 'Old Vic' style of acting. It is natural to be most impressed by what you see for the first time when young, but I really believe the acting we saw then was superior to much of the stuff that is served up now at Stratford and the National. For one thing, even from the back of the gallery, we could hear every word. We weighed the talents and form of John Neville, Paul Rogers, Barbara Jefford, Derek Godfrey, Paul Daneman, Maggie Smith and the up-and-coming film star Richard Burton, as if they were players in our local football team.

We somehow missed Sir Donald Wolfit giving his Lear and Macbeth at the Camden Palace, but we did catch him depicting a rather slippery Cardinal in the West End. We weren't all that impressed. Croft nevertheless invited him to come to the school and judge the poetry reading prize. To our surprise Wolfit accepted. Edward Upward, one of the few masters to own a car, albeit a pre-war one, was dispatched to Stockwell tube station in his rickety Rover to pick up the knight and his lady wife. I can still see Sir Donald mounting the school steps, like Tamburlaine entering Persepolis, wearing thick tortoise-shell framed glasses and pink silk handkerchief bursting from his breast-pocket. Stride and Hampton had left by then. I'd never won a prize the entire time I was at school; I really thought this time I was in with a chance. I gave what I thought was a rousing rendering of Browning's *How They Brought the Good News from Ghent to Aix.* I went off Sir Donald completely when he awarded it to some little swot called Algie, who did, what I considered, an extremely abstruse passage from Wordsworth's *Lines Composed a few miles above Tintern Abbey.* Years later I spent several days with Wolfit on the film *Becket* and found him a charming companion. I forced myself not to mention the prize.

I watched Glover, Stride and Farrington win scholarships to RADA under Croft's tuition, but was not sure if I had enough talent to follow them. 'You'll see more dinner times than dinners,' was my stepfather's response whenever the subject was broached at home. I hung on at school

– Croft told me to wait until I was eighteen. I was good at English and History by then, but there was no hope of university. You couldn't read the Arts without O-level Latin and I was hopeless at that; it was RADA or nothing. Then Croft's novel, *Spare the Rod,* became a bestseller and he decided to quit teaching to pursue his original ambition of becoming a full-time writer. I and many others felt desolated and abandoned – the centre of our universe was being taken away. I'm sure Croft had already carefully planted it in our minds, but we discussed it at school before a handful of us went to his flat in Lordship Lane one Sunday morning and begged him to put on a play in the school holidays. That was how the National Youth Theatre began.

King Henry VI
(Parts One, Two and Three)

'Few playwrights are more regularly done so badly as Shakespeare.'

Memories: Ironically enough these first acknowledged plays marked the humble beginning of my professional career. It was the summer of 1960 and I was finishing my National Service at Woolwich, waiting to return for my final year at RADA. My regiment, still equipped with heavy anti-aircraft guns that had been obsolete since 1942, was finally being disbanded, and there was little for me to do. There never had been much. I had been a terrible soldier: a senior officer once told me I was the reason why the Government had decided to abolish National Service. Peter Dews, a chubby bundle of Yorkshire wit and exuberance, who bore a strong resemblance to both Tweedledum and Tweedledee, had persuaded the BBC to let him televise all of Shakespeare's history plays from *Richard II* to *Richard III*, in live, one-hour episodes. Nothing quite like it had been attempted before and most certainly will never be attempted again. They went out fortnightly over thirty weeks and the viewing figures never dropped below five million. Peter called the series: *An Age of Kings*. The more effete members of the ensemble cast, revelling in unaccustomed long-term employment, called it affectionately, *An Eternity of Queens*. It was nevertheless groundbreaking television, with some outstanding performances, not least from young Sean Connery as an extremely Scottish Hotspur. One could almost feel sorry for Andrew Faulds, the future rabble-rousing M.P. who was playing Angus, the official Scot – how could he possibly compete? Two years before Bond, Connery had a charm and romantic innocence that no other Hotspur I've seen since has been able to equal. Richard Burton once told me that only great actors can play kings and Robert Hardy certainly could. In my opinion his Henry V was the second only to Olivier's. Eileen Atkins, then married to

Julian Glover, made the most of her first break on television as a freakily sexy Joan of Arc.

There was an excitement, terror and immediacy about acting live on television that young actors today can only guess at. The Duchess of York was depicted by Violet Carson, who was soon to don a hair-net and become a national treasure as Ena Sharples in *Coronation Street*. One transmission night she assumed that she had finished, got changed and took a bus home. As she passed through Shepherd's Bush, she glanced idly at the television sets flickering in a Rediffusion window and, with increasing horror, watched a scene she'd forgotten she was in. She needn't have worried; the other actors, being seasoned pros, simply worked the lines without her. On another occasion an unscheduled royal broadcast was suddenly announced on the night of the Agincourt episode of *Henry V*. Her Majesty could not be kept waiting and fifteen minutes had to be taken out. Robert Hardy, who had the bulk of the lines, was commanded to make last-minute, unrehearsed cuts. A floor manager laid them on the floor in front of him – if you look closely you can see Hardy casting the odd glance down. But none of it mattered, the plays and performances carried all before them. Thankfully they have been captured, albeit crudely, on DVD. In those non-digital, non-video days, someone had the foresight to point a cine-camera at a TV monitor and hope for the best. I watched some episodes again recently. It is like peering through grey soup, but Shakespeare is alive and shines more brightly than in the recent dour and humourless BBC films (Jeremy Irons' superb Henry IV excepted).

Peter Dews had originally wanted me to be in the ensemble, which included my old school-fellows, Farrington and Glover, having seen me perform with the Youth Theatre at the Edinburgh Festival in 1958, but Queen and Country had first call. I thought I was going to miss out completely, but Peter decided he needed proper acting from the extras, and members of the cast were encouraged to call in their out-of-work chums. It was a great idea – pity it never caught on. I told Ken Farrington I thought I could get time off, he put my name forward and I entered the series as they staggered up to *Henry VI*. The plays were unknown to me and practically everyone else in the country. Though popular in Shakespeare's lifetime they had been neglected for centuries as being thought unworthy of his pen. They had been virtually rediscovered by Douglas Seale in 1953 when he mounted the entire trilogy at the Birmingham Rep. Peter Dews had seen them and had based his television production on them, he was even using some of Seale's cast.

I must have been the only Second Lieutenant in the entire British Army working part-time for the BBC. We extras were called in for the crowd and battle scenes to rehearse for two days in a drill hall at Shepherd's Bush, before moving up the road to the fantastically exciting studios of the brand-new Television Centre. It was doubly exciting for me being with professional actors for the first time: listening to their outrageous Rabelaisian tales – in stark contrast to the military experiences I'd been hearing nightly in the Officers' Mess. Peter Dews himself, despite the colossal pressure, could never pass up an opportunity of telling a theatrical anecdote. Some mornings seemed to be entirely spent exchanging jokes. He could do this because the core of his cast, actors such as Frank Windsor, Geoffrey Bayldon, William Squire and Edgar Wreford, veterans of the Old Vic and Birmingham Rep, had been bred on Shakespeare. They spoke it by instinct and didn't seem to need much rehearsal. Being with them, even in my lowly capacity, made me even more convinced that this was all I wanted to do. I was a little perturbed when I heard some of my fellow crowd-artistes lamenting how long they had been out of work: a year or more in some cases. In the smugness and certainty of youth, I decided I was far too good for that ever to happen to me.

I showed up each fortnight and carried a spear for both York and Lancaster, at Barnet, Towton, and both battles of St Albans. I rebelled with Jack Cade, enacted by a fearsome Esmond Knight; was present at the beheading of the Duke of Suffolk and the stabbing of the Duke of York; led the Duchess of Gloucester to her exile on the Isle of Man and the doomed King Henry to the Tower. I featured most prominently perhaps, as the Son that has been killed by his Father. This is a truly affecting scene where the hapless King Henry watches the battle of Towton from a windmill, whilst a father bewails the son he has unknowingly killed, and a son laments having mistakenly slain his own father. Needless to say my part of the Dead Son was non-speaking. It was even non-breathing, but I felt it just the same. I even got a close-up.

Green Room Tattle: (The Green Room is traditionally a spot close to the stage where actors gather and gossip between entrances and exits. There is no clear explanation of the origin of the term. Scene Room – where actors waited for their scenes? Green baize was originally spread on the stage for tragic heroes and heroines to die on. Even in those days the costumes were more important than the actors. When I first started I often heard old stagers say, 'See you on the Green.') In 1963, John Barton, the resident scholar and dramaturge of the newly formed RSC, condensed the three parts of Henry into two plays, which he renamed *Henry VI* and *Edward IV*, and joined them with *Richard III* under a new title: *The Wars of the Roses.* Peter Hall chose my good friend and RADA contemporary, David Warner, a lanky and nervous twenty-three-year-old, to play King Henry, and fifty-three-year-old Dame Peggy Ashcroft to play Margaret, his Queen. Barton solved the historical problem of Henry being older than Margaret by adding a new line for the Duke of Suffolk: *'Although in years she be older than your Grace.'* It was one of more than 1400 that he added, creating entirely new scenes whilst cutting over 5000 lines of early Shakespeare. Some claimed it was hard to tell Barton from Bard.

Both the early productions of that season had been critical disasters and Peter Hall's newly formed RSC was heading for financial ruin. Laurence Olivier was about to open the National Theatre and a debate was raging as to whether the country could afford, or indeed even needed, two great theatrical companies. The future existence of the RSC virtually depended on the success of these little-known plays. During rehearsals Hall collapsed from stress and overwork and it was left to John Barton and Dame Peggy to hold the company together. Against all the odds the trilogy turned out to be one of the RSC's greatest-ever successes. The designer, John Bury, under the influence of the then fashionable Brecht, created a massive rusty set, made largely from scrap metal, which with his black and grey costumes of no discernible period, made out of unbleached calico and floor cloth, established the new RSC style. The actors were made to speak in a sharp, direct manner, driving the story relentlessly forward. There were some great performances: David Warner's Henry, described by Michael Billington as 'a lean, gangling, Dostoyevskian holy fool'; Ian Holm, who made Richard a 'snickering psychopath'; and Donald Sinden, until then considered to be merely a minor British film star with a very stiff upper lip, reinvented himself as a classical actor with his Duke of York. Queen

Margaret is a mammoth part with 847 lines in the four plays, ageing from eighteen to eighty, and Dame Peg, as she was affectionately known, was a true leading lady – the Judi Dench of her age.

Peggy Ashcroft had a lifelong passion for cricket and arranged weekly matches for the company, including one classic encounter between York and Lancaster. The teams were led by cricketing greats – Len Hutton of Yorkshire and Lancashire's Cyril Washbrook. Neville Cardus, the doyen of cricket correspondents, and J.B. Priestley provided the commentary. There was an extremely embarrassing moment when Sir Leonard Hutton, then holder of the record for the longest innings in Test history, was bowled for a duck by the Second Murderer. During that summer a very exciting Test series was played against the newly formidable West Indies, and Dame Peg took to listening to the radio commentaries on a tiny transistor radio under the helmet she wore in the never-ending and extremely noisy battle scenes. At appropriate moments she would relate the latest score to her soldiery in a Shakespearean stage whisper. Eventually an officious stage manager felt obliged to report her to Peter Hall, who was reluctantly forced to reprimand 'la grande dame' who'd saved his bacon.

On certain days all three plays were performed – a punishing twelve-hour marathon for actors and audiences alike. I know only too well, having sat through one. David Warner remembers the veteran, Paul Hardwicke, who was giving his good Duke Humphrey, flagging on one such occasion. A certain look came into his eye and David knew that he'd gone. Most old actors have some cod Shakespearean lines to get them through such emergencies, such as:

'I'll hie me to the market-place,
And there in one hour hence I'll meet with thee.
Until that time, farewell.'

If poor Hardwicke had one, he was so far gone he couldn't even remember that. The line in question was:

'The purest spring is not so free from mud,
As I am clear from treason to my Sovereign.'

Eventually all that tumbled out was: '*My mind is clear as mud.......*' His fellow actors were holding their bladders tight – unable to speak. The silence was broken by an American lady whispering in the stalls: 'So that's where that came from...'

I saw the three plays in their original state in 1977 with Alan Howard as Henry; he had the monopoly on playing all the kings at Stratford at the time. His queen was a real sex kitten, the young Helen Mirren. It was one of the few occasions she managed to keep all her clothes on.

Titus Andronicus

'One of the stupidest and most uninspired plays ever written.'
T.S. Eliot (1888-1965)

Tattle: Although it was almost certainly written and acted earlier, the first record of this play is an entry in Philip Henslowe's diary noting a performance, probably at the Rose Theatre, on 24 January 1594. It was published in Quarto the same year, making it the first of Shakespeare's plays to be printed. It is certainly the most violent and bloody, containing 'unprecedented depths of savagery and inhuman perversion: Fourteen killings (nine on stage), six severed members, one rape (or two or three, depending on how you count), one live burial, one case of insanity, as well as a bit of cannibalism – an average of 5.2 atrocities per act, or one for every ninety-seven lines.' The Longleat Manuscript, belonging to the Marquis of Bath, gives the only contemporary illustration of a Shakespeare play in performance. It depicts Timon and Tamora dressed in Elizabethan clothes with classical attachments, together with a pitch-black Aaron. This must prove that some attempt was made at costume – you can't just say Shakespeare's plays were all performed in Elizabethan dress.

Though it was Shakespeare's first box-office hit, which may be a sad reflection on the prevalent taste of Elizabethan audiences at the time, *Titus* was considered unperformable for over three hundred years until the young tyro, Peter Brook, directed Laurence Olivier and Vivien Leigh in it at Stratford in 1955. Geoffrey Bayldon, the future Catweazle, played the noble Roman, Aemilius. He remembers Peter Brook telling those chewing the veal and ham pie that stood in for boiled Goth, to stare out front and dare the audience to laugh. There was not a single titter throughout a triumphant European tour on both sides of the Iron Curtain. Maybe that was down to the bad reputation of English cuisine.

Like a London bus, after waiting for more than three and a half centuries, another major production came trundling along almost at once. The following year the Old Vic presented *Titus*, with a Grand Guignol performance from Robert Helpmann as the Emperor Saturninus, as part of an unlikely double bill with *The Comedy of Errors*. Even though *Comedy* is the shortest of all the plays, *Titus* has 2523 lines in its entirety, roughly the same length as *The Merchant of Venice.* Even with drastic cuts it must have been an unbearably long evening. More recent productions by Trevor Nunn and Deborah Warner, and a samurai version by Yukio Ninagawa, have won the play respectability. Michael Billington believes that instead of being dismissed as a primitive Marlovian gore fest, it should now be seen as 'a prolonged lament for the suffering imposed by an imperialistic society.' I'm not sure about that. Giles Gordon, a fellow critic, once said: 'Billington seems temperamentally incapable of not finding a great deal to praise in almost anything he sees. He gives the impression of having been at a party every evening.' But there's not much wrong with that. Billington genuinely loves the theatre. In recent years he has become my favourite critic and I can now read him online every day without having to offend my slightly right-of-centre principles by buying *The Guardian.*

Talking of critics I don't know why actors and directors fear them so much. To slightly misquote Hamlet: 'they would better have a bad epitaph than their ill repute while they live.' Croft used to warn us: 'If you believe 'em when they say you're good, you've got to believe 'em when they say you're bad', although he assiduously courted them himself. I can understand how vital good reviews are to the box office of commercial managements, but Sir Trevor Nunn and the hierarchy of the RSC, with the feather bed of public funding and all performances sold out in advance, delayed the opening night of *King Lear* at Stratford in 2007 for two months because Goneril, in the shape of Frances Barber, had injured her knee by falling off a bike. They were terrified that the perfectly adequate understudy would attract adverse criticism. Rubbish! The critics would have appreciated the drama of the occasion and would have leant over backwards to be understanding. I've met and liked most of them over the years, with the exception of Nicholas de Jongh, who always seemed perverse to me, and Milton Shulman, once described as 'arguably the dullest theatre critic in the history of the world'. Shulman remained in the job for almost forty years and all too often sounded bored to death. Before the advent of the Internet they both carried a lot of weight because they wrote for *The Evening Standard* and came out a day before the others. But Irving Wardle, Benedict Nightingale (a man of fine discernment – he supports Chelsea FC), Michael Coveney, Charles Spencer, young Henry Hitchings, even Quentin Letts, are all real softies compared with their savage predecessors, as the following pages will reveal. I don't honestly know how they stand going to a play every night and still retain their enthusiasm. They spend more evenings with each other than with their wives. I can say this in my retirement; I don't expect another notice in my life, so nobody can accuse me of buttering the buggers up.

Memories: Not surprisingly this is one of the plays I have missed out on, but Michael Croft took a few of us to the first night when Brook's production arrived at The Stoll Theatre in 1957. Michael's novel had become a bestseller, the film rights had been sold, and he was temporarily in the money. (He confidently expected Trevor Howard to play the lead; a character he'd based upon himself, and was mortified when it eventually went to Max Bygraves.) We were more than thrilled when, in the foyer, he introduced us to Kenneth Peacock Tynan, in plum-coloured velvet jacket and cigarette languishing between third and fourth finger. Michael always described Tynan as a man who could make money out of throwing his own party. He had directed Croft in several plays at Oxford and Michael had duly acquainted us with Tynan's weekly criticisms in *The Observer*, which we read as avidly as the football reports. The Stoll, a magnificent opera house at the bottom of Kingsway, was about to be demolished for the monstrosity that now stands in its place – indeed Olivier reported that the builders began their wrecking during the last week of the run, and bits of plaster fell sporadically from the ceiling on either side of the curtain. (Plaster rained down from the roof of the Apollo recently and there wasn't a builder in sight.) I was still a schoolboy and Olivier was God to all would-be actors of my generation. It was the first time I had seen him on stage and I can still recall the thrill of hearing his voice declaiming his opening lines: *'Hail, Rome, victorious in thy mourning weeds!'* Vivien Leigh, we now know, was suffering from nervous breakdowns. She looked a trifle bored that night as she drifted around the stage with blood-red rolls of silk hanging from her shoulders in the style of Japanese theatre. You couldn't really blame her: Lavinia is not much of a part. She loses her tongue very early in Act Two. Tynan, never a fan, wrote the following Sunday: 'when she was ravished on the dead body of her husband, Miss Leigh gave the impression she would have preferred a Dunlopillo mattress.' I've since read that Olivier blamed Tynan's caustic comments for some of Vivien's mental problems; he was even slightly scared of him himself. When he took over the embryonic National Theatre Olivier made sure he got Tynan on side by making him dramaturge. I think Tynan would have lived longer if he had remained a critic. I have recently re-read his diaries – his fall is almost Shakespearean. The brilliant wit and perceptive mind ends up wallowing in self-exoneration and sadomasochism. He died from emphysema at the age of fifty-three. His vision of a permanent ensemble, like those in Russia and Germany, would never have worked in Britain. We have too many good actors – they all deserve a chance of playing in our National Theatre. Moreover, actors have families and mortgages and the best ones will always be tempted away by the higher salaries of films and television.

The performance that impressed me most that night at The Stoll was Anthony Quayle's Aaron. Quayle had a fantastic physique, as anyone who has seen the film *Ice Cold in Alex* will recall. It looked doubly good in shining black body paint. Aaron is a great part. It's a shame that the many excellent black actors we have nowadays are deprived of the chance of playing it because it features in such a rarely performed play. Aaron's soliloquy beginning: *'Now climbeth Tamora Olympus' top,'* is a wonderful audition speech for any black actor. At least it makes a change from Othello.

The Two Gentlemen of Verona

'A youthful, unfinished, minor exercise, full of inconsistencies with chasms in the text.'
Anon

Tattle: There is no record of a first performance but it heads the list of twelve plays that Francis Meres, a Lincolnshire rector, attributed to Shakespeare in 1598: 'For comedy witness, his *Gentlemen of Verona*, his *Errors*, his *Love Labour's Lost*, his *Love's Labour's Won*, his *Midsummer Night Dream* and his *Merchant of Venice*. For Tragedy his *Richard the 2., Richard the 3., Henry the 4., King John, Titus Andronicus* and his *Romeo & Juliet.*'

Two Gents had hardly ever been performed until John Kemble put it on at Drury Lane in 1790. It was not a success, as a note in his diary testifies: 'A very ineffectual piece and I am sorry I ever took the trouble to revive it. NB It was very ill-acted into the bargain.' Though it contains the Shakespearean theme of the attainment of self-knowledge through the power of love, *Two Gents* is hardly more than *Babes in the Wood* mixed with *Robin Hood and his Merry Men*. There has, as yet, been no breakthrough, blockbuster production as with the other minor plays. I have yet to sit through it without dozing off. It contains Shakespeare's first well-known song: *'Who is Sylvia?'* and it is the first time he introduces one of his favourite ploys – the boy actor playing Julia disguising himself/herself as a boy. It has only sixteen characters, the smallest cast list of any of his plays.

Although I firmly believe William Shakespeare, the actor from Stratford, was responsible for all the works attributed to him, I'm not convinced that he wrote all the lines, particularly the comic lines in prose. I think he left a lot to his comedians – in these early plays to the broad humour of Will Kempe, who would have played Launce. The best part in this play is the dog, Launce's dog, Crab, who has extremely unsociable habits. Perhaps the original Crab was Will Kempe's own pet, whose flatulence disrupted rehearsals? Strangely enough Shakespeare uses farting – a beloved source of English humour – very little. Indeed apart from Falstaff threatening to 'break his wind' on Gadshill (although I believe he is referring to himself as a tired old horse running out of breath), the only other instance I can recall is in the same play, *Henry IV Part One*, when Hotspur likens the earth trembling at the birth of Glendower with '*the imprisoning of unruly wind within her womb*.' Shakespeare uses over 17,600 words in his works and has belches aplenty, but I've never come across another fart. Other Elizabethan dramatists drop them frequently. Thomas Dekker gives a non-speaking character in *The Shoemaker's Holiday*, the unfortunate Cecily Bumtrinket, '*a privy fault, she farts in her sleep*.' The diminutive Denise Coffey always got the biggest laugh of the night at the Mermaid in 1964 when she glowered up, an abject spectre of resentment, at her accuser, John Woodvine's blustering Simon Eyre. My suggestion of an appropriate sound effect each time she entered was disregarded.

Michael Aldridge was a fine actor. I spent a couple of days with him filming *The Masque of the Red Death* – he was painted yellow at the time. When he was cast as Launce at the Bristol Old Vic in 1951, he found his Crab, an uncouth mongrel, at the Lost Dogs Home in Bath. The dog was so grateful, he faithfully obeyed every instruction Aldridge gave him on stage and got every possible laugh in the book. Michael became so attached him during the run that it was rumoured he preferred Crab to his wife, who I think was giving her Sylvia. Dogs, like everything else, are not the same today. In a recent RSC tour the part of Crab was taken by a spoilt professional, who arrived at the theatre every night with his chaperone in a chauffeur-driven car. The beast had one of the three dressing rooms to himself, whilst the rest of the cast were crammed into the other two. On top of that, on several occasions, he disgraced himself on stage, to the huge enjoyment of the audience but to the mortification of the poor player who had to lie down on the same spot in the following scene.

Memories: In 2003, when I was well into my sixties, my agent phoned to say that the young lady who was about to direct this play in Regent's Park wanted to know if I was interested in the small part of Sir Eglamour, who appears in two scenes with only twenty-nine lines. Despite the fact that I had directed and played Falstaff and other leading roles at the Open Air Theatre in the dim and distant past, the job appealed to me. I had never appeared in the play and it would be another one to tick off the list.

Furthermore, acting in the Park is a very pleasant way of spending the summer and I would have plenty of time to sit in a deckchair watching the swallows. I phoned Clifford Rose, who has been in every Shakespeare play but one (I've forgotten what one it is) and must hold the record, knowing he had once played Sir Eglamour. Clifford advised me to play him as the White Knight in *Alice through the Looking Glass*. I bore this in mind when I went to meet the young lady, thinking it was just a formality. We spoke for about ten minutes; I confidently expounded on Clifford's theories and never heard from her again. It is one of the many things that actors find hard to accept – and they accept a lot, believe you me – but if they have taken the trouble and time to go to an audition, how long does it take to send an email saying: 'Thanks, but no thanks'? I must admit to a little schadenfreude when the production was awarded only two stars by *The Guardian* (but not by Billington – the second strings are always more severe).

The Comedy of Errors

'Shakespeare appears to have bestowed no great pains on it.'
William Hazlitt (1778-1830)

Tattle: There is no record of where it was first acted or by whom, although a performance given at Gray's Inn on 28 December 1594 by 'a company of base and common fellows' resulted in 'great disorders and abuses'. The resulting public inquiry blamed it on the actor playing the sorcerer, Dr Pinch. It must have been one hell of a performance as Pinch has only twelve lines! Shakespeare transforms two Greek comedies by Plautus into a knockabout farce, but whereas Plautus has one set of identical twins, Shakespeare adds a second. It would have made a great comic movie with Oliver Hardy playing both brothers Antipholus and Stan Laurel as the Dromios, but there is an underlying humanism as well: the theme of forgiveness and reconciliation that Shakespeare follows through to *The Winter's Tale* and *The Tempest* at the end. In spite of the complex plot it is the shortest of all his plays – only 1778 lines. Hamlet has 1569 of his own.

In 1938 Rodgers and Hart adapted the play into a musical, *The Boys from Syracuse*, which became a Broadway hit containing classic songs such as '*This Can't be Love*' and *'Sing for your Supper'*. I saw Bob Monkhouse and Ronnie Corbett in it at Drury Lane in 1963 (needless to say they were not playing twins). Casting one let alone two sets of identical twins is extremely difficult, especially from an ensemble. In 1955 the Old Vic cast as the two Dromios: John Fraser, slender, Scottish, perhaps the most handsome young actor in Equity at that time, and Dudley Jones, a short, squat, bald Welshman. John suggested that they should black up and play it like a couple of Jamaicans – you could do that without offence then – but Dudley could not master the accent. John then suggested they should brown up and play it Indian, as Welsh and Indian accents have a similar lilt. This was finally agreed upon, although Dudley's accent never drifted east of Swansea.

The play had never been regularly performed until 1962, when Clifford Williams, a real man of the theatre, directed it for the RSC in commedia dell'arte style, with the considerable talents of Ian Richardson, Alec McCowen and Diana Rigg. It was so popular that the production became the mainstay of the RSC for years, constantly revived whenever the company was in need of a sure-fire commercial success. Numerous productions have followed; it has been set in Edinburgh, the New Orleans waterfront and the West Indies. My favourite rendering was Trevor Nunn's semi-musical version in 1976, set around a Greek taverna. With choreography by Gillian Lynne, it was Nunn's first step towards *Les Mis*, *Cats* and all the rest. Judi Dench was Adriana and my old RADA chum Michael Williams was hilarious as Dromio of Syracuse. Nickolas Grace matched him as the other one – I can still see him breaking plates, dancing on and off tables with the energy and élan of Gene Kelly.

For several decades, before cruise ships became the thing, wealthy Americans, many of whom were not regular theatregoers, made pilgrimages to Stratford to see a play. It didn't really matter what play, so long as it was by Shakespeare. Used to watching television and making comments at will, their mutterings in the stalls were often heard by the actors on stage and became RSC legends. One such lady had sat through *The Comedy of Errors* with her spouse sleeping at her side. When the Dromio twins, Michael Williams and Nickolas Grace, ran on stage from opposite directions for their curtain call, she nudged her husband in the ribs and exclaimed: 'Gee! There are two of them!' One wonders what she'd been making of the plot.

Memories: I wish I had some. I've never been in this play. I still have hopes for the aged Aegeon – I'm far too aged for anything else.

The Taming of the Shrew (Loves Labour's Won?)

'A wretchedly poor farce,
with a theme unworthy of Shakespeare.'
Anon

Tattle: It is probably the mysterious *Love Labour's Won* in the aforementioned list of Frances Meres. I've always found it hard to comprehend that Shakespeare was surpassed in popularity in his own lifetime by Beaumont and Fletcher, and for more than half a century following the Restoration of 1660 was considered no higher than or indeed inferior to Ben Jonson, Webster or Massinger. Actors, being actors, considered him fair game for improvement and painstakingly adapted his works to suit themselves. James Quin, despite his heavy, laboured delivery and ponderous movement, was considered the leading actor before David Garrick and is a case in point. A contemporary wrote: 'Mr Quin had during the course of his acting, from his judgement in the English language and knowledge of the history of Great Britain, corrected many mistakes which Shakespeare, by oversight or the volatileness of his genius, suffered to creep into his words.'

Even though Garrick is credited with restoring Shakespeare, he could not resist writing his own version of *The Shrew* entitled *Katherine and Petruchio*. Garrick's acting was far more animated than Quin's, and during one performance he accidentally ran a fork through the finger of his unfortunate leading lady, Kitty Clive. The play has always been accident prone. It became extremely popular throughout the nineteenth century and henpecked husbands may have watched with quiet satisfaction as subsequent Kates were battered and bruised by over-enthusiastic Petruchios. Now that wife beating is rightly no longer considered a joke, even more disturbing to some feminists is Katharina's blind obedience and sanctimonious lecture to the other women in the final scene. I don't see the problem, it is easily overcome if acted tongue-in-cheek. Strangely enough, I read that Germaine Greer, the untamed shrew herself, approves of the play. She holds it is: 'not a knockabout farce of wife-battering but the cunning adaptation of a folk-motif to show the forging of a partnership between equals'. I agree with her on that.

Alfred Lunt and Lynn Fontanne, the so-called King and Queen of Broadway, had a long-running success with the play in 1933. Their outrageous antics on and off stage were the inspiration of Cole Porter's *Kiss Me, Kate*. In more recent times the roles of Petruchio and Katharina have attracted such stars as Peter O'Toole and Peggy Ashcroft, Alan Bates and Vanessa Redgrave, and, not least, Richard Burton and Elizabeth Taylor. Strangely enough, Olivier and Gielgud never played Petruchio, nor did Paul Scofield or Albert Finney, nor have any of our present crop of theatrical knights. Olivier did play Katharina whilst at school; perhaps even then he knew it was the better part.

Memories: In the vanity of youth I considered myself to be a natural swashbuckling Petruchio. I only ever played him once, rather unsuccessfully, in my early days at RADA. I had duly auditioned and thanks to Croft's coaching been accepted by the Academy with a scholarship: all fees paid and a grant of £4 a week, which as I lived at home was more than sufficient. I could eat lunch every day in a greasy spoon and drink bottled Double Diamond in the nearby Marlborough Arms, where I would discuss the state of the theatre with my fellows, not least a cherub-faced 'scouser' called Michael Williams. As well as being extremely talented, I've never forgotten a brilliant mime play he created about coal-miners trapped underground, Michael was the kindest of men. Dame Judi Dench was very lucky to get him. I also had enough of my grant left over to see any play I wished, albeit from the back of the balcony. Life was extremely good.

The structure of the Academy was entirely different then. It was a two-year course with three intakes of sixty per term, divided into three classes of twenty, ten of each sex. Not all of them finished the course, but potentially three hundred and sixty students were given a chance to shine. Now, I gather, the course is three years and only thirty students are admitted each year – that is a maximum of ninety. I believe this is wrong. Nobody really knows who will make it or not, whose talent will develop or those whom luck will smile on. The other major drama schools have adopted RADA's selective policy which has given rise to a proliferation of minor drama schools and University courses throughout the country. Surely it is better to have large centres of excellence where students are taught by the very best? Having said that, I don't think you can teach acting – there are many 'methods' of achieving a performance – the only real way is practice. You never stop learning. Play as many parts as you can, before an audience if possible. We were lucky in 1957; we could do that in rep. Young actors and actresses today are forced to put on their own productions in pubs, where audiences are all too hard to find.

I'm afraid I don't subscribe to this modern fad of calling us all 'actors'. What on earth is wrong with being called an 'actress'? It was good enough for Sarah Siddons, Edith Evans and Vivien Leigh, to name but three. The argument that actors are actors in the same way that doctors are doctors and lawyers are lawyers irrespective of sex – just doesn't hold. If you are sick or in legal difficulties you just need the best doctor or lawyer you can find, or afford, sex doesn't matter. But if I am directing a play with four male and three female characters, I need four actors and three actresses – not four male actors and three female actors. Strangely enough 'actresses' come back soon enough whenever the awards come around.

It is estimated that over ninety-three per cent of Equity are unemployed at any one time. I believe it is higher if you count gainful employment. It has got even worse since Equity was forced by the European Court of Human Rights to abandon its closed shop policy in 1988. (You couldn't work as a professional without an Equity card and theatre companies and other establishments were only allowed to issue a limited number of cards each year. This led to all sorts of abuses with producers giving cards to their girl or boy friends, and young actresses having to work in striptease clubs. But all too often the poor young things still have to strip today. Nothing brings an audience into a small pub theatre like a full frontal. I was in a play at the Finborough recently and studied the lascivious looks on the faces of both sexes packed into the front row, surveying the impressive equipment of the naked young actor I was working with.) I don't really know the answer but the flow of aspiring drama students grows every year and the competition ever fiercer. As Evelyn Waugh said of literature, acting 'offers scope for profound and prolonged laziness, and in the event of success gives rewards quite out of proportion to industry,' but there can never be enough work for everybody.

Gower Street was less than five miles from Brixton but it seemed a world away in 1957. For one thing it was full of girls, not all of them up to my expectations, but they were girls all the same. Under Sir Kenneth Barnes RADA had earned a reputation for being a finishing school for the well-bred 'gels' that inhabited the drawing-room comedies of the West End stage and the films of J. Arthur Rank. John Fernald had recently taken over as Principal, and was trying to introduce more ordinary types to suit the new wave of British films and the 'kitchen sink' dramas emerging from the Royal Court. I think he somewhat overdid it. Apart from Susannah York and the exquisite Amanda Grinling there was hardly a flicker of glamour. Mind you, I can't seem to remember many Paul Newman types amongst us men.

As is the usual practice in drama schools the leading roles were divided up, so that as many students as possible got a chance to play them. I was given the first act. My Kate was a gamine type from New York, the first American girl I'd ever got close to. Try as I might, I was unable to create much chemistry between us. She didn't seem to like it when I manhandled her or slapped her pert behind on the line *'What, with my tongue in your tail?'* which I thought was quite inventive at the time. Years later I was told she was a lesbian – I don't think I would have understood what the word meant in 1957. We were directed by a ferocious, hunch-backed, old woman called Winifred Oughton, who had played male roles at the Old Vic during the First World War. 'You'd better learn to type, dear,' was one of her kinder comments to the girls, many of whom she reduced to tears. She was obviously not impressed by my attempts at virility – standing legs apart with my hands on my hips, chest thrust out, pretending to be Errol Flynn or Burt Lancaster in *The Crimson Pirate*. The harder I tried the less funny I became. Her report at the end of the year, when I went off to do my National Service, was brief and to the point: 'Good luck, David, and come back to us a man.' I wondered how many poor souls she'd sent off to the Somme with a white feather. I always fancied having another go at Petruchio but never got the chance. In later years my ambitions switched to Grumio or Gremio, then to Baptista or even Christopher Sly. I am still awaiting the call.

Trevor Nunn's production in 1967 was the best I've seen. It began with a troupe of itinerant actors coming into a barn out of the snow, like figures in a Bruegel painting. A very young Nunn had arrived in Stratford from

Coventry with a pretty blonde girlfriend whom he'd cast as Bianca. Within weeks Katharina had taken centre stage in every sense and Janet Suzman was well on her way to becoming the first Mrs Nunn. We had no idea that little Trevor would achieve so much. He was quite nondescript, indeed a trifle scruffy; someone described him as looking a bit like a Vietnamese waiter. I seem to remember him wearing a terrible jacket with a silver thread running through it; he had yet to adopt his talismanic jeans and matching shirt. I don't think he did much 'Treving' in those days either. (I received a hearty hug only yesterday when I encountered him in Lupus Street, Pimlico, where he was rehearsing his current project. He never stops.) He would quietly sit at our table in the Dirty Duck, sipping his half pint, whilst Alan Howard and I related our outrageous stories of filming in Norway with Kirk Douglas and Richard Harris. (I still remember most of them, but they belong to another book.)

Some Shakespeare plays are fun to be in even if you have very little to do; others make you dread going into the theatre. There were two companies at Stratford that year: we were battling through a turgid *Coriolanus* on alternate nights to Trevor's fun-filled *Shrew.* Needless to say, most of us would have preferred Padua to Rome. Michael Williams established his reputation with his rough but kind Petruchio. Roy Kinnear, a warm and lovely man, was hilarious as Baptista; I can't really remember Patrick Stewart's Grumio or Frances de la Tour's Widow – hardly surprising as the Widow has only eleven lines. Christopher Sly was played by a rumbustious, one-eyed thespian called Morgan Shepherd. I shared a dressing room with him later in the season: whilst I gingerly applied the mascara to my lashes, he boldly plucked out his eye, spat on it and polished it assiduously before popping it back.

Richard III (Dick De Turd)

'Richard is not a man striving to be great, but to be greater than he is; conscious of his strength of will, his power of intellect, his daring courage, his elevated station; and making use of these advantages to commit unheard of crimes, and to shield himself from remorse and infamy.'
William Hazlitt

Tattle: Richard is a mixture of conspirator, tyrant and sardonic comedian, a diabolical but likeable monster. It is the first star role in the canon, the second longest part after Hamlet. It needs a great actor and Shakespeare had one in Richard Burbage, who from this point would create all the leading roles. There is no contemporary record of Burbage's performance apart from a diary entry of John Manningham, a student at the Middle Temple: 'Upon a time when Burbage played Richard III there was a lady grew so far in her liking for him that before she went from the play she appointed him to come that night unto her by the name of Richard III. Shakespeare, overhearing their conclusion, went before, was entertained and at his game ere Burbage came. Then message being brought that Richard III was at the door, Shakespeare cause return to be made that William the Conqueror was before Richard III.' I hope that story is true. Actors haven't changed much. A friend of mine went all the way up to Sunderland to play Romeo with a Juliet he fancied and was mortified when she went off with Mercutio.

Young David Garrick made his London debut in the role in 1741. It says much of the parlous state of the English stage before his arrival that he was complimented for continuing to act when he wasn't speaking. 'He is attentive to whatever is spoken, and never drops his character when he has finished a speech by looking contemptuously on an inferior performer, unnecessary spitting, or suffering his eyes to wander through the whole circle of spectators.' In 1813 Edmund Kean's Richard banged open the doors to his fame. *The Morning Post* declared 'his attraction was unprecedented in the annals of theatricals'. Lord Byron, a director of Drury Lane, exclaimed: 'By Jove he is a soul! Life – nature – truth, without exaggeration or diminution. Richard is a man and Kean is Richard.' Byron was so taken with the performance that he presented Kean a sword with an engraved Damascus blade. After Kean's death it came into the possession of an actor in his company by the name of William Henry Chippendale. Years later Chippendale presented Irving with another sword, the sword that Kean actually wore on stage. That sword then came via Ellen Terry to Gielgud. Sir John, with typical generosity, gave it to Olivier after seeing his Richard III. Olivier should have passed it in turn to Scofield after his awe-inspiring Lear, but clung on to it until his death. I read somewhere that Lord Larry kept it under his bed. There is an unfounded story that Emma Thompson (then Mrs Branagh) phoned Joan Plowright after Olivier's death, and suggested that she give it to her Ken. Miss Thompson, a delightful lady, was summarily rebuffed. Strangely enough I have just read in *The Daily Telegraph* that Olivier's family didn't want Ken at the funeral. For some inexplicable reason the engraved sword given to Kean by Byron, now rests at Birmingham University. It should be with our leading Shakespearean. Branagh seems to have lost his passion for the Bard in recent years; I suppose 'Serena' McKellen is the leading candidate, although that would not be to everyone's taste. Actors are a bitchy lot. What about Judi Dench? Nobody has a bad word to say about her – as far as I know.

Sir Henry Irving may have inherited Kean's sword but his Richard failed to win over Bernard Shaw, who declared: 'Irving was not, as it seemed to me, answering his helm satisfactorily; and was occasionally out of temper with his own nervous condition.' Sir Henry was furious, believing Shaw was accusing him of being drunk. This could be the root of the famous 'Wait till you see the Duke of Buckingham story', which has been attributed to Sir Donald Wolfit, Wilfred Lawson, Robert Newton and various other imbibers. For the extreme minority who haven't heard it: 'Leading actor staggers on stage with wig aslant and begins a much laboured rendering of '*Now ish the w-inter of hour dis-con-tent…*' After a few lines someone shouts from the gallery: 'You're pissed.' The actor looks up with baleful eye and declares: 'Wait until you see the Duke of fucking Buckingham!' But perhaps the story originated with George Cooke. A noted toper, he had been the acclaimed Richard before Kean until the bottle took over. In 1809 a wag wrote of his performance at Drury Lane during the riots over the new prices:

'Though Mr Cooke King Richard play'd
None listened to a word was said.
'Twould not have mattered much I ween,
Had he, this night, as usual been –
That is, had he been non se ipse
Or in plain English, had been tipsy'.

Poor Cooke died a pauper in America and had the indignity of having his skull used as a prop in a performance of *Hamlet* in New York. Kean made amends by erecting a monument over his grave, which still stands in St Paul's Churchyard in Manhattan.

His detractors say Olivier held on to Kean's sword out of vanity: jealously and selfishly guarding his reputation against his younger rivals. But for my generation he had no rivals, especially when it came to Richard III. Peter Sellers notwithstanding, we all had our own imitation of him. The British Film Institute considers Olivier's 1955 film has done more to popularise Shakespeare than any other work. Patrick Troughton, a future Dr Who, played Tyrell the murderer and stood in for Olivier whilst he directed. Gerry O'Hara, the assistant director, told me they began by filming the battles in Spain, on bull runs in Andalucía. Would-be toreadors were posted to keep the bulls away. In the film Bosworth Field looks a very parched and dusty brown and there are distant mountains that are definitely not the Cotswolds. Olivier was determined that Richard's charge should surpass that of the French at Agincourt in his previous film, *Henry V*. To that end he hired 500 of General Franco's finest cavalry and brought over the Queen's Archer with an especially accurate bow. His task was to fire an arrow that would hit Olivier's horse exactly plumb on a heavily protected area under the carapace, so that it would rear up on a precise cue. Unfortunately the bow, or the archer, was not as accurate as promised, and on the take the arrow pierced Sir Larry's rubber armour and stuck in his leg. '*A horse! A horse! My kingdom for a horse!*' became the exceedingly un-Shakespearean, 'Pull the fucking thing out!' Stanley Baker, who was playing Richmond, had mainly worked in films and thought the great man was over-acting. Nevertheless Olivier was nominated for an Oscar and the film has been shown continuously on television throughout the world ever since.

Since Olivier cast his giant shadow over the part there has been a plethora of Richards: Derek Jacobi's was a pussy cat; Simon Russell Beale's a venomous toad; Antony Sher's a spiky-legged tarantula; whilst the impeccable Henry Goodman made a rare mistake in trying to play him as Mr Punch. Ian Holm was a terrifying psychopath with a surgical boot, and Anton Lesser, Ian McKellen and Robert Lindsay all bore the hump with distinction. But we have nevertheless missed out on some great Richards. Why did Albert Finney, Richard Burton or Peter O'Toole never play him? Anthony Hopkins at least gave us a glimpse of his Dick in Hannibal Lecter.

Memories: I'd always seen myself as a genial Buckingham but it was quite late in my career before I was offered anything in this play. In 1982 I went to meet Richard Eyre at the National when he was about to direct Ian McKellen in the title role. Eyre seemed quite keen for me to do either Stanley, who has some good moments, or the Lord Mayor of London, who has hardly more than a cough and a spit. I rather think I would have ended up with the Mayor, and was not too disappointed when circumstances forced me to turn it down. Nevertheless I was duly mortified when it blossomed into a huge success and went on to a World Tour and then was made into a highly successful film. However, I did end up playing Stanley, but in far humbler circumstances.

In 1994 I came across young David Babani in the Long Bar at the National. I'd met him a few years before when, as a schoolboy, he'd helped with the lighting on my one-man play *Falstaff* when I performed it at Highgate School. David informed me that he was now a producer and was about to put on *Richard III* and asked if I would like to be in it. I wasn't all that keen, as there appeared to be little or no money involved, but Babani has great persuasive powers and I found myself agreeing. A few days later my agent rang me to say I had been offered Stanley, on a profit-share basis. It was the first time I had heard of such an agreement and was filled with foreboding, knowing all too well that profits are virtually non-existent in the theatre. The following week I found myself outside a rundown building in a yet to be gentrified part of Clapham. A group of rough-looking characters were loitering around the door on their mobile phones. They eyed me suspiciously. I asked them if they knew where the actors were. My heart sank when they told me they were the actors.

The oldest of them was at least twenty-five years younger than me – I would have nothing in common with any of them. There would be no old cronies to reminisce with, which for me is so much of the pleasure of being in a company.

Eventually we were summoned into the rehearsal room, a damp and ill-smelling hall, where the young and seemingly bored director proceeded to fill us in. The up-and-coming actor Eddie Marsan was going to play Richard in a 1950s Kray-like gangster setting. The action was largely to be set in a pub, *The Duke of York*. A rival gang were based in another pub, *The House of Lancaster*. The play was to be put on at some remote corner of North London that I had never heard of, in a new venue called the Pleasance. In this production Stanley was going to be the pub landlord. The part was combined with Brakenbury, normally the Keeper of the Tower, which would entail me keeping prisoners like Clarence and the Little Princes in my cellar. I wondered why on earth I had agreed to do it. I thought about walking out, but had been taught never to do that once I'd given my word and started a job. (I wish I hadn't. On one occasion I'd just begun rehearsing at the Young Vic on £95 a week, when I was offered £20,000 for the first Kentucky Fried Chicken Advert, a huge sum then. The miserable, mean-spirited young director, who has since justly sunk without trace, refused to release me for two days. I should have told him to get stuffed and taken the days off, but foolishly kept my so-called integrity. My kids didn't get much of a holiday that year.)

During the first few days at Clapham I endeavoured to get better acquainted with my fellow actors. They were working-class lads from all over the country, apart from one public schoolboy type who was cast as Harry Buckingham, a shady entrepreneur. Their toughness and villainy were so realistic I began to wonder if they were actors at all, and inquired which drama schools they had attended. They were mostly institutions in the East End or the North of England of which I had never heard. I became aware how much the profession had changed. When I was at RADA most of us aimed at getting into a theatrical company, staying several years, working our way up the cast list. The most ambitious aimed for the fledgling RSC, the Old Vic, or the about to be born National. Now all these actors seemed to want, if they couldn't get into films, was regular roles in *EastEnders, The Bill* or *Coronation Street.* They seemed in a terrible hurry to make it before it was too late. They were on their mobiles at every conceivable spare moment: each morning as soon as they arrived at rehearsal they would recharge them in every available socket. After the first week I felt so out of it that, against all my previous resolutions, I persuaded myself to purchase my first mobile phone.

I was particularly fascinated by the biggest and roughest member of the cast, nicknamed Chopper. In the opening scene he garrotted the rival gang leader, aka Henry VI, with such unbelievable ferocity and expertise that I began to believe he'd got his nickname for some axe-murder or worse. I was therefore very relieved and delighted when I discovered that he called himself after his hero, the Chelsea legend, Chopper Harris. From that point on we became firm friends with our shared interest in the finest London soccer club, and had daily discussions on the merits of the then up-and-coming team.

Although as I expected *'profits did not accrue'*, it was one of the most enjoyable jobs I've ever done. The director, contrary to my expectations, knew what he was doing. Eddie Marsan's hunch-backed bartender was mesmerisingly evil, and that cast of roughs attacked the play with a vigour and energy that put many of the National or RSC productions I've been in to shame. The second half opened in the pub with Richard celebrating his coronation as leader of the mob, singing *'New York! New York!'* on the karaoke. It was as exciting a moment as I've ever experienced on stage. We were all completely immersed in the same world. The production met with critical approval, and I'm sure if it had been put on at the Cottesloe or Swan if would have achieved even greater recognition. We did however take it on two short tours to Germany. When we assembled at the airport for the second tour, I was disappointed to see that Chopper was not there. I learned that he was inside for GBH.

One of our dates was in Chemnitz, formerly Karl-Marx-Stadt, in East Germany. We played at the Schauspielhaus, part of a vast five-theatre complex that had enjoyed heavy subsidies under Communist rule. It was like working in the local town hall. There was no energy or excitement. The permanent actors and stage hands, who had been there enjoying comfortable employment for years, regarded our energetic young hooligans with amazement. But, in my mind, it is the fact that a British or American actor's life is so precarious that makes them the best stage actors in the world. You have to try your hardest, give your best, every single night, or you will be out in the cold. Another heavily subsidised amenity was the health club at the modern hotel where our company was billeted. To the profound delight of all the young lads and one old man, frauleins of all shapes and sizes disported themselves naked in the swimming pool. It wouldn't have happened in Cheltenham.

David Babani is now a highflying producer on both sides of the Atlantic; Eddie Marsan has also gone on to better things. He seems to have cameos in every British film that is made these days. The chirpy Jay Simpson deservedly works regularly, but I don't think I've seen any of the others since. On the other hand I never watch *EastEnders* and the other soaps, so they may be nationwide celebrities for all I know. I often wonder what happened to Chopper. I sometimes scan the faces of the crowd in the Matthew Harding Stand at Stamford Bridge, where the die-hard Chelsea fans congregate, but have never seen him.

(There is nothing new under the sun, as far as Shakespeare is concerned. I have just read Billington's review of David Haigh's *Lear*, 'transposed into the world of 1960s East End gangsterdom'. The concept suits *Richard III* better.)

Love's Labour's Lost

'There are many passages which are tedious and impossible, though we all pretend to like them.'
George Bernard Shaw (1856 – 1950)

Tattle: More suited to a stately hall than a common theatre, *Love's Labour's Lost* is recorded as having been performed for Queen Elizabeth in 1598, and also for Queen Anne of Denmark, wife of James I, at the Earl of Southampton's house in 1605. This is attested by a surviving letter written by Sir Walter Cope to Robert Cecil: '*Burbage is come, and says there is no new play that the queen hath not seen, but they have revived an old one, called Love's Labour's Lost, which for wit and mirth, he says, will please her exceedingly.*'

The quick pace of the play was entirely unsuited to the huge theatres of the late eighteenth and nineteenth centuries, which required slow and loud declamation. There was no big leading role for the actor managers and the play was more or less ignored until 1932, when Tyrone Guthrie staged it at the Westminster Theatre. The young Paul Scofield played Don Armado at Stratford in 1946; Michael Redgrave resembled a character in a Hilliard miniature when he gave a noted Berowne for the Old Vic Company in 1949. I witnessed a surprisingly docile Glenda Jackson giving her Princess of France for the RSC in 1965. I have sat through the play several times since, but must confess I have often found the brilliant verbal exchanges fly too fast for me. The clearest production I've seen was by Ian Judge, not normally one of my favourite directors, who set it in Oxford just before the First World War. The play works beautifully in the open air and I've seen excellent productions in Regent's Park. I thought Cole Porter's songs were the best thing in Kenneth Branagh's film.

Memories: My own participation in the play was tenuous in the extreme. For his final productions at the National, Trevor Nunn decided to direct a very young company in *Love's Labour's* in conjunction with Cole

Porter's *Anything Goes*. They were all highly talented singers and dancers but there was nobody to understudy Holofernes. I was about to join the National in *Henry V* and I was asked if I would like to do it. It meant being on salary a few weeks early and I willingly agreed. It was the only time I have been a walking understudy – that is understudying without actually appearing in the play. I have never discovered why it is called 'walking'. Perhaps in the days of the strolling players there was only so much room in the cart and the poor understudy had to walk behind. The text of *Love's Labour's* is very intricate and Holofernes' comedy is perhaps the most difficult of all. Coming into rehearsals late, I missed the long and painstaking explanations and investigations of the script that Trevor usually gives, so never really understood all that I was saying, not least because of the Italian, or was it Latin? Latin has always been Greek to me – I failed my O-level ignominiously. I had no idea how to deliver lines like: '*Fauste, precor, gelida quando pecus omne sub umbra Ruminat*', or '*Novi hominem tanquam te*'. I drummed the words into my head by rote, with the aid of a keen young assistant director. I only played the role once and followed Dame Edith Evans's dictum: 'Stare out front and think dirty'. I was gratified and more than surprised when the laughs came, almost on cue. Even at this early stage Shakespeare, or his comic actors, knew exactly what they were doing.

There are moments in some Shakespeare plays when everyone is caught up in a unity of purpose and emotion. The most notable is being in the English army at Agincourt when Henry delivers his St Crispian Day speech. Other examples are at the beginning of *Lear* when almost the entire cast wait for their mass entrance, knowing the marathon that lies ahead of them all; and watching Bottom's play in *The Dream*. I discovered a similar moment in the last scene of *Love's Labour's*. Trevor had the entire cast singing the song that ends the play: I have never been a singer, but I stood among those bright and talented youngsters and sang my heart out:

'When icicles hang by the wall,
And Dick the shepherd blows his nail,
And Tom bears logs into the hall,
And milk comes frozen home in pail,'

I was so happy to be part of it. I'm not sure whether it was the song, Trevor's direction, or the pretty young things I stood among.

Romeo & Juliet

'It is the worst play I ever heard in my life.'
Samuel Pepys (1633-1703)

Tattle: Though printed twice in Shakespeare's lifetime there is no record of any performances, *Shakespeare in Love* notwithstanding. Which role did Burbage play? Romeo is not for a mature actor. Who was it first said: 'I don't know whether to play Mercutio and go home early, or play the Friar and keep my trousers on'? Capulet's line that Romeo: '*bears him like a portly gentleman*' has led some to believe that Burbage was a bit overweight. Gertrude says a few years later that Hamlet is '*fat and scant of breath*', but portly and fat had different connotations then. John Dryden, leading poet and playwright of the Restoration, alleged that Shakespeare first played Mercutio. I find this highly unlikely – if he was anyone he was Friar Lawrence. One thing that has always puzzled me is who first played the Nurse? She ranks a little below Falstaff as a comic masterpiece. Surely she was not originally played by a boy? Why not Will Kempe? It is commonly assumed that he was the bland and obvious clown, Peter, because of the prefix attached to some of Peter's lines. Could this not be just a misreading by an early editor? I like to think it was.

Unlike dancers in Prokofiev's ballet, no actor has made his name as Romeo. Olivier, who had an infallible eye for a good part, observed: 'You spend the whole evening searching for sympathy – but anyone who lets an erection rule his life doesn't deserve much sympathy does he?' In the ballet Juliet comes down from the balcony and the lovers dance passionately together to the most sublime music. In the play they hardly touch. Romeo's charm is his youth; part of the drama is his change from youth to maturity forced upon him by sudden tragedy. It is far easier for a good young actor to portray maturity than it is for a mature star to act young. Most of the mature stars who have attempted Romeo have come a cropper.

Garrick, who had the effrontery, or courage, to attempt Romeo at the age of forty-eight, was a case in point, despite following his usual custom of doctoring the part to suit himself. He even changed the ending so that Juliet awoke just before Romeo expired. No dramatist, living or dead, was safe from Garrick's pen.

The fiery Edmund Kean was never a Romeo. *The Morning Post* reported: 'He exaggerated every passion and tore them to tatters. A rotatory movement of the hand, as if describing the revolution of a spinning jenny; multiplied slaps upon his forehead, and manual elevation of his fell of hair; repeated knocking upon his own breast, and occasional rapping at the chests of others; opening of his ruffles, like a schoolboy run riot from the playground, and a strange indistinct groping inside of his shirt, as if in search of something uncommonly minute, filled up the round of his action, while a voice most unmusical, exerted to a harsh and painful screech, afforded the finishing touch to a Romeo decidedly the worst we ever witnessed on the London boards.' Later in the century, Max Beerbohm regarded Sir Henry Irving's suicide in the vault of Capulet a merciful release.

Juliet has to combine bubbling adolescence with great depth of feeling for the later tragedy. The play could be well called *Juliet and Romeo* – she virtually carries the second half on her own whilst Romeo is languishing in Mantua. In the nineteenth century only mature actresses were considered capable. For the most part they proved profoundly unsatisfactory: Miss O'Neill's Juliet was 'endowed with an opulence of figure remarkable for fourteen even in Italy', whilst Mrs Patrick Campbell, 'lay down beside Romeo and revolved herself right over him like the roller of a mangle, leaving his chiselled profile perceptibly snubbed.'

Olivier and Gielgud, then respectively twenty-eight and thirty-one, alternated Romeo and Mercutio in 1935 – the only time they ever appeared together on stage. It was Olivier's first classical role, till then he had been just a fashionable West End actor. He wrote later that he saw himself and Gielgud as two sides of the same coin – Gielgud the poetic, ethereal side, himself earth and animal passion. Olivier conceived Romeo as a fervent Italian teenager and acted the part rather than declaiming the poetry, only to receive a lethal collection of criticisms from the traditionally-minded press: 'Olivier plays Romeo as though he were riding a motor bike'... 'His blank verse is the blankest ever heard'. He was so hurt that he had to be persuaded to continue in the part. Gielgud, adopting his usual poetic approach, was more successful, but still had to suffer Ivor Brown in *The Observer:* 'Mr Gielgud has the most meaningless legs imaginable.' Their Juliet, the thirty-year-old Peggy Ashcroft, was treated more kindly; indeed it was the part that made her a star. Alec Guinness had seven lines as the Apothecary. I suspect he had a field day with his makeup. He confided in his diary that he thought Olivier was 'vulgar and gimmicky, and looked and behaved like the leader of a dance band.' It's hardly surprising that Olivier never asked him to be in any of his Shakespeare films.

It was not until 1960 that Franco Zeffirelli had the sense to cast young but talented unknowns as the tragic lovers and let the story speak for itself. He believed that as 'all cultures acknowledge Shakespeare as the world's greatest playwright – even in translation. His dramatic insights were more valid than his poetic ones.' I'm not sure I entirely agree, but I count myself fortunate to have been in the Old Vic on the opening night. It began with the stage misty with dry ice to suggest dawn breaking over the piazza; the balconies were hung with washing instead of the customary dangling wisteria. It was no chocolate box production – Zeffirelli had personally gone round with a spray, suggesting dogs' pee on the walls – but the stage overflowed with red-hot Italian passion. Romeo was a robust lad in the shape of my schoolboy hero, John Stride. Olivier, seeing perhaps a trace of what he'd intended his own performance to be, believed Romeo's boyish passionate intensity had never been bettered – and the blessed Judi Dench was sublime as Juliet. I was amazed when next morning the more conservative critics were as hostile as they had been to Olivier's interpretation twenty-five years before. But Kenneth Tynan came riding to the rescue the following Sunday with a rave review, declaring, 'it was not so much a revelation but a revolution.' Such was the weight of his opinion that it immediately became one of the biggest successes in the Old Vic's history. Tynan had done exactly the same in 1956 with *Look Back in Anger* when he declared: 'I doubt if I could love anyone who did not wish to see this play.'

One would have thought the lesson had finally been learned, but although Ian McKellen was considerably younger than Garrick when he gave his Romeo at Stratford in 1976, he was still too old for Sheridan Morley, who opined: 'The two lovers, played by Ian McKellen and Francesca Annis, are not only star-crossed but visibly into their thirties which makes one wonder during duller moments why they aren't out looking for work or worrying about their children's education.'

Memories: I returned to RADA in the autumn of 1960 after completing my National Service. Harold Macmillan had made his 'You've never had it so good' speech and most of us still believed what our Prime Ministers told us. There was definitely a whiff of optimism in the air, especially among actors. New theatres were being built, more funding for the arts was on line, new plays and new writers were popping up all over the country and on television. On top of that I had acquired a prestigious part-time job. Paul Scofield's performance in *A Man for All Seasons* at the Globe (now the Gielgud) was the talk of London. During the summer I had been playing Mark Antony in the NYT production of *Julius Caesar* next door at the Queen's. Scofield's dresser became ill and the stage door keeper of the Globe asked his opposite number at the Queen's if one of the young lads of the Youth Theatre would fill in until he recovered. I was asked if I would like to do it and volunteered at once. A dresser has more or less the same duties as a batman. I knew exactly what they were – even a National Service Second Lieutenant had a batman in 1960. In little more than a week I went from having a batman to being one. I made Scofield his tea, brushed his clothes, helped him with his changes and kept his dressing room tidy – a piece of cake. He had a very relaxed attitude to acting that I could not but admire – I can vouchsafe he never went in for vocal warm-ups, not at least in that production. He was kind and considerate, although not over-generous with his weekly tip, and I revelled in the excitement of being in a big West End hit. Every night we played to packed houses, and I would pour drinks for the well-known visitors who came to pay homage in the dressing room. One particular night my hand shook as I filled the glass of Vivien Leigh.

John Fernald's new broom had been busy at RADA during my absence. The older teachers had exited to Denville Hall and other sanctuaries for aged thespians, to be replaced by young directors like James Roose-Evans and current West End actors such as Gerald Harper and Peter Barkworth. In spite of the kitchen sink revolution, plays were still being written with French windows and drinks trays. Barkworth duly taught us the stage technique of mixing cocktails, flicking Ronson lighters and smoking cigarettes. However, many of the students would have been more at home in a public bar – Ian McShane, John Hurt, David Warner and John

Alderton were typical of the new sort of actor Fernald was endeavouring to produce. There were working-class girls as well, notably the shapely and down-to-earth June Ritchie; although Roedean was still represented by a wide-eyed nymphet called Sarah Miles. I first saw her in the canteen eating lunch with her mouth open. I presumed they didn't teach table manners at the best schools.

I was delighted and quite surprised to find I had acquired a bit of a reputation. Many students and teachers, including John Fernald, had seen my Mark Antony at the Queen's. It was probably the reason that I was cast as Mercutio in a full production in the Vanbrugh Theatre. I think Mercutio is the best male role in the play. Tynan dubbed him 'a lovely piece of downright cursing flesh,' with the first really tragic death scene in the entire Shakespearean canon. But Bernard Shaw had a point when he wrote: 'It took a long time for the Bard to grow out of the provincial conceit that made him so fond of exhibiting his accomplishments as a master of gallant badinage. The very thought of Berowne, Gratiano, Mercutio and Benedick must, I hope, have covered Shakespeare with shame in his later years.' Many of Mercutio's jokes are quite incomprehensible but still get laughs if delivered with enough panache. I played him, as I still tended to play most parts at that time, in the swashbuckling style of Errol Flynn. Mercutio's big hurdle is the Queen Mab speech. I have seen it interpreted many ways, but I played it straight. He uses Queen Mab to debunk Romeo's romantic dreams and his imagination soars higher and higher as he describes the course of her nightly journeys. He has nearly run out of steam when Romeo cuts him off with:

'Peace, peace, Mercutio, peace!
Thou talk'st of nothing.'

Mercutio replies:

'True, I talk of dreams,
Which are the children of an idle brain,
Begot of nothing but vain fantasy.......'

Simple really.

We were given the choice of the stock RADA Shakespearean wardrobe. I elected for black tights with a customary thick pair of socks stuffed into my jockstrap, and a loose white shirt open almost to my navel, with liberal dollops of body make-up smeared across my chest. There was an anaemic Romeo and Benvolio couldn't do much with the role – I had the same problem later. We did, however, have an excellent Tybalt, who wore his dagger and rapier like a gunslinger. He was a Californian called Larry Linville, who went on to become famous as Major Frank Burns in *Mash.* I always hoped that I would catch up with him again someday, but he died of cancer in 2000.

The dress rehearsal was one of the turning points of my life. We had assembled on stage afterwards for notes when a very attractive girl, dressed all in black, with high leather boots and a trilby pulled over one eye, came up to me.

'You are a very good actor,' she said, sounding like Marlene Dietrich.

That was all that any red-blooded drama student needed.

'How about a cup of coffee?' I enquired.

'I must tell you I come from a very good family,' she replied.

'I come from a very bad family. We sell fish and chips in Brixton market.'

'And what is fish and chips?'

And that was how it began. I soon learned that she was Jewish, a survivor of the Holocaust who had spent part of the war in a Bulgarian ghetto. She had escaped through the Iron Curtain to become a solo dancer in the Vienna Opera, but had fallen off a rostrum and injured her back so badly that she couldn't dance again. She had come to London without speaking a word of English and had auditioned for RADA by learning her audition speeches by rote. Her name was Dora Reisser and I have been with her, with a few breaks here and there, ever since.

1962: After completing a season at the Manchester Library Theatre, to my great surprise I was cast as Romeo in an ITV schools version of the play. I'd never in a thousand years have considered myself right for it; on top of that it was the first big television part I'd ever played. At that time ITV took its educational programmes very seriously and a lot of money went into the production, which was shown in five half-hour episodes. Unfortunately money was not spent on a director, and a very nice middle-aged lady from the schools department was put in charge. I don't think she'd ever directed a play before, let alone Shakespeare, but she would sit and watch us with a benevolent smile on her face. I rather think she was partial to gin. One afternoon she dropped off whilst I was rolling on the floor bewailing my cruel fate to the Friar. (I've heard Sir Peter Hall has been doing that for years. On one occasion a renowned Dame is supposed to have led the company out of the rehearsal room and left him there for the night.) Thanks to Zeffirelli, young Juliets were all the rage and mine was a Pre-Raphaelite looking girl of fourteen, with long red hair. Her name was Jane Asher. This was a few years before Paul McCartney – I don't think at that time she'd been properly kissed. Considering her lack of experience she made quite a good stab at it, but it was difficult for me. Even though I was only twenty-two myself, I felt like a cradle-snatcher and couldn't work up much passion. Good job I didn't in the light of recent scandals.

I also found Romeo a bit of a wimp – I only really enjoyed the clash with Tybalt after Mercutio's death, the Apothecary scene, and the great speech in Juliet's tomb: '*How oft when men are at the point of death,…*' which is as good as anything of Hamlet's. The problem was the sex. Like Juliet, Romeo is supposed to be a virgin. They bring to their one night together '*a pair of stainless maidenheads.*' Romeo is a hot-blooded Italian youth; even though he can't get it away with Rosaline at the beginning of the play, I couldn't believe that he hadn't knocked off a serving wench or two.

1967: It was five years later, the summer of love and *Sergeant Pepper*, and I was playing Benvolio with the RSC at Stratford-upon-Avon. I had been busy in films and had done quite well, with feature parts opposite Richard Burton, Peter O'Toole, Kirk Douglas, Dirk Bogarde, Richard Harris and Vincent Price, and even a starring role for Walt Disney, but I still had yearnings to become a classical actor. I remembered Richard Burton telling me that if you wished to have a proper career you should concentrate on the stage. So, even though I had been offered a contract by the legendary Hal Wallis, I accepted a very average line of parts by the newly formed RSC. Sad to relate I never really got back into films again, although Dora is convinced I'd be long dead from sex or drugs if I'd gone to Hollywood in 1967. Ironically enough she was herself in Hollywood that year, working on *The Dirty Dozen*. We were having one of many trial separations.

Stratford was still a market town in 1967. The main street was lined with ancient inns and a butcher's shop where each week unfortunate sheep trooped in for the slaughter. Every time I watched them I thought of those lines in *Henry IV*: '*And as the butcher takes away the calf…*' and Shakespeare didn't seem too far away. I rented a thatched cottage at Ettington and settled in with my Dalmatian dog, Kosher, intending to be a conscientious and long-serving member of the RSC.

Romeo was directed by the renowned Greek director Karolos Koun, who hardly spoke a word of English. Sometimes he would weep with frustration at his inability to express himself, but that didn't matter terribly as he had an intense understanding of the play and also of the use of atmospheric lighting, far ahead of his time. Lighting designers were virtually unheard of then; lighting effects being the preserve of the director and chief electrician. Unlike Peter Hall and John Barton, Koun did not fuss about the verse. He was forced to leave the acting to his experienced cast, concentrating on setting the atmosphere from which the play emerged. I found it a truly liberating experience. Ian Holm was Romeo, Norman Rodway Mercutio, Elizabeth Spriggs the Nurse, and Estelle Kohler, a South African actress, Juliet.

Ian Holm had been hanging about the RSC since 1953. Because of his size – he was not much above five and a half feet high – he had not been considered for leading roles, apart from the Fool in Charles Laughton's *Lear* and Puck in *The Dream*. His psychopathic Richard III in *The Wars of the Roses* changed everything. He had just won a Tony on Broadway for his performance as Lenny in Pinter's *The Homecoming*. Romeo was his first romantic role. I could sense his ambition; he was restless, feeling he had already spent too much time at Stratford. He was eight years older than me and quite envious of the films I had done – especially as I had played his stage role in *Becket*. He was about to make up for lost time. Within a few years he had won an Oscar nomination for *Chariots of Fire* and has never been out of the movies since, still finding time to play a great Lear at the National, which earned him a well-deserved knighthood.

I could never fathom the formidable Elizabeth Spriggs. She had recently married Marshall Jones, a small-part actor in the company, who had been a mature student at RADA with me. I sensed the marriage was already on the rocks. One afternoon we were both free after rehearsal and she suggested that we should go and drink a bottle of Asti Spumante together at the thatched cottage she was renting at Shottery. I was very shocked and hurt when after a couple of glasses she proceeded to tell me what a terrible actor I was. I made my excuses and left before the bottle was finished – I've never liked the taste of Asti since. My pride was a little restored when I discovered later that she had lambasted many of the young actors in the company in a similar fashion. But I still began to think, being a typical insecure actor, that maybe she was right. Up until then I had always played showy parts in Shakespeare and been noticed and praised, but try as I might, there was nothing much I could do with Benvolio. All he really has is a short poetic speech in the first scene, grief over Mercutio's death and a tearful explanation of Romeo's fight with Tybalt, which the audience has just witnessed. He disappears completely in the second half.

'For never was a story of more woe.
Whatever happened to Benvolio?'

He's the only young one left alive at the end. Zeffirelli had him weeping over the bodies of Romeo and Juliet as the final image of his renowned production, and I was rather hoping that Koun would do the same. I remember suggesting it on more than one occasion. But that was not to be. I spent a very relaxing second half sunbathing on the balcony overlooking the Avon, reading in the dressing room, or chatting up the bored local housewives, who'd been brought in to make up numbers in the ball scene. Sometimes it went a bit further than flirting. I seem to recall a fervent session in a dark corner under the stage whilst Romeo was departing for Padua above. I was not alone. The place was heaving with rutting Capulets and Montagues. Voluminous Renaissance dresses were easily raised and codpieces were undone and put to their proper use. It was like a scene from Boccaccio, but don't forget, this was the summer of love: carefree sex at last – thanks to the pill and penicillin. We had no idea the nightmare of AIDS was waiting in the wings.

It was nevertheless a wonderful production. Ian Holm's lack of inches worked perfectly for Romeo; although he was thirty-seven years old, he still looked like a boy. There was a most touching moment in the balcony scene when he stretched up on tiptoes and couldn't quite reach Juliet's hand. At the same time he had the experience to explore the passion-racked depths of the role, which even John Stride had not reached. Holm had a sense of danger and wildness about him. His father had been superintendent of an East London mental hospital and Ian had studied the patients in his youth. He had, and has, a quality of spontaneity and surprise in his acting: Each time I pulled him away from his berserk savaging of the dead Tybalt, I wasn't quite sure if he would turn on me. Estelle Kohler was a moving Juliet, despite having her surly American husband hanging around, complaining to all and sundry that he should be playing Tybalt. Sebastian Shaw made Friar Lawrence a manly figure, not the usual doddering old fool. He had played Romeo at Stratford in 1926. That was the famous season when the original theatre burnt down and the company had to play in the local cinema. Norman Rodway, given free rein, was 'the most foul-mouthed' of Mercutios. Rodway who always depicted himself as 'a broth of an Irish boy' was in fact born in Dublin of English parents. Elizabeth Spriggs's bespectacled Nurse was said to have 'effaced the memory of Edith Evans herself'.

At that time the RSC was campaigning feverishly for a permanent London home and only the best productions at Stratford were taken down to the Aldwych Theatre at the end of the season. (I still find it unbelievable that Adrian Noble threw away the Barbican after all the struggles his predecessors went through to get it, but that is another story.) We were the first major production of *Romeo and Juliet* since Zefferelli's at the Old Vic in 1960 and we should have gone. On top of that Koun's production was universally acclaimed: 'One of the great Shakespearian productions of our generation,' ...'by far the best of an uneven season'... 'it reaches a standard that we have not seen for too long.'...'the play seems more powerful than I have ever known it'. But Karolos Koun was not a staff director so his production played for only a couple of months in Stratford, whilst Hall's ill-fated *Macbeth* and Barton's undistinguished *All's Well* were transferred to the Aldwych. In spite of their loudly proclaimed socialist egalitarian principles, RSC directors seemed to me just as grasping and ambitious as the most selfish West End star. Actors were becoming less important, even less sexy – the directors were pulling the best girls.

In the sixties, young actors hoped to remain with the RSC for several years as an Associate Artist and work their way up through the ranks. That had been what I had fully expected to do, but I grew to dislike the claustrophobic atmosphere. It seemed to me that everyone was perpetually sucking up to the directors and Maurice Daniels, the all-powerful head of casting, and I've never been any good at politics. I only wish I had. And I tried, believe you me. You could tell the people that were 'in'. Alan Howard was a case in point. We had become quite close during the filming of *Heroes of Telemark* or *Carry on Kirk* as we called it; I'd even introduced him to his first wife, the beautiful Stephanie Beaumont, who'd shared a flat with Dora. I had had a much bigger part in the film, I was billed just behind Michael Redgrave, Alan was way down among the other ranks; but at Stratford he quite deservedly moved straight into the upper echelons.

Helen Mirren was 'in' the moment she walked through the stage door. She had every director salivating at her feet. Ben Kingsley and Patrick Stewart also quickly found favour with the powers that were, but I began to realise that I wasn't 'in'. Even Pam, the formidable Mistress Quickly of the Dirty Duck, never asked me for a photo to put on her wall. I couldn't understand it. Mind you, I was dabbling with one of her nubile barmaids. It was the first time I hadn't been 'in'. I had been 'in' at the NYT, at RADA, at Manchester, the Mermaid, and the films I'd made – but not here. It was a sobering moment.

Nevertheless I made the most of that summer. I drove a fire-engine red Mini-De-luxe, sported a loosely tied silk scarf and shining patent Chelsea boots, and went everywhere with Kosher: I considered myself the very image of a swinging sixties actor. And the sixties really did swing: girls, from every known continent, came to Stratford that summer in microscopic mini-skirts, eager and fully equipped. I endeavoured to oblige as many as I could, although I suspect that Kosher was the real attraction.

1968: I was about to finish my first spell with the RSC, when one morning my agent rang and told me I had to go immediately for a voice test. I went to some small place in Bayswater and as I was waiting in the outer office, a smiling and confident Ian McKellen walked out of the studio with Dyson Lovell, whom I'd last seen playing Pericles at RADA, clad in a skimpy loin cloth, frantically banging a drum as he waited for me to lower the curtain. (That story will come later.) I was relieved he did not seem to remember me. He told me he was Franco Zeffirelli's assistant on the film of *Romeo and Juliet* and had been sent to find a new voice for the actor playing Benvolio. Though McKellen was not yet a star his reputation was such that I immediately presumed that he'd got the job. Nevertheless I recorded Benvolio's poetic speech in the opening scene and thought no more about it. A couple of days later I was very pleasantly surprised when my agent rang to say that Zeffirelli had liked my voice and wanted me in Rome immediately.

Dubbing was, and is, the norm in Italian cinema. Sophia Loren's voice was always dubbed in Italy because her Neapolitan accent didn't go down too well in Rome. But I had no idea why Zeffirelli should want a new voice for his Benvolio, who was played by a young actor called Bruce Robinson. I even felt a bit sorry for him. I looked forward to meeting two old acquaintances: Tybalt, in the shape of Michael York, who I had known for years in the NYT when he was Michael Johnson, a broken-nosed, blonde boy from Bromley; and Romeo himself, Leonard Whiting, who'd been my young cockney side-kick in the Dick Turpin film I had made for Walt Disney.

I got to Rome and was driven to the studio early, before Zeffirelli arrived, where a young, doe-eyed sound editor screened some of the scenes I had to dub. I was stunned by the beauty of the settings and costumes. Tybalt is an eye-catching part, but Michael York was giving the best performance of his career, including *Cabaret*. Leonard Whiting looked like a beautiful Renaissance painting, as did Bruce Robinson. Moreover, in my opinion there was nothing wrong with the way Bruce said the lines, which I was all too familiar with. Leonard, on the other hand, sounded strained and false. I wondered momentarily if they had made a mistake and wanted someone to dub Romeo. I asked the Italian technician if he knew why Benvolio had to have a new voice. He winked and said, 'He didn't do what Franco wanted.' Was it to be Groundhog Day for me? I had been propositioned by a film director in Rome the last time I had been there, when I played Mark Antony in 1961. I had responded then in the same way as Bruce, and had not the slightest doubt that I would do the same again. I wondered how long it would be before I'd be on the plane back to London. My unease increased when the phone rang and the Italian's handsome face creased into a worried frown as he listened to an excited voice at the other end of the line. He shot a few glances at me and nodded with what I took to be pity. He put the phone down and said: 'You'd better take an early lunch. Franco wants to record someone else this morning. Come back at two.'

I was convinced that Ian McKellen had arrived in Rome and was going to dub Benvolio after all. I ate a miserable seafood linguini, wondering if I would still be paid – I'd heard terrible tales about tricky Italian producers. The red light was on when I got back to the ante-room. I expected to hear McKellen's mellifluous voice intoning the familiar lines, but it was somebody else and the lines certainly weren't familiar. There were curses, cries, coughs and groans. Triumphant laughs and agonised howls. I listened awe-struck. I was even more awe-struck when the red light eventually went out, the door opened, and Zeffirelli emerged with his arm around the shoulder of Sir Laurence Olivier himself. I learnt later that the great man was in Rome filming an epic, *The Shoes of the Fisherman,* and having a free day had offered to supply Franco with his range of voices for the soundtrack.

When he eventually got round to me, Zeffirelli didn't seem to fancy me at all. I'm not sure whether I was relieved or hurt. However, he made me feel relaxed and confident, explaining what he wanted in the simplest terms. I spent a very enjoyable couple of days with him. Leonard Whiting had changed greatly in the four years since we'd filmed together. Then he'd been an effervescent cockney lad, hot from playing the Artful Dodger in *Oliver!* Now he was hesitant and uncertain of himself. I learned that he had been sent away from his home at Olivier's suggestion, to live with the family of the gentleman actor, Anthony Nicholls, to improve his speech and accent. I think he would have had a better career if they had left him alone.

I needn't have worried about doing Bruce Robinson out of a job – within a few years he was nominated for an Oscar for writing *The Killing Fields* and had directed the iconic *Withnail and I.*

1970: I thought I had finished with Benvolio, but two years later John Tydeman, the doyen of radio directors, asked me to play the boring bugger again. It was an all-star cast with Ian McKellen as Romeo. I trotted out the same old lines once more, although I never told McKellen that I'd dubbed them in Rome.

I always fancied playing Capulet, which is an extremely good part. A mini-Lear in some ways, but it never came my way.

Richard II

'Richard "plunges his nose with zest into the bouquet of humiliation" but he grows up the moment he is about to be cut down: "I wasted time, but now doth time waste me."'
James Agate (1877-1947)

Tattle: First printed in Quarto in 1597 without the deposition scene – very understandable as that scene was considered treasonous and was to play a crucial part in the Essex conspiracy. In spite of the famous victory of 1588, England was still at war with Spain. Fresh Armadas were sent in 1596, 1597 and 1601. This is reflected in the extreme patriotism of Gaunt's dying speech, which looks a doddle but is extremely hard to do. The throwing down and picking up of the gauntlets and the scene between the Duke and Duchess of York and their son Aumerle can easily appear ridiculous. They are often played for laughs, but I'm not entirely sure that this was Shakespeare's intention.

Richard is one of the great lyrical roles; his long, seemingly everlasting speeches are almost arias. The play was rarely performed until the young John Gielgud played the petulant king in 1929. Harcourt Williams, a revered director at the Old Vic whom I always think of as the mad French King in Olivier's film of *Henry V*, declared: 'Gielgud's playing of the abdication scene will live in my mind as one of the greatest things I have ever seen in the theatre.' Gielgud has left his explicit instructions on how the role should be played: 'The actor playing Richard cannot hope at any time during the action to be wholly sympathetic to the audience. Indeed he must use the early scenes to create an impression of slyness, petty vanity, and callous indifference. But he must also show himself to be innately well-bred, sensitive to beauty, lonely in his aloof position of kingship, young, headstrong, frivolous, and entirely out of sympathy with the older men who try so vainly to advise him and control his whims.'

Michael Redgrave, who played Bolingbroke when Gielgud played Richard again in 1937, wrote: 'John was as near perfect as I could wish or imagine. Ninety per cent of the beauty of his acting was the beauty of his voice, and to this day I can see no way of improving on the dazzling virtuosity of the phrasing or breathing which was Gielgud's.' Redgrave played Richard himself in 1951. Tynan reviewed it in his inimitable fashion: 'Redgrave, still missing the real heights by an inexplicable inch, makes a fine sketch of Richard, using a shaky tenor voice, a foppish smile, and damp, uncertain eyes to summon up the poor man's instability. In the early scenes, clad in sky-blue doublet and cloak of palest orange, he looked exquisitely over-mothered, a king sculpted in puppy-fat.'

Since then Richards have been practically tumbling over each other. Nearly all our leading actors have had a go. Paul Scofield, directed by Gielgud, deliberately sought to de-romanticise the role. John Neville saw him as a playboy. Harry H. Corbett, a stalwart of Theatre Workshop at Stratford East, long before he found universal fame in *Steptoe & Son*, depicted King Richard as a raving queen. David Warner's nervous smiles and loose-limbed awkwardness were described very harshly by one critic as 'bloodless as a vegetarian dinner'. Ian McKellen has been quoted as saying that classical drama is only worthwhile if closely tied to the current world. In 1968, in keeping with the times, he created a young and frivolous king, surrounded by student-type friends, rebelling against the established order. It was his first great Shakespearean success. Derek Jacobi returned to the romantic interpretation and enjoyed almost universal acclaim on stage and on television with Gielgud as Gaunt. Back at the RSC, Ian Richardson and Richard Pasco brilliantly switched Richard and Bolingbroke on alternate nights. I thought Alan Howard sounded rather like a Dalek when he included Richard in his round-up of Shakespearean kings; Jeremy Irons was excellent, as he usually is, but David William in *An Age of Kings* was the best I've seen. He was regal but truly dangerous, a megalomaniac and a tyrant. It is easy to forget that before the play opens he has been deeply involved in the murder of his uncle Gloucester.

Gloucesters are to be found throughout the histories, one even turns up in *Lear*. The choice for older actors is which Duke: Gaunt or York? Gaunt has a great but very difficult speech then goes home early, unless he has to double with the gardener. York hangs on ineffectually throughout the play but has some touching and comic moments.

Memories: I left RADA with the Special Medal, which made some amends for Wolfit's failure to award me the reading prize at Alleyn's. (RADA stopped awarding medals about the same time competitive sport was banned in schools. I can't for the life of me understand why. Acting is the most competitive business that there is, with awards and gongs galore.) I went back to Gower Street recently and found my name on the honours board, sandwiched between Sir Tom Courtenay and Sir Anthony Hopkins, both of whom I must confess have done slightly better than me. But I was brimful of confidence in that summer of 1961. Three top agents had been begging me to sign with them and I was certain I was on my way to stardom. It was a most exciting time to be a young actor. The RSC had just been formed; Olivier was about to launch the National Theatre at Chichester; new regional theatres were being built all over the country; even though we had only two channels, there was first-class live drama on television nearly every night; and a new wave was bursting over the ailing British film industry. I already had a job promised in the autumn – a season at the prestigious Manchester Library Theatre – so when Michael Croft obtained the Apollo on Shaftesbury Avenue for a month at extremely reasonable terms and asked me to do Bolingbroke, I willingly agreed. It was a wonderful shop window. Croft had directed *Richard II* earlier that year with the OUDS – the renowned Oxford University Dramatic Society – and intended to repeat his production with Richard Hampton remaining in the title role.

By then most of the NYT had been together for five years; one critic said we were the only real ensemble company in the country apart from Joan Littlewoods's *Theatre Workshop*. We had a great cast including John Shrapnel as Mowbray, Martin Jarvis as the Earl Marshal, Ian McShane as Hotspur, Neil Stacy as York, Simon Ward as Aumerle, Hywel Bennett as Bushy, and a newcomer, Michael Pennington, as Salisbury. Some of the original OUDS cast also took part, bringing with them a calypso, of which I can only remember the refrain:

'Who is the Queen?
Is it Bushy, Baggot or Green?
Or is it one of the pages?'

The colourful costumes, overflowing with mediaeval pageantry, from the previous year's production at the Old Vic, were superb. I had a scarlet tabard with the rose of Lancaster emblazoned across my chest, and armour which made my shoulders wider than an American footballer. How could you go wrong with a get-up like that? Bolingbroke is a great role and one of my favourites. He starts off with a fiery slanging match with Mowbray and then is extremely macho in the lists at Coventry, followed by a tender farewell to his aged father. Then he has an act off before he returns hell-bent on claiming his rights. It is up to the actor to decide when Bolingbroke resolves to go for broke (I didn't intend that pun) and claim the crown itself. Power begins to corrupt him and at the end of the play he senses the growing hostility of his strongest allies, Northumberland and Hotspur. The only thing going against Bolingbroke is that he has to stand around for hours on end like everyone else, as Richard laments his misfortunes. Unfortunately, although we had good reviews, the novelty of boys playing Shakespeare in the West End was wearing thin and we played to very poor houses.

Forty-four years later in 2005 I was in the play again – albeit in a much less prominent position. Kevin Spacey had taken over the Old Vic and wanted Trevor Nunn to direct him in a leading Shakespearean role. The obvious choice would have been Richard III, but Trevor persuaded him to go for Richard II. It did not really matter – there was a touch of the hunchback in Kevin's performance anyway. As soon as I heard Trevor was going to direct it, I followed the actor's time-honoured formula of writing a letter asking to be in it. I would have loved to play Gaunt, but realised that a 'name' actor would be required for that important character, and therefore suggested myself for the good but subsidiary role of Northumberland. The following week my agent informed me that Northumberland was already cast but that Trevor wanted me to be in it, and was offering me the small part of Willoughby plus the understudy of Northumberland. It still sounded an exciting proposition and I'd always wanted to act at the Old Vic, so I accepted.

Kevin Spacey was not present at the first day's rehearsal – he was still in Australia finishing a Batman movie. The rest of us spent the day listening to Trevor lugubriously expound his ideas on the play. It was going to be a modern dress production using lots of state-of-the-art multi-media. Trevor had adapted the opening and completely cut the lists at Coventry, so that the first act took place in a crowded House of Lords. He therefore needed a large number of mature actors to fill the benches. I looked around and saw lots of old familiar faces and knew it was going to be an enjoyable job with plenty of gossip and reminiscences. Our star arrived a bit jet-lagged the following day and we started off by reading the play. Kevin, having done little Shakespeare, must have been a little anxious reading before such a quizzical, knowledgeable throng. He read very well, his only mistake was when he came to the line: *'You, who with Pilate wash your hands,'* which he pronounced if we were doing our ablutions in the manner of a fashionable exercise. There were superior smirks all round.

Trevor devised a marvellous opening in which all we old farts tramped on in our long, authentic, House of Lords robes to the music of *Zadok the Priest.* I told Jeffrey Archer about it and he generously offered to lend me his Lord's robe for the production, as he didn't think he'd have much use for it in future. It duly arrived in pristine condition, far superior to the somewhat bedraggled robes that had arrived from the costumiers. I was rather miffed when it was issued to Bolingbroke. My old school-fellow, Julian Glover, was John of Gaunt, and did the famous speech as a sort of television party political broadcast. Remembering the eternal standing about from the production of my youth, I elected to play Willoughby as a hunting/fishing type complete with shooting stick, which I sat upon at every opportunity. Trevor always strives to give actors a line through the play, no matter how small their part. I became the old reactionary who stuck with Bolingbroke to the bitter end. I enjoyed it very much, always remembering the old adage I'd been taught at RADA: 'There are no small parts, only small actors.' I got several laughs and even a notice. Ben Miles was outstanding as Bolingbroke.

The production was only a qualified artistic success but played to packed houses. I have nothing but admiration for Kevin Spacey. Despite bad notices and some adverse publicity when he first took over, he doggedly stuck to his task and, without any Government grant, has firmly established the Old Vic on a sound financial basis. He will be an extremely hard act to follow. Kenneth Branagh would be my choice. But whenever a theatre is modernised or refurbished it is the non-theatrical departments that expand. There was always a shortage of dressing rooms at the Vic, but now many are occupied by such things as publicity, marketing and corporate hospitality, things which never existed in my youth. I, together with the Bishop of Carlisle and the Gardener, was stuffed in an airless sort of cupboard under the stage.

The following year the production was invited to a Shakespeare festival in Recklinghausen, a small town in Germany near the Ruhr. Oliver Cotton, who had played Northumberland originally, rang to tell me he would not be going because of other commitments. I therefore told my ineffectual agent, 'the dregs of that dull race', that I naturally assumed that as I had been the understudy I was going to be offered the part. She rang the Old Vic and was told that it was their policy that 'major' parts such as Northumberland would only be offered to 'name' actors. It was at that moment I fully realised how far down the pecking order I'd fallen. I was even more disillusioned when the two young actors who had been understudying Mowbray and Hotspur were given the roles. I sent Trevor an email, saying how let down I felt. Trevor replied immediately saying he was no longer involved as he was now working on his next project. The production had been taken over by the associate director, it had nothing to do with him, and he would never intentionally hurt my feelings. I wondered if he was doing a 'Pilate'.

I considered telling them to stuff Willoughby, but have never forgotten an old actor telling me when I was starting, that he'd very rarely regretted accepting a job, but he'd often regretted turning jobs down. The money was good and the company would be staying in an attractive old German hotel. I decided to swallow my pride and take Dora along for a holiday. I was glad I did. The Germans looked after us very well; we played in a sort of miniature Glyndebourne, before very intelligent and appreciative audiences. Spacey, unlike most stars, stayed in the same hotel and entertained the company every night.

Northumberland was taken over by a competent actor of whom I'd never heard, nor have heard of since.

A Midsummer Night's Dream

'It is the most insipid, ridiculous play that ever I saw in my life.'
Samuel Pepys. Again!

Tattle: Titania describes the unusually bad weather of the summer of 1594, which gives rise to the belief that the play was written to celebrate the marriage of William Stanley, Earl of Derby, to Elizabeth Vere in January 1595. In 1691 Purcell turned it into an opera, *The Fairy Queen,* with words by the actor, Thomas Betterton. *The Dream* only really became popular in the latter half of the nineteenth century. Sir Herbert Beerbohm Tree gave a spectacular production with real rabbits and Mendelssohn's music. Alas it failed to enchant Bernard Shaw: 'As Titania, Mrs Tree plays prettily, but is scarcely fairy-like. It is a fairy from South Kensington, whose revels are limited to Queen's Gate, and whose rings are to be found in Kensington Gardens. Mrs Tree gives one the notion that Titania has smart friends somewhere, and is only out in the wood because it happens for the time to be a society fad. As Theseus, Mr William Mollison was admirable; we cannot tell why, but we can always hear Mr Mollison, whereas with most other actors we have to listen. We imagine the reason to be that Mr Mollison is one of the few actors on stage who have really learnt to speak; the others, for the most part, only talk.' The same could be said of many actors at the National and RSC today, mainly because they are only ever taught to act in small theatres.

Charles Laughton offered up his ample Bottom at Stratford in 1959, but Tynan thought his performance had nothing to do with acting. Peggy Ashcroft, Vivien Leigh and Judi Dench have been beautiful Titanias, whilst Vanessa Redgrave, Diana Rigg and Helen Mirren have taken their tumbles as Helena and Hermia. The four lovers are usually very grateful for the long sleep Shakespeare thoughtfully provides at the end of the frantic and very tiring quarrel scene in the forest; but pretending to sleep on stage can be very dangerous. Sebastian Shaw told me he dropped off completely playing Lysander in 1929, as did Amanda Grinling as Helena in Regent's Park in 1962. She woke from a pleasant slumber and squealed to behold a strange man bending over her in the dark.

Memories: I have dim recollections of my grandmother taking me to see a matinee in Regent's Park during the war. It would have had to be a matinee because of the blackout. The legendary Robert Atkins must have been playing Bottom but all I can remember is that it rained and most of the play was performed in a tent. The seating was not raked and I hardly saw a thing. The first performance I remember is a truly magical one at the Old Vic, despite Tommy Steele, the biggest pop star before the Beatles, being a painfully gormless Puck.

We did the forest scene in my first term at RADA in 1957, where I had finally arrived, pumping teenage testosterone, from my all-boys grammar school. I had had expectations of beautiful, nubile, female students, all looking like young Vivien Leighs, but on the very first day, realisation brought me harshly down to earth. There were ten girls in my class with not a whiff of Lady Olivier about any of them. For that matter I don't suppose there was much of Sir Larry about us men. I was cast as Demetrius, the first time I'd played a lover, albeit quite a nasty one, and tried in vain to engender passion for my Helena, an earnest Oxbridge graduate, with a face which always made me think of a startled horse. Hermia, the first target of my affections, was an Australian girl with acute acne and very inflated opinion of her very limited talents. Titania was a large female member of the communist party from some northern university with no visible sense of humour. Oberon, from New Zealand, was what we then called very 'camp'. Puck was played by a pleasant little cockney lad who had appeared in lots of Boy Scout Gang Shows, and it showed. Bottom, the part I coveted, to my great chagrin, was given to Kenneth, a fat chap from Leeds, who wore the same unwashed shirt for most of the term. He also had an unpleasant habit of breaking wind in the Academy's sole telephone cubicle. I always seemed to go in directly after him. He had been a leading light in the Yorkshire am-dram world, and considered himself to be the next Charles Laughton. I thought at the time that he would be, but like most of that class he has sunk without a trace. In fact the only other one who has lasted in the business was handsome Robin Hawdon, now a playwright with a string of successful comedies to his credit, who was giving his Lysander. We were directed by a frail old actress called Nell Carter, affectionately nicknamed 'Nell of Old Drury'. She had worked with Sir Frank Benson and been directing Shakespeare at the Academy almost since then, giving the students exactly the same moves and intonations year after year. It was all so different from the virile Youth Theatre productions I had grown up with.

I always thought I'd do Bottom one day, but it was not to be.

In 1978, after being his assistant on several occasions, David Conville invited me to direct *The Dream* and play Theseus at the Open Air Theatre in Regent's Park. It was not really my production; I merely rehashed an earlier, successful one of David's. He had set it in Byronic Greece with the lovers in attractive Regency-style costumes, the mechanicals as Greek peasants, and Theseus dressed as the Duke of Wellington, in scarlet tunic, tight white trousers and black shining boots. Together with Lysander and Demetrius I was even given a Byronic perm. Although Theseus has the most lines in the play, I don't think it is a really interesting part unless he is combined with Oberon. On the other hand, although I could give a good manly rendering of the Athenian Duke, I was never cut out to be the Fairy King. Also, as Theseus appears only at the beginning and the end of the play, it was much easier to direct. Not that I had all that much to do. The mechanicals, led by the indestructible Ian Talbot as Bottom, and the Quince of Anthony Sharpe, a West End veteran of the old school, had played their parts for several years and knew how to squeeze out every possible laugh. All I had to look out for were the young lovers and the very attractive fairies.

The Dream is the ideal play for the open air. Darkness falls in June and July at exactly the right time – in the middle of the lovers' quarrel. *Hamlet* and *Macbeth* never work in the park because they both require darkness in the opening scenes. The poor sod giving his Macbeth has enough problems seeing the dagger leading him to Duncan's murder without the sun shining directly into his eyes. How can the Ghost stalk the battlements of Elsinore amongst summer foliage? Likewise how can Lear imagine the storm and 'poor naked wretches' on a balmy summer's evening? And believe me, no matter how bad the English summer, there are plenty of balmy evenings in Regent's Park. On average only four performances a year are cancelled because of inclement weather.

By this time, Dora had decided we needed a regular income and was busy with her dress-designing. We had two small sons and I was often required to look after them during their summer holidays. As we lived in Camden Town, a stone's throw from the park, it was usually not too difficult. On matinee days I would take the boys and their Yorkshire terrier with me, and they would read or play chess with the other actors backstage or play cricket in the park, quite happily without any trouble. Then one day I was informed that we would have to take Jeremy with us, because Jeremy was coming for a 'sleepover' – I think it was the first time I had heard that particular Americanism. Jeremy was my least favourite of all the obstreperous brats that made up my sons' circle of acquaintances. I considered him rude and noisy and I don't think he thought much of me either. Nevertheless I took him along together with my boys and the dog that hot August afternoon. As Jeremy had never seen the play I suggested that they might like to watch it by sitting on the grassy bank at the side of the stage. Jeremy shrugged and showed little enthusiasm, but the play began with them all in place, apart from the dog, who was being looked after by one of the fairies. The trouble with matinees in the Park is that you can see the audience quite distinctly. As I began to declaim I was aware of Jeremy gazing superciliously at me – he obviously thought I was a real 'plonker'. The boys had had enough by the end of the first scene and went off to play cricket. They came back just as we were about to go on for Bottom's play. 'Why don't you take Jeremy back out front and watch this scene?' I asked with all the kindness and enthusiasm I could muster. 'It's very funny.'

Jeremy shrugged again and they traipsed round to the auditorium. They were back in their positions on the grassy bank as I made my entrance. The scene opens with Theseus's best moment of the play, '*The lunatic, the lover, and the poet*' speech, which I never really got right. (It was the director's fault, of course.) As I gazed soulfully and meaningfully out front I caught Jeremy yawning out of the corner of my eye. I couldn't stop myself looking at the brat throughout the rest of the speech. He was looking around. I knew he was planning something. Bottom and his troupe came on and began to perform their play. Howls of laughter rang down the steep ranks of the auditorium. I looked back towards Jeremy, expecting to see at least a trace of amusement on his face. The little sod had disappeared, together with my boys. I continued with the scene, in what ducal dignity

I could muster, whilst casting anxious eyes around the auditorium, until I noticed a rustling in the shrubbery on stage left. The bushes parted and I beheld Jeremy's superior sneer, framed by the amused grins of my two sons. I deliberately turned my head but couldn't stop myself looking back a moment later. Jeremy stuck out his tongue and put his fingers to his ears and waggled them. The audience were too busy laughing at Ian Talbot's antics to notice, but I'd had enough.

Edward Hibbert, playing Philostrate, my major-domo, his days in *Frasier* well ahead of him, had seen it too. 'Get those little bastards out of there' I commanded in a not very well-disguised stage whisper. Edward duly bowed and exited hastily up the steps at the back of the stage as if he were going into the palace. A few moments later there was a violent rustling in the bushes and the three little faces were dragged out of sight. Edward deposited them with the stage management and rushed back to finish watching Bottom's play. That was the last time I took my boys to the Park that summer. The last I heard of Jeremy he was earning lots of money in the City. I'm not surprised.

David Conville invited me to direct *The Dream* again the following year, which I did with the same crew of mechanicals – it was like a pension for them, they turned up every year no matter who was directing it and gave the same performances. Then in September Michael Croft asked me to direct it for the National Youth Theatre at the Roundhouse. Joe Davis' lighting was wonderfully atmospheric, with the forest depicted by shadows on the floor of the huge round playing space. Tony Howes, who was an irrepressible Puck – and has been irrepressible ever since – tells me Colin Firth made one of his earliest appearances as Mustard Seed. Apparently I failed as a director to inspire much life into him, and made him stand at the back, pretending to be a tree. I must state that my normally excellent memory has no recollection of it.

The Merchant of Venice

'A curate's egg of a play – or rather a rabbi's egg.'
Kenneth Tynan (1927-80)

Tattle: The play was influenced by Marlowe's *Jew of Malta* and the trial and execution in 1594 of Queen Elizabeth's physician, Rodrigo Lopez, a Portuguese Jew who professed to be a Christian. Shakespeare knew all about usury – his father indulged in money lending at twenty per cent, double the legal rate. A recent theory, propagated mainly on the Internet, is that he was also influenced by Aemilia Bassano, a possible contender for the Dark Lady, whose father was reputed to be a Jewish musician from Venice. (If you delve deeper you can even find fanciful claims that she was the true author of the Complete Works.)

Following the Restoration the play was rewritten as *The Jew of Venice* in which Shylock was played for laughs by low comedians with red beards and long noses. Charles Macklin, in 1744, reverted to the original and was reputedly the first to play Shylock with 'fearsome dignity'. He was certainly fearsome: he once killed an actor in the Green Room at Drury Lane, by thrusting his cane into the poor chap's eye. They were having a quarrel over a wig, of all things. Macklin was perhaps the father of naturalistic or even 'method acting': he went about the streets and markets of London studying how Jews spoke and behaved. He had peculiar habits; he used to wash himself all over every night in brandy. That may explain his longevity – he was still playing Shylock in 1789 when he was well into his nineties.

When the poor strolling player, Edmund Kean, was given a chance at Drury Lane in January 1814, he chose to play Shylock as his debut. Kean had had barely a couple of hours' rehearsal with the rest of the cast, who treated him disdainfully as a provincial parvenu. He was short and almost insignificant in appearance and wore a black wig and beard – even Macklin had worn the traditional red. When he stepped on stage the theatre was freezing cold and more than half empty, but as soon as he spoke his first line, *'Three thousands ducats, – well,'* he is reputed to have had the audience in the palm of his hand. His Jew hated and suffered with equal passion, he inspired loathing and pity, fear and contempt, with an infinite variety of expressions and gestures. There was such variety and expressiveness in his gestures that it almost appeared as if his body thought. His triumph was so great that he positively acted Shakespeare off the stage and the audience refused to let the play continue after his final exit in the trial. William Hazlitt, who was the only critic present, declared in *The Morning Chronicle*: 'His style of acting is more significant, more pregnant with meaning, more varied and alive in every part, than any we have ever witnessed.'

Later in the century, Sir Henry Irving went even further, seeing Shylock as a symbol of a persecuted race, more of a gentleman than anyone else in the play. He struck his bargain with Antonio as a jest; it was only after Jessica's betrayal that he fell to the irresistible temptation to use it as a weapon of revenge. The problem with this interpretation is Shylock's speech earlier in the scene: *'I hate him for he is a Christian.... If I can catch him once upon the hip, I will feed fat the ancient grudge I bear him.'* David Thacker, who directed an otherwise excellent production for the RSC, solved the problem by simply cutting the lines. I hardly think that is the answer. My personal belief is Shakespeare began by writing Shylock as a villain but the sheer force of Shylock's character took control of his pen.

I have seen Ralph Richardson play Shylock like a perplexed schoolmaster and Laurence Olivier as a Rothschild with a double set of false teeth. I have been told on good authority that when Robert Helpmann played the Jew, he would regularly roll up his 'Jewish gaberdine' at curtain call and display his bare bum to the rest of the cast. I would have paid a few ducats to see that.

Memories: This is an extremely unpleasant play to be in. Judi Dench loathes it – she thinks everyone behaves badly and wouldn't cross the road to see it. Unless you are Shylock or perhaps the Prince of Morocco, the characters haven't an ounce of sympathy. Antonio is an anti-Semitic bigot – he admits he has spat on Shylock and called him dog, and swears he will do it again. He refuses Shylock's offer of friendship when the bond is first agreed. Bassanio and Lorenzo are shallow money-grabbers, Gratiano is little better than a fascist, Portia is a blue-stockinged goody-goody and Nerissa her sycophantic acolyte. Jessica is a selfish, faithless daughter and Gobbo is perhaps the least funny clown in all Shakespeare. He could have been the reason Will Kempe left the company in a huff and jigged to Norwich.

Frank Dunlop, who always reminded me of a mischievous imp on speed, was a product of the golden age of Repertory. He had run both the old theatre and the newly-built Nottingham Playhouse before going on to become one of Olivier's lieutenants at the National and then founding the Young Vic. I worked for him many times over the years and found him a bold and inventive director. If he had a fault it was that he was usually juggling three balls in the air at once and left a lot of the actual directing to his assistants. Not all of Frank's ideas came off, but it was never dull when he was around. When he offered me Antonio in the early eighties I was very happy to accept. Frank went against form and opted for a straightforward Elizabethan production: I was dressed more or less as Sir Walter Raleigh and tried to find the latent homosexuality and loneliness within the character. Antonio is *The* Merchant of Venice, the one above all that Shylock wishes to ingratiate himself with or bring down. I endeavoured to play Antonio as if he was the leading role, which is rather difficult because Shakespeare seems to lose interest in him as he becomes more and more fascinated with Shylock. He never fully explains why Antonio is so sad at the beginning of the play, although I am certain it is because of his unrequited love for Bassanio. There is also the debate about Antonio's attitude to Shylock at the end of the trial. At first glance, stipulating that Shylock must become a Christian is the cruellest punishment of all, but Antonio could be trying to save Shylock's soul if he believes that only Christians can enter Paradise. I tried to play it as if Antonio had been truly moved by Portia's speech on mercy, losing the hatred he feels at the beginning of the scene. In the same vein he asks the court to give Shylock half his money back, provided that he, Antonio, manages the other half for the benefit of Lorenzo and Jessica. Having seen how badly Antonio has managed his own affairs, one wonders how much the newly-weds will eventually get.

The first thing Lear looks for is a lightweight Cordelia to carry on at the end, likewise Antonio needs a Bassanio he finds attractive even in a heterosexual way. I was fortunate because my Bassanio was played by the good-looking son of Jack Hawkins. Derek Francis, an Old Vic stalwart, was a straightforward Shylock. My most vivid memory of the production is the performance after *The Mousetrap* anniversary.

During the run at the Young Vic Agatha Christie's potboiler achieved some new landmark on its inexorable run and Peter Saunders, the producer, threw a great lunch-time drinks party at the Savoy. An old friend was in the cast at the time and invited me along. It was a truly wonderful affair, packed with acquaintances and the odd ex-lover I hadn't seen in years. Glasses of champagne seemed to evaporate miraculously as I swapped reminiscences and anecdotes with old chum after old chum. The time flew and I suddenly realised the party had gone on to half past five. I stumbled out into the Strand and made my way across Waterloo Bridge to the Young Vic. It was a cold evening and I realised to my horror that I was drunk and the performance was less than an hour and a half away. When I was young I'd heard that some actors could not perform unless they were half-cut. Richard Burton drank so much beer one night whilst playing Prince Hal that he pissed in his armour. I'd often had a few glasses of wine before a show but I'd never been like this. I was, as Bernard Shaw had said of Sir Henry Irving, 'not answering my helm satisfactorily'. I am never nervous before going on but that night I was terrified. Would I remember the lines? Let alone give a responsible rendering of the part? I was letting down my fellow actors and more importantly the audience. I drank several cups of black coffee then lay on the concrete floor of the dressing room in my doublet and hose and mumbled to those who asked what the matter was: 'Don't worry. I'll be there.' I got there and got through the performance although I can't remember a thing about it. I've barely touched alcohol before a show since.

The following spring we took the production on a ten-week tour with a largely new cast, and a new director as Frank was busy with something else. This time Bassanio was played by the sturdy Michael Simkins. We were now dressed in Italian Renaissance costumes complete with Veronica Lake wigs to our shoulders. Michael, as well as being a wonderfully amusing writer, is an excellent actor for whom I have the greatest admiration; but every night, try as I might, he singularly failed to arouse me when he ambled towards me in the trial to take his final farewell. I can still see him, dressed in baggy pantaloons, a flat Tudor-style cap stuck on top of his flaxen tresses, his face screwed up like a dried prune. He looked like a hefty girl from the hockey team. It was during that tour that I realised I was no longer 'one of the lads'. Younger actors now organised the parties. I began to find the music too loud, the lights too dim and the dancing grotesque.

I had known for years that I was never going to make it big. I fooled myself each time I got a job that this was the one that would make the difference. This was the one where my talent would finally be discovered or I'd meet the director who would release my potential. But nothing really changed. The acting profession is like a sieve – every year thousands pass through it and are washed away without a trace. I look now through the cast lists of old programmes, remember keen young faces and promising talents and wonder what happened to them. Where did they all go? Every actor blames the downturns in his career upon his agent. I was no exception. I quit my first agent, a very powerful one, following my first long spell out of work and went into a downspin after that. As they say, changing agents is like swapping deckchairs on the Titanic. I had racked my brains, trying vainly to think of an alternative profession, before realising that there was nothing else that I could do or wanted to do. I had therefore resolved to swallow my pride and take anything that came along, so long as I could remain an actor. I wasn't going to be washed away. So when George Murcell asked me to direct *The Merchant* at St George's, a redundant Victorian church in a yet to be gentrified corner of North London, I accepted at once.

By chance, St George's, which had a circular nave, had been built in similar dimensions to Shakespeare's Globe and Murcell had valiantly endeavoured to transform it into an Elizabethan playhouse. George was a rumbustious character who made quite a good living playing snarling villains in movies. He could do German, Russian, Turk or Greek or whatever – George could snarl in any accent. He was a Tsarist prison guard in *The Fixer*. I still can hear him say 'Spread' and see his eyes sparkle with anticipation as the naked Alan Bates bends over for his inspection. George was always running off doing little jobs to subsidise his beloved obsession. I remember he was delighted one day when a female casting director he had never really got on with asked him to fly immediately to Rome for three days filming. He came back in a fury: 'The bitch didn't tell me. Three days! Three fucking days! Hanging on a bleedin' cross, bollock-naked behind Jesus. The cow did it on purpose.' On another occasion he returned from some location bloodied and bruised after diving into a swimming pool and failing to notice the absence of water.

George was such a traditionalist that he refused any lighting effects. (Which I'm sure Shakespeare would have made good use of if he'd had them available. He constantly altered his style and went with the changes.) Also, by financial necessity as much as tradition, George used the same costumes and wigs for every production. In the first season, when such stars as Alan Badel and Eric Porter were around, they were fine, but over the years things became decidedly tatty. There was a particular female wig which resembled Miss Piggy's that went from production to production. Anna Sharkey, an award-winning musical actress, was my Portia. Unfortunately she had done little Shakespeare and was extremely nervous. On the first performance, which was a schools matinee, she hurried off from the trial, put on Miss Piggy over her tightly pinned hair then rushed back on for the romantic finale at Belmont. I was watching, director fashion, from the back when I noticed, to my horror, that each time Anna tossed her head, which she seemed to do on every line, Miss Piggy was creeping further and further back up her brow. Finally, I knew it was coming, Anna gave one toss too many and Miss Piggy flew to the floor like a dead cat. The young audience broke out in gleeful cheers. It was the most entertaining moment of the entire afternoon. Anna stood frozen with her hair in pins, like Cinderella stripped of her finery at the ball, before squealing in dismay and fleeing from the stage. The rest of the cast were doing all they could to control their hysteria. Nerissa was in danger of wetting herself. Peter Gale's Bassanio saved the day by picking up Miss Piggy and declaring: 'Come friends, let us go in and sup.' The production never really recovered after that. I should have followed Irving and ended the play at Shylock's exit from the trial.

George was as devious as they come but deep down he had a good heart. With his devoted assistant Suzie, he valiantly kept St George's open for thirteen years without any subsidy; like Micawber, he was always expecting backers to turn up. There were many false dawns, but they never appeared. Nevertheless more than 250,000 pupils attended his performances and workshops, and St George's was the first theatre in the country to appoint an education officer. George Murcell was a buccaneer like Bernard Miles, Michael Croft and Frank Dunlop. Though their productions may be looked down on by the subsidised elite of today, they kept the fire burning and gave many actors a chance to play great roles in big spaces. A few went on to better things.

I had had several offers to return to the RSC over the years, but was loath to uproot my boys as they were doing so well at their respective schools. Moreover I was able to subsidise my meagre acting earnings during the summer months by being an official Blue-Badge tour guide. On more than one occasion I delivered a whole bus load to St George's to augment a thin house. It wasn't so bad – at least I was sitting comfortably in the front of the bus; I used to see poor Edward Petherbridge leading bemused Americans on walking tours of Hampstead in the rain. But by 1992 both my boys were ensconced at university, and as they were among the last to enjoy grants and free tuition, I was able to afford to return to Stratford. However, I found myself way down the batting order. I'd been offered the role of George V in a new play about Elgar, and as a sort of makeweight, was cast as Balthazar in *The Merchant*. I wasn't over-excited as I couldn't even remember Balthazar in the previous productions I'd been in.

Stratford, like me, had changed markedly since the sixties, and not for the better. The market town had become a pure tourist destination. The ancient inns and shops of the High Street had been converted into chain stores and shopping malls. The butcher's, where each week the doomed sheep had walked down the ramp of the farmer's lorry, was now a branch of W H Smith. The RSC had changed as well. Under the torpid hand of Adrian Noble, who I considered had been in the job too long, there was little excitement or crusading zeal about the place. The directors did the play allocated to them as they came round in the cycle, not plays they fervently wanted to direct. The actors seemed more serious, there was less talk of sex and booze, though I was quite shocked when I heard of substances being taken, even one unbelievable tale of leading actors sniffing lines of coke across the stage. I'd never dabbled in drugs, apart from one unsuccessful puff at a joint in Malaga. I was already feeling old. The only thing that hadn't changed was Pam, who was still running the Dirty Duck. She greeted me without much affection – perhaps still remembering my 1967 dalliance with her barmaid. My photo never made it to her wall.

The Merchant was a modern dress production. The set resembled a tower at Canary Wharf, full of glowing computer screens and sharp-suited bankers rushing around with mobile phones. Balthazar was beefed up by giving him various lines from other messengers and turned into Portia's trustee, a sort of family lawyer, dressed in a smart Armani suit, who kept the keys to the caskets and made the various suitors sign legal documents before they made their choice. I was on stage for a hell of a long time, exchanging earnest glances with Penny Downie's extremely earnest

Portia. One night the glances became more than earnest when I tapped my jacket and realised that the Wardrobe Department had sent the suit to the cleaners and had not put the key back into my pocket. I whispered my dilemma into Penny's ear as I passed by on my way to usher in the Prince of Morocco. Horror spread slowly across her face: we were not sure if the casket would open without the key. When Ray Fearon, the Prince of Morocco, proffered his hand on the line *'Here do I choose, and thrive I as I may!'* I could only fumble in my pocket and pretend to pass him something. A look of acute bemusement spread across Ray's handsome features. He then in turn mimed putting a very, very, small key into the lock as Portia, and now Nerissa, looked even more earnestly on. The relief on stage was palpable as the lid opened and Morocco took out the death's head with the scroll in its eye. It was perfect for the scene, it was the best we'd ever done it, but I've never forgotten to check my pockets since. We had an excellent cast with Owen Teale as a manly Bassanio and David Calder a fine Shylock. Christopher Luscombe even managed to be funny as Gobbo when he pressed the wrong button on Shylock's computer and every system on the set crashed.

That was a good production but a few years later I was to be slightly involved in an even better one. I was a member of Trevor Nunn's ensemble at the National and originally was not in his superb *Merchant* set in Fascist Italy, which was first presented in the small Cottesloe Theatre. When it moved into the Lyttelton I was asked if I would mind understudying Antonio and the Duke. I personally thought that Antonio was the one weak link and was glad to have a chance of showing how I thought the part should be played. However, I never went on for Antonio, though I did do a few performances of the Duke, a good role, lots of sitting down. It was mesmerising being on stage and passing judgement on Henry Goodman's heart-wrenching Shylock, which I think will never be bettered. When it was filmed I managed to get roped in for a couple of days as a drunken patron in the night club scenes.

That film version was really nothing more than a record of the stage production, and Henry's Shylock lost a little of its brilliance. I think this was mainly due to the editing, particularly in the trial when the camera seemed linger on Portia when it should have been on Shylock. There is a full-blown film, beautifully set in sixteenth-century Venice directed by Michael Radford, with Al Pacino as a dangerous but deeply moving

Shylock. He had been spied more than once at the National watching Henry. Jeremy Irons is the perfect Antonio and Joseph Fiennes is the best Bassanio I've seen. In my mind there is one mistake. I think when Portia goes to court all she has in her locker is the plea for mercy. The loss of blood only comes to her as an inspiration once Shylock has refused all the offers. Otherwise she is blatantly cruel. The film does not show that sudden moment of realisation.

King John

'Three hours that passed like thirty.'
Bernard Levin (1928-2004)

Tattle: Shakespeare wrote it around 1596, the year his eleven-year old son, Hamnet, died. That may well be the reason for the inferior quality of the play. Was he lamenting his own loss when he gave Constance the following lines?

'Grief fills the room up of my absent child,
Lies in his bed, walks up and down with me,
Puts on his pretty looks, repeats his words,
Remembers me of all his gracious parts,
Stuffs out his vacant garments with his form…'

King John was regularly performed in the nineteenth century. Constance was considered one of Sarah Siddons's greatest roles. Actors and directors are always thinking they have discovered a new way of achieving truth, but someone has always been there before. Sarah Siddons's notes on playing Constance have more than a hint of the Method: 'Whenever I was called upon to personate the character of Constance, I never, from the beginning of the play to the end of my part in it, once suffered my dressing-room door to be closed, in order that my attention might be constantly fixed on those distressing events which I could hear going on upon the stage, the terrible effects of which progress were to be represented by me. Moreover, I never omitted to place myself, with Arthur in my hand, to hear the march, when, upon the reconciliation of England and France, they enter the gates of Angers to ratify the contract of marriage between the Dauphin and the Lady Blanche; because the sickening sounds of that march would usually cause the bitter tears of rage, disappointment, betrayed confidence, baffled ambition, and above all, the agonising feeling of maternal affection, to gush into my eyes. In short, the spirit of the whole drama took possession of my mind and frame, by my attention being perpetually riveted to the passing scenes.'

After years of neglect, *John* is coming back into some sort of favour. Modern directors have treated it as a satire on the corruption of power and politics, a mixture of farce and tragedy. It is almost Brechtian.

Memories: I have only a distant recollection of seeing Sir Donald Wolfit playing King John on television, looking like a mangy old tomcat, and that superb character actor, Maurice Denham, floundering at the Old Vic.

Greg Thompson is an excellent director who makes a habit of putting on lost and obscure plays in the most unlikely places. He once persuaded me to appear in *The Play of the Weather*, an entertainment written for Henry VIII, in the Banqueting Hall at Hampton Court – where the blessed Shakespeare himself performed. Greg believes *Look About You*, an anonymous Elizabethan play featuring a younger version of John, is one of Shakespeare's earliest works. Greg arranged a dramatized reading of it at the Orange Tree in Richmond, in which I played Sir Richard Faulconbridge, a cheery old knight whose wife is being rogered by young Richard the Lionheart. Hence the Bastard Faulconbridge in the later play. There are many Shakespearean touches – it begins, like *Lear*, with old King Henry II foolishly dividing his kingdom between his sons. The good Duke of Gloucester, like Kent, warns the King against it and is banished for his pains. Greg claims no other Elizabethan writer but Shakespeare uses the phrase *Look About You,* as well as other words and images in the text. It is also very funny. It ends with nearly every character in disguise – even Robin Hood turns up in drag. I'm not convinced it was by Shakespeare so I'm not claiming this one, but knowing Greg, he'll put it on somewhere.

Henry IV Part One

'The Falstaffiad'
Professor Harold Bloom (1930 –)

Tattle: Lord Hunsdon, the patron of Shakespeare's company, and incidentally the father of an illegitimate child with the aforementioned Aemilia Bassano, died in 1596 and was succeeded as Lord Chamberlain by Lord Cobham, a strict Protestant, who strongly disapproved of theatres, actors and playwrights. He was descended from Sir John Oldcastle, a follower of John Wycliffe, who fell out with Henry V and suffered a martyr's death. Shakespeare originally called his fat disreputable knight Oldcastle – a trace survives in Act One Scene Two when Hal addresses Sir John as '*my old lad of the castle*'. Was Shakespeare deliberately lampooning Cobham by depicting his ancestor as a whore-mongering thief? One thing that no commentator has ever mentioned, as far as I know, is that Shakespeare has Oldcastle/Falstaff commit his robbery, the only real crime we see him do, on Gadshill, a few miles away from Lord Cobham's ancestral home, Cooling Castle. That was really rubbing salt into the wound. After a few performances Cobham made his displeasure vehemently known and the name was changed to Falstaff, again taken from an historical figure, Sir John Fastolfe, who fought ignominiously in the loss of France. Shakespeare would in all likelihood have spoken the Epilogue at the end of *Part Two*, and would have thus made his forced apology on stage: '*Oldcastle died a martyr and this is not the man.*' But Shakespeare and his fellows did not have to endure Cobham long. He died the following year and the more benign George Carey, Lord Hunsdon's son, was appointed Lord Chamberlain in his place.

Will Kempe was probably the original Falstaff, although the character is on a different planet from Bottom and Dogberry, roles that Kempe definitely played. Although a miserable few find the fat old knight an unfunny and unpleasant old fart, the renowned American scholar,

Harold Bloom, ranks Falstaff alongside Hamlet, Rosalind and Cleopatra as Shakespeare's most profound creations, claiming he speaks the best and most vital prose in the English language. Others see him as the quintessential Englishman, with many of our virtues and our faults. John Fraser, once the handsomest juvenile in Britain, played the old fat man throughout Africa and Asia; time and again he was told by the natives that he was just like some Englishman they knew.

Strangely enough there have been very few memorable Falstaffs. Sir Ralph Richardson is generally accepted as the 'best Falstaff there ever was,' but alas there is no record apart from Rembrandt-like photographs. Richardson is said to have ignored the low comedy aspects of the role – the puns, the belches, and galumphing horseplay, beloved of Elizabethan groundlings, but which are often perplexing to refined modern audiences (the present-day frequenters of the Globe excepted). He played him with an absolute presence of mind, triumphing over every challenge until his rejection. Harold Bloom, who does seem to go in for hyperbole, considered Sir Ralph's bounding up on *'Embalmed!'* after his supposed death at the Battle of Shrewsbury, was the most joyous representation of secular resurrection ever staged. Richardson himself observed: 'Not until you play Falstaff do you realize how small the mere actor is... It's like trying to play a huge organ with too vast a keyboard to reach the steps at the top and down at the bottom at one and the same time.'

Orson Welles saw Falstaff as symbolising 'Merry England where the hay smelt better and the weather was always spring-like and the daffodils blew in the gentle breezes.' He somewhat perversely went on to make a dark, melancholy film with an international cast in the middle of a Spanish winter. Welles looks every inch, or ounce, Falstaff; but there is something missing. His mind seems to be wandering elsewhere – perhaps he was pre-occupied with his usual financial problems with finishing the picture. On stage I have seen fine actors such as Brewster Mason, Michael Gambon and Robert Stephens sweating and puffing away, but have yet to find the true old rascal. Roger Allam brought out all the low comedy to the delight of the groundlings at the Globe, but missed out on the pathos. Simon Russell Beale gave a perversely unfunny reading recently on television. Queen Elizabeth would never have requested another play about the mawkish character Beale presented.

Combined these two plays have to be my favourites. All England, not only Merry – the stews and the taverns as Shakespeare knew them – are crammed within them. They are bursting with energy, humour, poetry and passion. Kenneth Tynan considered the Shallow scenes to be the most naturalistic in all Shakespeare. It is hard to understand why there have been so few outstanding productions. The best I've seen was at the Old Vic in the mid-1950s. The vigour and comic life of the Boar's Head, the elegiac magic of Justice Shallow's orchard and the heartbreak of Falstaff's rejection, are still etched firmly in my mind. And what a cast: Robert Hardy as Hal, Eric Porter as King, Paul Rogers as good a Falstaff as I've seen, Paul Daneman giving the performance of his life as Shallow, and John Neville, a rip-roaring cockney Pistol: '*'ave we not Irene 'ere?*'

Memories: Ian Mullins ran the Everyman at Cheltenham, a beautiful theatre designed by the great Frank Matcham, as a very successful fortnightly rep, putting on a mix of plays that would have been a worthy repertoire for the National. In the autumn of 1965 he offered me Prince Hal together with a line of such tempting roles that, even though there were television parts in the offing, I could not refuse. It was to be my only experience of what being a member of a repertory company in a smallish town used to be like. The theatre and the actors were truly part of the community, albeit a middle-class one. It was Cheltenham after all. There was a colonel, ex-Indian Army, a bachelor, who never failed to invite the prettier actresses to a curry supper at his grand house, every second Thursday after he had seen the play. They told me he behaved impeccably throughout the entire evening. There were the well-bred ladies who took coffee in the theatre bar each morning, eager to give comments, usually appreciative, on one's performance. The girls of the famous Ladies' College were regular patrons and had wild crushes on the younger male members of the company. Billets-doux and little gifts were always to be found at the stage door. I did particularly well as some had recently seen me as Dick Turpin in my Disney film. The actors and actresses were known and welcomed in nearly every shop or pub in town. And Cheltenham was still a lovely town then, before it was ruined by traffic schemes. The Polygon was filled with elegant shops, Cavendish House was a miniature Harrods, and we downed schooners of sherry whilst we ate our steaks at the new and very trendy Berni Inn. My theatrical lodgings consisted of a large comfortable room in a fine Regency house overlooking an elegant square.

The Cotswold Hills lay ten minutes' drive away, where I walked Kosher, my Dalmatian dog, and learned my lines by declaiming them to the wind. Life was good on £30 a week.

But there were sad things too. One was an old actor, named Frank, who played fathers, vicars and other distinguished types. He was gay but fearful of revealing it in case it prevented him getting heterosexual parts. It was still not fashionable or completely legal to admit to being gay in the swinging sixties. He had spent his entire career in rep, going from one town to another, never having fixed roots or a permanent partner. He was also suffering from the old actor's nightmare – he was finding it more and more difficult to remember his lines. He was cast as Glendower and his hands were shaking in rehearsals as he struggled to stammer out the Welsh. He never got it right. I was very relieved not to be in that scene. It was pitiful hearing him take prompt after prompt throughout the run; it was doubly sad in that he knew his time was up. He couldn't cram any more lines into his poor old brain. I was on tour a few years later and came across him in a tatty boarding house in Birmingham, where he had become a permanent resident. His hands were shaking more than ever as he ate his lonely, greasy breakfast. I said hello but he didn't remember me.

Prince Hal came towards the end of the season sandwiched between Dick Dudgeon in *The Devil's Disciple* and Lophakin in *The Cherry Orchard*. Ian Mullins, a conscientious director, had been an actor in Anthony Quayle's production at Stratford in 1951. He gave me as much of Richard Burton's performance and moves as he could remember. (Many of the traditions and much of the business in playing Shakespeare have been passed down from actor to actor through the centuries, all the way back to Burbage.) We had less than ten days to rehearse, whilst I played Dick Dudgeon at night. There was no time for discussion or finesse: all I could do was learn the lines and try to speak them with clarity and pace. Hal is a difficult part; he is outshone by Hotspur's valour and Falstaff's wit. The jokes are for the most part obscure and difficult to put across. He is an unpleasant prig, playing cruel practical jokes, watching and waiting for his moment. The role is only fulfilled when both parts are played together with Henry V. Richard Burton made his name when he did the trilogy at Stratford in 1951; Ian Holm followed him in 1964; Robert Hardy was memorable on television. I can't really think of any other great Prince Hals. It wasn't really my part, I'd wanted to play Hotspur, but that was taken by a very experienced repertory actor, who considered himself to be the leading man. He modelled his performance on Olivier, who is supposed to have been the first to have played Hotspur with a stutter. Olivier justified this because Lady Percy describes her husband as 'speaking thick'. She probably meant he spoke with a northern twang, but as the poor chap dies trying to say 'worms', Olivier decided that Hotspur had trouble with his double-u's. This can put ten minutes on the running time and my Hotspur eked out every last second. Each night he got slower and slower, especially in the final scene, when he became extremely loath to die and leave the stage to me. Indeed the night his mother came he inexplicably parried my final thrust at his vitals and we had to go through the complete fight again. He eventually emigrated to South Africa and pursued his art there. The young Antony Sher witnessed one of his performances. He was reputedly still over-acting.

But there were some very good things about that production. The standard of acting and performance in a good three-weekly or even fortnightly rep was not too far behind some of the stuff offered these days at the National or RSC after months of rehearsal. Josephine Tewson, whose perplexed visage is known all over the television universe as Patricia Routledge's long-suffering neighbour in *Keeping Up Appearances*, was hilarious as Mistress Quickly, and Daniel Thorndike, a nephew of the incomparable Dame Sybil, had a good shot at Falstaff. Dan, who I worked with on several occasions, was one of the most decent men I have ever met, justifying the old adage about his aunt:

'Nobody loves anybody
Like Sybil loves everybody.'

1970: I eventually got my chance to play Hotspur in an open-air production at Ludlow Castle as part of the annual Festival. With memories of Cheltenham etched in my mind, I decided not to go for the stutter. The play was directed by an over-opinionated, over-weight chap just out of Cambridge. I was cast at the last moment, I think I was about his tenth choice, and we didn't get on from the start. The budget was sparse. The Festival was financed by a local committee who appeared to think the actors should be honoured to perform for them at minimum payment. I seem to recall that we didn't get paid at all during the three weeks of rehearsals in London. I was even more concerned that there was no money for a fight director. A fiery, brutal fight is crucial for the final confrontation between Hal and Hotspur, but our director insisted that he could arrange the fight himself. We soon discovered he couldn't. Hal was played by Michael Byrne, an acerbic actor, far more suited to Hal than I'd been, and we put together as good a fight as we could manage, practising ferociously in the railway yard beside my abode in Pimlico, to the consternation of the neighbours and passers-by.

Hotspur was not the piece of cake I'd thought, most parts never are, and I got little inspiration from the director. Three weeks passed all too quickly, and one sunny Sunday morning I found myself driving up to Ludlow in my bumpy Citroen Deux Chevaux, its roof rolled back, with my faithful Kosher and two young actors and their kit jammed into the rear. Ludlow is relatively unspoilt now, having avoided the fate of most small towns by preserving its individuality by banning the ubiquitous chain stores; but it was idyllic then, like stepping back into the pre-war England that only exists in black and white movies on afternoon television. Ancient inns served strong beer brewed on the premises, butchers and grocers were crammed with appetising hand-raised pies and sausages and cheeses, the stalls in the market square were overflowing with local produce – it's no wonder that today Ludlow is considered a gourmet's paradise with Michelin star restaurants. My delight quickly evaporated as soon as I walked into the castle courtyard and beheld the set. If there was one play at Ludlow that didn't need a set, it would be *Henry IV Part One*. Hotspur had lived in this very castle. He'd climbed those towers and watched from those ramparts and walked upon that greensward. They were crying out to be used; but a Cambridge friend of the director had spent almost all the budget designing a monstrous set of three separate metal stages, which obliterated all traces of the castle behind it. The three stages were supposedly areas for the three elements of society represented in the play – royalty, nobility and commons. The common or Falstaff area was in the centre and the other two areas raked down perilously towards it, linked by narrow catwalks. There were twelve edges of stage to fall off.

So began one of the worst weeks of my life. It was World Cup time again. On the Monday, after a frustrating day, slowly staggering through the play trying to put it onto that dreadful set, most of the company were crammed into a smoky room at the back of the pub we'd adopted, drinking the cheap but extremely potent local scrumpy, cheering on England as they swept to a seemingly triumphant two-nil lead against the old enemy, Germany. Life was suddenly great – it made up for me missing the 1966 final – I'd even forgotten about that damned stupid set – when Sir Alf Ramsey decided to take off the incomparable Bobby Charlton to preserve his energy for the next game. That was the turning point – it was unbelievable – before we knew it we'd lost two-three. (I have just read newly released allegations that the German team had taken illegal stimulants.)

The following morning, with sore heads and heavy hearts, we returned to the play. We had no help from the director or his designer friend as we worked out entrances and exits, which sometimes entailed frantic route marches behind the castle walls to get to the other side of the stage on cue. It was late afternoon before we got to the fight scene. The castle had been opened to visitors throughout our rehearsals and there were always a few watching us without any visible sign of comprehension. I think we may have both been trying to ignite their interest as Michael and I began our fight, which we waged with sword and dagger. We started tentatively, aware of the edges that suddenly came up behind us as we swept around the stage, but as the pace quickened, Hotspur took over. I parried with my dagger, snarled and swung around and found myself hurtling off the slippery metal stage on to the ancient stones five feet below. I fell onto a rock still holding the sword tightly in my left hand and broke my wrist.

The director was as useless in a crisis as he was at directing, but the extremely attractive young actress, fresh out of Oxbridge, playing my Lady Percy, took over. She produced a flask of brandy which I gratefully imbibed as she took me to the local cottage hospital in her car. They couldn't do anything for me and telephoned for an ambulance to take me to A & E in Shrewsbury. My distress was somewhat alleviated when Lady Percy insisted on accompanying me. I lay throughout the journey with my head on her lap, like a stricken warrior, while she stroked my fevered brow, her inviting breasts bobbing a few inches from my chin, pouring yet more brandy down my grateful throat. When we arrived at the hospital the first thing a forbidding matron asked was if I'd had any alcohol. When I replied in the affirmative – my breath would have told her anyway – she ordered me to go away for three hours until the effects had worn off.

My dutiful Lady P was still in attendance and suggested we pass the time in a cinema. We found one nearby where the latest James Bond film was playing. I've never been a great fan of Bond, but endured it until the villain twisted Sean Connery's arm and the throbbing pain in my wrist became unbearable. We hurriedly left the cinema and I staggered into the street to behold a plaque declaring: **The body of Harry 'Hotspur' Percy was hung here in chains after the Battle of Shrewsbury in 1402.** Hotspur was suffering again that night on the same bloody spot. Eventually, after sipping bitter lemons in the Falstaff Inn and trying to alleviate the pain by concentrating on the heaving bosom of my fair companion, the three hours were up and she delivered me back to the hospital where I was examined by a very young and very tired doctor from the Subcontinent. He didn't seem to believe me when I explained I'd got myself injured sword fighting at Ludlow Castle. I was given pain-killers at last, my wrist was reset and put in plaster, my arm put into a sling, and the ambulance transported me back to Ludlow with Lady Percy stroking my brow even more tenderly than before.

We opened the following day and strangely enough the injury helped my performance. I played most of the evening with my arm in the sling, as if it were a wound I'd suffered at the battle of Holmedon, which precedes the action of the play. I flourished it in my first scene when I said: *'I then all smarting with my wounds being cold,'* and used it as a cause of Hotspur's impatience and anger, especially in the scene with Lady Percy, which had suddenly come to life. Her line: *'In faith, I'll break thy little finger, Harry;'* got an unexpected and welcome laugh. It was even more appropriate at the end. I'd always found it hard to believe that Hal could beat Hotspur in single combat, after Hal had been spending all his time drinking and wenching in the taverns with Falstaff, whilst Hotspur had been in training, waging constant war against the Scots. I made a great show of taking my arm out of the sling before the battle, trying to hold the sword and then transferring it reluctantly to my other hand. The audience could see that Hotspur lost because he was fighting with the wrong hand. It made perfect sense although I'm not too sure if Michael Byrne liked me milking the sympathy.

The play went far better than I'd expected, and I thought things were beginning to look up, even though the randy old sods on the Festival Committee invited Lady Percy, who'd been looking more inviting by the day, to the Festival Ball and not me. But '*when sorrows come they come not single spies but in battalions*,' and a third disaster duly came at the end of the week. Kosher collapsed and died as he was happily running around a field. I couldn't understand it: he was in his prime. The local vet who examined him said he had a weak heart. He was buried on the farm where we were staying. He'd been my constant companion for seven years: at the Mermaid, at Cheltenham, Stratford and countless film locations. We'd been through so much together: 'Brothers and sisters I bid you beware of giving your heart to a dog to tear.'

I don't think Shakespeare liked dogs but Kipling did.

My wrist was still painful. It was examined by the local doctor who told me it had been set badly and I would have to have it broken again and reset. I didn't fancy another trip to Shrewsbury, so my agent arranged for me to have it done privately in London. It was done on a Sunday so I would miss only one performance, the only performance I've ever missed in my entire career – I never wanted to be off in case the understudy did it better than me. I wasn't too worried as on that occasion my understudy was very young and, I seem to recall, a little weedy. On my way back to Ludlow on the train (I couldn't drive the Citroen because of the complicated gear shift), my thoughts turned to Lady Percy. I had steadfastly withstood her advances, thinking it was about time I grew up and showed a little maturity and self-control, but the swinging sixties were barely over and I decided there and then that I'd suffered enough and deserved a little reward. But as the Bard says: *'There is a tide in the affairs of men, which taken at the flood, leads on to fortune.'* I'd definitely missed the flood. In my brief absence, my uncle, '*Saucy Worcester'* had stepped into the breach and was firmly entrenched.

There was nothing left for me but to concentrate on my performance for the rest of the run. The weather was dreadful, it rained every night, my armour became rusty, but the hardy Salopians remained on their deckchairs, steadfastly wrapped in their raincoats, to the bitter end. Trevor Nunn says that the exciting thing about acting Shakespeare is that one night you might get it right. There was one night before the battle as I addressed my followers and looked up towards the castle battlement with the rain dripping into my eyes, when I felt, for that one brief moment, that I had got it right. It is for moments like that, against all odds, that actors continue to strive.

I haven't heard of the director since. I expect he ended up teaching drama at some Mid-West university – so many of the bad ones do.

1985: It was another fifteen years before I revisited the play. I had vowed I would never work again for dear old George Murcell at St George's. The original costumes, which were still dragged out for every production, were becoming tattier and tattier, even Miss Piggy's wig was looking bare, indeed the entire project was tottering on its last legs. The funding cuts meant that the schools, which made up the vast bulk of the audiences, were no longer coming. It closed a few months later. But when George offered me Falstaff in *Part One* I couldn't refuse. I'd played him in *Part Two* and *The Merry Wives* and it would complete the trio. We put it on in ten days and I was very average. In a very thin house towards the end of the run, Michael Croft, ever-faithful, came to see me. He didn't say anything but I knew that he knew I would never fulfil the hopes he'd had of me when I first performed the role all those years before. It was the last time I saw him. Michael, the most companionable of men, the nearest man to Falstaff I've ever known, died alone on a Saturday night a few weeks later. He was my second father: I mourn him to this day. We'd heard the chimes at midnight again and again.

Henry IV Part Two

'Only one man in all of Shakespeare's thirty-six plays believes in life, enjoys life, thinks life's worth living, and has a sincere, unrhetorical tear dropped on his death-bed; and that man is Falstaff.'
George Bernard Shaw (A vegetarian teetotaller)

Memories: **1957:** Following the success of *Henry V*, the inaugural production of the NYT, or Youth Theatre as it was called then, Croft decided to follow it up with *Henry IV Part Two*. This play, so much concerned with old men and death, was a strange choice for the Youth Theatre, but Michael had done it a couple of years before at Alleyn's School, and most of the cast were still available, including Falstaff in the shape of yours truly. One vital member who was not available however was Richard Hampton, the original Prince Hal. He was away on National Service and a replacement had to be found. Up until then the Youth Theatre had been made up entirely from boys from schools in Dulwich, but there was no one suitable and the net was cast further afield. To Leytonstone in fact, where Michael had read glowing reports of a schoolboy Hamlet. And so Derek Jacobi became the first non-Dulwich member. We rehearsed during the Easter holidays in a Sea Cadets hall in Dulwich and each morning young Derek came all the way from Leytonstone by bus. I think he had to change four times. He was a good Prince Hal but didn't have a very good time. We probably didn't treat him very well; we'd been together so long and had our own in-jokes. He was always an outsider. Derek even claims that Richard Hampton's mother, who curled the boys' hair each night with hot tongs, put them on him when they were at their hottest. Most people stayed with the NYT for years but Derek never came back.

Later that year Manchester Grammar School suggested that we take the production to Manchester, which we did, with a new but very inferior Prince Hal from Dulwich College. We all drove up to Manchester in the Alleyn's School Cadet Force's very old army lorry, which pre-dated Dunkirk. There were no motorways then, the old truck was very slow and it was an exceedingly long and uncomfortable journey. We eventually arrived to find the assistance that Manchester Grammar School had promised was non-existent. The only support came from a little bright-eyed boy, called Ben Kingsley, who came with his mother, and was recruited to play a non-speaking soldier; and a slightly bigger boy called Robert Powell, who offered to sell programmes. There was no accommodation, we started off sleeping on the floor of a derelict house, but Croft was always adept at publicity and our plight was blazoned across a full page of the *Manchester Evening News*. The warm heart of the north was duly touched and offers of succour came in. Most boys found themselves in comfortable middle-class homes in Cheadle or Chorlton, but Colin Farrell (now called Col because some Irish parvenu stole his name) who was playing Justice Shallow, and I ended up in a house of dubious repute in Moss Side, along with most of the cast of an African dance troupe, playing at the Opera House. What we lacked in comfort was made up for by the sight of topless black beauties on their way to the bathroom. *Part Two* has never been as popular as *Part One* and even though Michael had us parading through Manchester's Piccadilly in full costume and make-up (it was a very hot day and I sweated off pounds beneath my padding) we had very sparse houses.

1998: My final association with these plays came at Chichester when Patrick Garland cast me as Bardolph in *Chimes at Midnight*, Orson Welles's amalgamation of both parts. In some ways it makes sense. There is much repetition. It was probably only the huge success of *Part One* that persuaded Shakespeare to write *Part Two*. Each contains a mammoth tavern scene, an act in itself, a rebellion, and a long reconciliation scene between Hal and his father. It seemed a good idea to take the best parts from both, which Welles did, and tag on a bit of the beginning of *Henry V* for good measure, including the death of Falstaff.

Welles had originally put in on at the Abbey Theatre in Dublin in the 1950s. It hadn't worked then, but the film version which he made in 1964 is considered a classic, by some. Keith Baxter, who had played Hal for Welles on stage and screen, was now Henry IV and Simon

Callow presented a Dickensian Falstaff. The wonderful old character actors, Timothy Bateson and John Warner, were the Justices Shallow and Silence; the Hostess was played by the talented and delightful Sarah Badel. Young Tam Williams was a natural Hal, and big Tristan Gemmill, in his pre-*Casualty* days, was every inch a warrior Hotspur. It should have been magnificent, but despite all Patrick's efforts it didn't work. Shakespeare always knows best. Nevertheless it was one of the most enjoyable jobs I've ever done. We were taught at RADA that there were no small parts, only small actors; and over the years, as the parts have indeed got smaller, I have found that to be increasingly true. I loved playing Bardolph. I understood him completely, I shared Falstaff's every emotion, and put as much feeling into: '*Would I were with him wheresome'er he is, either in heaven or in hell*', as if I were Hamlet lamenting the death of his father. Listening each night to Sarah describing Falstaff's death, one of the most moving passages in all Shakespeare, never failed to bring a tear to my eye. It was a delight sharing a dressing room with John Warner, whom I'd first met on *An Age of Kings*. John appeared gentle and effete but had deep inner courage. He'd been in command of a motor torpedo-boat on D-Day.

I also became very fond of Tam Williams – he gave everything he had to the part. One night at the end of the tavern scene, he literally flew down the stairs of the vomitary (the downstage exit) with a ringing: '*The land is burning; Percy stands on high; And either we or they must lower lie!*' Then those of us on stage heard a crash, followed by 'Oh! Fuck!' He had broken his ankle and the fight with Hotspur was only two scenes away. His understudy was the very thin, reedy boy playing Prince John. There was no way of telling the audience what had happened. Prince John was hurriedly strapped into Hal's armour and pushed on stage to do battle with the mighty Hotspur, who towered over him like a raging bull. It was the most terrifying ordeal for the poor young chap. I think he gave up the business soon after that.

FALSTAFF

Throughout the nineties I did over 120 performances of a one-man play based on Robert Nye's moving but extremely Rabelaisian novel, *Falstaff.* I began at the Other Place in Stratford in 1993 and ended at the Cottesloe nine years later. In-between I played most of the fringe venues and festivals in Britain as well as a few in Europe, and various colleges in America. I hardly earned any money but, thanks in no small measure to the direction of David Delve, a fellow actor, I think I got nearest to the character then and received some of the best notices I ever had. Doing a one-man show is a lonely existence, especially in front of thin houses as I did on more than one occasion. But sometimes in a small space you can establish an amazing contact with your audience. I remember one Saturday afternoon at the Southwark Playhouse when only one lonely man turned up. I could have cancelled the show but I felt even sorrier for him than I did for myself. I told Falstaff's story to him alone and it was one of the times I nearly got it right.

Henry V
(Hank Cinque)

'Henry is a very amiable monster in a very splendid pageant.'
William Hazlitt

Tattle: The Chorus's reference to Essex's expedition to Ireland dates it to around 1599.

'Were now the general of our gracious empress -
As in good time he may – from Ireland coming,
Bringing rebellion broached on his sword.....'

It is commonly accepted to have been the first play to be performed at the Globe. The lease at the old theatre in Shoreditch had expired and the landlord wanted more money. So one weekend – I've no idea how they did it – the actors, led by the Burbages, who were carpenters by trade, dismantled the timbers of the old theatre, transported them across the Thames and rebuilt them at Southwark as the Globe. If *Henry V* was the first new play to be performed there, I believe that Shakespeare played the Chorus (he had spoken the Epilogue for the previous play), and would thus have explained to his familiar patrons how they would see his new play through his words and their imaginations. (As far as I know, no director has thought of doing it that way.)

Henry V was one of Sir Frank Benson's favourite roles. Ever athletic, he would pole vault over the wall at Harfleur on *'Once more unto the breach.'* Donald Sinden told me that towards the end of his career Sir Frank became absent-minded. One night the old chap got his plays muddled and soared over the wall dressed as Shylock. John Fraser played the English soldier, Williams, when Richard Burton played Henry at the Old Vic in 1955. Burton's charisma on stage is legendary among actors. In the scene round the campfire John could always feel a thrill run through the audience when

Burton stared silently out into the night. John asked him how he did it. Burton said he simply looked down at the ground then raised his eyes very, very slowly until he reached the Gods. John tried it later when he played Romeo in Canada – Romeo spends a lot of time hanging around saying nothing. It worked – the notices said he gave a 'hypnotic' performance.

Memories: In 1956, Michael Croft launched what would become the National Youth Theatre with this play. He started without any funding; using the relatively small amount of money he'd recently received from his bestselling novel, *Spare the Rod.* The cast was made up of boys from Alleyn's School, playing parts they had played in a production Michael had directed two years before, plus a contingent from Dulwich College. Although both schools had been founded by the Elizabethan actor, Edward Alleyn, they were deadly rivals, and as the College boys considered themselves a bit above us, it was appropriate that they were largely cast as the French. I played Pistol, a part in which Croft had discovered certain bombastic comic possibilities in me I'd previously been unaware of. We played for two weeks at Toynbee Hall in the East End, drinking at *The Princess Alice*, a pub on the corner that was frequented by some jolly cockney types. One particularly big guy seemed to be especially friendly, particularly with the youngest member, Simon Ward, who was playing the French Princess. His name was Ronnie – Ronnie Kray.

During rehearsals W.A. Darlington, the revered critic of *The Daily Telegraph*, persuaded his paper to sponsor us. We began to get publicity – it was considered a newsworthy event for boys to put on Shakespeare. There was talk of a return of *'the little eyases'* mentioned by Hamlet. Michael, always adept at using publicity, persuaded several eminent members of the acting profession, such as Peter Ustinov and Flora Robson, to lend their names to his cause. Sir Ralph Richardson agreed to be our President and came to the opening with Richard Burton, who had recently played Henry V at the Old Vic. That night I had a rare moment of inspiration and decided to come on for the famous scene where Fluellen forces Pistol to eat a leek, wearing the Dauphin's helmet and various other pieces of armour that I imagined the French nobility had lost during the battle. This of course could never be done in the professional theatre – it would have to be cleared with the director, the designer, rehearsed with the other actors, etc.- it was in two words completely unprofessional – but I wasn't a professional then. My Fluellen, Ken Farrington, was very aggressive at the best of times, and the look of angry amazement on his face when I sauntered on to a big laugh, was perfect. He hit me with the leek, a particularly fat one with lots of soil still on it, fresh from Petticoat Lane. It knocked the Dauphin's helmet clean off my head, which got an even bigger laugh. As he advanced menacing towards me I fearfully knocked my knees together, forgetting that I had the Constable of France's armour on them. They produced a clanking sound that brought the house down. Farrington this time was really angry: 'Stop it, you bastard. I can't get my lines out!' he hissed in my ear, whilst stuffing half the leek down my throat. I nodded but forgot to stop my knees knocking. I think I was so carried away I wouldn't have been able to stop even if I'd tried. I came off at the end of the scene to thunderous applause. It was worth the bruises I had over all parts of my anatomy.

The whole evening was a phenomenal success. Richard Hampton was an excellent King, the Dulwich College boys were suitably effete as the French, and the Alleyn boys were bursting with vigour as the soldiery. The St Crispian Day scene was particularly moving. We all knew each other so well then and have remained friends to this day, although most have had non-theatrical careers. A dozen or so of us, even a couple from Dulwich College, still meet for lunch every month or two and '*remember with advantages*.' After the performance there was a knock at the door where about twenty of us were changing. Richard Burton walked in, came up to me and said 'That was the funniest leek scene I've ever seen. You must become a professional.' It was that and Ken Tynan's review, in which he particularly praised Ken Farrington and me, saying we were both 'up to scratch and down to earth', that finally persuaded me to apply for a RADA scholarship. After the reviews Ken Farrington quickly adapted to my reading of the scene, it got laughs every night, but never as many as the first.

Seven years passed and I was cast as Brother John in the epic screen version of Anouilh's *Becket,* opposite Richard Burton, now the biggest male star in the world. Every young actor in London had wanted that part. I couldn't really understand how I had got it. My agent told me it was down to the casting director, but I liked to think perhaps Burton had suggested me. Before filming started, the producer, the great Hal 'Casablanca' Wallis himself, summoned me to his house in Knightsbridge to meet the rest of the cast. I found myself in the middle of a cocktail party with half of the theatrical establishment. Sir John Gielgud, Sir Donald

Wolfit, Sir Felix Aylmer, Martita Hunt (looking as if she were still playing Miss Havisham in *Great Expectations*), Pamela Brown, Peter O'Toole and not least, Richard Burton with, reputedly the most beautiful and infamous woman in the world, Elizabeth Taylor. The only person I'd met before, apart from Sir Donald, whom I'd not yet forgiven for failing to award me the school reading prize, was Burton. He caught my eye and smiled. I was certain that he had asked for me.

I went confidently over to him and said, 'Well, I did what you told me.'

He reluctantly took his eyes off Elizabeth and demanded, 'What are you talking about?'

My mouth felt very dry. Perhaps he hadn't recommended me after all. 'Well, you came to the first night of the Youth Theatre a few years ago and you said I should become an actor.'

He gazed at me intensely before pulling on his cigarette. The smoke was making my eyes water. 'Oh, yes. I remember you well,' he said at last. 'You were very promising.' At this Elizabeth, who I think had resented my intrusion, began to show interest. She surveyed me with her renowned violet eyes. I noticed she had double lashes. I swelled with pride. Burton sipped his vodka, 'Yes, you were very, very good.' Elizabeth smiled at me. I was ten feet tall. It didn't matter that he hadn't recommended me. Burton nodded sagely and sipped his vodka, 'You were an excellent Henry V.'

It felt like a kick in the teeth. I thought for a moment that I should let him think that I had played the king, but found myself confessing, 'No, actually I played Pistol. Don't you remember? You said the leek scene was very funny.'

He lit another cigarette. 'Oh, yes. So I did. Yes, you were good too.'

Elizabeth's interest in me had evaporated. Throughout three months of filming it never came back.

1977: To mark the Queen's Silver Jubilee, David Conville decided to abandon the sure-fire comedies that patrons of Regent's Park love to this day, and mount a lavish production of *Henry V*. It was a very brave of him as he operated without any public funding and still managed to pay his actors a living wage. As well as being brave, David was also an extremely modest man, a far better director than he gave himself credit for. He felt he didn't know the play terribly well and asked me to be his assistant. Being an assistant director is usually a thankless task, but David took many of my suggestions, even letting me direct whole sections of the play. I left the leek scene alone, as it was in the very capable hands of Ian Talbot's Fluellen, although to my mind it never seemed to get as many laughs as we did in 1956. It was an excellent cast, led by the up-and-coming Clive Arrindell. Clive had all the makings of a star: looks, charisma and talent. He was one of the very best Henry V's I've ever seen and I was certain he'd have a big future. I worked with him several years later and his spark seemed to have departed. He'd become a Buddhist, nothing wrong with that, but I suspect he might have chanted his fire away. I've since heard he became the well-paid face of the Spanish Lottery. Celia Imrie made her debut in straight theatre as Mistress Quickly, and my friend, Esmond Knight, was Chorus, which he played as an old archer. Esmond who had played Fluellen in Olivier's film was, with the possible exception of Anthony Quayle, the bravest actor I have ever worked with. He had been Gunnery Officer on the bridge of *The Prince of Wales* when it was hit by a shell from the *Bismarck*. In his moving book, *Chasing the Bubble*, he vividly describes *The Prince of Wales* preparing for action as she steamed full speed ahead towards the mighty *Bismarck*. Things had changed little since Trafalgar:

'Two more seconds of unendurable ecstasy, then that pulverizing crashing roar, which for a second seems to knock one senseless – we had opened fire! We were blinded by a dense sheet of flame which rose before us, mixed with clouds of black, bitter-smelling smoke. For a second we closed our eyes till it dispersed; then, peering through binoculars, we gazed anxiously to see where the first salvoes had fallen. At this moment nothing was visible except the serene forms of the enemy ships. There was no change in what we saw; for our shells were actually still in the air, hurtling towards the enemy, who had not yet opened fire… From this moment on everything seems hazy, except that I remember hearing a great rushing noise, like the approach of a cyclone, and having a quite irrelevant dream about listening to a band in Hyde Park, and then being conscious of a high ringing noise in my head…'

Esmond was almost totally blind from then onwards but retained the enthusiasm and sexual appetite of a young actor just out of drama school, as well as managing to paint vibrant and exciting pictures of mediaeval battles and fighting ships. I look at the painting he gave me as I write. Esmond was determined that his blindness should not hinder or be a problem for others. He learnt his lines by having them read to him over and over again and was always word-perfect on the first day of rehearsal. He carefully measured his moves by the exact number of steps, which, because of the long distances, was extremely difficult in the Park. At times he had to appear on top of a scaffold high up in the trees, one step too far and he would have hurtled down, but he never gave it a thought. Esmond to me was the spirit of England and he brought a special quality to the play. There was a wonderful moment when he raised his sightless eyes to the heavens and said: *'Think, when we talk of horses, that you see them.'* He saw them indeed and so much more. Appropriately his granddaughter, Marianne Elliott, directed *War Horse*. Esmond was a war horse if ever there was one.

The King of France was played by another national treasure, Richard Goolden, the original Mole in *Toad of Toad Hall*. He played it in David Conville's annual Christmas revivals for so many years that he had grown to look like one. He lived a lonely, mole-like existence in a scruffy basement flat in Chelsea. I dropped him off one night and he invited me in to partake of his frugal supper of boiled lambs' hearts. I declined but had a glass of wine instead. He had particular problems remembering the long list of French nobility that the King summons to bar Henry's way at Agincourt. On the opening night his memory failed him completely and the Lords Orleans, Bourbon and Berri, Alencon, Brabant, and Bar became those of Chablis, Beaujolais, Macon, Sauternes and Châteauneuf-du-Pape.

It was an excellent production but it was one of the worst summers ever. Our gaiety and our gilt were truly besmirched with painful marching in the rainy field, and business was very bad. David should have stuck to *The Dream*.

2002: Twenty-five years later the Queen had another jubilee and I found myself in the play again. But this was nothing celebratory about this production. The invasion of Iraq was brewing and Nick Hytner chose to do a modern-dress version to open his reign at the National. I was already there in Trevor Nunn's company and survived the change of regime, although the parts I was offered, the Bishop of Ely and Sir Thomas Erpingham, would hardly tax my memory. I'd had a fondness for old Sir Thomas's few lines ever since Esmond Knight had doubled the role with the Chorus in the Park. I don't think Hytner had any real affection for the play but used it to push an extreme anti-war message, which to my mind, went against Shakespeare's more balanced approach. The simple speech deploring war that he gives Williams, the common soldier, is powerful enough. Though I've nothing against modern dress, I feel that tanks and modern weapons go against the sense of the play. Shakespeare's magnificent verse vividly describes horses charging against flights of arrows. There have been superb anti-war films, such as *Platoon* and *The Hurt Locker* in recent years – you don't have to muck about with Shakespeare to put over the message. The war proper began during rehearsals and we were suitably shocked when the desert battle fatigues that the wardrobe department had ordered from Angels, the theatrical costumiers, were recalled by the Ministry of Defence, as they didn't have enough for the Task Force.

To be thoroughly up-to-date Hytner chose the excellent black actor Adrian Lester to play Henry, and had a smattering of black actors throughout the cast, including Pistol, the Hostess and the Queen of France. But there seemed to be little thought or sense behind it, as there was when Trevor Nunn had cast all the Trojans black in *Troilus and Cressida* a few years before. In a modern-dress production there is no reason why Henry should not be black – the House of Lancaster has grabbed the crown, they are parvenus, newcomers. But make the whole family black, Uncle Exeter and all. I am speaking against the trend: more enlightened people will tell me that race should not matter, only the actor. That is true in many cases. Black actors should be in all the Roman plays – Brutus, Antony and Cassius are crying out to be played by black actors – the Roman Empire spanned the world. The RSC have just done a superb black *Caesar* set in modern Africa. You can have black Benedicks, Bottoms and Petruchios, black Macbeths, Lears and Hamlets, as long as it is thought through. Lear's daughters should be black as well, so should either Gertrude or Claudius. As for Romeo and Juliet, it adds another aspect to the play if the two warring houses are black and white, or Jews and Muslims, or whatever. But the English history plays are different: Shakespeare was writing about specific historical times and I think they only make sense if they are depicted historically correct. I know I will be accused of racism and of being years behind the times, but if my simple logic was followed in casting, it would mean far more parts for black actors, instead of the token one or two that the RSC indiscriminately drop into every play.

Trevor Nunn always tries to give every character, even the smallest part, a clear line through the play. Hytner moved us around like chess pieces. Old Sir Thomas went from driving the King off to battle in a Land Rover

(I must say that was quite a thrill, although it was a very old Landrover and I was never quite sure whether it would start and make its stuttering progress across the vast Olivier stage), to having a sandbag over his head and morphing into a French prisoner waiting to be shot. I and several others had to spend what seemed like an eternity kneeling on the floor, in acute discomfort, with our hands tied behind our backs. I felt Nick was bending the play to make it look like a war crime. In fact, though a terrible thing in any age, killing prisoners was quite common and acceptable in mediaeval warfare if it looked likely that the enemy was going to attack again.

Hytner was faced with the mammoth task of putting bums on the seats of the massive tiers of the Olivier auditorium. Trevor Nunn had succeeded by putting on popular musicals but had been pilloried by some for doing so. Nick's plan was to get a sponsor so that he could offer a large quantity of tickets for £10 for every performance. One hot afternoon I was kneeling in the rehearsal room, trying to breathe through the sandbag and wondering just where my career had gone wrong, when Nick's secretary hurried in and informed him that the sponsor was on the phone. Nick looked very nervous, told us to take a tea break and followed her out. He returned twenty minutes later with a huge smile on his face, 'This wonderful man, Lloyd Dorfman, head of Travelex, has agreed to sponsor the entire season. I was afraid he would pull out because of the war.'

Lloyd Dorfman? He was married to my step-father's grand-daughter. We were related – sort of. I flourished my sandbag and said, 'Do you realise I am a member of his family? If it was an Italian family I wouldn't be kneeling at the back of the stage with a bag on my head. I'd be playing the Duke of bloody Exeter at least.' Nick stopped smiling. We haven't got the same sense of humour.

I was very put out when I saw that the National had abandoned its usual practice and had omitted the actors' names from the posters. From time immemorial, to Shakespeare himself, the names of the players have been on the bills. For the scholar, it is an invaluable method of discerning who appeared in what; for the small-part actor it is one of the few proofs he has of ever having been in the thing. When I asked the reason I was told it had been decided the poster would look more attractive without being cluttered by names – though of course the Director, Designer, Lighting Designer etc., were prominently displayed. I voiced my disapproval but seemed to be the only one who cared. The actors' names have never returned. Unless you are a 'celeb' nobody really listens.

Despite Adrian's excellent performance (my money is on him being the first black actor to be knighted), I felt the production never really came off. Penny Downie played the Chorus as a history scholar who becomes disillusioned with her subject. At one point she wandered through the peace conference in the last act, sadly shaking her head – another complication that the play did not need. I couldn't believe it when the Leek Scene, despite an excellent Fluellen, was cut. Old-fashioned David Conville in his damp Regent's Park had a greater understanding for *Henry V* than Nick Hytner, world-acclaimed director that he is. Only my opinion, others will strongly disagree.

However, I truly enjoyed the entire experience (apart from my cameo as the French prisoner). The casting department had found a tough bunch of young actors for the soldiery; little different, I suspect, from the real ones out in Iraq. It was a sobering thought to realise that I was the oldest member of the company. Until then there had always been someone like Esmond, Michael Bryant or Denis Quilley from an older generation; but not anymore, I was now in the front line, ready to go over the top. The younger actors treated me like an 'old sweat'. I was roped in with half a dozen of them to be sentries, standing in a line across the back, facing upstage, during the interminably long scene in the French camp the night before the battle. It seemed to go on forever. After a few performances one of the lads decided to break the monotony by emitting a sonorous fart. It was answered immediately by the man on his left. In a thrice it had come down the line to me – where it stopped. Over a few nights it developed into a sort of symphony. It was completely harmless, we were so far upstage that nobody could hear it, but I alone resisted, thinking it completely unprofessional. Then one night, after a particularly pungent prawn curry in the backstage canteen, Sir Thomas relented and ended the cadence with a soft bass. The next day the stage management posted a notice on the board, lambasting those concerned for puerile and disgusting behaviour. I never worked at the National again after that. I don't think it was because of the fart.

The Merry Wives of Windsor

It has been used as the libretto for at least nine operas. Thank God Shakespeare was forced to change the fat knight's name – can you imagine an opera called *Oldcastle*?

Tattle: It is the only play Shakespeare set in a small English town, with low-born citizens as the main characters. The schoolmaster scenes may well be based on Stratford memories and there are echoes of his father's trade when Mistress Quickly asks: *'Does he not wear a great round beard like a glover's paring knife*?' The legend of Queen Elizabeth requesting it, and of Shakespeare completing it in eleven to fourteen days, dates from 1702, but I like to think it is true. Had Kempe already left the company and could that be the reason, without his input, that Falstaff's wit is no longer as sharp? After the Restoration, Thomas Betterton and James Quin excelled in the role, although later actors such as Kean and Macready chose to play Ford.

In recent times a very well-known actor; almost a national treasure although not noted for Shakespeare, was cast as Falstaff by the RSC. He found, as I did, that being cooped up in the laundry basket whilst Ford berates his wife was extremely uncomfortable. One night Ford, played by a distinguished Shakespearean, not noted for his sense of humour, kicked the basket by mistake. There was a heartfelt groan from within which got the biggest laugh of the night. Ford was furious, thinking Falstaff had done it deliberately to kill one of his own laughs, and kicked the trunk even harder. An even bigger groan emerged, earning a veritable roar of delight. A whole series of kicks, groans and laughs ensued. Ford was now berserk with rage, assuming Falstaff was sabotaging his performance. Falstaff was likewise outraged, thinking that Ford was deliberately attacking him. They came off and had a virtual punch-up in the wings, only breaking off for their curtain calls when they came on together smiling, hand in hand. I'm told, on very good authority, that Leslie Phillips and Edward Petherbridge resumed hostilities the moment the curtain fell.

Memories: 1982: David Conville had initially cast Ronnie Fraser as Falstaff, but when a film came up halfway through the run, generously let him go and asked me to take over. I didn't have much time to give any fresh interpretation; in any case it would have thrown the other actors if I had. I watched Fraser several times and just learnt the lines. Ronnie should have been ideal for the Falstaff in *Merry Wives*, he was a brilliant comedian and I'll always remember him as a superb Bardolph, probably the best I've seen, at the Old Vic back in the 1950s. But he wasn't happy in the Park, perhaps he was ill, he died a few years later; his Falstaff came over as a bad-tempered old man. I don't suppose I was much better, but I enjoyed myself with two very sexy wives, Kate O'Mara and Pippa Conville, both of whom I'd worked with before. Anne Page and Fenton are allegedly the most insipid juveniles in all Shakespeare. Anne was played by a radiant Natasha Richardson, I think it was her first job, and Fenton was a gloomy young man who sloped about backstage as if he had the world on his shoulders. We never met during the course of the play and I never really got to know his name. I found out later it was Richard E. Grant, about to find fame and fortune in *Withnail and I*. At the end of the run we took the play for a brief season at Arundel Castle, beneath the Round Tower, which is almost identical to that at Windsor. David had had the brilliant idea of casting the incomparable Dora Bryan as Mistress Quickly, and when she appeared before me as Queen of the Fairies at the end of the play it was another of those rare magical moments. The tapers of the children playing fairies twinkled around the castle battlements, dulcet voices and evocative music floated down; I could sense the rapt enchantment of the packed audience. That night it was wonderful to be an actor.

Much Ado About Nothing

'Benedick's pleasantries might pass at a sing-song in a public house parlour; but a gentleman rash enough to venture on them in even the very mildest suburban imitation of polite society today would assuredly never be invited again.'
George Bernard Shaw

Tattle: 'Nothing' was an Elizabethan term for the vagina. I read somewhere that Shakespeare has more than a hundred other names for it in his works, including such eroticisms as: 'withered pear', 'nest of spicery' and 'salmon's tail'. For some reason (was the Bard just feeling un-poetic?) the majority of the text of *Much Ado* is in prose. It was probably written after 1598 as it is not mentioned in Frances Meres' list. Dogberry was the final part created for Will Kempe before he quit the company in a huff to jig his way to Norwich. The play has always done good business. Leonard Digges wrote in 1640: 'Let but Beatrice and Benedick be seen, in a trice the Cockpit, Galleries, Boxes, all are full.' In the early eighteenth century it was brought up to date and renamed *The Universal Passion*. David Garrick went back to the original and Benedick became one of his favourite roles; he went on playing it until he was fifty-nine. Henry Irving and Ellen Terry made the parts their own. Irving was said to be a soldier first, a lover next, and always a gentleman, whilst Ellen Terry was hailed as 'Shakespeare's Beatrice, the incarnation of the merry lady'. John Gielgud and Peggy Ashcroft had similar success in the 1950s. Gielgud, 'spoke the prose with a silken rhythm and did not let the man dwindle.' In 1965 Franco Zeffirelli followed up his *Romeo* with a hot-blooded Sicilian *Much Ado* at the National starring Maggie Smith and her then husband, Robert Stephens. My most abiding memory of it is Albert Finney's corseted Don Pedro blowing smoke rings with his cigar. The Benedicks of Christopher Plummer, Alan Howard and Derek Jacobi have all been justly applauded, but my personal favourite was Donald Sinden in a production set in the British Raj. Judi Dench was a moving Beatrice and John Woodvine a hilarious Indian Dogberry. It was such light-hearted fun that it was hard to believe that it had been directed by John Barton.

1961: My first part on leaving RADA was to play Don Pedro at the Manchester Library Theatre. It was a great start. Manchester was a much sought after place to be: three-weekly repertory, as opposed to the normal one or two. (The only other three-weeklies at the time were: The Bristol Old Vic, The Liverpool Playhouse, Birmingham Rep and the Glasgow Citizens. The Nottingham Playhouse was yet to open.) The artistic director was David Scase, a leading force of Joan Littlewood's *Theatre Workshop*, having been her stage manager as well as an actor. David was the son of a Fulham plumber and proud of his working-class roots. He was a man after my own heart, instinctive and anti-intellectual. His motto was do it – don't analyse. So different from the university educated directors I would encounter at Stratford and later at the National. He was all for zest and energy. In many ways he was similar to my mentor Michael Croft. They had both been sailors in the Second World War – David had been torpedoed in the North Atlantic. I suspect I got the job on Croft's recommendation. David had the reputation of being very fierce – a few years later he fired Anthony Hopkins – but I found him a pussy cat. He would direct with a beaming smile on his face, pulling on a cigarette, continuously hitching up his low-cut trousers.

David was an excellent director and did superb productions of *The Hostage* and *The Entertainer* that season, but unfortunately he did not think *Much Ado*, a romantic comedy, was really his cup of tea. He only did it because it was a set book that year, and we were left a lot to our own resources. I'd never done an entire Shakespearean comedy before and needed all the help I could get. I ended up playing Don Pedro as a bluff soldier and missed out on the darker side of the character. Why is he left alone at the end? Is he gay? I always wanted to go back and have another go at it – I was too young then. However, despite the bleak drabness of Manchester in those days and the extremely cold winter, I was content. I felt I was a real actor at last.

I shared a poky room with Claudio, my old sparring partner Ken Farrington, then better known as Billy Walker in *Coronation Street* and a big celebrity in the north. I always think Claudio is an unpleasant little shit. So is the Claudio in *Measure for Measure*. Did Shakespeare have anything against that name? For that matter why do all Shakespeare's Antonio's appear to be gay? Antonio is gay in *The Merchant* and in *Twelfth Night,* and he is very much an old bachelor uncle in *Much Ado*. I've never really fathomed the Antonio in *The Tempest,* but he definitely has a problem. But back to Manchester: our room was freezing cold and poky and the floor sloped alarmingly. I am reminded of it whenever I see a revival of *Look Back in Anger,* but Jimmy Porter's digs are always luxurious in comparison. There was a bed in two of the corners of the room, a sink and gas ring in the third, an old table and chairs in the fourth, and a dilapidated sofa in the middle. Isabel, a beautiful young ASM, who should have been playing Hero, had a crush on Ken Farrington and sometimes slept on the sofa if she missed her late-night bus to the other side of Manchester. One Friday evening Dora decided to make her first visit to the north and give me a surprise. After being attacked on the train by a drunken sailor, she arrived at our digs at about half past one in the morning and had to persuade our dubious landlady to let her in. As Dora crept across the lino towards my bed, Ken, hearing footsteps whispered: 'Is that you Isabel?' 'Isabel? Who is this Isabel?' Dora furiously demanded, leaping to attack. It took quite a while to pacify her. We left her in bed the following morning forgetting to explain that the gas fire, the sole source of heat, had to be fed by shilling pieces. It was one of the coldest winters on record and we returned that night to find her still in bed, shivering under a pile of coats. Apart from a solitary visit to the Edinburgh Festival, Dora has never ventured north of Stratford-upon-Avon since.

I found the Library Theatre itself to be a soulless place, tucked away in the basement of the Central Library. It smelt of over-brewed coffee – they didn't have a licence for alcohol then. I always think it is far harder to make an audience laugh if they haven't had a drink. But I enjoyed the camaraderie of the company: Colin Welland, who would win an Oscar for writing *Chariots of Fire*, was our Dogberry. He'd been a local art teacher who had applied to Scase for a job painting the scenery. David was about to direct Pinter's *Birthday Party* and could not find a Stanley. He took a chance on Colin and a career was born. Dogberry was the second part he'd played: he wasn't quite as bad as Michael Keaton in Kenneth Branagh's otherwise excellent film, but it was a close run thing. The best thing in the show was Beatrice in the shape of Jennie Goossens, hot from the Old Vic. Young Helen Fraser, with nary a trace of *Bad Girls*, was a homely Hero.

John Noakes, his Action Man days in *Blue Peter* way ahead of him, was Borachio, and John Normington, known to all and sundry as 'Nora', was playing the small part of Conrade.

John was not much older than me but had acquired a vast amount of experience in tatty reps. He'd even played daily rep one summer in Cornwall. I didn't believe him until he showed me the bills. His speciality was playing old men: that was his main function in the company and he was hurt that David had not given him Leonato. I think David thought that Shakespeare was a bit beyond Nora. There was a saying then that somebody was only a 'rep' actor. Little did we know that in a few years John Normington would become a stalwart of the RSC and one of the most sought-after character actors in the business. Ironically, he was playing Billy in *The Entertainer* at the Old Vic when he died in 2007. He had played the same part, most movingly, in that Manchester season. I can still picture him singing '*Onward Christian Soldiers*'.

I was on £10 a week but there always seemed plenty of money for drinks at lunchtime, tea and Kunzle cakes at the Kardomah cafe, and late night sessions at the New Theatre Inn, where we would mingle with the visiting actors playing at the Opera House. The highlight was the week when John Stride arrived with the Old Vic tour of *Romeo.* I also fondly recall one very rumbustious night with a purple-faced Trevor Howard. I believed, like Pinocchio, that it really was 'an actor's life for me!'

As You Like It

'Rosalind is not a complete human being; she is simply an extension into five acts of the most affectionate, fortunate, delightful five minutes in the life of a charming woman.'
George Bernard Shaw

Tattle: Not mentioned in Meres' list of plays so probably written around 1599. William Kempe had left the company and Touchstone was the first role created for the new clown, the more subtle Robert Armin. There is some evidence that Shakespeare originally played Old Adam. The play was rewritten after the Restoration and given the prosaic title, *Love in a Forest*. Rosalind, alongside Cleopatra, is generally considered Shakespeare's finest female creation. She became popular in the eighteenth century when 'breeches' parts, that is roles in which actresses were able to display their legs and thighs, were considered especially erotic. But Rosalind didn't suit the formidable Sarah Siddons, who is said to have strutted about the stage like Lady Macbeth. *The Morning Chronicle* reported: 'Mrs Siddons' costume was not that of either man or woman. Her Hussar boots with a gardener's apron and petticoat behind gave her a most equivocal appearance, which rendered Orlando's stupidity astonishing, in not making a premature discovery of his mistress. What caused Mrs Siddons to innovate upon the former representations of this character in the article of dress we cannot guess.' Maybe she had bad legs?

The Rosalind of the age was Dorothy Jordan, long-term mistress of George III's third son, the Duke of Clarence. Clarence, like all the royal brood, was up to his neck in debt and lived off Dorothy's theatrical earnings. She played Rosalind from 1787 until 1814 throughout ten pregnancies inflicted upon her by the randy Duke. There couldn't have been much doubt about the sex of her Ganymede, but she 'carried all before her' and was acclaimed by Hazlitt and others for the delicacy of her comedy. When Clarence moved up the pecking order and it began to look as if he might be King, for the sake of respectability and a legitimate heir, he was forced to abandon poor Dorothy. Her children were taken from her and she died in exile of a broken heart. Claire Tomalin has written an excellent book '*Mrs Jordan's Profession*', which one day will be made into an award-winning film. Mark my words – you read it here first. Dorothy's understudy, Harriet Melon, was luckier. She married the Royal Banker, Thomas Coutts, who died and left her his money, and she ended up as the Duchess of St Albans. (There was of course a theatrical connection as the Duke was a direct descendant of Nell Gwynn.)

Talking of films, Laurence Olivier played Orlando in a 1936 film of the play, which I've never seen. I don't think many people have, despite having music by Sir William Walton and being edited by the young David Lean. I did see a magical production by Wendy Toye at the Old Vic; I think she was the first woman to have directed Shakespeare there. Barbara Jefford was Rosalind, she played all the leads then, with the embryonic Dames, Maggie Smith and Judi Dench, as Celia and Phoebe. At Stratford, Vanessa Redgrave's lanky Rosalind made her a star, and Ronnie Pickup (a vastly underrated actor) was superb in the all-male version during the early and great days of the National. Sir Anthony Hopkins gave one of his most heartfelt performances as Audrey.

Memories: David William was a first rate director of Shakespeare. His productions were intelligent, clear and imaginative: he took special care to help his actors create a real living world on stage. When he directed *The Shoemakers' Holiday,* we spent an entire day at Lobb's, the historic cobblers in St James's Street, learning how to make shoes by hand. He made you aware of the full value of the words and poetry, but at the same time was meticulous in comic detail. He should have directed for the RSC and the National, indeed he was mooted as a possible successor for Olivier, but he spent most of his career at the other Stratford in Canada. In 1963 he took me out to lunch and offered me Orlando in his forthcoming production in Regent's Park, adding in his caustic manner: 'It's the only Shakespearean juvenile you could ever possibly play, apart from the younger brother in *Cymbeline*.' He may well have been right, although I think I could have done a good rendering of an on-the-make Bassanio; but a film came up and I opted for that. He was not best pleased and never asked me again, although we remained friends.

The nearest I got to Orlando was being disturbed in flagrante with Rosalind's understudy at Stratford by an assistant stage manager frantically banging on the door – Dorothy Tutin was in London and had forgotten there was a matinee. I was never a Jaques or a Touchstone; I thought I might play one of the Dukes. I'm past those now. All that's left is Shakespeare's own part, Old Adam. At seventy-five it would be an honour '*I dream not of*'.

Twelfth Night; Or, What You Will

'After dinner to the Duke's House, and there saw Twelfth Night acted well, though it be but a silly play…'
Samuel Pepys

'It is perhaps too good-natured for comedy. It has little satire, and no spleen. It makes us laugh at the follies of mankind, not despise them.'
William Hazlitt

Tattle: This last great comedy was written about 1600, possibly for Queen Elizabeth's Twelfth Night celebrations. The first recorded performance was in the Middle Temple Hall. John Manningham, who gave us the *Richard III* story of Shakespeare and Burbage, wrote in his diary on 2 February 1602: 'We had a play *Twelve Night* or *What you Will.*' To mark that occasion, the modern Globe Company, complete with Mark Rylance's pert Olivia, have performed the play there in recent years. (Great actor though he is, I think Rylance is a trifle greedy; there are too few female parts in the canon without them being purloined by leading actors. Dame Eileen Atkins is of a similar opinion, stating the parts were not written for middle-aged men, but for boys whose voices hadn't broken yet. Which, of course, was what Croft was doing with the NYT sixty years ago.) One of the unsolved mysteries is the almost impossible part of Fabian, who suddenly appears out of nowhere. As Feste is never on at the same time, I tend to think that he is really Feste and the editors misread the prefix to the character's name.

Viola gave Mrs Jordan another chance to display her legs. Charles Lamb gives a description of the spontaneity she was famous for: 'There is no giving an account of how she delivered the disguised story of her love for Orsino. It was no set speech, that she had foreseen, so as to weave it into an harmonious speech, line necessarily following line, to make up the music...but, when she had declared her sister's history to be a 'blank', and that she 'never told her love', there was a pause, as if the story had ended – and then the image of the 'worm in the bud' came up as a new suggestion – and the heightened image of 'Patience' still followed after that, as by some growing (and not mechanical) process, thought springing up after thought, I would almost say, as they were watered by her tears.'

That sounds very naturalistic and modern to me.

Memories: In the summer of 1983 *Twelfth Night* was playing in repertoire with the Scottish play at St George's and I was cast as Sir Toby and Macbeth. I'd always fancied playing Toby, mistakenly thinking he was akin to Falstaff. I couldn't have been more wrong. After the first two scenes Sir Toby becomes more and more morose. I also realised that Sir Toby doesn't have to be fat like Falstaff: he is a bitter alcoholic. Alcoholics are often thin. I tried to play him as a gone-to-seed swordsman; his defeat by Sebastian is not comic but a moment of realisation of what he has become: a sponging old trickster. He uses everybody – does he really feel any affection for Maria? He becomes very quiet towards the end of Malvolio's prison scene, as if he is disgusted with himself and Maria's trickery. I found that scene particularly difficult to play. Sir Donald Wolfit cut it entirely in his production, giving as his reason. 'I cannot learn it, and if I cannot learn it, Shakespeare did not write it.'

As ever at St George's there was no time and no money and both productions had to be rehearsed in little more than a couple of weeks. I naturally was concentrating on Macbeth and waited for the director, a fugitive from BBC Television, to give me some help or ideas. They never came. It was probably my worst Shakespearean performance.

Julius Caesar

'It abounds in admirable and affecting passages, and is remarkable for the profound knowledge of character, in which Shakespeare could scarcely fail.'
William Hazlitt

Tattle: A performance at the Globe is recorded in the diary of the Swiss physician, Thomas Platter, in September 1599. There are three leading roles, but Burbage would have played Brutus, a forerunner of Hamlet in the manner he soliloquises on the assassination of his friend. It was one of the favourite roles of John Kemble whose slow delivery and noble bearing were well-suited to stoic Romans. The play's republican sentiments have always made it popular in the United States. John Wilkes Booth, Lincoln's assassin, was in a production in New York in 1864, though ironically he played Mark Antony, not a conspirator. In 1937 Orson Welles played Brutus in his iconic Mercury Theatre production set in Fascist Italy, which is vividly recalled in the excellent film '*Me and Orson Welles*'. Cassius was one of John Gielgud's finest roles and has been preserved, alongside Marlon Brando's Antony, James Mason's Brutus, Louis Calhern's Caesar and Edmond O'Brien's Casca in the low-budget Hollywood version of 1953, one of the finest Shakespeare films ever made. The play is so good it can survive all manner of interpretations. In 2012, I saw an excellent all-black version set in Africa, but took care to avoid an all-female extravaganza set in a women's prison. (I may have made a mistake. People tell me it was brilliant.)

Memories: This ranks just behind both parts of *Henry IV* as my favourite play. Not only because of personal memories, but because it is exciting, accessible and has three equal leading parts, plus a great supporting role in Caesar himself, who you could say dominates the entire action. In the summer of 1960, H M Tennent, then the most powerful West End management, offered Michael Croft the recently restored Queen's Theatre on Shaftesbury Avenue for a month on extremely reasonable terms. Michael had always wanted to do a modern dress Caesar using a huge crowd, such as only the NYT could muster. I think he was partly inspired by what he had heard of Orson Welles's pre-war production in New York. Michael was well aware of my big voice and wanted me for Mark Antony. The only problem was I was still in the Army, doing National Service, until the end of September. I had managed to get odd days off to do the extra work on *An Age of Kings,* but I would be needed day and night for Antony. Fortunately, Sir Ralph Richardson, President of the NYT, was an old schoolfellow of my Brigadier, and by some miracle, I never quite understood how it was achieved, I was granted special leave. I was officially stationed in the Officers' Mess at Woolwich but took the train up to rehearsals in the West End each morning.

Croft was then at the peak of his powers before the booze began to take control. That summer he was bursting with invention and dynamism. He could handle huge numbers on stage like no other director I've ever worked with, as well as having a straightforward approach to the verse. As I intoned over Caesar's body: '*Are all thy conquests, glories, triumphs, spoils, Shrunk to this little measure?*', I can still hear him, rasping out, between puffs of his fortieth cigarette of the day: 'The spoils, David. Think about the spoils. What <u>were</u> the fuckin' spoils?' It was the first time the NYT went fully national and Michael had assembled a remarkable cast. Martin Jarvis was Cassius; John Shrapnel, Caesar; Neil Stacy, Brutus; Simon Ward, Octavius; Michael York, Messala; Hywel Bennett, Lucius, and Ian McShane, the first northern member from Blackburn, Lancashire, made his mark as Strato. Moreover, Michael had finally bitten the bullet and accepted girls. They were amply represented in the crowd, and Simon Ward's girlfriend, Jane Merrow, just out of RADA, was a very glamorous Portia.

My Antony in that production was perhaps the best thing I've ever done, which is rather pathetic as I was only twenty-two. Apart from Brando in the film, I've yet to see anyone discover more in the part than I did, or should I say that Croft found for me. I was very fit from my Army training and felt completely at ease, dressed in an American Parachute General's uniform. Antony, Brutus and Cassius are all fantastic parts, but Antony is the showiest, although he's only really on for the Third Act – but what an Act. His best friend has been brutally assassinated; he confronts the conspirators and manipulates Brutus into allowing him to speak in Caesar's funeral and then, when he has been left alone, vows vengeance over his friend's body. He follows that in the Forum, with one of the greatest sequence of speeches Shakespeare ever wrote.

Though I love traditional and authentic dress in Shakespeare, sometimes modern dress can add an extra dimension. It certainly worked with *that* Caesar. It opened with the crowd jiving to rock and roll music played on a juke box. The various professions and ranks of the conspirators could be designated by their clothes and uniforms. They all look alike if they are wearing togas. When it came to the battle scenes, the army of Antony and Octavius were clad as American GIs, whilst the forces of Brutus and Cassius were dressed bang-up-to-date as Castro-type rebels. Michael added wonderful inventive touches, such as Antony deliberately putting aside the microphone through which Brutus has addressed the crowd, so that he could appeal directly to their emotions; and lighting a cigarette, exhausted at the end of his oration before musing: *'Now let it work. Mischief thou art afoot, Take thou what course thou wilt.'* The production was rapturously received by the critics and I had some of the best notices I would ever have. On top of that three leading agents: London Management, Christopher Mann and Philip Pearman, the reputedly gay husband of Coral Browne, were clamouring for my signature.

However, my most potent memory of that production is the special performance we gave for the acting profession. Michael chose a day, I think it was a Tuesday, when no other West End theatre was doing a matinee, and invited all the casts to see us at the Queen's. In 1960, unlike today, the West End was not packed with musicals, and many illustrious actors attended, including Alec Guinness and my idol, Laurence Olivier himself. I was in the dressing room, putting on copious make-up, as we all did then, when Martin Jarvis looked out of the window and exclaimed in that immaculate voice: 'Oh, my God! Look at that!'

An army lorry had pulled up outside the Wellington pub and I saw my NCOs: Sergeant-Major Cooper, who'd been at Dunkirk, and Bombardier Pizzey, a veteran of the International Brigade in the Spanish Civil War, their breasts gleaming with medals, getting out of the cab, whilst most of the lads from my Battery were jumping out of the back. Unbeknown to me, Cooper had arranged a special outing to come up to London and support 'sir'. The moment I stepped on stage in the first scene a great cheer and stamping of army boots erupted from the balcony, to be repeated even louder when I exited a few lines later. I think Cooper and Pizzey became a tad disappointed when I didn't appear again for an hour or so, and decided to go for a drink in Soho. They didn't come back until the curtain. As we took our bow there was slight fracas in the wings before Sergeant-Major Cooper staggered on stage, his medals and beret slightly awry, clasping a huge bunch of flowers. He gave a bloom to Jane Merrow and another to Calpurnia, before thrusting the remainder into my arms and embracing me with a smacking kiss. At this cheers and stamping erupted again from soldiery in the gallery, to which Cooper responded with a slow and deliberate V sign as the curtain fell. Sir Laurence Olivier and Sergeant-Major Cooper arrived at the dressing room to congratulate us at the same time. I seem to remember Sir Laurence telling me not to strain my throat too much and that I should gargle with raw eggs and port, whilst Cooper was slapping him and me on the back simultaneously. Eventually the Gunners were rounded up and I thanked them, very emotionally, for their support before they were driven back to Woolwich. However, Bombardier Pizzey could not be found. It was not until Caesar's coffin was dragged into place to be brought on for the evening performance, that the old soldier was discovered sleeping sweetly inside it. Unlikely though this story sounds it can be verified by all surviving members of the cast.

Sir Alec was appearing as Lawrence of Arabia in *Ross* at the Theatre Royal Haymarket. That evening he remarked to fellow actor, Gerald Harper, 'You know, I saw something very odd at the Queen's this afternoon. I rather think Lawrence would feel quite at home in the army today.' I last saw Sergeant-Major Cooper when he was a Beefeater, conducting tourists round the Tower of London; I never came across Bombardier Pizzey again.

The following spring of 1961, during the Easter holidays, we took *Caesar* on an epic tour of Italy. Croft had done a deal with an Italian impresario and had dates for *Julio Cesare in Blue Jeans* to play in Turin, Genoa, Florence, Perugia and Rome. Michael's NYT would never have got off the ground in these days of 'health and safety' and 'political correctness' (nor would Lilian Bayliss's Old Vic for that matter). With hardly any public funding, Croft would be at odds with the Arts Council until his dying day, he dragged almost seventy kids round Italy in a clapped-out bus, singing Sinatra on the back seat with a bottle of brandy in one hand and smoking cigarette in the other. It was an educational experience we would never forget. (Brian Croft, getting his first experience a 'roady', went ahead, driving an old army lorry, with the scenery and stage crew.) In Genoa the very shady impresario had for some unexplained reason booked the girls and Mrs Hampton, the wardrobe mistress, into a brothel near the docks. Croft dragged them out after one night. Some of them seemed quite reluctant – Mrs Hampton said she had never slept on a more comfortable mattress.

One afternoon in Rome, Croft took us all on an expedition to the wine caves at Frascati, which developed into a dodgem car battle versus the local youths. Needless to say, the performance that evening was not one of our best. The impresario was very slow in paying the money he had promised, sometimes he only gave half. Michael had to have the cash to pay for our food and accommodation and travelling costs. One evening towards the end of the tour, Croft and five of us largest lads confronted the impresario in his office at the interval and refused to go on for the second half unless the money was paid in full. There were angry exchanges between us and some very dubious characters that answered the Italian's frantic phone call, before a flustered representative of the British Council arrived and the money was finally handed over. The curtain went up nearly an hour later than expected. The audience didn't seem at all put out: I've since been told that long intervals are quite common in Italy.

But my most vivid memory of that tour is one particular night in Rome. We had just finished the final performance when a phone call came for me from the stage door. A thick Italian voice said he was the chauffeur of a famous American film director and he had orders to take me to the director's apartment where he wanted to discuss a part in a film. I couldn't quite make out the director's name. It sounded an absolute con, but then you never know. A very good-looking and sweet-smelling young Italian in an Alfa Romeo drove me to a street near the Forum and stopped outside an expensive apartment block. He told me to press the top bell. I got out and obeyed. The door swung open as a voice told me to take the lift to the top floor. The lift opened inside a luxurious apartment and a little man in a grey suit with a face like a friendly gnome was waiting for me with open arms: 'Why, you're just a kid. You looked so big when you strode across that stage. How'd you get that walk?'

He poured me a huge whisky on the rocks in a chunky cut-glass tumbler, sat beside me on the biggest leather sofa I'd ever seen, and proceeded to tell me that his name was Irving Rapper; he'd been with Warner Brothers during the great years and was Bette Davis's favourite director. He rolled out a long list of films, some of which I'd heard of – I'd even seen a couple. He told me that he had invented the business of lighting two cigarettes at once for Paul Henreid in *Now, Voyager* and gave me an elaborate enacting of the process. He was now freelance and was directing an Italian epic, *Joseph and his Brethren*, here in Rome. His next project was a story of a patrol lost in the desert and he thought I would be just right for the youngest soldier. It all sounded too good to be true – it was the stuff young actor's dreams are made of. I listened eagerly and drank copiously. After a while he tapped me on the knee, got up, and went to the corner of the room where two huge windows met. 'Come over here. You can see the Forum down below. That's the actual spot where the real Mark Antony gave his speech, but I bet he didn't do it better than you did tonight.'

I dutifully went over and gazed down at the magnificent view of the floodlit Forum. As I turned back to speak to him I saw that his little arms were outstretched and his hands were pressing on the window panes either side of me. He looked up at me with soft brown eyes: 'How about a kiss?' I panicked. This is what my mother had always been frightened of. I told him in no uncertain terms that I wasn't that way inclined. He looked extremely disappointed but took it very well. I even felt a little sorry for him. He wrote down my agent's number in London, promised to call her, and phoned his driver to take me back to my hotel. As I went down in the lift I wondered if I had thrown my chance of stardom away. I needn't have worried. He did indeed call my agent but the film was never made, in fact Rapper never really made a film again. *Joseph and his Brethren* was a resounding flop. He came to London quite regularly over the years and never failed to ring me with stories of projects he had in mind and parts that I might play. At first I took Dora with me when I went to meet him and later I went with my two young sons – they called him 'sweet wrapper'. I grew very fond of him. He died in Hollywood in 1999 at the age of 101.

I thought I'd finally finished with Croft when I left RADA, but he had one last adventure for me. In September 1961, just before I was due to begin my professional career in Manchester, the NYT's production of *Caesar* was invited to be part of the West Berlin Festival. We left London by train during an East-West crisis, with all the costumes and props, which included fifty old WW1 303 rifles, with their firing pins removed, acquired from the Alleyn's School CCF. They were to cause undreamed of mayhem when we reached the East German border and were eventually confiscated and sent back as being possible weapons for counter-revolutionaries. Croft informed the British Council of our loss, and it was arranged that the British Army of the Rhine would provide fifty modern rifles, without ammunition for every performance. Each night an army wagon would draw up at the stage door of the Hebbel Theater and a squad of soldiers would carry out the weapons, which every young actor had to sign for under the stern gaze of a regimental sergeant-major. The Berlin Wall actually started to go up during our technical rehearsal. Portia and Calpurnia had a late call and on arrival at the theatre told us that a lot of the hotel staff had not turned up that morning. During our lunch break we saw East German soldiers running out the initial coils of barbed wire. They waved us away and shone mirrors in our eyes. We thought they were having a laugh. Everything in West Berlin seemed highly charged and fraught with danger: it was exhilarating giving vent to those great political speeches before rapt audiences whilst the wall was being built a few hundred yards away. The left-wing members of the company made dutiful daily forays over Checkpoint Charlie to the Berliner Ensemble, where they watched rehearsals of Brecht's 'sullen tracts of tedious didacticism', which were then all the rage. I remained firmly on the western side of the rapidly rising wall and, with other less politically-minded chums, sampled the beer halls with Croft.

Within six months I was back in the play again in more mundane Manchester. David Scase announced that *Julius Caesar* would be the second Shakespeare play of the season. I fully expected to give my Antony again, albeit in a toga, and was stunned when David told me I was going to play Brutus. I should have been grateful for the chance of playing an entirely different character, another of Shakespeare's greatest roles, but I considered Antony was my part and was considerably put out. David directed the play well; he had done it a few years earlier with Robert Stephens and Jeremy Brett, but I'm ashamed to admit that my Brutus was not all that different from my Antony. One evening I even began Brutus' measured speech to the crowd: *'Romans, Countrymen and Lovers'*, with Antony's impassioned *'Friends! Romans! Countrymen!'* Rick Jones, the actor playing Antony, was less than pleased. It is difficult for Brutus to play the extremely long scene in his orchard, soliloquising on Caesar's assassination, without being tedious. I was better in the heated quarrel with Cassius, the so-called 'tent' scene on the night before the battle. I wore my toga with aplomb and combed my hair forward in the style of Marlon Brando. I didn't know whether to be pleased or hurt when *The Manchester Guardian*, as it then was, said I resembled the newly-elected President Kennedy.

The following year, 1963, Peter Dews sought to repeat his successful *Age of Kings* with *Spread of the Eagle:* Shakespeare's Roman plays serialised with an ensemble cast. This time I was free and accepted eagerly, even though the parts offered were not what I had become used to. I found myself a member of an extremely 'camp' ensemble – we hardly used the word 'gay' then. I was one of the handful of heterosexual members. In *Caesar* I played the First Citizen and Young Cato, sometimes known as the Chinese part, because of his last line before he is killed at Philippi: *'I am the son of Marcus Cato Ho!'*. Peter Cushing, the kindest of men, taking a break from horror, was a superb lean and hungry Cassius, and Paul Eddington, his comic triumphs in *The Good Life* and *Yes Minister* years ahead, was a perplexed but noble Brutus. Antony was well cast in the shape of Keith Michell, the virile Australian actor who, having heard I had played the part, made the mistake of telling me to give him notes, and was slightly put out when I took him at his word.

We rehearsed in the old Drill Hall in Shepherd's Bush. One morning during coffee break, as Peter was regaling us with yet another of his theatrical anecdotes, the floor manager told me I had to phone my agent. 'Hollywood's calling,' someone, I think it was Paul Bailey, said rather bitchily. And it was, although it came via my agent. Sally Nichol, an elderly casting director who went around with her shopping bag and old hat eternally planted on her head, was casting the film *Becket*. It was the talk of London because Richard Burton and Peter O'Toole, hot from his triumph as Lawrence of Arabia, had been cast in the leading roles. Hal Wallis, the legendary producer of *Casablanca*, had instructed Sally Nichol to find an unknown young actor to play the young monk, Brother John, the third biggest part, which Ian Holm had played in the stage version. Sally had remembered my Mark Antony and had offered the part to me. It was the young actor's dream. I couldn't believe it was happening to me. I was dumbfounded as I went up the stairs to rejoin the rehearsal.

Peter eyed me quizzically: 'I 'ope it was bloody important? We've all been waiting for you.'

I savoured the moment. It tasted delicious. 'They want me to play Richard Burton's monk in *Becket*.'

From that moment everyone's attitude changed. It was as if they sensed I had some secret power behind me. I was taken seriously, people wanted me to have a drink or go to lunch with them. Even the older actors listened to my opinions and laughed at my jokes. I had a brief taste of what it must be like to be a star.

I was a sadder and wiser man in 1979 when David Conville, taking a break from running the Open Air Theatre in Regent's Park, asked me to play Brutus in an Arts Council tour. David was a much better director than he gave himself credit for. Unlike many far less talented directors he was basically a modest man – several times he asked me to be his assistant because he felt he didn't know the particular play well enough. He did a semi-modern dress production of *Caesar* and wanted me to play Brutus as a bespectacled university professor type. I resisted it and played it more or less as I had done before. I should have listened to Conville: I wasn't all that good.

We did that tour throughout the 'winter of discontent', the final months of Callaghan's government. As far as I can recall only Mark Antony and Calpurnia joined me in voting for Mrs Thatcher. But so did Peter Hall (according to his Diary).

Hamlet
(The Moody Dane)

'The Tragedy of Hamlet is a coarse and barbarous piece, which would not be tolerated by the basest rabble in France or Italy...one would think that this work was the fruit of the imagination of a drunken savage.'
Voltaire (1694-1778)

'Hamlet's airy compliments to Ophelia before the court would make a cabman blush.'
George Bernard Shaw

'Now might I do it, Pat.'
Does Hamlet have a silent Irish accomplice?

Tattle: In 1580 a young girl was found drowned in the Avon at a spot renowned for its willows. Her family succeeded in giving her a Christian burial, protesting that she was not a suicide, but had fallen into the river while getting water in a pail. The girl's name was Katherine Hamlett. Was she the inspiration for the death of Ophelia? A lost play *Hamlet*, possibly written by Thomas Kyd, was first performed in 1589. Some believe this lost *Hamlet* was Shakespeare's first draft.

Hamlet abounds with theatrical references. *'There is, sir, an aery of children, little eyases...'* refers to the popularity of the boy actors in the indoor theatre at Blackfriars. With lighting and scenery by Inigo Jones and plays by Ben Jonson, they were flavour of the month and were threatening the popularity of the Globe itself. Indeed it closed for several months and Shakespeare and his fellows were forced to go on tour during 1601, when the version of the play we have now was most probably written. The father/son relationship is strong throughout all the plays, but never stronger than this one. John Shakespeare died in September 1601, shortly after

William had attempted to restore the old man's honour by purchasing him a coat of arms. The Shakespeares were now gentlemen, but as Hamnet, Shakespeare's only son, was dead, there was no line to continue.

Hamlet is the longest of all his plays with 3930 lines and Hamlet is the longest part with 1569 of his own. It was printed in 1603 (the Bad Quarto) and 1604 (the Good Quarto) before the 1623 Folio. They are in fact three distinct versions with different scenes, and some characters have different names. Directors delight in delving in them all and mixing their own cocktail. It was first performed at the Globe around 1602 with Burbage in the title role. We have no idea how Burbage played the Prince, but Betterton, some sixty years later, had been instructed in the part by Sir William Davenant, who claimed to be Shakespeare's illegitimate son. Davenant had seen Joseph Taylor, who had taken over Burbage's roles on the great actor's death in 1619. Betterton, who would still be playing Hamlet when he was well into his seventies, 'opened with a pause of mute amazement; then rising slowly to a solemn, trembling voice, made the Ghost equally terrible to the spectator as to himself.' Though corpulent and 'clumsily made' he must have had a formidable stage presence: 'upon his entrance into every scene he seemed to seize upon the eyes of the giddy and inadvertent.' That stern critic, Samuel Pepys, considered Betterton's Hamlet to be 'the best part that ever man acted'. In the following century, we learn that Garrick, 'at the sight of the Ghost, staggered back two or three steps with his knees giving way under him; his hat falls to the ground and both his arms, especially the left, are stretched out to their full length, with the hands as high as his head, the right arm more bent and the hand lower, and the fingers apart. In this strained position, supported by Horatio and Marcellus, he spoke at last, not at the beginning, but at the end of a breath, with a trembling voice: "Angels and ministers of grace defend us!"' Macready was reputed to have played the scene with such terror that he frightened the ghost.

It may have been the strain of playing Hamlet, or the strong liquor he was partial to, that induced John Kemble, whose Prince was acclaimed for his restraint and aristocratic bearing, to attempt a dressing room rape on his Ophelia, the aptly named Miss De Camp. Her screams for help brought succour from Kemble's wife, Priscilla Brereton, who was giving her Gertrude. Priscilla was a very average actress herself, it was said that she was never known to draw either a smile or a tear, but was very understanding, like many actors' wives have had to be – describing the incident as 'more of a jest than an enormity.' Miss De Camp eventually became her sister-in-law when she married John's brother Charles.

Irving's melodramatic Hamlet was one of his major triumphs. Bernard Shaw, always reluctant to give Irving his due, claimed it was because of Hamlet's long soliloquies: 'Remember the nation is trained to hear sermons.' Forbes-Robertson, John Barrymore, and above all, Gielgud, were the Hamlets of their time. Sir Michael Redgrave may have hung on too long. He played the Dane when he was fifty. After the dress rehearsal, the note given by the director, Glen Byam Shaw, was: 'Splendid, Michael, splendid – but just a touch too young.' But Brian Croft, the tough roadie of The Rolling Stones, was Assistant Stage Manager for all of Sir Michael's sixty plus performances, and says that the beauty and clarity of Redgrave's verse speaking remains with him till this day. I've heard that when the excellent comic actor, Richard Briers, played Hamlet he went so fast that when he expired the audience assumed it was the interval.

Memories: In the spring of 1960 the NYT's production of *Hamlet* was invited to Paris as the official British entry in the Theatre des Nations Festival. I was still in the army, but I was only stationed in Gravesend, managed to get a seventy-eight-hour pass, and went along to give my Marcellus. I had only been able to attend a couple of rehearsals, but Marcellus is not on for long, he disappears after Act One. It is not a bad little part: he is up there on the battlements with Horatio when Hamlet meets the ghost and he has the Christmas card speech at the end of the first scene:

'Some say, that ever 'gainst that season comes
Wherein our Savour's birth is celebrated,
The bird of dawning singeth all night long:
And then, they say, no spirit dare stir abroad.
The nights are wholesome; then no planets strike,
No fairy takes, nor witch hath power to harm,
So hallowed and so gracious is that time.'

Michael Croft chartered what looked like a very old aeroplane; I think it was a Dakota from WW2, and the cast and set, plus a few odd family members and friends piled into it. We rocked and rolled our way over the Channel to give four performances in the historic Sarah Bernhardt Theatre in the heart of Paris. Richard Hampton, then current President of the OUDS, was a fine Hamlet, Ken Farrington, about to graduate from RADA, a virile and devious Claudius. The Youth Theatre was no longer confined to Dulwich: John Shrapnel added his purposeful attack as Laertes and Michael York his Rupert Brooke-like looks as Voltemand. I remember walking along the Seine with him as he asked my advice on whether I thought he should turn professional after Oxford. With the experience of one year at drama school, I condescendingly told him to give it a try – you never know. It was the last Youth Theatre production when the female parts were played by boys. Simon Ward had forsaken his skirt to play Rosencrantz, so Ophelia was played by a stunning blonde by the name of Hywel Bennet. He took certain members of the Parisian Intelligentsia by storm, but not the critic of *L'Humanite*: 'As soon as Ophelia appears the thought comes to your mind that this girl wouldn't make a *sou*.' Nevertheless we received standing ovations, and they didn't do it just for show then. *Le Monde* enthused: 'It was the *Hamlet* that we wished to see, and we saw him.'

It all seemed too easy.

One hot summer's day in 1964, I was summoned to a Nissen hut somewhere near the south end of Blackfriars Bridge to meet my idol, the great Olivier himself. As I sat sweating nervously on a wooden fold-up chair outside his office, the door opened and Ken Tynan hurried out and gave me an encouraging smile. My heart was thumping as I was ushered in. Olivier was wearing horn-rimmed spectacles and peered over them at me like a benevolent headmaster. He remembered my Mark Antony and wanted to know if I would be interested in playing Fortinbras in his inaugural production of the National Theatre at the Old Vic. I could hardly believe it as I stammered out my profuse delight. He then added there was only one proviso: John Stride, my schoolboy hero, was the first choice, but he was under contract to do a play with Gielgud at the Haymarket. If the play flopped, (which of course it wouldn't – how could it with Johnnie G and Irene Worth?) the part would be Stride's. If not it was mine. The play was *The Ides of March* by Thornton Wilder, it closed in ten days and John Stride duly played Fortinbras. I often wonder how my career would have gone if I'd been at the National with Olivier from the very start. To have been directed by God would have been enough. However, despite

God's direction and a cast that included Peter O'Toole as the Prince (in baggy pantaloons looking like an overgrown Lord Fauntleroy), Michael Redgrave as Claudius and Derek Jacobi as Laertes, that *Hamlet* was a big disappointment. When Peter Hall took over from Olivier, he directed Albert Finney in an uncut version lasting over four hours, but was no more successful.

The old Birmingham Rep had been opened in 1913 by Sir Barry Jackson as the first purpose-built repertory theatre in the country. It had nurtured the talents of most of the hierarchy of the British Stage from Olivier, Ralph Richardson and Edith Evans, to Paul Scofield and Albert Finney and a host of others in-between. But following the death of Sir Barry in 1961 it had lost a little of its sheen. Peter Dews was invited to take it over and re-establish its reputation. In 1969 Peter was inspired to invite Doctor Kildare, aka Richard Chamberlain, then the most famous television star in the world, to play Hamlet. To everyone's surprise Chamberlain accepted and exchanged Beverly Hills for the Bull Ring. When Peter offered me Laertes, though I was getting plenty of work on television, I accepted at once. Peter had assembled a strong cast including Gemma Jones as Ophelia; Brian Oulton, who at that time played concerned and fussy vicars in nearly every British film that was made, was a concerned and fussy Polonius; and a superb character actor, Desmond McNamara, made up to resemble Sir Henry Irving, was the best Player King I've ever seen. As *Hamlet* is set at the end of a dynasty, Peter devised a thrilling Russian-style production in the last days of the Romanovs.

No American had played Hamlet in England since the great John Barrymore. Chamberlain, then a very shy, nervous young man, was only too aware of what he was letting himself in for. Throughout rehearsals Peter, who had a short fuse at the best of times, continually lost patience with his star, and rebuked him as if he were an errant schoolboy: 'For fuck's sake, wake up Richard! How many times have I bloody told you?' Chamberlain took it all, without a sign of resentment. I soon discovered Laertes was not all that much fun. After two short appearances he is away in France for most of the play. After two hours in the dressing room he returns to find his father dead and his sister mad. He barely gets over that when she drowns herself. He is out-grieved by Hamlet at her funeral and then goes into the fight with the audience knowing he is a cheat. That fight is the main thing Laertes has to worry about, it is hanging over him throughout the evening, an accident waiting to happen. Hamlet has enough on his plate – the fight is down to Laertes. I remembered Robert Hardy showing me the scar on his forehead from a misplaced cut from his over-zealous Laertes. Macduff has the same problem. Our duel had been arranged as a vicious fight with sabres. Chamberlain conscientiously rehearsed with me every day and then every night during the interval when the play was running, despite being nearly exhausted. I had nothing but admiration for him.

Every London critic and several from New York were coming up for the first night prepared to lambaste the presumptuous Hollywood soap star who had dared to play Shakespeare's greatest role in the heart of England. We did a dress rehearsal in the afternoon and Chamberlain was in a terrible state of nerves. He did everything wrong, including the duel – he made an unscheduled cut to my head which I just managed to duck. Peter had chosen some stirring Tchaikovsky to accompany the four captains bearing Hamlet's body from the stage, but that afternoon as they bore an exhausted, sweaty Chamberlain up a steep flight of stairs, down wafted the all-too familiar strains of the title music of *Doctor Kildare*. Chamberlain's eyes opened in horror: he thought he was having a nightmare. We could hear Peter chortling in the stalls at his little joke.

But it may well have had the effect that Peter wanted, for that evening Chamberlain gave a near-faultless performance. He spoke with passion, sense and clarity. He was considered old-fashioned by some following David Warner's recent gangly sixties student, but to others he epitomised '*the glass of fashion and the mould of form*.' The critics were almost unanimous in their praise. I was particularly gratified when the *New York Times* found space to admire 'the fine and fiery Laertes.' We were packed to the rafters every night; West End producers began falling over themselves offering theatres for limited runs. But the balance of power had changed. Brian Oulton and I had the dressing room next door to Chamberlain's and we could hear the nightly exchanges between him and Dews:

'Richard, luvy, they've offered us a couple of months at the Haymarket. It's the best theatre in London. How about it, ducks?'

'No, Peter. I don't really think I'm ready for London, do you?'

And we never went. Chamberlain did do Hamlet eventually on television, but without Peter and wasn't nearly as good. Gemma Jones (an extremely powerful Ophelia, some nights she scared me to death in her mad scene) had developed a strong platonic bond with Chamberlain and was the only member of our cast to be in it. By some strange coincidence, her brother played Laertes.

During the run at Birmingham, as I was lying dead in the final scene, I began to hear the younger male members at the back of the stage corpsing and sniggering at Hamlet's line: *'Absent thee from felicity awhile.'* Brian Oulton, who was a professional of the old school, became very concerned and one evening sent me up to the lads' dressing room on the top floor to discover the reason for their mirth. They told me there was a very attractive girl called Felicity, who was working part-time in the wardrobe next to their dressing-room, who was extremely generous with her favours. I reported this back to Brian who was more concerned than ever and gasped: 'Do her parents know?' I always think of her and Brian whenever I hear that line.

In the autumn of the same year I found myself in the play again, this time as Horatio to Michael York's Prince at the newly-opened and ultimately ill-fated Thorndike Theatre in Leatherhead. Throughout this period many reps, which had existed in simple buildings, often converted halls with the minimum of staff, were persuaded to build grandiose modern theatres with all sorts of departments and huge running costs. The Thorndike is one of many that have floundered and now stands empty for much of the year.

Michael York had followed my advice, and I'm sure that of many others. He was already an established film star, but had had precious little stage experience. He didn't quite make Hamlet – at that stage of his career he would have been a good Laertes or Horatio. I found Horatio to be the better part of the two. Although he doesn't have Laertes' big dramatic moments, he is there with Hamlet throughout most of the play: *'the man that is not passion's slave.'* However, there was one moment I could have done without. Our director was the distinguished actor, Joseph O'Connor. As a Catholic he believed the play was about Catholicism, and the set was duly dominated by a huge green Celtic cross. He is not alone in this. John Nettles, taking a break from solving *Midsomer Murders,* holds the belief that: '*To be or not to be…*' is a Catholic call to arms. O'Connor had the misplaced inspiration that the self-same soliloquy should be delivered by Hamlet to Horatio as a students' debate. I duly sat uncomfortably at the base of the cross and registered various unrealistic expressions of agreement and surprise throughout the run.

Laertes was excellently portrayed by Ian Ogilvy, who briefly followed Roger Moore as the Saint before becoming a member of Hollywood's English Tribe. I trace his daily doings on Facebook. During rehearsals Ian went for several tests and meetings for the forthcoming film of *Cabaret*. Michael, ever the gentleman, never failed to ask how things had gone. Of course York eventually got the part; I suspect he knew all along. He was perfect for it. Apart from Tybalt in the Zeffirelli film it was the best thing he's ever done. But Ian would have been very good as well. Careers hang on things like that.

I must be the only actor who never wanted to play Hamlet. My inner sense told me correctly that it was not for me. Richard Digby Day once offered it to me whilst he was running the Pavilion Theatre at Bournemouth. He was furious when I turned it down to do a play on television and never offered me a job again. Claudius was the role I wanted. I thought once I was going to get it, but that story goes with another play.

Troilus and Cressida

'The real problem about the play is the failure of most critics to appreciate it.'
Kenneth Muir (1907-1996)

Tattle: The Quarto of 1609 states '*it was never clapper-clawed with the palmes of the vulgar.*' It was probably performed not in a public playhouse but before a sophisticated audience at the Inns of Court. It is the first of the so-called 'dark' comedies, or 'problem' plays, marking the change in Shakespeare's outlook and philosophy. The Quarto edition called it a 'history'. In the 1623 Folio it is included among the tragedies. Or is it a comedy? It ranks with *Timon* as his most savage play. It is anti-heroic, anti-war, saturated with pessimism and obsessed with disease. Some critics declare it is a failure on a grand scale; a minority consider it one of his greatest achievements. Its mockery of war and cruel knowledge of life have made the play more popular since the bloodbaths of the last century. It has been avoided by nearly all the great actors because there is no star part, although it contains more good roles than practically any other play. I somehow missed Tyrone Guthrie's satirical rendering at the Old Vic in 1956, set at the beginning of the First World War. His Trojans were glass-smashing cavalry officers; the Greeks were scarred and monocled Prussians, and Thersites a scurrilous war-correspondent. In 1960, in the first season of the newly-formed RSC, Peter Hall and John Barton created the famous Sand Pit production. The up-and-coming Peter O'Toole played Thersites and is reputed to have fallen asleep on stage during the interminable night scene in the fourth act. It was not until the abolition of the Lord Chamberlain's power of censorship in 1968 that the homo-erotic relationship between Achilles and Patroclus was fully explored. It has been given full licence ever since.

Memories: This difficult play was an unlikely choice for the third production of the NYT, which we took up to the Edinburgh Festival of

1958. Michael Croft chose it because it was a rarity and offered a wide range of parts. By then we had been together so long that the play cast itself. Richard Hampton, back from playing his flute in the band of the Royal Artillery, was Troilus, Simon Ward, still our leading lady at sixteen, made a seductive Cressida, Colin Farrell was Thersites, and I attempted Hector, with a Grecian nose that I had learned to fashion by courtesy of make-up lessons at RADA. I had completed my first year at the Academy, which had not been entirely the hedonistic experience I'd expected, and was due to be called up for my National Service in September. We rehearsed for three weeks in a youth club in Pimlico before our company of thirty-six piled into the old army truck once more, for the twenty-hour haul up to Scotland. When we finally got there we camped out on the floor of a redundant elementary school on the outskirts of the city and played at the Worthington Hall on the Royal Mile.

Troilus, we soon discovered, is bloody hard work on both sides of the curtain. There are no Agincourt moments. There is some comedy in the Ajax – Thersites scenes, and Pandarus can have some fun, but it leaves a bitter and sour taste. It is moreover a very long play, longer than *Lear* – some nights it can seem as long as the Trojan War itself. I tried to play Hector heroic, but I found him to be somewhat of a vain fool. He starts off by condemning the war and urging that Helen be returned to the Greeks, then turns on a sixpence and decides to keep her on the lame excuse:

'For 'tis a cause that hath no mean dependance
Upon our joint and several dignities.'

I defy anyone to make much out of that. I now think he is the epitome of the Victorian public schoolboy, 'Play up! Play up and play the game!', and should be played for laughs.

The Edinburgh Festival of 1958 was a mere whimper compared to the commercial monstrosity of today: there were only twenty-seven shows on the Fringe that year. When we didn't attract much of an audience, Michael gave an interview to the *Edinburgh Evening News* complaining there were far too many shows. One of them was a production of *Measure for Measure* by Leyton County High School. Derek Jacobi, then a Cambridge undergraduate, had gone back to his alma mater and was giving his Angelo, sporting an even worse false nose than mine. We all went to see one of his matinees, as far as I can recall he never came to see us. But the renowned

Shakespearean scholar, Professor J. Dover Wilson, did. One evening he was a member of our sparse audience and came backstage afterwards to congratulate the cast. Talking to the youngest member he asked, with a glint in his eye:

'Well, is it a tragedy or a comedy?'

'I don't know, sir', replied the servant of Paris.

'Neither do I – and I have been studying the play for fifty years.'

Another fringe show, playing opposite us on the Royal Mile, was a student production from Oxford of a new play by Willis Hall entitled *The Disciplines of War*. It was later re-titled *The Long and the Short and the Tall,* and became the launch pad of the careers of Albert Finney, Peter O'Toole, Robert Shaw and Michael Caine among others. That first production was directed by Peter Dews and starred a young student by the name of Patrick Garland. Our two companies became very friendly, sharing the same pub, and one evening I was astounded and delighted when Peter Dews asked me if I would like to be a member of the ensemble he was putting together for his forthcoming television series *An Age of Kings*. It was the first time anyone had offered me a job, an all too rare occurrence during many of the years to come. Still my most striking memories of that early Festival, (I put it down of course, to the lust and decadence of the play) were my dogged attempts to lose my virginity to the young actress playing Saint Bernadette in a rival attraction in the Haymarket. Perchance the Blessed Virgin herself intervened, for I was ultimately unsuccessful. Each night I understood exactly what Troilus was going through:

'I am giddy; expectation whirls me round.
Th' imaginary relish is so sweet
That it enchants my sense…'

But it wasn't much help for Hector.

Achilles, in the beefy shape of P.R.R. Jackson, was being more successful. We shared our venue with some drama students from the Rose Bruford College (a sedate establishment in Sidcup, which was devoted to teaching actors to teach and teachers to act), who were putting on a children's play in the afternoons. Ignoring the homosexual tendencies of his character, Jackson became carnally entangled with a freckled girl who was playing a cat. We could not forbear making jokes about his 'pussy.'

The Festival finished on the Saturday of the first week in September and Jackson and I were due to report to Oswestry to commence our National Service the following Monday. Croft was suddenly offered a week at the Lyric Hammersmith and he somehow inveigled the Military to postpone our enlistment – I've no idea how he managed it. Jackson and I eventually arrived at the depot, long-haired and feeling distinctly feeble, to be greeted by a wrathful Bombardier, who turned out to be the tough elder brother of Tommy Docherty, who was then playing for Arsenal. He didn't warm to me when I told him I was a Chelsea fan. I'll never forget his stinging rebuke on my first efforts at drill: 'Gunner Weston, when you were born they threw away the baby and kept the after-birth!'

Nevertheless those three months of basic training were good times. Jackson and I mixed with lads from all sorts of backgrounds from all over the country: Welsh miners, shipbuilders from the North-East, factory workers from the Black Country, cockney spivs and public schoolboys. There were even a few newly-arrived West Indians. We all got on very well and learnt from each other. I know I sound like an old fart – but it's a pity there's not something like it today.

1999: Forty years on, having turned down the National several times because I did not consider the parts offered were good enough, I eventually bit the bullet and joined Trevor Nunn's ensemble. I will be forever grateful that I did. The following eighteen months, working with an extraordinary group of talented actors, were among the most fulfilling of my up and mostly down career. Although I had known Trevor for more than thirty years it was the first time I'd been directed by him. I found his way of working much more to my taste than the dry, academic approach favoured by his fellows, Peter Hall and John Barton. Trevor concentrates on the text just as much as the other two, but is not a verse fanatic, believing the sense will naturally give the correct rhythm. He directs from the heart and endeavours to make everything simple and understandable to his actors. He is at times pedantic, you don't win many arguments with him, but he constantly encourages, never making you feel a fool. If an actor is confident he is more than halfway there. I only wish I had worked with him years before.

I was cast as the Chorus, who describes himself as '*a Prologue armed*'. For some reason I was clad in full Elizabethan armour whilst the rest of the cast were dressed as Ancient Greeks. It was the first time I had acted in the vastness of the Olivier, which my late friend, Sheridan Morley, once described as 'a space which might seem over-large for a full-scale revival of Ben Hur on ice.' Being an old ham I had no qualms belting out my excellent lines into the dark vastness. For years I had been suggesting that that the NYT should attempt this play again with the Trojans played by young black actors. This not only helps illuminate the story but also gives the feeling that the Greeks are invading colonisers. Trevor had had the same idea but for some reason cast Pandarus white. I never understood why, particularly as the excellent Clive Rowe, who would have been so right for Pandarus, was in the ensemble and ended up being hopelessly miscast in the Victorian comedy *Money* instead. Trevor spiced up the action by inserting battles at the faintest opportunity. Never a man to waste an actor, however old, he duly threw me into the front rank, alongside the even more aged Nestor, the incomparable Denis Quilley. Denis was a man after my own heart, many evenings we would fortify ourselves with a glass of burgundy in his dressing room whilst the more conscientious members of the cast warmed-up on stage. We needed it as the Trojans were all young, big and fit, and came at us each night without fail like bats out of hell. The designer had decided for a reason best known to himself that we should be bare-footed, and had spread the stage with a sort of rubber substance that resembled red-hot coals. They were agony to walk on, especially when desperately defending yourself with a heavy iron shield from the vigorous cuts and swipes of Troilus, Paris et al.

In the final act, just before Hector is killed, there is a stage direction: *Enter One in (Greek) Armour.* Hector sees him, fancies his armour and duly kills him. This is usually overlooked but for some reason Trevor attached importance to it and decided that I should appear in the middle of the battle in golden armour. Never one to forfeit the spotlight I felt quite honoured to be chosen, assuming Trevor thought I would cut an impressive figure. We never really had time to rehearse that bit. Indeed we gave our first preview without even dress rehearsing the second half. That night I was duly clad in golden helmet, armour and shield, still wet with gold paint, and appeared with martial tread out of the dry ice at the back of the vast stage, feeling as if I was stepping from the pages of Homer himself. I exchanged impromptu blows with the gigantic black Hector and died, I thought, valiantly. Hector tore off my golden helmet, looked down at me and intoned:

'Most putrefied core, so fair without,
Thy goodly armour thus hath cost thy life.'

It was the first time I had really taken in what he was saying: '*putrefied core*? Had Trevor picked me out because I looked seedy? After that I never felt Homer's touch again.

Hector was indeed a magnificent specimen – six foot six, with a body like a Greek god. Moreover, he was handsome, had a good voice and spoke well. I couldn't imagine the part being played better and thought he was set for big things; but some actors have a self-destruct button waiting to be pushed. He disappeared after a few performances and his smaller understudy took over. The battles were never the same again. We were eventually told that he'd been offered a part in Baz Luhrmann's film *Moulin Rouge!* and had flown off to Australia. I thought it must have been a very good part to walk out on Sir Trevor Nunn. I could hardly believe it when I saw the film the following year. He appeared in one shot when he caught Nicole Kidman as she fell from her trapeze. He didn't utter a bloody word – to think he gave up a career at the National for that.

It was nevertheless a very good production. Sophie Okonedo and Peter de Jersey were excellent as the lovers. I thought he was the more talented of the two but she has gone on to award-winning films and nominations. It's a funny old business. Roger Allam was a superb Ulysses: his control of those long, often very dry speeches was an object lesson to any actor. I shared a dressing room with Paris and Aeneas – two bright young black thespians, bursting with testosterone. I felt like the old stag at the end of *Bambi,* but we became close friends even though one supported Spurs and the other was a 'Gooner'.

All's Well That Ends Well

'The bed trick demands a suspension of disbelief which even Shakespeare's skill and language are powerless to achieve.'
Osbert Lancaster 1908-1986

Tattle: There is no record of any performance in Shakespeare's lifetime and the play has always been one of his least popular works. Was it just a 'pot boiler'? Were the company pushed for a play and he quickly put together something from Boccaccio's *Decameron,* he hoped the Globe audience would like? Though he shows some knowledge of medicine, perchance because his daughter Susannah was being wooed in Stratford by her future husband, Doctor Hall, the plot creaks and groans with improbabilities. Bernard Shaw thought that the Countess of Rousillon was 'the most beautiful old woman's part ever written', but Kenneth Tynan observed, more succinctly, that she is merely the only mature woman in Shakespeare that is neither a scold nor a murderess. Others have considered her a domineering old monster. She also has a very dirty mind. The greater part of her scene with Lavache, her clown, is taken up with a discussion on his penis: '*It must be an answer of most monstrous size that must fit all demands.*' Notwithstanding, alongside Coriolanus's mother, Volumnia, she is the only decent part in the canon for any lady over fifty. Peggy Ashcroft and Judi Dench have played her in recent decades; Maggie Smith and Vanessa Redgrave duly wait in turn. James Agate, a critic of the old school, considered Bertram an appalling cad and Helena Shakespeare's most unlikeable heroine: 'she thrusts herself upon him and plays a most unlady-like trick, declaring she shall be his mother, mistress and friend, but can't see he doesn't want her in any of those categories'. The cowardly Parolles is the most vibrant character. It is a part I would have liked to play. An Elizabethan Del Boy, whose plans and pretences are always doomed to go wrong, he is humiliated like Malvolio but does not feel the same pain. He will soon bob up again with a new scam. He has self-knowledge like Falstaff: '*Simply the thing I am shall make me live.*'

Memories: Most improbably *All's Well* always makes me think of Mike Leigh. I had known him at RADA where he had been the youngest student by about ten years. He was also the smallest by a mile. I can remember him, hunched like a little dormouse, as the boy in *Six Characters in Search of an Author*. He'd left acting, gone to art school and had been working with amateur actors at the Midland Arts Centre before he was engaged by the RSC as an assistant director in 1967. A thankless task at the best of times but Mike really hated it. He found the way the RSC worked old-fashioned and hide-bound, and would sit and watch rehearsals with arms folded and a bored smirk. When Peter Hall went down with shingles and *Macbeth* was postponed, it left a few of us who were not rehearsing *All's Well* with nothing to do. I was working with Mike on my understudy of Coriolanus one morning, when he asked me if I would like to be in an improvised play. I had never improvised in my life, but I felt sorry for him and agreed. The cast he eventually assembled was a bit like the *Dirty Dozen*, although as I recall there were only seven of us. We definitely weren't the *Magnificent Seven*. I was the only one who was playing a line of parts; the others were simply spear-carriers or understudies. As far as I can recall they were: Louis Mahoney (it was the first year that the RSC had engaged black actors. It caused quite a stir in the town); Peter Rocca, half-Sicilian and very eccentric, who spent most of his time in the *Dirty Duck* in largely unsuccessful attempts to find a Julie Christie look-alike; a gormless-looking chap from the Home Counties who had a deft touch with comedy – he was Monty Python before it was born; an intense bearded bloke from the North-East; a young, eager, bushy-tailed Australian; and a little waif of a girl from Glasgow, who always seemed to be in a slough of despair. We were the first professional actors Mike Leigh had ever worked with.

For several days he made us sit apart in the rehearsal room and think about a character. I can't recall how we first arrived at the character, but Mike would sit with each of us like a psychiatrist, arms folded and head bent, and probe our thoughts and feelings; gently nudging us in certain directions. By the end of the first week he had nudged me into being a none too bright racist – I think that had been his intention from the start. I've no idea why. The next stage was sitting with two of us at the same time, finding out what our reactions to each other were. After he'd firmly established all of us in our characters, he put us into our setting; a seedy Italian cafe run, naturally, by Peter Rocca. It soon all fell into place. We entered the café in our characters, as customers or looking for a job. I was the mechanic from the garage next door; the girl a lost soul just off the Glasgow train; Mathew O'Sullivan, the young Aussie, became a mad poet who declaimed his dreadful verses on table-top; Louis a recently arrived immigrant. The intense lad from the North East was dreaming of founding a Utopian Arts Organisation, something I suspect that at that time was after Leigh's own heart. The organisation in question was called, I think, North Eastern New Arts Association – NENAA, which gave the piece its name. It is listed in Leigh's biography as his first play. We spent another week or so refining it, cutting and changing until Mike was satisfied. This method works for Leigh and the type of play/film he makes, but most people I know prefer a script. One of the problems of improvisation is that the quick-witted and those good at repartee end up with all the best lines. My mechanic remained obdurately surly and unlikeable.

We performed it one lunchtime in the big rehearsal room, which is now the Swan Theatre. The cast of *All's Well* together with John Barton, Maurice Daniels, the all-powerful casting director, and the various heads of department made up our audience. We had no idea what their reaction would be. It succeeded beyond our wildest dreams. Peter Rocca was hilarious – he gave the performance of his life – indeed I don't think he really ever gave another. All the rest of us were real and believable. We were loudly cheered by our fellows at the end. Some said it was the most truthful acting they'd seen at Stratford that season. We all thought our futures in the RSC were assured – but none of us, including Mike Leigh, were invited back the following season.

I never worked with Mike again. Over the years students from various film schools have got in touch, offering me non-paid work in their student films, saying my name had been recommended to them by Mike Leigh. Each time I had to refuse because of other commitments. I am still waiting for my racist mechanic, albeit now well past retirement age, to feature in a Mike Leigh film.

Measure for Measure

'When your baby is pleading for pleasure, let her sample your Measure for Measure.'
Cole Porter (1891-1964)

Tattle: Although it had probably been previously seen at the Globe, the first recorded performance is found in the Revels Accounts listing *'Mesur for Mesur by Shaxberd,'* acted before James I on 26 December 1604. *'Shaxberd'* may be explained by the mispronunciation of a Scottish secretary of the newly arrived King James, who would have approved of the play as it maintains, to some degree, his favourite hobbyhorse: the Divine Right of Kings. Though the plot is set in Vienna, the whores, bawds, pimps and brothels are vivid depictions of the stews of Southwark where Shakespeare was now living. Why do nearly all the characters have Italian names? William was never all that good at geography; did he confuse Vienna with Venice?

Following the Restoration, the aforementioned Sir William Davenant did a version adding Beatrice and Benedick to liven things up. Isabella was one of Sarah Siddons's favourite roles and she continued playing her when she was well past her sell-by date. She became so fat that it took two attendants to raise her up from her knees. But I suppose audiences looked on their favourites then in the same way as overweight opera divas were regarded until quite recently. It was the passion that counted. Claudio and Isabella have some very good speeches, laughs can be extracted from the low-life scenes and Gielgud had a success with Angelo, but the play has never been really popular. Marius Goring told me that once, over lunch at the Garrick, he had asked Wolfit why he had never given his Angelo. Sir Donald took a mouthful of claret, swirled it round his mouth, smacked his lips and replied: 'The problem with yer Angelo, is yer Duke.'

Well-meaning public bodies are constantly sending Shakespearean productions to the most unlikely places in order to spread the word, as

I know only too well having done more than my fair share. Jonathan Miller once took his production of *Measure,* set as you would expect in Freud's Vienna, and 'formalized according to the rhythm of a Schoenberg Sonata', to a working men's club in Barrow-in-Furness. He was asked by the manager if he would like a microphone to introduce the acts.

Memories: None, apart from a numb bum during several boring productions.

Othello

'Just declaim a few lines from "Othella"
and she'll think you're a heckuva fella...'
Cole Porter – he's too good for only one quote.

Tattle: There were many 'Moors' in Elizabethan London, driven out of Spain by the Inquisition. They were Arabic, not Negroes. There is an existing portrait of a Moorish Ambassador from the King of Barbary who visited Elizabeth's court in 1600. Othello is an outsider like Shylock. Is it a coincidence that both come from Venice? First performed before King James at the Banqueting House, Whitehall, *Othello* is a domestic tragedy, more in keeping with the smaller indoor theatres which were then just coming into vogue. (It will be fascinating to see this play and Macbeth performed in candlelight at the new Jacobean theatre at the Globe.) Othello has been one of the most consistently popular of all Shakespeare's plays and was among the first plays performed when the theatres reopened following the Restoration. Margaret Hughes, who played Desdemona, is reputed to be the first actress to appear on the English stage. Iago is the third biggest part in all Shakespeare, surpassed only by Hamlet and Richard III. He has 1117 lines to Othello's 888, but the Moor has always been considered the leading role. We know Othello was the part written for Burbage because verses written at his death in 1619 declare:

No more young Hamlet, old Geronimo,
King Lear, the grieved Moor, and more beside,
That lived in him, have now forever died.

Othello needs physique and physical power. It used to be looked upon as the final hurdle before the Becher's Brook of Lear in the steeplechase of the great Shakespearean roles: Romeo – Hamlet – Henry V – Macbeth – Othello – Lear – and the easy final hurdle of Prospero. Now it is reserved exclusively for black actors, and a good thing too. Apart from Edmund Kean, who had 'a lighting flash of power that set Drury Lane a-tremble', Othello has been a death trap for white men. Even Kean did not escape the curse. He collapsed into the arms of his son Charles (who was playing Iago) during a performance at Covent Garden in 1833. Kean never acted again and died a few weeks later.

When Charles Macready attempted the role he was said to resemble 'an elderly negress, of evil repute, going to a fancy ball.' In 1876, Sir Henry Irving's Moor was described as resembling 'one of Fennimore Cooper's Mohawk braves wrapped in his blanket'. Sir Donald Wolfit's was said to 'want a banjo' and Sir Ralph Richardson's was considered 'an almost total failure'. Kenneth Tynan's description of Orson Welles's performance was headlined 'Citizen Coon', unprintable and unthinkable in these enlightened times. The same critic described Richard Burton's portrayal as: 'The Chocolate Soldier who resorts to forced bellowing and perfunctory sobs.' (Burton shared the role with John Neville, swapping with Iago. They came back from a boozy lunch one day and both walked on stage un-blacked-up, ready to play Iago.)

The opening night of Gielgud's *Othello* in 1961, according to his director, Franco Zeffirelli, was: 'the most disastrous and ill-fated in the whole history of English, and possibly world, theatre.' This was in part due to Zeffirelli's huge operatic scenery, which swamped everything. The scene changes took so long that the play ran for over four hours. Moreover it was painted largely brown so that Gielgud's brown Othello disappeared against it and, to top it all, Sir John's beard kept falling off. Michael Billington observed that if *Hamlet* was the tragedy of a man who could not make up his mind, Gielgud's *Othello* was the tragedy of the man who could not make up his beard. The illustrious knight looked like an Indian civil servant having a bad day and struggled to find the jealous passion. There is an apocryphal story that Peggy Ashcroft, who played Emilia, finally exclaimed in exasperation: 'Surely, John, you must have been jealous of something or somebody in your life.' He thought for a moment and then said: 'Well, I did cry once when Larry had his big success as Hamlet.' Sir John later admitted: 'I have neither the voice nor the power for Othello, and I should never have attempted it.'

Laurence Olivier was undeterred by his old rival's failure, and decided to black up at the Old Vic in 1964. *The Sunday Telegraph* duly reported:

'Olivier's Othello is the kind of bad acting of which only a great actor is capable. His hips oscillate, his palms rotate, his voice skids and slides so that the Othello music takes on a Beatle beat.' In 1975 Sir Robert Stephens tried to master the role in the open air at Regent's Park. Unfortunately it was a very hot summer. *The Times* noted: 'His Othello suffers from a make-up that sweats off in drops like blood.' In 1979 yet another knight, Donald Sinden, played Othello with a frizzy wig, looking and sounding like a country squire who had been blackened by a very bad electric shock. I can still see him feverishly inspecting Desdemona's sheets as he dragged them from the laundry basket. Paul Scofield took up the challenge on the immense Olivier stage in 1980, only to be told: 'He has an accent which makes him sound less like a Moor and more like a man wrestling with a new set of National Health teeth.' James Agate thought the part went against the English grain: the Moor's way of treating infidelity was definitely not cricket.

But not all black actors have found it easy. In 1930, even though he had young Peggy Ashcroft as his Desdemona, the great Paul Robeson was hampered with 'a pretentious dud' of a director, who happened to be the producer's wife, and the producer himself playing Iago. When he attempted it again at Stratford in 1959 he was too old. Tony Richardson, the director, sought to inject a feeling of savagery by having Othello arrive at Cyprus accompanied by a pair of black panthers. The designer objected that black panthers would clash with the golden hues of the set and costumes. They compromised on a pair of cheetahs. It was decided that cheetahs were props, and the Prop department were told to obtain them. The Pet Department at Harrods did not have any cheetahs in stock and so the roles eventually went to a pair of golden Great Danes, for whom a special dressing room was constructed near the stage. They came under the jurisdiction of the youngest Props ASM, my old school-friend Brian Croft, who was unfairly blamed when the beasts farted and howled throughout the performance. They were eventually banished to a hut in the Bancroft Gardens.

Robeson was not the first black actor to play Othello on the London stage. Ira Aldridge, known as the 'African Roscius', born in New York, grandson of a slave, performed the role at Covent Garden in 1833. The critic John Cole wrote: 'Novel, imposing, and sublime was the first sight of the Moor, personated as he was by the sable African. His intonations of deep and sweet melody were however soon added to by the grandeur of his personal appearance, and every trait of the noble-minded and generous Moor was afterward presented in appropriate and conspicuous style. We consider Othello as played by the African Roscius, a performance enriched with brilliancy of genius.' Unfortunately not all critics were so sympathetic. The bill abolishing slavery was about to pass through Parliament and there was still bitter opposition. Some held a black man to be incapable of expressing artistic sensibilities equal to the white. There were other, more basic, prejudices as well: 'In the name of propriety and decency we protest against Desdemona, an interesting and decent girl in the person of Miss Ellen Tree, being subjected to the indignity of being pawed about by a black servant.'

Slavery was duly abolished but Aldridge was forced to ply his trade in the provinces and eventually in Europe, where he gained great distinction. He was honoured in France, Austria, Prussia and Russia, playing 'white' parts such as Lear, Macbeth and Shylock, indeed the Stanislavskian method of natural acting is said to have originated from Aldridge. He fought against slavery and for equality throughout his life – there is a great film waiting to be made. Robeson intended to do it himself: he was coached as Othello by Aldridge's daughter, and a script was prepared at Ealing Studios. Tragically Robeson fell foul of the McCarthy Un-American activities investigations and was refused permission to leave the United States. Find that script Denzel Washington, and an Oscar awaits you. (Since I wrote that I have seen the award-winning *Red Velvet* and Adrian Lester's heart-wrenching performance as Aldridge at the Tricycle Theatre. I was told by one of the cast that it couldn't be transferred to the West End because, ironically, Lester was already contracted to do Othello at the National. If anyone had had any imagination the plays could have run on alternate nights, same actors in both plays. That would have been truly exciting. The National has resources aplenty – it was founded for such projects. Perhaps they will do it on Broadway.)

In 1985 Sir Ben Kingsley did a halfway house Othello, playing him as an Arab, but since then there has been a conveyor belt of talented black actors, bursting to play the Moor: David Harewood, Willard White, and against all odds, Lenny Henry. One of the finest I've seen was Ray Fearon at the Barbican. In 2007 Chiwetel Ejiofor won an Olivier for his performance at the Donmar. This brings me back to Olivier himself. I think I have been unjust to him. In 1964 most people considered his performance to be truly great. I saw it at the Old Vic and was bowled over. I was therefore amazed to hear my sons ridiculing it as they watched it on video in the mid-eighties. They were studying the play for A-Level. I watched it with them and, perhaps because it was a film, so much in close-up, reluctantly began to see the flaws; but I will remain forever faithful to Olivier nevertheless.

He is the subject of my favourite Othello anecdote. Maggie Smith was his original Desdemona and he had taken her to task for her strangulated vowels. On the first night as he was daubing himself all over in his specially prepared black make-up, she pushed open his dressing room door, perused him carefully, before pronouncing in her inimitable style: 'How now, brown cow!'

Memories: In 1982 Frank Dunlop put on a trilogy of plays set in Venice, at the Young Vic: *The Merchant,* Byron's *Marino Faliero*, of which the less said the better, and *Othello.* Kenneth Haigh, the original Jimmy Porter in *Look Back in Anger*, was cast as the Moor. I played Antonio in *The Merchant*, a decent part in the Byron, and the undemanding role of Ludovico in *Othello*. In fact all Ludovico really does is come on towards the end with letters that are vital to the plot. The part was described by the legendary Robert Atkins as 'the cunt that forgets to bring on the letters'. (I have done that but not in this piece.) The plays were performed in repertoire and I will never forget a Saturday night towards the end of the season. I arrived at the Young Vic to find all in consternation. Kenneth Haigh was down with gastroenteritis and the company, going through financial difficulties, had not been able to run to the expense of understudies. There was a full house and the Young Vic couldn't afford to refund the money and lose a whole night's takings. Frank Dunlop asked me if I was willing to go on with the book.

It was a mixture of vanity, not wishing to let the side down, and an inordinate love of the limelight that made me foolhardily agree. Within minutes I was sitting in Haigh's chair applying chocolate-coloured liquid to my face and all visible parts of my body. There were no make-up ladies at the Young Vic, so it was all left to me. I had grown a beard for Antonio, which I duly blackened with Haigh's mascara. I struggled into the loose robe Othello wore in the first Act, and then glanced at Haigh's black curly wig, perched jauntily on a wig stand, as if daring me to put it on. I put it on, pulled it down over my own untidy locks, and peered into the mirror, hoping to get some confidence. Through the thick foliage of Haigh's 'Good Luck' cards, I looked like a second-rate Abenazar. Desire for limelight was draining out of me.

Over the Tannoy I could hear the stage manager explaining the situation to the audience. I heard a groan of disappointment which eroded the remains of my confidence. The stage manager went on to explain that I had agreed to stand in and read the part, so that they would at least have the chance to see the play. There were more mutterings, but I detected some sounds of approval and a ripple of applause. There was no turning back. I pulled on a pair of thick black leather gloves and picked up my Penguin edition of the play. Before I knew it I was standing in the wings, whilst the opening scene was being played, being given kisses of encouragement by Amanda Boxer, who was giving her Desdemona. I saw to my horror that the mascara on my beard had smeared a black trail over her fair cheek. She hastily ran to amend her make-up and kept away from my face for the remainder of the evening. The opening scene finished all too quickly and I strode on stage, with what I considered sweeping grandeur, Penguin in hand. To begin with it seemed easy. I had been doubling as a senator in the Senate scene, so I was familiar with the lines. I put on a deep voice and enjoyed myself reading Othello's poetic account of how Desdemona came to love him. The only trouble was the gloves made it difficult to turn over the pages. I decided to discard them for the next scene, the arrival at Cyprus, and liberally daubed my hands with more of Mr Haigh's dark liquid. At first all went well; I could now turn over the pages easily, but then the black make-up began to come off my hands and left smudges all over the text. To make matters worse it gradually dawned on me that I had no idea what Othello did in the middle part of the play, because I had hardly seen it. I turned the page and saw a long, long speech stretching before me, with not the faintest clue of how it was going to end. My black finger prints had practically obliterated several lines; I couldn't quite see what they were. I paused, shook my head and moaned *'Oh, the pity of it, Iago!'* then pondered Othello-like, until I worked out a rough idea of what I had to say. I reached the interval and was congratulated by all and sundry backstage – even poor George Sewell, whose subtle Iago I had ruined by ploughing on through all his pauses. I refreshed myself, in the style of Sir Donald Wolfit, with a pint of Guinness whilst desperately trying to read the second half. I caught a glimpse of myself in the mirror: the wig was perched on the top of my head like a black beret; pink streaks of sweat were shining through the make-up. If any casting director had been out front it would have been the last nail in my ailing career. The call for the second half came through the Tannoy. I felt like a beat-up boxer staggering out to take further punishment. All too soon I was rolling on the floor, Penguin still in hand, affecting an epileptic fit; but that was nothing to the last scene when I stalked on to smother Desdemona laden with scimitar, candle and the inevitable Penguin. But succour was at hand. Way back in 1957 I had chosen Othello's magnificent '*Put out the light*' speech for my RADA audition. I have found that once Shakespeare is really embedded in your brain it never leaves you. I laid the book on the bed beside the long-suffering Amanda Boxer, and for a few moments was able to act unheeded. Desdemona woke and I attempted to carry on with a sort of improvisation, but despite my work with Mike Leigh, it proved inadequate and I was forced to fumble amongst the bed clothes to retrieve my faithful Penguin. In a daze I smothered my wife, stabbed Iago and with a profound relief, which no doubt the audience wholeheartedly shared, I put Othello and myself out of our misery. As far as I know no white actor has attempted the role on a major London stage since.

Macbeth (The Scottish Play)

'There isn't really a curse on Macbeth – it's just so bloody hard to get right.'
Anon

Tattle: It was not printed until the 1623 Folio but was probably first performed before King James and his brother-in-law, the King of Denmark, in the banqueting hall of Hampton Court Palace in 1606. The Porter's references to the '*equivocators*' of the Gunpowder Plot of November 1605, are another nail in the coffin of the supporters of the Oxford heresy: the Earl of Oxford died in June 1604. *Macbeth* is the shortest of the tragedies. Some scholars believe there was an earlier, fuller version, and the play we have now was assembled from the prompt book of that performance before King James. Knowing the King's fascination with witches, Shakespeare added the Hecate scene for his benefit. They hold much of it was taken down from memory, scenes were omitted and mistakes made in the text. Most actors would disagree, the play works thrillingly as it stands and it has never failed to do good business. It has all the right ingredients – murders, witches, a ghost and a bloody battle. Dr Simon Forman, a shadowy astronomer and alchemist, records a visit to *Macbeth* at the Globe on 20 April 1610, and gives a very accurate description of the plot. All the great actors have attempted Macbeth but as with Othello, very, very few have succeeded. Is there really a curse on it? Some claim Shakespeare used real black magic in the witches' chants. Others say that accidents occur in the fight at the end because Macbeth is exhausted, but Hamlet has an equally demanding fight in a much longer play.

After the Restoration Sir William Davenant, keeping with the taste of the times, rewrote the tragedy as semi-opera with comic flying witches. Thomas Betterton played the Thane as a stately gentleman with cocked hat and full wig. Davenant reworked the original lines to suit the refinement of his age, so that: '*The devil damn thee black, thou cream-faced loon. Where got'st thou that goose look?*' became: '*Now friend what means thy change of countenance?*' The play was adapted even further to the extent of making Macduff the leading role, but the great David Garrick went back to Shakespeare, although he played Macbeth dressed in the uniform of an officer in the Grenadier Guards. He could never resist dying on stage and wrote himself a long death speech ending:

> *It is too late, hell drags me down. I sink,*
> *I sink – Oh! – My soul is lost for ever!*
> *Oh!*

Nevertheless his portrayal was considered one of his finest and has been captured to a certain extent in paintings by Zoffany and Fuseli, although a contemporary described Zoffany's depiction of the dagger scene as looking like 'a cook and a butler quarrelling over the kitchen knives'. Garrick indulged in an almost 'twitter-like' correspondence with his audience, who were not always complimentary: 'The last dress in which you played Macbeth was that of a fine Gentleman; so that when you came among the Witches in the 4th Act, you looked like a Beau, who had unfortunately slipped his foot and tumbled into a night cellar, where a parcel of old women were boiling tripe for their supper.' Unlike some of the 'celebs' of today, Garrick never failed to render a courteous reply.

The Irish-born Charles Macklin was the first to play Macbeth in some sort of Scottish dress. John Kemble was the first star to decide he didn't want to be upstaged by Banquo's ghost in the banquet and so cut it. This misguided practice is still occasionally followed. Kemble's sister, Sarah Siddons, was the first Lady Macbeth to mime washing her hands in the sleepwalking scene. Hazlitt considered it her supreme achievement: 'It seemed as if a being of a superior order had dropped from a higher sphere to awe the world with the majesty of her appearance. Power was seated on her brow, passion emanated from her breast as from a shrine; she was tragedy personified. In coming on in the sleepwalking scene, her eyes were open, but their sense was shut. She was like a person bewildered, and unconscious of what she did. Her lips moved involuntarily – all her gestures were involuntary and mechanical. She glided on and off stage like an apparition. To have seen her in that character was an event in everyone's life, not to be forgotten.'

It is surprising that Macbeth was not one of Edmund Kean's more successful roles. Dickens's friend, Charles Macready, was considered the best of his age, even though it was reported that he stole into Duncan's chamber 'like a man going to purloin a purse, not like a warrior about to snatch a crown.' Macready was notoriously ill-tempered. One night, finding no dresser waiting with a bowl of fake gore to incarnadine his hands after Duncan's murder, he punched a nearby stagehand on the nose and helped himself to the poor chap's blood. Always argumentative, he fell out with Edwin Forrest, the American tragedian and in 1849 played Macbeth in opposition to him in New York. A riot broke out between their rival supporters which left twenty-four dead outside the Astor Place Opera House – surely the most tragic example of it being an unlucky play.

Sir Henry Irving, Sir Herbert Beerbohm Tree, Sir Johnston Forbes Robertson and Sir Donald Wolfit all attempted the Thane, but according to James Agate, the esteemed critic of that period, the most successful was rather surprisingly Sir Frank Benson, who played him as an improbable cross between Richard II and Henry V. Dame Edith Evans refused to play Lady Macbeth, declaring: 'I would never impersonate a woman who had such a peculiar notion of hospitality.' Dame Sybil Thorndike played opposite her husband, Lewis Casson saying: 'You must be married to play the Macbeths.' Charles Laughton, then an internationally acclaimed film star, gave his Macbeth at the Old Vic in 1933. He was slumped dejectedly in his dressing room following a disastrous first night, when Lilian Bayliss, the legendary founder of the theatre, swept in, dressed in full academic robes (she had been made an Honorary M.A. of Oxford University). She gave a laugh of embarrassment, beamed benignly through her glasses and said: 'Never mind, dear. I'm sure you did your best. And I'm sure that one day you may be quite a good Macbeth.' Laughton went back to Hollywood.

The first Macbeth I ever saw was Sir Ralph Richardson. It was one of his greatest failures, possibly because he'd been driven to distraction when he discovered that Malcolm, in the shape of parvenu Laurence Harvey, was knocking off his leading lady, Margaret Leighton. Ken Tynan wrote: 'Richardson's Macbeth is slovenly; and to go further into it would be as frustrating as trying to write with a pencil whose point has long since worn down to the wood.' Sir Ralph was just as hard on himself: 'Lend me a fiver, cocky, or I'll put it about that you were in my Macbeth.' His friend Laurence Olivier called the part 'this impossible monster'. His first attempt in a stylised production at the Old Vic in 1938 was in his own words, 'not an apparelled success.' It lived up to its unlucky reputation when Lilian Bayliss died on the second night. Olivier was more successful at Stratford in 1958. Always the master of artifice, he had concealed steps painted into the scenery so that he could literarily climb up the wall at the sight of the dagger. Not everything went as smoothly. Geoffrey Bayldon played Duncan and still remembers Vivien Leigh's whispered greeting at Inverness: 'You look a cunt in that wig!'

Sir Alec Guinness, who would always have been an unlikely Macbeth, played him in a perverse production at the Royal Court Theatre in 1966, which has passed into the legends of theatrical disasters. It was staged in modern dress, with no scenery, bright lights, three black witches, and the renowned French film star Simone Signoret as the Lady. One of the kinder critics said she had need of subtitles and microphone. I had the misfortune to see the production and few nights later had supper with Simone Signoret in Buckstone's, the beloved actors club, long-defunct, opposite the stage door of the Haymarket Theatre. Off-stage she was charming and magnetic. She lambasted the critics, lamenting: 'You English cannot understand this play because you have never been occupied.' I didn't want to say that Shakespeare had likewise never experienced it. But we English have always been sceptical of foreigners having the temerity to attempt our beloved Shakespeare. The benign John Gielgud supposedly said of Ingrid Bergman: 'She speaks five languages perfectly and can't act in any of them.'

Peter O'Toole superstitiously called the play 'Harry Lauder', after the famous Scottish comedian, but that still didn't do him much good. One of his kinder critics wrote: 'His performance suggests he is taking some kind of personal revenge on the play.' O'Toole's *Macbeth* became notorious, a sort of Shakespearean *'Springtime for Hitler*,' and broke box office records. Felix Barker could not even remember Anthony Hopkins' name when he savaged his Thane in *The Evening News*: 'John Hopkins is a good miniaturist, but without the inches or grandeur for a major performance … This cocky genial fellow sometimes sweats apprehensively and occasionally bellows, but frequently he gives the impression that he is a Rotarian pork butcher about to tell the stalls a dirty story.' Hopkins, in the grip of his well-documented alcoholism eventually withdrew suffering from nervous exhaustion, abandoning his Lady, Diana Rigg at her sexiest.

Banquo, in the shape of the steadfast Denis Quilley took over. Years later Denis told me, he sensed that Macbeth becomes sexually aroused at the thought of Banquo's murder. To that end he invented a piece of business which entailed him putting his hand down the front of Diana's dress and fondling her nipple whilst uttering:

'Good things of day begin to droop and drowse,
Whiles night's black agents to their preys do rouse.
...So, prithee, go with me.'

He then, figuratively, took her off to bed. I must say that interpretation appeals to me, especially with Diana Rigg.

In 1976, Trevor Nunn, having failed with Nicol Williamson and Helen Mirren in the main house at Stratford, did a minimalist production in a corrugated iron hut known as The Other Place, with Ian McKellen and Judi Dench. It became the most successful in living memory and has been preserved on video.

Memories: Lennox, or 'Bollox' as my friends in the fourth form insisted on calling me, was my first real part in a school play. In that at least I followed in the steps of Olivier. I received my first notice from Donald Fitzjohn of the British Drama League: 'Amongst the Scottish Lords I particularly liked the attack of D.C.Weston as Lennox.' The die was cast. The play lived up to its unlucky reputation when the mother of the master assisting Croft died on the night of the dress rehearsal.

1964: Sir Bernard James Miles, Baron Miles of Blackfriars, son of a farm labourer and a cook, was the second actor to be awarded a life peerage after Olivier. As far as I know Richard Attenborough has been the only other one so far. Julian Fellowes was given his peerage for services to the Conservative Party. Despite Miles's genial buffoonery and his successful career in music hall, he was far from being a bucolic fool, having won a scholarship to Oxford in his youth. He appeared in practically every film ever made to help the war effort, as well as being a heart-warming Joe Gargery in David Lean's '*Great Expectations*'. In 1959 he cajoled and charmed the bosses of major businesses to help him open the first theatre in the City since the seventeenth century. The Mermaid, by the wharf where Shakespeare took his wherry to the Globe, was a beautiful 600-seat theatre with the biggest stage in London. Bernard was among the first to realise that a theatre should be used throughout the day and made the Mermaid the social centre of Blackfriars. It had a restaurant overlooking the river and an attractive bar in the lobby which was the haunt of journalists from the nearby offices of *The Observer*. The soulless road and tunnel had yet to be built and Upper Thames Street had changed little since Elizabethan days. Little alleys and by-ways led down to the river; there were no parking restrictions and I left my Mini unheeded every day in Trig Lane, where Middleton set a scene in *The Chaste Maid in Cheapside*.

Bernard put on two shows every night: at 6pm to catch the City commuters before they caught their trains back to the outer suburbs; and 8.30pm for theatre-goers from other parts of London. This was hard on his actors, to whom by necessity he paid meagre wages, and was particularly hard when they played in repertory as we did in that summer of 1964. It meant we went in to rehearse at ten in the morning and did not stagger out till eleven at night – Equity rules were laxer then. Bernard kept us going between the shows by coming round the small and crowded dressing rooms with a huge saucepan of soup, which I always suspected was made up from the left-overs of his restaurant. His direction was democratic in the extreme. I remember one occasion, protesting against a move he had given me. His eyes twinkled behind his glasses. 'Is your mother coming to a preview, David?' I nodded. 'Well, if your mother doesn't like the move you won't have to do it.' It is hard to imagine Peter Hall or John Barton relying on maternal advice. On hot evenings we would sit on the steps of Puddle Dock, drinking in what fresh air we could, the dirty Thames lapping at our feet, whilst Bernard regaled us, his pet parrot on his shoulder, with his inimitable tales of touring the Hebrides in wartime – I only wish I could remember them. It was on such an occasion that Bernard was supposed to have spied a barge passing by. Determined to impress the young actors with the power of his voice, he bellowed across the water: 'Whither sailest thou, bargee?' 'Fuck off, you silly old bugger!' came floating back. I loved him.

1964 was the 400th Anniversary of Shakespeare's birth and Bernard put on a season of Elizabethan and Jacobean plays to celebrate the event. *Macbeth* was the only one by Shakespeare and the least successful. It was directed by Julius Gellner, a distinguished German director who had twice escaped the clutches of the Gestapo. During the war he had directed acclaimed productions at the Old Vic, including *The Merchant of Venice* and *Othello* with Bernard as Iago. Gellner may have been inhibited by the inflexible Elizabethan setting that was used throughout the season, but he never seemed confident with the play or his actors. Perhaps he had supped too much with real horror. *'Out, out brief candle, and soon I hope,'* was the headline in the long-defunct *Empire News*. The Macbeth of the ever-dependable John Woodvine, who would later be the best Banquo I've ever seen in the Trevor Nunn/Ian McKellen version, was generally slated. Now, if your Macbeth is slated, as so often happens, the critics usually find something to praise in either Malcolm or Macduff. I was the leading young man of the company and what *The Times* described as my 'ringing' Malcolm did particularly well. You can either play Malcolm as an innocent boy growing into kingship, or a scheming politician. The latter is more popular today, with the witches often gathering again as the curtain falls. I think this is wrong. Shakespeare nearly always ends in reconciliation and Malcolm swears '*by the grace of Grace*' to cure Scotland's ills. Shakespeare wrote the play to be performed before King James, who would know that historically Malcolm and his English Queen Margaret ushered in one of the few periods of peace in his country's barbaric history. I therefore played him as a 'goodie', forcing myself, in that interminable England scene, to voice my pretended vices to test Macduff's honesty, even though I pitied his disillusionment.

That summer was one of the best times of my life. I had just finished two major films, my career was surpassing all my expectations, and more and more girls were going on the pill. Malcolm's lines: *'Your wives, your daughters, your matrons and your maids, could not fill up the cistern of my lust,'* was particularly apt as I worked my way through the young ladies of the wardrobe and stage management. Or did they work their way through me? Those days are long gone – for me and the poor old Mermaid. She stands empty and marooned as the traffic endlessly swirls around her. Lord Bernard deserved better.

1966: Two years later I had another go at Malcolm, this time on radio with Paul Scofield and Peggy Ashcroft as the Macbeths. Scofield's dresser was proud and honoured to be in such exalted company. Scofield's inimitable voice effortlessly caught the poetry as well as the savagery, 'the mighty opposites of fear and courage', which so few Macbeths have managed to combine. Dame Peggy, although she never really liked playing evil parts, '*screwed her courage to the sticking place,*' and was irresistible as she drove him to murder. My Malcolm was 'ringing' again, this time accompanied by the crystal-clear diction of Alec McCowen's Macduff.

The following year, Scofield agreed to do the play at Stratford; it was expected to be one of the greatest triumphs of his career, following on from his ground-breaking Lear and his Oscar-winning performance in the film of *A Man for All Seasons*. I was in it again but in the minor role of Menteith, or was it Caithness, Argyll or even Cromarty? It didn't really matter. I'd never played a small part before and quickly found they are far harder than big ones. I consoled myself that Malcolm was to be played by Ian Richardson, one of the stalwarts of the RSC, and I had bigger parts in other plays. Furthermore, *Macbeth* was set to go on a world tour and then was scheduled to be made into a film. It was directed by Peter Hall himself. I never really got on with him, especially after he remarked that he thought there might be a classical actor lurking inside me somewhere, and the RSC would endeavour to get it out. I thought this a bit much after I'd received excellent notices from major critics. I found him an intellectual director without heart, only concerned with the speaking of the verse and the marking of end pauses. He would spend much of the rehearsal looking down at the text and not at his actors. On other occasions he would take Scofield into a corner and deliver long whispered lectures. Scofield was an instinctive actor; he gradually felt his way into a part and then made it unique. I sense he saw Macbeth as basically a good man driven to destruction by the forces of evil. Hall seemed to want to impose his own interpretation – that Macbeth was evil before he even met the witches.

Lady Macbeth was Harold Pinter's then wife, Vivien Merchant, at that time highly regarded for her performances in her husband's plays. It was soon apparent to me that she had very poor diction when she spoke fast. Pinter must have been aware of this and wrote his plays to suit her speech patterns. Alas they didn't fit into Lady Macbeth's. She trivialised and fidgeted and, unlike Dame Peggy, was a poor spur to her husband's ambition. Scofield appeared unhappy and uncertain. Hall meanwhile was overdoing things, directing his first feature film as well as running the RSC and overseeing the planning of the Barbican. After a few weeks he went down with shingles:

Daily Mirror: 29 June 1967: '*Macbeth* is traditionally an unlucky play. Actors will not mention the name in dressing rooms. Even Sir Laurence Olivier has fallen its victim. He was once stabbed during rehearsals. Now *Macbeth* has struck again. It was supposed to open as the highlight of the season at the Royal Shakespeare Theatre, Stratford-on-Avon on July 13.

The choice of date caused mutterings among the company. Then director, Peter Hall got shingles of the left temple. The play was postponed until July 26 (please note a double 13). Something else had to happen. And it did. Yesterday it was announced that the play is now postponed to mid-August. Hall's doctor says he must rest for at least another five weeks. Fans with an eye for auguries may take comfort from the choice of one of the plays replacing *Macbeth* for the time being. The company are staging extra performances of *All's Well That Ends Well.'*

Hall eventually returned after nearly losing an eye but the production never recovered and was dealt further blows by the set and costumes, which John Bury did in his brutal *Wars of the Roses* fashion. The floor and walls of the stage were draped in red carpet. Half the cast were beneath it as the curtain rose, with more red carpet on their backs, swaying side to side to represent blood-stained heather. It was considered a great status symbol to start the play above the carpet. At least I had that gratification. There was an effective moment when the witches rose out of the carpet to greet Macbeth, but after that it just got in the way. To make matters worse it slid about on top of a steeply raked bone-coloured, plastic floor. Scofield slipped and tripped on it on several occasions. He was saint-like in his patience and never complained until one night towards the end of the run. He suddenly stopped acting and walked silently around the stage deliberately arranging every single piece of the dreaded carpet. The costumes and curved helmets, which made us all look like garden gnomes, were made of thick PVC that John Bury treated to look like leather. It was a very hot summer and we soon found ourselves drenched in sweat beneath it. After a few performances we all had to be issued with salt tablets, before all the plastic costumes were scrapped and replaced, at huge cost, by leather. The iron shields and swords were so heavy they could hardly be lifted, let alone used. Macbeth's fight with Macduff, which should be savage and furious – *'I'll fight, till from my bones my flesh be hacked'* – was no more than a half-hearted exchange of blows. There was no excitement. The highlight of the show for us thanes was the practical banquet. The RSC was profligate in those days and huge chunks of ham and cheese were served each night with freshly baked bread. Most of us took it for our evening meal and judiciously attempted to do justice to it before Lady Macbeth ushered us out after the second appearance of Banquo's ghost. Some nights certain thanes were more intent on the ham on their platters than Macbeth's fearful behaviour and departed with bulging cheeks and masticating jaws. Scofield had been very friendly with me when I had been his dresser. I hoped it would continue but we never became close. He carefully preserved his privacy and never really mixed with the company, although he was not above the odd little wink upstage in the banquet. The radio version was repeated one night during the run. We listened to it in the dressing-room almost simultaneously as Scofield came up live on stage over the Tannoy. The performances were chalk and cheese. On the radio he was heart-rending, his rich, gravelly voice full of unexpected modulations of tone. On stage, after three months of Hall's direction, he was dull, lifeless, and uncertain. Garry O'Connor in his biography of Scofield says that it is hard to imagine anyone else being able to match that radio performance, which thankfully can still be heard today. The critics were kind to his stage version but Scofield knew he had failed by his own impeccable standards. I remember driving along a country lane one wet Sunday afternoon and seeing him walking through the rain, alone and disconsolate, sucking on his pipe. The film was cancelled, the world tour curtailed to Helsinki, Leningrad and Moscow.

We left in bleak midwinter, hardly the ideal time to visit such northern climes. Some of us had keen expectations of Helsinki. Scandinavian girls were then considered the sexiest and most liberated of all, and we had heard arousing stories of naked multi-sex sauna bathing, beatings with birch bark twigs, and steaming bodies frolicking in the snow. On our first free afternoon my roommate, Peter Rocca, who had temporarily abandoned his search for a Julie Christie look-alike, suggested an excursion to the local sauna. He had fantasies of having his bare bum tickled with birch twigs. It sounded like a good idea at the time so I readily agreed. After much embarrassed questioning of the very respectable-looking natives, we were directed to a rundown-looking establishment in a side street. We paid our money to a hard-faced middle-aged lady, were handed a towel and directed to the changing room. We swiftly disrobed and went into the sauna, expecting to see nubile blondes lying naked on the benches. It was as empty as the Sahara and ten times as hot. We were the only punters there. We sat steaming for ten minutes or so – watching the door, hoping that Britt Ekland would come wafting in – until we could stand it no more. Rocca by then looked like a parrot-faced lobster. We staggered out and made our way to the steam room and threw ourselves down on stone slabs. We'd missed out on girls in the sauna but at least we'd have the birch twigs, I could see a bunch in an adjacent bucket. The door opened. I licked my salty lips in anticipation. Out of the steam, like two creatures in a Hammer horror, came two vast females in white coats. I closed my eyes as one hosed me down with ice-cold water before slapping soap all over my back and nether regions. I heard moaning from Rocca's slab, but it didn't sound like ecstasy. I looked over: his formidable ice maiden was scouring his bum with a scrubbing brush that would have taken the skin off an elephant. I'd had enough. I thanked my own lady, who was now advancing menacingly towards me with her own implement of torture, made my excuses and fled with Rocca at my heels. As we came out of the establishment we passed several middle-aged members of the company slipping furtively in.

We had a bumpy flight to Leningrad in what looked and sounded like a converted propeller-driven bomber. Russia was very much a forbidden country – I think we were only the third British theatrical company to visit since the war. We had been advised that the Soviet Union, the leader of the Space Age, was suffering from a shortage of bath plugs. We all had dutifully come with our own. I can't remember if we ever needed them. Again our expectations were high. The film of *Doctor Zhivago* had been released two years previously and some of us were hoping to find a Lara of our own. (They are now clustering in abundance in every designer shop in Sloane Street.) On our arrival we were given earnest instructions from a representative of the British Consul – his main concern being that we did not attempt to take religious icons out of the country – we'd be arrested if we did. We were then handed over to representatives of 'The House of Friendship', young ladies who were going to look after our sight-seeing requirements. I suspect that they were all Government officials or daughters of high-ranking party members. I was assigned to a stern and stolid wench who looked as if she was halfway to becoming a shot-putter. The Soviet Union was producing plenty at the time. I can't remember if she had a moustache.

We were driven from the airport in a Red Army bus. The architecture of Leningrad was as beautiful as we had imagined, but the shops and the people along the Nevsky Prospect were extremely drab. We were housed in the plush, pre-revolutionary Astoria Hotel, where Hitler had intended to hold his victory banquet. (The Red Army found the unused invitations in

Berlin.) An old lady sat at the end of each corridor in the hotel, seemingly noting who went in and came out. We were certain that our rooms were bugged. Rocca had a talent for breaking wind at will and always managed extraordinary explosions when entering our cavernous bathroom, his intention being to blast the ears off the listening KGB. He may well have succeeded. On our first free morning my young lady from the House of Friendship arrived and announced she was taking me to the Gulf of Finland. I had been expecting a visit to the Hermitage but assumed she would know best. I wasn't with Lara, but the crowded train we got on came straight out of *Zhivago.* The toilet was literally a hole in the floor, up which blew icy blasts. If you'd sat on it long, your vitals would have frozen solid. I attempted a conversation with my guide but didn't get very far. Meanwhile the train was passing through an ever-more frozen and desolate landscape. It stopped eventually at a seemingly deserted station and my companion indicated that we should get off. She then began to lead me through thick snow towards a dark forest. I'd never been so cold in my life; it really did cut through me like a knife. I was wearing jeans and trendy suede boots, which quickly became sodden. She appeared to be very warm and comfortable in her fur coat, hat and boots. I finally demanded to know where we were going. She pointed through a gap in the trees towards a frozen sea. It was a remarkable sight, but I would have much preferred to be viewing paintings in the warmth of the Winter Palace. Before I could say anything she grabbed hold of me and literally threw me against a tree. 'Kiss me!' she demanded as heaps of snow fell upon my head from the branches above. I was as petrified as a spinster seeing her first prick. Was she trying to compromise me? I'd seen *From Russia with Love*. But what secrets could SMERSH wish to extract from me? Did they know I had been a National Service Second Lieutenant in the Royal Artillery? I gave her a half-hearted peck, said I wasn't feeling well and insisted that we went back to the hotel.

When she came to take me to some Russian play the following evening I made sure I took Rocca with me. She seemed a little put out when she saw him clamber into the taxi beside me. As we drove along the Nevsky Prospect she made a grab for my hand. I evaded her as gently as I could. She became furious, ordered the driver to stop and literally threw me out of the car. It sped off with Rocca peering anxiously out of the back. I think he must have toed the party line. She was no Julie Christie but he wore a satisfied smile for the rest of the week. To this day I haven't a clue what her intentions were. Was she really an agent or just frustrated?

We went to Moscow on the overnight train, the Soviet equivalent of the Orient Express, or so we were told. We were billeted in the Ukraine Hotel, a monstrous skyscraper, built on the orders of Stalin himself. It was then the tallest hotel in the world. The only problem was that the packed lifts took as long to descend through all thirty-four floors, as a London bus making its way through Oxford Street in the rush hour. On the first night when Rocca and I got in on the twentieth floor at about a quarter to six, we found Scofield pressed against the back. We had been told to be in the lobby precisely at 6pm to catch the special bus that was to convey us all to the theatre. It would not wait for latecomers. The lift stopped at every floor. The door took an eternity to open and shut. People got out, changed their minds and got back in. I caught a sad twinkle in Scofield's eye. 'I hope the understudy took another bloody lift,' he murmured.

We played that night at the famous Moscow Arts Theatre. It was a gala occasion. Scofield's Lear had been revered in Russia and a 'Red Carpet' *Macbeth* seemed highly appropriate. Khrushchev had been replaced as leader, but we could make out his bald head watching from a box. Kim Philby was also present – I trust the sod had a boring evening. The performance was followed by a reception at, I think, the Soviet Academy of Actors. Iced vodka and Russian champagne were consumed in prodigious quantities, and effusive speeches were made by our hosts. Scofield said a few brief words in reply. Vivien Merchant's marriage to Harold Pinter was falling apart and she did not feel up to making a speech. It was given instead by the First Witch in the shape of Elizabeth Spriggs, who with tears streaming down her cheeks, pledged her ever-lasting love to her dear, dear, dear, Soviet colleagues. The bus eventually took us all reeling back to the Ukraine.

I got into the same lift as Elizabeth Spriggs together with a smartly dressed little man, who apologised in English as he bumped against her. Elizabeth turned towards him. She had the same look in her eye as when she'd been at the Asti Spumante. I hoped she wasn't about to tell him he was a bad actor. 'Are you an American?' she demanded. The Vietnam War was at its height and anti-Americanism was just becoming popular.

'Yes, I am, ma'am,' he politely replied.

'And what is your name?'

'Hiram S. Garner.'

'And what were you doing in 1940, Hiram S. Garner when Coventry was bombed? I was in Coventry that night. Our city was destroyed. The English looted – they had never looted before.'

I was hoping the poor little chap would get out, but the lift made its slow, inexorable progress, stopping at every floor.

'And what did you do, Hiram S. Garner, when we asked you for aid?' she continued. 'You sent us parcels of powdered egg. What good were powdered eggs against the bombs?'

Mr Garner continued to smile politely, until we reached the tenth floor. He raised his hat before he went out: 'I'm sorry you feel like that, Ma'am, but it wasn't exactly a bed of roses in the Pacific.'

Every morning throughout that week we were taken to view various shining examples of the Soviet system. An orchestra rehearsal, a visit to the Moscow Circus School, the Kremlin, Red Square, the odd factory where, believe it or not, the manager gave us a lecture on productivity, and the Museum of the Great Patriotic War – which somehow managed to avoid any mention of Stalin. He had recently been denounced by Khrushchev. I was astounded that some of the more radical members of the company refused to see anything bad in the system. All they seemed to care about was the profusion of subsidised orchestras and theatres – albeit heavily censored ones. They happily bought their souvenirs in the official party shops, which were off limits to ordinary Muscovites. The highlight for me was a visit to Stanislavsky's house. We were given a tour by the great man's ancient valet, still living there fifty years after the Revolution. Only about half a dozen of us felt up to it that morning – Ian Richardson was the only senior member of the company present – but the old chap appeared to be honoured by our presence and treated us all, including Rocca, as if we were the leaders of our so-called profession.

On our last morning in Moscow Don Henderson, who had briefly been an unlikely policeman before becoming an actor, came into breakfast white-faced, holding something wrapped in newspaper. He'd met a Russian the previous evening and they had ended up drinking vodka in his room. He'd found the package when he woke. We looked inside and saw an icon. The company manager frantically summoned someone from the Embassy who came and speedily took it away. We supposed the Soviet authorities had seen Don's previous occupation on his passport, assumed he was an agent and sought to compromise him. Perhaps my lady in Leningrad had had ulterior motives after all.

We came back to London in time for Christmas and did a few weeks at the Aldwych before the ill-fated production was put to rest.

(Since I wrote the previous passage my editor has informed me that Peter Rocca died in 2009 of breathing difficulties at the age of seventy-two. We had lost touch over the years. I hope he found his Lara, but fear he never did.)

Although Scofield would give acclaimed performances in Ibsen and Shaw and other classics, he never touched Shakespearean heights again. Was it yet another example of the curse of *Macbeth*? In 1978 Peter Hall tried again at the National with Albert Finney, but still couldn't get it right. His diary entry of 7 June begins: 'The notices are as terrible as any I have ever had…'

In 1970, after directing the play at the Roundhouse for the NYT, Michael Croft sent me off to Sunderland to repeat the production for the Northern Branch. I am told that Derek Hatton, future Commissar of Merseyside, played one of the murderers. I cannot recall him or any militancy. I finally said goodbye to Malcolm in Michael Jayston's television version. Though it was initially made for schools it was not at all bad, with Barbara Leigh Hunt a formidable Lady M. This time it was set in the correct historical period, which meant I played Malcolm (still ringing!) in a Veronica Lake style shoulder-length wig. The performance just about survived it.

In 1978 David Conville was asked by the Arts Council to take a rough and ready *Macbeth* to places where Shakespeare was not usually performed. I was his assistant director and, my juvenile days over at last, also played Macduff. It was a very simple production indeed, with a cast of 10. Everybody, apart from Macbeth, had to double parts; Lady Macbeth was also the First Witch. I doubled with the First Murderer, which I found rather hard to motivate as I had to murder my own wife and children. Every time I'd played Malcolm I'd thought how much easier Macduff was. It is a common fallacy; the other actor's part always looks easier than your own. Macduff is extremely difficult at the best of times and includes a famous tank trap: '*all my pretty chickens and their dam at one fell swoop*', which is rumoured to have been delivered as: '*all my shitty chickens and their pram at one swell poop*'. At least I managed to avoid that. The scenery was made of hollow blocks of wood of various shapes and sizes which the cast arranged in different positions to suggest a gateway, or table or throne. Even worse, for long periods, when we were not actually acting in the current scene, we had to sit on the bloody things and watch, thumping them with our hands and whistling to create sound effects. On top of that we were dressed in baggy tracksuits of blue, green or brown. Even though I was the assistant director, I never did discover the significance of the colours.

Everything went quite well until we got to Cornwall. It was the middle of winter and we played in a theatre virtually on the beach at Newquay, where concert parties took place in the summer. The sound of the Atlantic thundering outside added to the atmosphere. Unfortunately Cornish schoolchildren were not used to watching plays and on our opening performance a large party of them talked and laughed incessantly throughout the first scenes. Macbeth was played by a short-tempered Scottish actor, who stormed up to me after the disruptions in his dagger speech and yelled: 'You're the fucking assistant director – do something about those little sods. Otherwise I am not going to bloody continue.'

Macduff tentatively appeared out of Duncan's bedchamber to raucous hoots and hisses. I raised my hand and quite unexpectedly silence fell. 'I have acted all over the world,' I faltered, 'and I can honestly say that you are the most ill-behaved audience I've ever come across. If you don't want to see the play, go outside and let those who do, watch it in peace.' There was not a sound or titter as I sloped off to the sanctuary of the wings. We continued in complete and utter silence, to the disgust of the Porter, who failed to raise his usual laugh on his urine line. They didn't even laugh when I came on with Macbeth's head, but we had loud and prolonged applause at the curtain. Next morning the headline across the front page of the local paper proclaimed: 'Actor says Cornish Children are Worst-Behaved in World!' A letter from the headmaster was waiting for me at the theatre, apologising profusely, and promising that the ringleaders were being sought out and would be severely punished. I had visions of crosses going up all over Cornwall with children hanging from them like at the end of *Spartacus*. I was very relieved when we crossed back into Devon.

The tour went on through the winter and early spring. It took us to Snowdonia and as far north as Aberdeen. By now Dora had become a successful dress designer and my two young sons had to accompany me during their Easter holidays. I am very glad that they did, being cooped up in stuffy dressing rooms and staying in tatty digs put them off the theatre for life, and they are both gainfully employed in sensible professions. Eventually we wended our way back south and ended up in the Leas Cliff Hall in Folkestone, which reminded me of a Wild West Saloon. I had been driving back and forth from London every day that week and was getting very tired. One night, before a sparse house, I came on in the final scene with Macbeth's head and looked around the stage. The other cast members were an unprepossessing crew in their baggy tracksuits, particularly the young chap playing Donalbain, who had a profile like a fish. I began my speech to Malcolm beginning: *'I see thee compassed with thy kingdom's pearl…'* and thought that if this lot are the pearl what must the rest of the buggers be like? For the first and only time in my career I began to corpse on stage. I tried to stop myself but tears rolled down my cheeks. I hoped the audience would think I'd been overcome with emotion. Malcolm and the rest presumed I was having a fit. At last I broke off and managed to put myself out of my misery by shouting triumphantly: *'Hail, King of Scotland!'* I never dared to look at Donalbain on stage again.

I finally played the Thane himself in 1982 when George Murcell offered it to me at St George's. It is only when you actually play a part that you fully appreciate the difficulties. How can a mere actor hope to do justice to the immensity of such lines as?

'And pity, like a naked, new-born babe,
Striding the blast, or heaven's cherubin, horsed
Upon the sightless couriers of the air,
Shall blow the horrid deed in every eye,
That tears shall drown the wind…'

As Trevor Nunn says you can only try and hope that tonight might be the night you nearly get it right. Like others before me, I found the tortured poet difficult if not impossible to realise, so concentrated on rendering *'Bellona's Bridegroom'* and was duly commended for my '*soldierly*' Macbeth by the perceptive critic of *The Daily Telegraph*. Most of our audiences were schoolchildren. There is no sterner test than playing Shakespeare before schoolchildren and preventing them laughing at you. It is invaluable training for any young actor. You must grab their attention and act with pace and energy. I was never a great Macbeth but I always prided myself that at least the little buggers never laughed at me – until one afternoon.

I had got to the banquet and had just seen Banquo's ghost for the first time when gales of laughter erupted in front of me. I put on more pace and energy but to my consternation the laughter grew louder. I couldn't understand it – I thought for a moment my flies were undone. I turned upstage to check and saw to my horror that a cat had wandered in from the street and was walking slowly along the banquet table. I thought there was something strangely eerie about it, but Ross, Lennox and the rest were having convulsions. It was impossible to continue. For the second time in my life I stopped the play and announced jokily: 'It must belong to the witches. We'll catch it and then start the scene again.' There were huge cheers but it was easier said than done. The cat became extremely lively, evaded all our attempts to capture it and eventually ran off into the wings. There was nothing to be done but start the scene again. The thought that the cat might reappear at any moment gave added tension to the scene and it was one of those occasions when I nearly got it right. The cat was never seen again. I wonder if it really did belong to the witches?

After being in the play so many times I ended up practically knowing it by heart. I devised a one-man version and toured it around various colleges in Texas. Apart from a torrid encounter with the Head of English at a Dallas University – she reminded me a bit of Doris Day in *Calamity Jane* – I failed to set the West on fire.

King Lear

'I was so shocked by Cordelia's death that I know not whether I ever endured to read again the last scenes of the play till I undertook to revise them as editor.'
Dr Samuel Johnson (1709-1784)

Tattle: Hardly festive cheer, *Lear* is reputed to have been first performed on 26 December 1606, with Burbage playing the leading role at the age of thirty-nine, roughly the same age as Paul Scofield when he gave his definitive Lear in 1962. After the Restoration, Thomas Betterton acted a version by Nahum Tate, the Irish-born Poet Laureate, which had no Fool, a love affair between Cordelia and Edgar, and a happy ending. David Garrick did an adaptation of Tate's version saying: 'The distress of seeing the original play would have been more than any audience could bear.' Kean and Macready went back to Shakespeare but Lear was not amongst their greatest triumphs. Bernard Shaw, as was his wont, did not think much of Sir Henry Irving's efforts: 'Irving's Lear is slow and has a habit of avoiding his part and slipping into an imaginative conception of his own between the lines.' But since then, unlike Macbeth and Othello, most actors have succeeded as Lear. To my mind it is not a difficult part – you just play Lear, and as long as you have the energy, the emotion will carry you through. The nineteenth-century American actor Edwin Forrest declared: 'Play Lear! I play Hamlet, Othello, and Macbeth; but by heaven, sir, I am Lear!' Olivier thought the same: 'Frankly Lear is an easy part. We can all play it. It is simply bang straightforward. He's like all of us really; he's just a stupid old fart. He's got this frightful temper. He's completely selfish and utterly inconsiderate. He is simply bad-tempered arrogance with a crown perched on top.' John Gielgud found it such a doddle that he did the Charleston in the wings each night before carrying on Dame Peggy to 'Howl! Howl! Howl!' The notoriously self-effacing Donald Wolfit (ho! ho! ho!) considered Lear to be, 'The Jewel in my Crown.'

In 1967, late in his career, Charles Laughton came to Stratford to give his Lear. Ian Holm played his Fool and became very close to him. Ian told me Laughton soon realised he had not the stamina to play Lear on stage, but some nights he would take Ian out to the Rollright Stones, a prehistoric stone circle in the Cotswold Hills about twenty miles south of Stratford, where he would act out the storm scene to the elements. Late one night in 1967, after a bottle of wine – driving after a few drinks, like smoking, was not so frowned on in those days – Ian took me out to the Stones and gave me his impression of Laughton's Lear. It was an amazing experience in the moonlight, surrounded by the Stones. According to legend, they are a king and his knights frozen to stone by a witch. I could swear that night that some of the Stones moved. Julian Glover, who played Cornwall in that production, has told me since that he had to take Laughton and Holm to the Stones in his car, since neither of them could drive. Glover remembers Laughton lying on the grass in the centre of the circle like a big brown blob. Ian's own Lear at the National in 1998 was considered one of the finest, and there have been many in recent years. I suspect some of it came from those nights by the Stones with Laughton.

I was in the company at Stratford in 1993 when Robert Stephens gave his acclaimed Lear. He was a very frail and sick man by then. It was terribly sad seeing him waiting for the bus to Coventry each night to catch the last train back to London. It is rumoured that at that time some directors of the RSC were flying first class, but they couldn't even provide Sir Bob with a taxi. Such is the value of actors.

Memories: The hedonism and excitement of the sixties dissolved all too quickly. It was during the winter of 1974/75 that I began to realise that the glittering career I'd once confidently expected was never going to arrive. It was like being in a waiting room and watching my fellows – Martin Jarvis, Ian McShane, John Shrapnel, Michael York, Simon Ward – being called in whilst I remained outside in the cold. I'd endured months out of work; afraid to leave the phone in case my agent rang (the mobile phone is one advantage the actor of today enjoys). I had two small sons and Dora's career as a dress designer was yet to get off the ground, so I was forced to swallow my pride and drive a minicab. It was one of the worst periods of my life. One day I was sent to an elegant Georgian house behind Westminster Abbey and to my astonishment Sir John Gielgud slipped into the back of my rather shabby Ford Zodiac. I'd played a scene with him in the film

Becket. Kingsley Amis had mentioned us both in the same sentence in his review in *The Observer.* I noticed Gielgud studying me through the driving mirror and remembered Richard Burton telling me that Sir John thought I had a very interesting face. I screwed my courage to the sticking place and blurted out: 'You may remember me, Sir John. We worked together on *Becket.*' He wrinkled his nose and looked out of the window. 'Really? What were you? One of the extras?' I'd heard of his unintentional put-downs but it hurt nevertheless and made me determined to get back into acting no matter what. So when I was offered the part of Edgar in a production of *Lear* at the Palace Theatre, Westcliffe, I snapped it up – even though it would pay less than a third of what I got from minicabbing.

The Palace, a proper theatre, an old Palace of Varieties, was a two-weekly rep run by Leslie Lawton. Leslie was very good at getting bums on seats, he went on to run more esteemed theatres in Liverpool and Edinburgh, but his main talent lay in comedy and farce and he was to work as Ray Cooney's assistant for many years. I don't think that at that time he'd ever been in a Shakespeare play; for that matter I don't think he's been in one since. He not only took it upon himself to direct *Lear* in 10 days but also decided to play Edmund. I'd have preferred to play Edmund myself, his famous 'bastard' speech had been one of my audition pieces for RADA and I considered it to be the more showy part, although very few actors have made their names in it. Edmund starts off well and then seems to fade away. Edgar is far deeper. He has a journey through the play to maturity and self-awareness, but it was extremely hard to explore in ten days. I found the '*Mad Tom*' scenes especially difficult. I crammed the gibberish into my head without having time to discover what was behind it. Leslie, ever aware of the box-office (the provinces like nothing better than a flash of bare flesh), wanted me to play those scenes naked apart from an old blanket. I refused; dreading to think what the schoolgirls of Southend would make of it, and settled for a loincloth. If I'd had the nerve I would have beaten Ian McKellen in the buff stakes. A few months later the future knight played Edgar and revealed his considerable all in a more prestigious production. Thirty years later he got his mighty manhood out again when he gave his Lear. He must be the only actor to have shown his part in both parts.

I hardly rehearsed the scenes I had with Leslie, as he was always busy dashing around directing everybody else and arranging the sound effects, which he did with an old stagehand who claimed to have done the storm for the legendary Irish actor, Anew McMaster. Metal sheets, wind machines, thunder runs and cannon balls were constantly being purchased and purloined and carefully positioned under the stage. Leslie was convinced it would be the making of the production – although I can't seem to recall ever hearing any of it during a performance. Lear was played by a solid actor called Antony Webb, who went around the reps playing kingly roles. Lear was part of his repertoire. We had a great shock at the dress rehearsal when Leslie appeared for the first time with a shoulder length wig and fluttering false eyelashes, looking like a cross between Danny La Rue and King Rat. His main preoccupation was his death scene, for which he had a large packet of fake blood taped to his body. It was enough for a sizeable transfusion. Each night when I stabbed him in the lamentably unrehearsed fight it spurted out over his white shirt in an uncontrollable fountain, to the hilarity of the audience. It was not one of the peaks of my career, but better than driving a minicab.

I'd always thought that the stalwart Kent was my part in *Lear* and jumped at it when Frank Dunlop offered it to me at the Young Vic in 1981. Like most parts it is far harder than it looks. After a rousing opening he next appears in an unlikely disguise, and then spends the rest of the play in great discomfort, supporting Lear from one travail to the next. Nevertheless it was an excellent production and a very rewarding experience. Frank always cast well and having thought out the initial concept left it to the actors. He had done the unexpected as was his wont, and cast James Bolam, a fine and versatile actor, but forever famous as the better half of *The Likely Lads,* as the tyrannical old king. James put his own stamp on the role and was extremely convincing. In fact he was so good that the production was invited to Hong Kong. James is a near contemporary of mine and we have always got on very well. We got on so well in fact, that we spent most of the long flight to Hong Kong reminiscing on mutual acquaintances. The British Airways stewardesses were then exceedingly generous with the alcohol, and when the plane landed in Calcutta to refuel, we were so full of bonhomie that the Captain wanted to leave us behind. We were fortunate that the pleas of our matronly stage manager prevailed.

Though it was still officially a British Colony the entire trip had been arranged and financed by the local Chinese government and we played to packed houses of immaculately behaved, beaming schoolchildren. As we declaimed, a translation in Cantonese slowly descended on a screen by the side of the stage. We were eagerly received, so much so that the authorities decided to put on an extra matinee without informing James. It is an unwritten law in the theatre that no actor should be asked to perform Lear twice in a day. James was furious but his protests were simply met with implacable smiles from the benign Chinese officials. James was forced to do the matinee, but he did it at double speed – the Cantonese hurtled down the screen as if it were tumbling off Niagara Falls. The Chinese still beamed – they didn't seem to notice.

When I got back to London I read that Jonathan Miller, who had been ploughing through the entire works on television, was going to finish off with his own production of *Lear,* with Sir Michael Hordern as the king. I had been trying unsuccessfully to get in the series from the beginning. The actor is forever being put off with: 'You're not quite right for the part.' I couldn't believe that there was not one single part in the entire canon that I was right for. I therefore wrote a long letter to Miller stating the reasons why I thought I would be an ideal Albany. I went for Albany because I was sure he would have somebody firmly in mind for Kent. I was pleased and surprised to receive a reply within days asking me to meet him at the BBC Centre. When I got to his office he stared at me with those sad basset hound eyes and apologised for not giving me anything in the past: I was just the sort of actor he'd been looking for throughout the series. *Lear* was all but cast, even Albany had gone. All he could offer was Burgundy, but he would make sure I'd be paid the same as if I were playing a major role. Beggars can't be choosers so I accepted.

The following Monday I made my way to what the actors used to call the Acton Hilton – the tower block by the side of the A4 where the BBC used to rehearse all its shows. In those days everything was still meticulously rehearsed, not shot in a couple of days as now. I arrived early, as is my wont, and entered the rehearsal room to find the floor managers running round in great consternation. Kent, in the shape of John Shrapnel, my old sparring partner from the NYT, had been filming *Wagner* with Richard Burton, and was stuck up the Matterhorn. How were they going to block the opening scene without Kent, who features so prominently? Dr Miller and the rest of his distinguished cast began to arrive. Most, had worked with him before, some had been in his previous television version. There was further consternation. I thought twice before I modestly remarked that

I'd just finished playing Kent at the Young Vic and would be more than happy to stand in. My offer was accepted. I thought I did it quite well – Michael Hordern congratulated me at the end of the day, so did several of the others. I was a bit miffed when Jonathan Miller said nothing. Shrapnel arrived safely the following morning in his usual bouncing, vigorous form, and rehearsals continued as planned.

At the weekend I bumped into Miller in Camden Market. To my surprise and delight he said: 'You are a very good actor. I think I might have something for you when this is over.' He ignored me again throughout the rest of his entertaining and fascinating rehearsals. As is his wont, he was more interested in the mental state of Lear than the smaller details of production. He gave me no notes as Burgundy and I just played it as written. Trevor Nunn, on the other hand, strives to give the smallest part substance. In his production he made it clear that Burgundy and Cordelia were into some sort of romance before the play started, which made his rejection of her when he discovers she has no dowry even crueller.

When we got into the studios, I realised most of my small part was going to be shot from the back of my head. I thought Miller had forgotten all about our conversation in Camden Market, until he came over to me in the canteen and said: 'I'm about to do *Hamlet* in town. Come to the Piccadilly Theatre next Friday. Have a look at Claudius. *"O, my offence is rank..."* My secretary will phone with details.' It sounded too good to be true. I thought my luck had finally changed. Claudius was the one part I knew I was right for at that time. I was ready for it. It could kick start my faltering career. The following Friday I went along to the Piccadilly and gave what I considered a good rendering. I had recently played Macbeth at St George's and there is much of him in that guilt-laden speech. When I'd finished Miller clambered up on stage and said, 'That was really excellent. There's just one other person. I'll make up my mind over the weekend.' I was on tenterhooks for a few days until I received a letter, in which he said it had gone the other way, but he would endeavour to cast me in a major role in the future. I wish I had a pound for all the parts I didn't get – but that one hurt more than most. I wondered why he'd raised my hopes so much – he could have offered me something else – I'd have been very happy with the Player King or the Ghost or even Marcellus.

It was no real surprise when Claudius ended up being very well played by John Shrapnel – he'd worked for Miller several times before. I am still waiting for the promised major role. I am grateful to the good Doctor for one thing however: he did put me on the upper pay level. I have received substantial cheques for repeats and sales of that *Lear* ever since.

1987: I eventually played Albany in Sir Anthony Quayle's touring production. Quayle was a great man, a patriot and visionary, whose contributions to our theatre have been grossly undervalued. He is largely remembered for his appearances in a seemingly never-ending line of war films – *The Guns of Navarone, Ice Cold in Alex, Lawrence of Arabia, The Battle of the River Plate* – to name but a few. He was so memorable in those roles because he was, to a large extent, re-enacting his own experiences. He gave up a soft job as aide-de-camp to the Governor of Gibraltar, where he mingled with the paladins of the Allied cause, to volunteer for Special Services and spend months behind enemy lines with partisans in the Albanian mountains. Such was his bravery and sense of duty that after he had been invalided out to safety he insisted on going back and rescuing the men he had left behind. Then back in austerity-hit Britain he turned down a million-dollar Hollywood contract to run what was then the Shakespeare Memorial Theatre for £30 a week. He did it because, as he told me one morning when we were walking over the Derbyshire Dales with his Jack Russell, he wanted to give the country something to savour after six years of terrible war. To that end he persuaded his friends, Olivier, Gielgud, Richardson and the rest, to play the great roles at Stratford, which up until then had been merely a provincial theatre.

He was the first to realise that to be a major international company the theatre at Stratford would have to have a permanent London base and function throughout the year. He would turn in his grave if he knew how Adrian Noble and others had thrown the Barbican away. In his seventies, after a long and profitable career in films and commercial theatre, he decided to give something back again. He thought the provinces were being starved of major theatrical productions so he sold his boat and founded *Compass,* his own touring company.

He loved actors – Richard Burton, Robert Hardy, Alan Badel are among those who owed the beginning of their careers to him – and he had assembled a great company for *Lear,* including Tony Britton as Gloucester, and Kate O'Mara and Isla Blair as the evil daughters. I soon discovered that Albany is a very good part. He has a clear line through the play: at the beginning he is completely under Goneril's thumb, not knowing what is going on, but eventually the penny drops, the worm turns; he takes control and is quite heroic by the time the curtain falls. We played almost exclusively in large auditoriums designed by Frank Matcham – the Christopher Wren of theatre building. Even today, after a century of assaults by cinema, television and bingo, nearly every large provincial city still has a Matcham theatre. Not only are they beautiful but unlike so many modern theatres – the Olivier to name but one – their acoustics and sightlines are impeccable.

Some say that Quayle was not a great actor. He was in the second tier below Olivier, Gielgud, Richardson and Guinness, but the older members of the public held him in special affection. They sensed his basic decency – he had endured and gone through war and privations with them. In the second half of the play Lear's lines: '*fawning politicians…they are not men of their words… a man may see how this world goes with no eyes…change places, and which is the justice, which is the thief?*' took on deeper meaning for them. Quayle's Lear was lamenting the demise of the England they believed they had been born into.

One unexpected bonus was that there were no Saturday matinees, even Quayle could not be expected to do two Lears a day at seventy-four, so I was free to attend the nearest major football match. Even though I never caught up with any away games of my beloved Chelsea, I visited such cathedrals as Ibrox, Elland Road, Old Trafford and Anfield, together with more minor shrines in Leicester, Huddersfield and Aberdeen. We played at Belfast for two weeks during the troubles. Indeed the Opera House, yet another Matcham masterpiece, had suffered bomb damage the previous year. There was no football game that Saturday but Quayle, ever mindful of the morale of his troops, arranged a coach trip to the Giant's Causeway and a visit to the Bushmills Distillery.

I noticed one morning that I had developed a rash on one side of my face and, having little else to do, decided to visit the theatre doctor. He was a wizened old fellow who strongly resembled the Hollywood character actor, Barry Fitzgerald. As he examined my face he enquired:

'And what is your occupation?'

'I am an actor.'

'Are you working at the moment?'

'Yes, I'm playing in *King Lear* at the Opera House.'

'Does anything happen to your face during the play?'

'Well, now you mention it, Kate O'Mara does slap it in Act Five.'

'Put it down to an industrial disease.'

Quayle was always so hale and hearty, a veritable tower of strength, but cancer claimed him within two years. He died on the very day Olivier's Memorial Service was held in Westminster Abbey. Larry upstaged him even in death.

2007: Twenty years later I was in the play again with yet another knight. My experiences of going round the world with Ian McKellen have been thoroughly dealt with in my book *Covering McKellen.*

Timon of Athens

'Many passages of the play are perplexed, obscure and probably corrupt.'
Dr Samuel Johnson

Tattle: Not surprisingly this is Shakespeare's most neglected play. Timon's passions are full of poison with no promise of eventual forgiveness and compassion; he ends in a slough of total despair, there is no reconciliation and hope of peace as at the end of *Lear*. It was a late addition to the 1623 Folio, possibly because it had never been performed. It seems likely that Shakespeare never revised the play as there are gaps in the narrative. Professor Harold Bloom thinks it is a pity Socrates wasn't included in the plot along with Alcibiades, holding that Socrates' wisdom, wit, self-knowledge and sense of reality would have added a Falstaffian quality and a bit of entertainment to the proceedings. Thomas Shadwell, an unlikely Poet Laureate, adapted Timon in 1678, modestly declaiming: 'It has the inimitable hand of Shakespeare in it, yet I can truly say I have made it into a play.' His rival Dryden aptly observed:

'The rest to some faint meaning make pretence
But Shadwell never deviates into sense.'

Another version added a love interest and music by Purcell. It was more or less ignored until Tyrone Guthrie dug it up at the Old Vic in 1952. Kenneth Tynan felt that Timon's everlasting railings were being played by a stuck gramophone needle. In 1956 Sir Ralph Richardson attempted Timon on a set described by Milton Shulman as looking as if 'it might have been left behind by a Wolverhampton production of *Babes in the Wood.'* Another critic thought Sir Ralph played Timon like a scoutmaster betrayed by his troop. In 1965 I saw Paul Scofield, at the height of his powers, directed by the Oscar-winning John Schlesinger. Scofield wrote later that there were exquisite passages in the second half of the play that had real meaning for him as well as a violent beauty. He thought that Shakespeare was expressing some great personal betrayal and that the play was a journey of expiation and final reconciliation. I have to admit I was bored stiff. When Trevor Nunn directed David Suchet as Timon in 1972, he added 200 lines of his own. Some critics said it was the first time they had really understood the play. Although Simon Russell Beale and Nicholas Hytner's up-to-date, anti-City production received almost universal acclaim, I still found the play tedious, predictable and banal. On top of that, the stage was full of unattractive voices. Surely the voice is the most important requirement of an actor – in the theatre at least? Beale gabbled away as is becoming his wont. I've admired him greatly in the past, but am I the only person who now has difficulty in understanding what he says? I'd had enough by the interval. 'Simon' of Athens had already daubed himself and his guests with shit – I couldn't stomach watching him eat his roots, so I made my excuses and left.

Coriolanus

'Shakespeare's finest comedy'
George Bernard Shaw

Tattle: In 1605 King James referred to some members of Parliament as: 'Tribunes of the people whose mouths could not be stopped.' The play was probably written in 1608, following widespread rioting in the Midlands caused by enclosures, bad harvests and shortages of food. The First Citizen complains of those who have '*their store-houses crammed with grain*' – exactly what Shakespeare himself was doing in his own barns in Stratford. Volumnia is the most powerful mother in all the works – 1608 was the year Shakespeare's own mother, Mary Arden, died. Following the Restoration Coriolanus became a favourite role of Thomas Betterton, and later was well suited to the neo-classical style and deliberate declamation of John Kemble. It was considered Kemble's highest achievement, even though his abstracted air, contracted eyebrows and suspended chin, reminded Hazlitt of a man about to sneeze. But until quite recently the part was avoided by most of the great actors, possibly because it lacks sympathy and introspection. Granville-Barker described him as an 'incorrigible boy'; whilst the scholar, Kenneth Palmer, considered him 'essentially the splendid oaf who has never come to maturity.' Modern left-wing critics such as Wyndham Lewis deemed Coriolanus 'a demented aristocrat and the incarnation of the violent snob, the typical product of an English public-school.' Lewis chose to ignore that Shakespeare, impartial as ever, shows the fickleness and faults of the people and their Tribunes in equal measure. It could be seen as 'the struggle of wrong and wrong.' In the twentieth century it was used by Fascists and Communists alike to propound their political theories. Brecht wrote his own version of the play for the Berliner Ensemble.

Richard Burton took a lot of persuasion from his mentor, Philip Burton, before he agreed to play the part at the Old Vic in 1954. He'd just returned from filming *My Cousin Rachel* in Hollywood. On the opening night as the Volscians were tearing him to pieces, screaming: *'He killed my son – he killed my father – he killed my cousin Marcus,'* a rather effeminate actor was heard declaiming: *'He killed my Cousin Rachel!'* Nevertheless Burton's cold detachment and Celtic fury fitted Coriolanus like a glove. Laurence Olivier considered him to be the greatest he'd ever seen. Olivier had played it himself in 1937 and it had been one of his less successful roles. Perhaps it was Burton's performance that gave Olivier the itch to have another go, which he did triumphantly in 1959. Unfortunately there is no record of that performance. Kenneth Tynan's review can only give a taste: 'The voice is soft steel that can chill and cut, or melt and scorch… he leaps up a flight of precipitous steps to vent his rage…a dozen spears impale him. He is poised, now, on a promontory some twelve feet above the stage, from which he topples forward, to be caught by the ankles so that he dangles, inverted, like the slaughtered Mussolini…' I remember the actor who caught him – I've forgotten the poor bugger's name – telling me how each night he was terrified shitless he'd drop 'the nonpareil of heroic tragedians' on his neck. Eventually it was Olivier's cartilage that snapped and he had to miss a few performances. (Another version is that he had to take time off to finish filming *Spartacus.*) His understudy was a young actor called Albert Finney, who normally played the First Citizen. *Coriolanus* is an exhausting play for the run and mill of the company, who go from citizens, to soldiers, to Volscians and back. They riot, fight battles, riot again, fight more battles and finally tear the hero to pieces. When Olivier returned he asked Finney if he'd enjoyed playing the leading role. 'Well, it's much less tiring than the First Citizen,' was Finney's response. Edith Evans played a forbidding Volumnia in that production – when asked the secret of her performance she replied 'I just face front and think dirty.'

Coriolanus is now frequently performed. Ian Richardson, Nicol Williamson, Alan Howard and Charles Dance have all done him justice, but a beefed-up Ian McKellen at the National in 1984 delved into the homo-erotic element of the play and was probably the most acclaimed.

Memories: I'd never seen the play before I appeared in it on television in the *Spread of the Eagle* series in 1964. I'd heard all about Albert Finney and had set my heart on playing the First Citizen. I was therefore a tad disappointed when Peter Dews cast me as the Second. To make amends he cast me as the First Citizen in *Julius Caesar*, which is not nearly as good a part. The play was divided into three hour-long episodes and went out with a rousing signature tune to which the ensemble quickly added lyrics, which we sang lustily as the captions rolled:

'You've never seen an anus,
There's never been an anus
You have never seen class
Till you've seen the arse
Of Corio-lane-arse!'

The Coriolanus in question was Robert Hardy, who'd been one of the Tribunes in Olivier's production. He played it in the same heroic style and impressed me immensely. Robert, or Tim as he's known to his friends, wanted to have the same spectacular death as Olivier, but unfortunately the actor hired to arrange the fights was not up to it – on one occasion refusing to fall from the walls of Corioli on to some cardboard boxes because he claimed to feel vertigo coming on.

The series never took off as *An Age of Kings* had: something was missing, probably the underlying link of history. Peter Dews, perhaps becoming aware that it was not going to be the overwhelming success he had hoped, began to lose his geniality. He would sometimes go into furious red-faced rages and look for a whipping boy. I have seen several directors do this; it is extremely unpleasant as well as cruel. I once witnessed a 'sharp-tongued little despot', reduce a veteran of Dunkirk to tears. But Peter's anger was not spiteful and would quickly cool, although there was one poor chap called Ben Harte whom he always seemed to pick on – he even fired him one day for forgetting a move. Ben was quickly reinstated, although the ensemble could not resist singing (dolce voce):

'You've got to have heart!'

Five years later I was in it again. It was the first play of the 1967 season, the first time it had been performed at Stratford since Olivier's triumph. I'd been cast as Titus Lartius, and following in the steps of Albert Finney, now a huge star, felt honoured to be also understudying Coriolanus. Titus, or 'Titty,' Lartius, is usually played as Coriolanus's young lieutenant. I had visions of giving my virile juvenile in a short tunic with loads of body make-up on my legs and other extremities. I was therefore very disappointed when John Barton informed me on the first day of rehearsal that I was to depict him as a gnarled old warrior. I was even more disappointed when the wardrobe department fitted me for a hump! That was the nearest I ever got to playing Richard III.

John Barton I found to be ever the academic, with little feeling or understanding for the ordinary actor, whom he treated like rather backward undergrads. Hector Ross, a good, experienced thespian in his forties, playing a line of middling parts, had a wife and family in London, whom he naturally drove down to visit at weekends. One Monday morning he was held up by traffic – there was no motorway then – and arrived twenty minutes late. Barton berated him before the entire company for being 'unprofessional'. Poor Hector had to stand before him blushing, with head bent. It was certainly not a way to invoke company spirit. Barton was a bear of a man who always seemed to gaze at life through a haze of cigarette smoke. He smoked and drank coffee incessantly. It was rumoured he also chewed razor blades but I never witnessed it. At rehearsals he would sit with the front legs of his chair off the ground and rock backwards and forwards as he studied the text. One day, as he was smoking and rocking furiously, we watched spellbound, whilst his chair edged slowly towards his coffee cup on the floor in front of him. We all hoped the chair leg would end up in the cup of coffee. It did.

Barton's production was slow and cumbersome; despite Ian Richardson's excellent Coriolanus there was little inspiration or excitement about it. We struggled through the long evenings under John Bury's heavy costumes and armour. One of the few pleasures was watching the young Helen Mirren snarling away amid the Roman mob. She was following the path of another Dame, Diana Rigg, who'd been in the mob in the previous production. Albert Finney had invented a special piece of business for her in the sack of Corioli. In a short simple scene two soldiers enter with loot. One says *'This will I carry to Rome'*; the other replies *'And I this'*. Finney had come on with Diana Rigg over his shoulder and slapped her rump on the line. I suggested to John Barton that someone should do the same with Helen Mirren – he wrinkled his nose and shook his head disapprovingly as if I'd broken wind in church.

The assistant director was a little dormouse of a fellow, the aforementioned Mike Leigh. He was very frustrated and unhappy; Shakespeare, or at least the way we were playing it, was definitely not his cup of tea. I listened without a great deal of interest when he told me of the improvised plays he'd been doing with some amateur group in Birmingham. He asked me, I think out of boredom, if I would like to work on my understudy of Coriolanus with him. I readily agreed: with Albert Finney constantly in my mind, I wanted to be sure I was more than ready to go on. We spent many hours on it together, the great speeches became firmly imbedded, but he offered me no new insight into the part. I suspect that working from established texts was never Mike Leigh's metier.

Aufidius, the best part in the play, was played by an extremely intense and surly young American actor. He was only in the RSC because he'd recently married Estelle Kohler, who was playing Juliet. I shared a dressing room with him and like most of the company found him extremely arrogant, but we may have been just jealous. He was deep into the 'method' and got carried away completely in the savage sword fights. So much so that he constantly managed to slash and stab poor Ian Richardson's legs. Some nights Ian could hardly walk; on several occasions I was told to stand by and be ready to go on. I was more than willing. One night I was actually in his dressing room, putting on the costume, when Ian limped in. He was a trouper of the old school: he'd literally have to break a leg before he'd miss a performance

Antony and Cleopatra

'Cleopatra is the daughter of Falstaff'
Professor Harold Bloom (Step up to the plate Dawn French?)

'An actor can no more make his mark as Antony in London, than a stone in the round pond in Kensington Gardens.'
George Bernard Shaw (I couldn't agree more.)

Tattle: The play was entered in the Stationers' Register, an early form of establishing copyright, in May 1608. Although Dryden's version *All for Love* was popular during the Restoration and after, there is no record of any performance of Shakespeare's full text until the middle of the nineteenth century. Some have averred that Cleopatra, 'the most sacred and exacting of all Shakespeare's female roles', would have been beyond the capabilities of even the most talented of boy actors. Shakespeare allows her to say that she will not see some *'squeaking Cleopatra boy her greatness*.' However, when I was in the play at school, playing Enobarbus, Richard Hampton, a blue-chinned, hearty heterosexual if ever there was one, was so convincing as the serpent of the Nile that he won plaudits from W.A. Darlington, the renowned critic of *The Daily Telegraph*. My dear mother was never quite sure of Richard's sexuality from then on. Cleopatra is Shakespeare's '*lass unparalleled*'; in her he appears to love women again. Is she a posthumous portrait of the Dark Lady? All the great actresses have sought to capture her but she has evaded most of them. If you weren't Ellen Terry, Bernard Shaw could be very cruel: 'Even Duse could do nothing with Cleopatra. It was like seeing her scrub a scullery. Whilst Janet Alchurch's Cleopatra gave me an afternoon of lacerating anguish, spent partly in contemplating her overpowering experiments in rhetoric, and partly in wishing I had never been born.'

In more recent times Tallulah Bankhead's Cleopatra was deemed to have 'barged down the Nile and sunk'. Kenneth Tynan thought Edith

Evans played Cleopatra like Lady Bracknell, cruelly starved of cucumber sandwiches, and that Vivien Leigh 'picked at the part with the daintiness of a debutante called upon to dismember a stag.' Peter Dews directed Margaret Leighton at Chichester in 1969. As he left the theatre one evening he heard a local lady remark, 'Yes, and the funny thing is, exactly the same thing happened to Monica.' Was the poor girl bitten by an adder in her Sussex garden? When Glenda Jackson, the future MP for Hampstead, played the Egyptian Queen, Milton Shulman opined: 'Miss Jackson's danger of succumbing to absolute passion was no closer than Mrs Thatcher's likelihood of weeping at Cabinet meetings. She gave the impression that Antony didn't really appeal to her.' Glenda did better when she played Cleo with Morecambe and Wise. Vanessa Redgrave had four goes over three decades. On one occasion Irving Wardle wrote in *The Times*: 'By the end, with a long showy gown added to her red wig, she came to resemble no one so much as Danny La Rue – a dubious interpretation of the word "queen".' Dame Diana Rigg was compared to an angry headmistress at morning assembly. Dame Helen Mirren and Frances de la Tour attempted to add sexuality to the role by flashing their tired old tits and bits, but 'cloyed the appetites' of several critics.

The main problem with staging the play is the Monument. It was easy enough at the Globe where Cleopatra and her maidens appeared on the balcony above, but modern designers build vast artefacts that are well-nigh impossible to get into or get out of. Judi Dench had to wait so long in her Monument on the vast Olivier stage that one night she picnicked on champagne and dressed crab whilst her Antony, Anthony Hopkins, endeavoured to run himself through. She must have tasted fishy when she gave '*the poor last of many thousand kisses*.'

Very few actors have left their mark on the Antony of this play. Olivier, as usual, came nearest, although he considered the hero: 'an absolute twerp. A stupid man. Not a lot between the ears…the young man who had orated so brilliantly over Caesar's body is now a middle-aged lap-dog. It is Cleopatra's play – she has wit, style and sophistication, and if played well, no Antony, however brilliant, can touch her…she has him firmly by the balls.' Trevor Nunn's production with Janet Suzman and Richard Johnston was the best I've seen.

Memories: In 1963 *Antony and Cleopatra* was the final play in the *Spread of the Eagle* series and was divided into three episodes. Keith Michell looked magnificent as the ageing Antony but failed to discover any depths of tragedy. Possibly because Mary Morris, whose feline viciousness had made her a wonderful Margaret of Anjou in *An Age of Kings,* was woefully unsexy as Cleopatra, at least to heterosexuals. She very much resembled the actor William Squire. In the final episode of *Kings* they stuck a beard on her as a joke and she went on next to Squire in a crowd scene. No one could tell them apart. The Enobarbus was dull. David William's Octavius came out best. Octavius usually does.

In the three episodes I played Demetrius, Canidius and Diomedes – an assortment of Romans and Egyptians. Perhaps understandably, I failed to make an impression in any of them. The only thing I can remember is that I had Tyrone Power's name on my boots. He'd recently died on the set of *Solomon and Sheba*. They must have pulled them off him whilst he was still warm.

In 1978 Michael Croft was struggling to run the Shaw Theatre, a soulless place beneath a public library in the traffic-filled Euston Road, which seemed to cut if off from the theatre-going part of London. Michael was a buccaneer: being tied down by bricks and mortar drained away his zest and spirit. He was no diplomat and his continual battles with the Arts Council led to cuts in his funding. His drinking problems had already brought on two heart attacks and the vigorous, innovative leader I and so many others had revered and loved was crumbling before our eyes. *Antony* was a set book that year, and when Michael told me he wanted me to be in a cheap modern dress version of the play, I thought he would cast me as Enobarbus, which I had done for him at Alleyn's more than twenty-five years before. I had mixed emotions when he told me he wanted me to play Antony.

'Who's going to play Enobarbus?' I asked.

'I am,' he replied.

'Who's going to direct?'

'I am of course.'

I'm not sure if he knew death was approaching and wanted to have a final blast at acting before he went. Though one of the finest directors of Shakespeare I've ever come across: he was superb at showing how to point a line, finding true emotion, and could manage huge crowd scenes with astounding pace and vigour, he was never a good actor. Moreover this strong, hearty ex-sailor and sportsman had lost his magnetic energy. Each night, when he jumped on the table during the Egyptian Bacchanals, I thought he was going to die. He had no strength to direct and we simply learned the lines and did our best. As has already been noted, though this play has some of Shakespeare's finest poetry it very rarely comes off on stage. Ours was no exception; we had a vivacious, blonde Cleopatra in the shape of June Ritchie, an old girlfriend from RADA. She had vitality, spark and passion aplenty. My Antony was pronounced in the press as a 'bluff soldier'. I didn't expect any more. Though Antony is described as '*the noblest prince of the world*', he displays a singular lack of nobility throughout most of the play. He has gone to seed and is indeed a '*strumpet's fool.*' I had some fun on Pompey's galley, whipped up fury and jealousy during the flogging of Thidias, but still found him to be a bit of a plonker. Even at the end, after he has shown generosity to Enobarbus and forgiveness to Cleopatra, and embarks on a poetic and heart-rending suicide, he goes and mucks it up – even Brutus and Cassius manage that successfully. Antony plunges the sword into his belly, falls to the floor, then looks up and cries: '*Not dead! Not dead!*' With a theatre packed with schoolgirls there was a laugh waiting every performance. I got round it by rasping it in the softest of whispers. I then had to suffer the discomfort of being hauled and pushed up by my bum into the monument, before finally dying in June's familiar arms. Bernard Shaw was right. I should have played Enobarbus.

It was after one very average performance that I first encountered that dreadful modern phenomenon: 'Questions and Answers with the Cast.' It's like having a discussion with the surgeon after he's cut out your haemorrhoids. Some things are best left a mystery. I have nothing but the greatest respect for the audience that have given up their time and money to see a play. The actor owes them the best he can give, every single night – not all actors, I'm afraid, subscribe to that dictum. But trite conversations after the curtain are a pain for all concerned. The company stagger awkwardly on stage, clutching tepid glasses of cheap wine – compliments of the management for taking part. (Theatre wine is always dreadful.) More 'acting' is about to be emoted than during the entire play. Some actors act exhausted, as if they've just gone ten heroic rounds with Mike Tyson. Others affect a modest aura – shy smiles and eyes fixed on the stage before them. Actresses put on a voice which makes them sound even more 'actressy,' and fervently expound upon their modest art as if it were more complicated than brain surgery. The audience, most of whom are worried about missing the last train home, come up with such banalities as: 'Have you ever had any embarrassing moments on stage?' or 'How do you learn the lines?' It's a complete waste of time. I've endeavoured to avoid them ever since – not that anyone wants to question a boring, ill-tempered old fart.

Shortly after I finished at the Shaw I was up for a part in Charlton Heston's film version. I went down to Pinewood to meet Chuck himself. I may have oversold myself as I told him my intimate knowledge of the play. When I informed him that, in my opinion, Antony was not the greatest of parts, his face set in that familiar expression of disapproval, which always made me feel he wanted to be sick. I didn't get employed but I doubt it would have made any difference to my waning career. One tabloid reviewed the film under the headline: 'The Biggest Asp Disaster in the World'. Chuck should have listened to me.

Pericles

'Some mouldy tale like Pericles'
Ben Jonson (1572-1637)

Tattle: Pericles is a sort of mediaeval Ulysses. The convoluted story contains some of Shakespeare's favourite themes: shipwrecks, a lost daughter (Marina) and ultimate reconciliation, plus lots of bawdry. Its admirers say that it has rich romance, a sense of adventure and a child-like dream quality; the reconciliation scene between Pericles and his daughter is almost as moving as that between Lear and Cordelia. Others hold that it 'stumbles along from improbable incident to preposterous coincidence like an old man telling a half-forgotten tale.' There is a theory that Shakespeare was part-author with the minor playwright, George Wilkins, who wrote a novel entitled: *The Painful Adventures of Pericles Prince of Tyre*. Wilkins was also an innkeeper of ill repute, charged with violence and keeping bawds. If he was involved, the brothel scenes in the play are likely to be extremely authentic. First published in quarto in 1607, it was the only one of Shakespeare's acknowledged thirty-seven plays not to appear in the 1623 Folio. This is difficult to understand because after *Henry IV Part I* and *Richard II* it was the third most popular play in Shakespeare's lifetime, being reprinted twice in 1609 alone. It was still successfully playing at the Globe in 1631 and was the first play by Shakespeare to be performed after the Restoration with Betterton in the title role. Dryden believed it was Shakespeare's first play – I find it hard to see why.

Memories: When I started at RADA in 1957, first-year students were obliged to do Assistant Stage Managing for the senior students' public performances in the Vanbrugh Theatre. This was all part of the training as most young actors then expected to be assistant stage managers in reps for the first year or so of their careers. I was never suited to it, being inept at electrics and anything technical. I was therefore relieved when I was consigned to the flies. All this entailed was climbing up to the gantry high above the stage and pulling on the ropes to raise and lower the curtain or scenery when the red light turned green. Even I could manage that.

I was assigned to a production of *Pericles* and had not been paying much attention to the action as I sat on my stool up in the dark, conscientiously watching the red light. I was thinking I was much too talented to be obliged to do anything so menial as this, when I glanced casually down and saw that the stage was full of scantily-clad girls. There were so many would-be actresses at the Academy then and it was always a problem to find enough parts for them to be seen in. Unbeknown to me the director had decided to use a dozen of the more voluptuous ones in the brothel scene in Act IV. In a desperate effort to attract agents and producers most of the girls had made sure they were displaying plenty of bosom and thigh. From my viewpoint above I could see right down their cleavages. I was transfixed, mesmerised, awe-struck. My eyes went slowly from one girl to the next. They looked almost as good as the girls at the Palace Theatre, Camberwell. I forgot all about red and green lights. I did not even notice there was silence on the stage below or that the girls were looking even more embarrassed, until the actor playing Pericles came clambering up the iron stairs in a fury. The green light was flashing like a dervish: 'Drop the curtain, you bloody fool! They've got to change the scenery for Tarsus!'

I was extremely unpopular with all that cast, especially the ladies, for the remainder of the term. Thankfully for all concerned, I was never required to be Assistant Stage Manager again.

Cymbeline

'Cymbeline is for the most part stagy trash of the lowest melodramatic order, in parts abominably written, throughout intellectually vulgar and, judged in point of thought by modern intellectual standards, foolish, offensive, indecent and exasperating beyond all tolerance.'
George Bernard Shaw

Tattle: The play contains elements of the masque, with songs and special effects, including the most ambitious stage direction in the canon: '*Jupiter descends in thunder and lightning, sitting on an eagle. He throws a thunderbolt.*' Some hold that the Bard only wrote it to amuse himself. There are some hidden gems however, such as the evocative dirge:

'Golden lads and girls all must,
As chimney-sweepers, come to dust…'

It is one of my favourite passages in all Shakespeare. I can still remember Richard Burton's resonant, mournful voice reciting it on television following the Aberfan disaster, when coal sludge burst down the mountain and engulfed the village school. *Golden lads* and *chimney-sweepers* were Warwickshire names for dandelions. Surprisingly the bland Posthumus was one of David Garrick's favourite roles. His friend and mentor, Dr Johnson, refused to waste criticism upon 'such unresisting imbecility, upon faults too evident for detection, and too gross for aggravation.' The play achieved its greatest popularity in the nineteenth century. William Hazlitt and John Keats numbered it among their best-loved plays. Kean, Kemble, Macready, Phelps and Irving all staged lavish productions. Ellen Terry achieved incomparable success as the pure and chaste Imogen. She chose it as one of her last performances at the Lyceum in 1896. The usual suspects – including Peggy Ashcroft, Vanessa Redgrave, and Judi Dench – have followed her in more recent times.

Memories: My most abiding memory of this play is a sumptuous production at the Old Vic in the 1950s. I can remember being erotically aroused (mind you it didn't take a lot to arouse me then) when Iachimo, the excellent Derek Godfrey, clambered out of the trunk, lifted a sheet, and described a mole on the breast of the sleeping Imogen (Barbara Jefford). I couldn't see a thing – his acting and my imagination were enough. Now tits are flashed all over the place, actresses can't wait to get the poor things out, and nobody gives a damn. The wicked Queen, all in black – I think it was Coral Browne – came straight out of *Snow White*. The battle scenes were spectacular, with scarlet-cloaked Romans battling Ancient Britons – I can't recall any woad.

We did a few scenes from the play during my first year at RADA. I really fancied having a go at the oafish Cloten but was disappointed to be cast as Cymbeline. I must have been bad. It has been obliterated from my memory.

The Winter's Tale

'A play of two halves.'
Jimmy Hill? (1928 –)

Tattle: Shakespeare scorns geographical accuracy and chronological order, alluding to the Delphic oracle, Christian burial, an Emperor of Russia and an Italian painter of the sixteenth century. It has six songs, more than any other Shakespeare play. The aforementioned Simon Forman records seeing it at the Globe in the spring of 1611. He particularly liked Autolycus, who was probably played by Robert Armin. The play was presented at Court in February 1613, for the wedding of King James's daughter Elizabeth to Frederick, Count Palatine of the Rhine and briefly King of Bohemia. It is more than likely that Shakespeare re-wrote parts of the play to suit the occasion. Was Polixines originally king of another country – one that was not landlocked? Ironically Elizabeth would become known as the 'Winter Queen' because the couple lost their throne after that one short season, an event that precipitated the Thirty Years' War.

David Garrick cut the first half entirely, rewrote most of the second and renamed the play *Florizel and Perdita.* Mrs Robinson, who had been forced on the stage to pay off her husband's debts, made such an impression as Perdita in 1779, that the seventeen-year-old Prince of Wales (the future George IV) sent her love letters signing himself Florizel and offering her £20,000 to become his mistress. She succumbed after much persuasion, but the young bounder soon tired of her and never paid. His father, George III, eventually gave her £5000 for the return of the letters. (The Royal family has been attracted to actresses ever since Charles II clapped his eyes on Nell Gwynn. Who can really blame them? I've heard that one actress, of a certain age, claims to have slept with two direct generations of the House of Windsor.)

John Kemble went back to the original text and Hermione was the last Shakespearean role his sister, Sarah Siddons, created. It nearly finished her off. Standing on a pedestal, applying her immense concentration on being the statue, her flowing robes blew over some candles at the back of the stage. She failed to notice and was engulfed with flames before a plucky stagehand beat them out with his bare hands. One of Sir Henry Irving's early roles was the twenty-four-line part of Cleomenes. He had the actor's nightmare: he dried, froze with fright, and fled the stage to cat-calls.

Memories: In 1966 Frank Dunlop founded Pop Theatre, the precursor to the Young Vic, and offered me Florizel, in a production that was to be part of that year's official Edinburgh Festival. Florizel isn't the greatest of parts, but there was nothing else on the table apart from a horror film, and it sounded as if it might be fun. Frank had a unique talent for putting together exciting casts and he'd certainly done it this time. Leontes was to be played by the Hollywood star, Laurence Harvey; Perdita by Jane Asher, now fully grown and with Paul McCartney in tow, perhaps the most famous and envied young lady in the land. Pop star and comedian Jim Dale, who'd just written the No 1 hit song *Georgie Girl*, was to make his straight debut as Autolycus; Moira Redmond, a well-known face on television, was to be Hermione; and West End veterans Diana Churchill and Esmond Knight were cast as Paulina and Camillo. Way down the batting order was a deep-voiced chap with eyes like hard-boiled eggs, who'd been cultivating roses ever since he'd left drama school, having married the niece of Harry Wheatcroft, the famous horticulturalist. He had just separated from her and was struggling to get back into show business. Among his several small parts was that of the Bear. His name was Tom Baker.

We rehearsed in a seedy ballroom in Strutton Ground, Victoria, just around the corner from Chadwick Street Labour Exchange, where half of Equity used to sign on, but I must confess that throughout the four weeks we spent rehearsing my mind was mostly elsewhere. Graham Bateson, a genial Cambridge soccer Blue I'd met at a party, had somehow acquired the official rights of 'World Cup Willie', the little lion mascot of the 1966 World Cup. In those innocent days before 'marketing' had taken over everything, the entire commercial outlets of the World Cup were Graham's four small stalls along Wembley Way, where he sold an assortment of key-rings, pens and woolly toys. Graham recruited all the friends he had to help him sell the stuff – there was no payment involved, only a free top-price seat in the main stand for every game played at Wembley throughout the tournament. As England were based at Wembley it meant I saw every England game. So naturally I found it hard to concentrate purely on the play. I thought I would have plenty of time free as Florizel doesn't appear in the first half, and was therefore a trifle miffed when Frank asked me to play Archidamus, a Bohemian lord. He opens the play with a short exchange with Camillo but then has to remain on stage during the extraordinary long scene whilst Leontes becomes insane with jealousy. It also meant I would have to stick a beard on every night, something I've always hated doing. Bernard Shaw considered Leontes a magnificent part, worth fifty Othellos, but Othello has three acts of Iago's villainy to provoke his jealousy, Leontes does it cold. Laurence Harvey soon found how difficult it was. He didn't seem to get a lot of help from Frank, who was perhaps a little in awe of his star. We spent many a long, hot afternoon on that scene, with Esmond Knight and myself standing way at the back of the stage, murmuring to each other as actors are wont to do. Despite the difference in our ages, we got to know each other extremely well. It was the beginning of a long friendship.

Robert Stephens wrote in his memoirs that: 'Laurence Harvey was an appalling man, and even more unforgivably, an appalling actor.' I would disagree with Sir Bob on both points. Harvey was excellent in a part that suited him, you don't get Oscar and BAFTA nominations if you're completely useless; and I found him to be an extremely pleasant and generous man. I believe there was resentment in the higher echelons of the 'profession', that Harvey, born Zvi Mosheh Skikne, a Lithuanian Jew, should have married Margaret Leighton, one of England's most esteemed actresses, then dumped her to boot. Before that, whilst barely out of his teens, he'd lived with Hermione Baddeley, a popular character actress, more than twenty years his senior. She got her supporting actress Oscar nomination in *Room at the Top* for telling him on screen what a shit he was – it was said at the time she wasn't acting. But there was a sadness hanging over Harvey that summer, as if he sensed his days of international stardom were coming to an end. Indeed he'd just finished filming *The Spy with the Cold Nose*, opposite a dog! It must have been a let-down after Elizabeth Taylor, Jane Fonda and Barbara Stanwyck – I hope the dog wasn't a bitch. I also think he was already suffering from the stomach cancer that would kill him at the age of forty-five in 1973. He smoked incessantly from a long cigarette holder, drank copious amounts of his specially bottled Pouilly-Fume, though he hardly ate anything and sometimes had tears in his eyes from pain. In spite of this he was managing to conduct simultaneous affairs with Mrs Cohn, widow of Harry Cohn, boss of Columbia Pictures, one of the most powerful men in Hollywood, and Paulene Stone, a beautiful fashion model, one of the faces of the sixties. He ended up marrying both of them – he certainly packed a lot into his brief life.

Meanwhile England continued to progress through the various stages of the Cup. If you were a Chelsea supporter in those long, lean years before Abramovich, you were an engrained pessimist, and I was convinced that each game I attended, after dashing up from rehearsals in Victoria in my Mini, would be England's last. But they kept on managing to scrape through. One magic night I sat next to Jimmy Greaves as we both watched Bobby Charlton score a fantastic goal against Portugal and, against all my expectations, we had made it to the final against the old enemy, Germany. The biggest match in England's history would be played that Saturday. Tickets were as scarce as gold dust and being sought and exchanged at unbelievable prices, and I had one in the main stand. We were due in Edinburgh the following Monday, and Frank had said there would be no rehearsal on Saturday so that we could prepare for our move north. On the Friday the opening scenes went worse than ever and Laurence Harvey decided he wanted an extra day's rehearsal. I couldn't believe it. I would miss the final. I thought by then that I was some sort of talisman, and that Bobby Moore and the boys would lose if I wasn't there. I contemplated doing a 'sicky', but I've never done that, and besides it would have been too obvious. Reluctantly I gave my ticket to a friend, even though the bugger supported Arsenal, and made my reluctant way to Strutton Ground.

Nevertheless I celebrated England's amazing victory that Saturday night and drove up to Edinburgh with a heavy head on Sunday morning. Jim Dale had invited me to share a posh flat he'd rented just off Princes Street, which belonged to a dentist who was about to go on holiday with his family. Jim was not going up till Monday and I had to get the keys from them before they departed that evening. I had agreed to give a lift to an actress who was appearing in a show on the Fringe. Dora and I were going through one of our trial separations, and by the time we'd reached Rugby the lady and I agreed it would be a good idea to share accommodation. Jim had underlined that it was important that I made a good impression on the landlords as they were a very respectable family and were hesitant renting their home to irresponsible actors. I flogged the Mini very hard throughout the day and arrived at the agreed hour. The family were duly waiting, packed and anxious to leave for the airport. They were expecting Jim Dale, so in an effort to impress them with my respectability, I introduced myself with: 'I'm Jim's friend, David Weston, and this is my wife.' A look of shocked horror spread across the dentist's face. He lowered his voice and whispered in my ear: 'Your wife has just phoned you from London!'

It wasn't the best of starts and when the play opened a few days later, although I had several good notices, the one in the *Financial Times* will be forever engraved on my very soul: 'Jane Asher is not helped by her chubby Florizel.' I had missed England's triumph for that! Being an actor, I blamed the designer, Carl Toms, who insisted that I dyed my hair peroxide blonde and wore the briefest of Grecian tunics which barely reached my bum. There must be something about Florizel. Dinsdale Landen had played him at Stratford a few years before. Bernard Levin had rewarded him with: 'Last night Mr Landen as Florizel managed to destroy the magic of Bohemia in a minute, nay seconds.'

Although the critics were not very enthusiastic about Harvey's performance and the first half in general, Jim Dale's Autolycus won rave reviews and stole the show. Frank Dunlop was always happier directing comedy, and the long 'sheep-shearing' scene, one of the longest in Shakespeare, was another unforgettable 'Agincourt' moment. I can still hear Jim's delightful songs and see Tom Baker's popping eyes, as he danced like a giant stick-insect among the shepherds and shepherdesses. I wore a sort of haystack and, at Frank's insistence, spoke my tender vows of love to Perdita in a mock 'mummerset' accent. I don't think it really worked. After reading the notices Harvey suggested, I think half-jokingly, that as so many characters in the play are in disguise, Autolycus is really Leontes looking for his daughter, and that he should play both parts. In fact, Harvey would have made an excellent Autolycus: there was nothing precious about him. There were no showers or even wash-basins in the Assembly Hall of the Church of Scotland where we performed. He would stand in a bowl of tepid water, like the rest of us, and endeavour to wash off the body make-up we were all daubed in.

The whole job from this point onwards was a sheer delight. The apartment was extremely comfortable, I got on very well with Jim; my passenger turned out to be an excellent cook, causing Florizel to get even chubbier. We partied every night at the Festival Club, which in those days was a very exclusive establishment in the Assembly Rooms with not a Fringe show in sight. Indeed the only Fringe I attended was a late-night performance of a new play, *Rosencrantz and Guildenstern are Dead,* put on by Oxford University students and written by an unknown writer called Stoppard. I have to admit I fell asleep, but that may have been due to the hectic life I was living rather than the super-clever text. The engagement was extended when Harvey arranged for us to go to Venice and play at La Fenice, the most beautiful of theatres and a complete contrast to the dour Assembly Hall. It was a unique experience to arrive at the stage door by gondola and stand on that vast stage and see oneself reflected in the myriad of mirrors at the back of the boxes. Harvey treated the entire company to supper at an exclusive restaurant with walls covered by Picasso sketches and full of characters out of *La Dolce Vita.* I took Jane Asher to a more humble establishment where we shared the first pizza I had ever tasted. We never became very close. She's a lovely lady, but I've always found it hard to talk to her.

We came back to London and did a season at the Cambridge Theatre. I arranged a first night party on stage; Harvey could not attend because Mrs Cohn was in town. The party went on longer than expected and we ran out of wine. I was well into my cups and, feeling extremely generous, was certain Harvey would not mind if we borrowed a couple of cases from his dressing room. Someone brought them down and they were swiftly dispatched. We had a matinee the following day (there's nothing worse than a matinee after a first night) and I woke with a hangover, which got worse when I read the notices. They were especially bad for Harvey and I remembered we'd taken his wine. When I arrived at the theatre I went straight to his dressing-room and knocked at his door. He called me in. He was sitting at his dressing table, smoking from his long cigarette holder as he carefully applied mascara to his lashes.

'What can I do for you, dear boy?'

'Well, Larry, we ran out of wine at the party last night and we borrowed some of your wine.'

'Yes, I noticed a couple of cases had gone. You can only get it from Wheeler's in Old Compton Street. Just go in and ask for Mr Harvey's Pouilly Fume. You'd better take your cheque book.'

I made discreet enquiries and found out that Pouilly Fume was more than £4 a bottle. Some of the lower-paid cast members were on £15 a week – I was only on £50 – but that was a good salary in 1966. I went around the cast collecting contributions and the following day parked my Mini in Old Compton Street outside Wheeler's. There were no parking restrictions in Soho then. I went to the bar and asked for two cases of Mr Harvey's Pouilly Fume.

'Getting my wine are you? Make sure it's the Pouilly Fume 62.' I turned and beheld Harvey with Paulene Stone. He was delicately chewing a sliver of Dover sole 'You'd better join us for lunch now that you're here.'

I had a large plate of whitebait and a couple of glasses of Pouilly before I wrote a cheque and collected the two cases from the bar.

'Leave them in my dressing room, dear boy.'

That I duly did and when I returned to the theatre that night was surprised and touched to find that Harvey had gone round and left a bottle of Pouilly Fume with a personal note on the dressing place of everyone in the company. Mine said 'Thirsty Work, love Larry'. I've kept it till this day. Whatever his critics say, I think Laurence Harvey had class.

There was a further extension when Harvey arranged for the production to be filmed. It was in the very early days of video filming on tape, Harvey directed it himself. The end product wasn't good and has rarely seen the light of day. I read recently that Harvey's funeral in 1973 was sparsely attended. I for one would have been there if I'd known.

Shakespeare has Time, as Chorus, '*slide o'er sixteen years*' between the two halves of the play; it was nearly twenty before I was in it again. Frank Dunlop, who had never lost faith in me, was coming to the end of his tenure at the Young Vic. He'd invited the veteran Hugh Hunt, who had run the Old Vic after the war, to direct the play, and recommended me to him for Leontes. Hunt was a gentle and self-effacing man, despite being the brother of Lord Hunt, the conqueror of Everest, but he was out of tune with the current state of the theatre, having spent years in academia, establishing drama departments in Bristol and Manchester. Remembering Harvey's tribulations, I wasn't all that sure if I would make a good Leontes and was honest enough to tell Hunt. He was very perturbed at this, and asked me if I would like to play anything else. Fondly remembering Esmond Knight's performance I opted for Camillo. Frank Dunlop was furious with me – he couldn't understand why I'd turned Leontes down. Looking back I can't really understand it myself. Bernard Shaw for one would have thought me insane. I should have gone for it. I was rarely offered leading parts after that. But it was not a good production, Hunt had been away too long.

I tried to get the darkness of Camillo, which Esmond had found; there is something sinister about him for Leontes to suppose he will poison Polixenes. I wasn't very good – but neither was the actor who played Leontes. Oh, and I also played the Bear. I was the only one free at the time. It was the same bear that Hofmeister had been using on a long-running television advert. I staggered on stage each night to hoots of recognition. It was the highlight of my evening.

The Tempest

'The last work of a mighty workman.'
Henry Norman Hudson (1814-86)

Tattle: The exact date of the first performance is uncertain, but Shakespeare's imagination is thought to have been fired by the 1609 wreck of *The Sea Venture* on the supposedly inhospitable Bermuda Islands. The crew survived quite comfortably for several months before they repaired their ship and sailed on to Virginia. Their story was published in 1610 and the Revels Accounts list the play as being acted at Court by the King's Men in November 1611. That fact alone puts it beyond the Earl of Oxford's pen as he died in 1604. *The Tempest* was not printed until the 1623 Folio, where it appears as the first of the comedies and is therefore the first play in the book. In 1667 Sir William Davenant and Dryden adapted it under the title *The Enchanted Island*, giving Miranda and Caliban sisters called Dorinda and Sycorax. This became one of the most popular plays of the Restoration. It was later adapted into an opera by Thomas Shadwell which was performed throughout the eighteenth century. Macready was the first to revert back to Shakespeare's original. It was not immediately popular. Even Charles Lamb didn't like it: 'To have the conjuror brought before us in his conjuring gown, with his spirits about him involves such a quantity of the hateful-incredible, that all our reverence for the author cannot hinder us from perceiving such gross attempts upon the senses to be in the highest degree childish and inefficient.'

Prospero is a safe role for ageing actors; perhaps Ralph Richardson was too young in 1938. His friend John Gielgud came backstage and declared, 'I think I hated you more in the first half than in the second.' An aggrieved Richardson asked why? Gielgud replied with a typical faux pas, 'Because there was more of you in the first half.' In these final plays Shakespeare has rediscovered his skill at creating innocent, enchanting young girls, but his young men are a hopeless lot: Ferdinand is an even sloppier juvenile than Florizel. It was one of Richard Burton's first roles at Stratford and even he failed to make much of an impression, declaring: 'Ferdinand is an unplayable role – if you happen to be rather shortish as I am, tottering about, with nothing to say of any real moment. He is bloodless, liverless, kidney-less, a useless member of the human race.' Next time he was in the play at the Old Vic, he sensibly chose to play Caliban, but even then he was not an unqualified success. *The Sunday Express* deemed that he looked like a miner with a tail coming up from a coal face.

Memories: I first saw this play at Drury Lane in the late fifties, incidentally the last time Shakespeare was performed in that vast theatre. The young, avant-garde Peter Brook directed, as well as designing the sets and costumes and composing a musique-concrete score. John Gielgud, still at the height of his powers, was Prospero, which he had played to great acclaim in previous productions. Although Tynan wrote that Gielgud was 'the finest actor, from the neck up, in the world today,' other critics were not so kind with the production. The long defunct *Star* pronounced: 'No doubt with the object of appealing to the modern child, Mr Brook has given the enchanted island a space age touch. A sputnik moon hangs in the sky, the goddess Juno arrives by spaceship and Shakespeare's opening "sweet airs" are like the sound track of a science fiction film with an X certificate. It all adds up to a rather superior Panto. But it is rather hard on the Bard.' I must admit to being unimpressed, but then I was a drama student at the time and they tend to look down their noses at everything.

I appeared in *The Tempest* late in my stuttering career. The RSC offered me Alonso in a touring version that was scheduled to play in the round in sports halls and other places where Shakespeare was not usually seen. As well as Gateshead, Cleveland, Ellesmere Port and Telford, more exotic and attractive dates were scheduled in Japan and the Far East. I thought it was a dream job especially when Ken Farrington, my old schoolmate and long-time friend, was cast as Gonzalo.

It went wrong from the start. The director, David Thacker, very good at modern, political plays, had no feeling for the magic. You always know a production is in trouble when actors get fired, and Ariel was replaced at the end of the first week. I never found out why, I thought she was the best thing in it. Prospero, a favoured member of the RSC, wanted to quit a week later – Adrian Noble literally had to beg him to stay. Some strange lady, I think a friend of the director, was engaged to make us move in a special way. We spent agonising hours lying on a dirty floor in a very depressing hall in Clapham. It soon became obvious that Thacker had given up. His one note to me was: 'Be natural. I want to see David.' I pointed out that David was not a shipwrecked king, mourning the loss of his only son, on an enchanted island. We'd got on well before but I never worked for him again.

I knew my costume was wrong as soon as I saw the design, especially the shoes with red high heels and white stockings. Olivier famously said somewhere that you can't act unless your feet are right. Alonso is at sea – he would wear sea-boots. As it was I tottered around on wobbly heels with socks that refused to stay up, which was hardly regal. We opened at the Young Vic, before it was air-conditioned, in a heat wave. When you play in the round you observe the audience with great clarity. There's nowhere to hide – the buggers are all around you. I lay on the stage in a supposed enchanted sleep and watched the reaction of the critics through half-closed eyes. It was worse than that scene in *The Producers*. A shirtless Nicholas de Jongh rubbed ice-cubes on his chest with a look of horror on his face; dear Michael Billington suffered but still managed to smile beatifically, whilst my friend Sheridan Morley snored gently behind him. To my mind, there was not an edifying thing in the entire production. The comics were not funny, the lovers were not attractive, the Alonso plot as boring as ever. The ethereal Ariel ended up by being played by a large Scandinavian girl whom I've never heard of since. For some reason the director had cast two elderly ladies to play the Goddesses – one of them was a leading amateur from Bolton. I couldn't understand why she was there representing the RSC, reputedly one of the most prestigious professional companies on the planet.

Within days of our opening the Far Eastern part of the tour was cancelled, to be replaced by further dates in the North of England. The furthest east we got was a week in Warsaw – where a reception was held in our honour at which even the British Ambassador seemed embarrassed. Caliban was played by a very talented but highly eccentric actor, who insisted on living in a tent throughout the entire British part of the tour. It was a very cold winter but he stuck it to the bitter end. I'm not sure what substance he used to keep himself warm; I don't think he got much sleep. He spent the first twenty minutes of the play on stage in a trunk, only emerging on Prospero's line – '*What, ho! slave! Caliban! Thou earth, thou! speak!*' On more than one occasion there was utter silence. Caliban, enjoying unaccustomed warmth and comfort, was fast asleep and only reluctantly emerged after Prospero had viciously kicked the trunk.

At least I had that old devil Ken Farrington with me. We shared digs each week as we had in Manchester all those years before. But this time there were no girls and gaudy nights. We got back from the sports hall or wherever the RSC had booked us, cooked each other meals and watched TV like a happily married couple. Ken was responsible for my most poignant memory of the tour. When we got to Stratford we played a couple of weeks in a proper theatre, the Swan. We had just finished a matinee when a message came over the Tannoy: 'Mr Farrington. There's a lady to see you at the stage door.' He returned a few minutes later a changed man. The irascible, wise-cracking Farrington was visibly shaken. In true Shakespearean fashion he had just met a daughter he'd never seen before. As he spoke I remembered the story, a youthful indiscretion, and the shame of having an illegitimate child in those days before abortion on demand. The girl had married another admirer and gone to Australia. The daughter, now in her late thirties, had watched her father through the years as Billy Walker in *Coronation Street*. She had come to Stratford as a tourist and by chance had seen his name outside the theatre. She came back to our cottage that evening. Their reconciliation was as touching as that of Lear and Cordelia.

Henry VIII (All is True)

'Shakespeare stands by himself alone in Heaven as the greatest writer in any language in any country in any time in the history of the world.'
Jack Kerouac (1922-1969)

Tattle: It is a sprawling chronicle, most of which was probably written by John Fletcher, with only four really good scenes: the downfalls of Buckingham and Wolsey, and the trial and death of Katharine of Aragon. Henry is an enigmatic figure; it would have been dangerous for Shakespeare, or whoever he wrote it with, to have portrayed him as anything else. Katharine of Aragon is treated very sympathetically, possibly because King James wanted peace with Spain. It was first performed at the Globe on 29 June 1613, when cannon fire called for in Act I, Scene 4 (line 47) ignited the thatching on the roof and the famous theatre burnt to the ground. There were no fatalities although one poor chap's breeches caught alight and were only extinguished by a bottle of ale. It was later played at Blackfriars, in the great chamber where events in the play actually took place. It achieved its greatest popularity in the nineteenth century with spectacular productions by Charles Kean and Henry Irving. Wolsey was considered to be one of Irving's finest characterisations. Katharine is one of the few great roles Shakespeare wrote for older actresses. Ellen Terry, Edith Evans and Peggy Ashcroft have all duly triumphed. Charles Laughton played Henry at Sadler's Wells in 1933 under the auspices of Lilian Bayliss. James Agate wasn't impressed: 'Mr Laughton came to Sadler's Wells with all his blushing film vulgarities upon him.' Sir Tyrone Guthrie did a famous production at Stratford in 1949 with Gielgud as Wolsey and Anthony Quayle as the King. Trevor Nunn put his stamp on it twenty years later, with Donald Sinden as Henry and Peggy Ashcroft as Katharine.

Memories: Most actors have never even seen this play – I must be one of an extremely small number who have been in it twice. In 1998 the budget cuts affecting minor members of the Royal Family had forced the Duke of Gloucester to give up his country home at Barnwell Manor, in Northamptonshire. The lease was taken over by an antique dealer with the intention of using it to display his furniture. A chance encounter with Robert Hardy persuaded him to mount a Shakespearean production in the magnificent ruined castle in the grounds. Open-air Shakespeare in the English summer is extremely ambitious at the best of times, especially from scratch. It became even more of a financial risk when Robert elected to direct the relatively unknown *Henry VIII*. Robert had had his first job in Tyrone Guthrie's legendary production and had loved the play ever since.

He offered me Wolsey and I accepted at once. It was a most unusual engagement. The play has a huge cast – forty-three speaking parts. The plan was to have a nucleus of eight professionals in the main roles, the support being given by local amateurs. Because of the remote location the leading actors would be given accommodation and food at Barnwell Manor throughout rehearsals and the run. I was assigned the Duke's en-suite bedroom at the top of a tower. It still had the bomb-proof doors and panic buttons that MI5 had installed during the IRA threat, when there had been fears that the Duke was a kidnap target. One night Dora came down to keep me company. She woke horrified in the morning to find herself covered in little red bites. The Duke's bed was full of bugs. I couldn't understand why they hadn't bitten me. Perhaps they were used to blue blood and Dora's was more aristocratic than mine? But Robert Hardy, lodged in the Duchess's quarters, with quite a bit of blue blood in his veins, also escaped bug-free. They may have been deterred by his cases of excellent wine, which we all enjoyed every night over dinner and long after, discussing the play and talking of times past and friends departed. Notwithstanding the bugs it was an idyllic time.

Our boss, the antique dealer, proudly announced that he had engaged a leading film costumier to do the costumes. The man knew a lot about costumes but had little idea of the finances of theatre. Every day fresh hampers of expensive costumes would arrive with *ANNE OF A THOUSAND DAYS* or *CARRY ON HENRY* sewn inside. I was very relieved that my Wolsey robes bore the name of Anthony Quayle rather than Terry Scott. More and more villagers and country folk were engaged to wear all the finery. The play opened with a veritable parade. One advantage of using lots of people is that they will sell many tickets to their friends. I'm not sure if our cast had many friends, or if all their friends were already in the cast, but the vast auditorium never seemed to be more than half-full. On top of that it rained practically every night throughout the run.

It was the last major Shakespearean role I was to play. I was so grateful that I got one last chance. There is something mystical about playing the great parts, and Wolsey is a great part. Some nights you can almost feel Shakespeare flowing through your veins. Tim had given me the right thoughts and pointed me the right way. Wolsey is no namby-pamby priest or aristocrat, but the son of an Ipswich butcher. His fall was one of the most thrilling scenes I've ever played. He is proud, a savage dog at bay, then humiliated and pitiful. Robert and I discovered a wonderful moment in the final speech – Wolsey finds God again – he almost preaches a sermon. The play runs for another act after Wolsey's demise. I would retire feeling very satisfied to my room in the tower, drink a glass or two of Robert's wine and watch from above.

We had hoped that Shakespeare would become an annual event at Barnwell until the bill for the costumes arrived. It killed the enterprise stone dead.

In 2006 the RSC invited Greg Thompson, who had won a reputation for doing obscure and neglected old plays in the most unlikely locations, to direct *Henry VIII* as part of the *Complete Works Festival.* Greg believed that in this play Shakespeare held a delicate balance between Roman Catholicism and the newly founded Church of England. It could easily have been a staunchly anti-Catholic play, but Katharine is the most sympathetic character, whilst Cranmer is depicted as the most honourable man. Greg believed that Holy Trinity, Stratford, the old church which had nurtured both religions, and where Shakespeare himself was baptised and buried, was the ideal place to perform it. I was offered the Chorus and Sir Thomas Lovell, a bit of a come-down after Wolsey, but even though he had frizzy long hair down to his shoulders, I liked Greg when I met him, so I swallowed my pride and accepted.

At first I felt like a fish out of water. Practically all the company had worked with Greg before and were used to his way of working; we hardly did any acting for the first week. To my dismay there was a lot of singing and movement. To make matters worse, he had this awful idea of making all the spare men play Anne Bullen's ladies-in-waiting in Act II, Scene III. This is a charming little scene, which I'd never really noticed before, between Anne and a slightly bawdy old lady, who comments on her marriage prospects. Greg split the old lady's lines between half a dozen of us. We had to put on gowns and wimples, with no attempt to disguise our beards, and sew. We were even given sewing lessons. I've never been so embarrassed on stage in my life, but Greg has this strange magic – the audience loved it.

The play took on an ethereal quality in the church. I did the opening chorus, with the setting sun casting a myriad of colours through the stained glass windows, standing on Shakespeare's very bones. When I began with: *'I come no more to make you laugh…'* I almost felt the old boy stirring in the ground beneath me. The audience was arranged along the nave in opposing ranks of raked seating and we performed in the narrow aisle between them. We had to make entrances and exits by going out of the church and hustling through the graveyard as the Avon twinkled in the moonlight. I made one very dramatic entrance, pounding on the great west door until it was thrown open. Greg introduced stately and triumphant music, chants and singing, he even used the pipe organ; but the highlight of the evening was the christening of Princess Elizabeth in Act V. A local red-haired baby girl was cast as the future Queen. She seemed to love the attention and never cried when Cranmer applied water from the ancient font as the church bells rang out and through the open doors fireworks flashed in the starry sky. Everyone, especially Michael Billington, was entranced. Apart from the world tour of *Lear* the following year it would be my final appearance in any Shakespeare play. Not a bad one to go out on.

Afterthoughts

'Shakespeare we have always with us: actors we have only for a few seasons.' … William Hazlitt

I am one of a shrinking band of elderly actors and actresses that have a lifetime's knowledge of Shakespeare going to waste. I once suggested at a public discussion that there should be some sort of network set up where people like me could visit schools and talk about particular plays. The renowned scholar, Professor Stanley Wells, was present and shook his head in what I took to be disdainful disapproval. Nevertheless I have since tramped around and given the message to any educational establishment or club that wanted me.

I was very relieved when neither of my sons wanted to become an actor (one is a hard-nosed City lawyer who tells me I have never done a proper day's work in my life). As I've said before, it's so much harder to get work and even more economically perilous than when I started over half a century ago. The reps, good or bad, where we learnt our trade, have gone and have been replaced by non-paid Fringe. Multi-channel TV has failed to provide more work for the majority, and has managed to destroy the repeat fees which used to be their bread and butter. Accountants rule – everything is done quickly – a couple of weeks' filming is done in a day.

But there is a greater pain than financial anxiety. As that fine actor and writer, Michael Simkins, put it so eloquently recently in *The Guardian*: 'The cruellest aspect of the acting business is not that it's unfair, but that it's merely indifferent. It gives everything to some and nothing to others; talent, ambition and virtue have little to do with it. What's more, with no qualifications or tests to assess how good (or bad) you are, the only benchmark is success. Anxiety is thus your daily companion: you cannot escape the drudgery of comparing yourself with your peers.'

But I have no regrets. I have travelled the world, made dear and lasting friends, and spent more than my fair share of time with the greatest playwright that ever lived. Perhaps I would have been more successful if I had pushed harder, but on the other hand maybe I went as high as my talent warranted.

I remember an old actor once telling me: 'It's not how high, but how far you go.' I think I stayed the course.

Synopses

The First Part of King Henry the Sixth

Plot: The play opens in 1422 with the death of Henry V, swiftly followed by news of English defeats as the French seek to reconquer lost territories. A distinctly shop-soiled Joan of Arc relieves Orleans; the valiant Talbot is killed. Joan in turn is captured and burnt. In England there is friction between the young King's uncle, Humphrey, Duke of Gloucester and his great-uncle, the future Cardinal Beaufort. Then, in a quarrel in the Temple Garden, the followers of Richard Plantagenet, Duke of York, pluck a white rose for their emblem, whilst the followers of the Duke of Somerset, another member of the Beaufort clan, choose red: planting the seeds of the Wars of the Roses. The play ends in 1444 when the ambitious Duke of Suffolk goes to France and is enamoured by Margaret, the daughter of the lowly Count of Anjou. He brings her back to marry the young King.

The Second Part of King Henry the Sixth *(The First Part of the Contention betwixt the Two Famous Houses of York and Lancaster)*

Plot: The Duke of York strives to increase his influence but is opposed by the Beaufort clan. Both seek to usurp the power of the Protector, Humphrey of Gloucester. Margaret, the Queen, is another centre of intrigue. Her lover, Suffolk, is eventually banished and beheaded by pirates. Humphrey's wife dabbles in witchcraft and is disgraced. Humphrey himself is accused of treason and found dead. Cardinal Beaufort in turn dies, raving out a confession for Gloucester's murder. Jack Cade leads a bloody revolt of the common people, swearing famously, among other things, to kill all the lawyers, before he is killed himself. The Wars of the Roses begin in 1455, when York and his followers, Warwick and Salisbury, defeat the King's army at the battle of St Albans. York's sons Edward and Richard make their first appearances.

The Third Part of King Henry the Sixth

(*The True Tragedy of Richard Duke of York and the Good King Henry the Sixth*)

Plot: Henry, ignoring his own son, weakly concedes that Richard Duke of York has the right to succeed him on the throne. Margaret now leads the Lancastrian cause, and defeats and kills York at the battle of Wakefield. York's sons and Warwick continue the struggle. It is Henry's turn to be defeated and he flees to Scotland. Warwick proclaims Edward King. Henry returns from exile and is taken prisoner. Warwick goes to France to negotiate a marriage between Edward and the sister of the French king. In Warwick's absence Edward meets a pretty widow, Elizabeth Woodville, and marries her instead. Warwick, furious, changes sides, returns to England, releases Henry and restores him to the throne. Edward and Richard continue the struggle, and Warwick is finally defeated and killed at the Battle of Barnet. Richard murders the hapless Henry in the Tower.

Titus Andronicus

Plot: To celebrate his triumph over Tamora, Queen of the Goths, Titus, a Roman general, sacrifices one of her sons. Tamora is taken as wife by the Emperor Saturninus and then contrives, with her paramour, Aaron the Moor, to have two of Titus's sons beheaded and his daughter, Lavinia, raped and mutilated. Titus retaliates by slaying Tamora's remaining sons and serving them up to her at a banquet, baked in a pie, not revealing what is on the menu until Tamora has finished the main course. Definitely not kosher. Titus then kills Tamora. Titus is himself killed by Saturninus, who is in turn killed by Titus's remaining son Lucius.

The Two Gentlemen of Verona

Plot: Two friends, Valentine and Proteus, visit Milan accompanied by their servants, Speed and Launce. Both gents fall in love with Silvia, daughter of the Duke, although she is already pledged to the foolish Thurio. Proteus's former lover, Julia, follows him disguised as a boy, and becomes his page. Proteus treacherously induces the Duke to banish Valentine. He becomes leader of a band of brigands, who take Silvia by force. Julia leads the Duke, Proteus and Thurio to Silvia, but Thurio proves himself a coward. The Duke gives Silvia to Valentine, and Proteus, discovering Julia's true identity, falls in love with her again.

The Comedy of Errors

Plot: Twin brothers, both named Antipholus, with their twin servants, both named Dromio, are shipwrecked in infancy. They are rescued and brought up separately in Syracuse and Ephesus. Years later their father, Aegeon, searching for his son in Ephesus, is arrested as an alien. Antipholus of Syracuse also arrives in Ephesus with his servant Dromio and there follows a series of hilarious situations of mistaken identity, not least with Adriana, wife of the Ephesian Antipholus. It is only resolved by the late appearance of an abbess who turns out to be Aegeon's long-lost wife and mother of the Antipholus twins. A family is thus restored and lost children found – one of the Bard's favourite themes.

The Taming of the Shrew

Plot: It is a play within a play. Christopher Sly, a tinker, is found dead drunk by a wealthy lord, who dresses him in fine clothes, and assures him when he wakes that he is a nobleman who has been out of his wits. The play proper is then performed for his entertainment. Bianca, the sweet daughter of Baptista, is courted by Hortensio, the old but wealthy Gremio, and young Lucentio. Baptista insists that his eldest daughter, Katharina, known by her fiery temper and waspish tongue as the shrew, must be married first. Petruchio arrives with his servant Grumio, looking for a wealthy wife, and undertakes to woo Katharina. The wooing is long and brutal but she is eventually tamed. Lucentio wins Bianca and Hortensio consoles himself with a widow.

The Tragedy of King Richard the Third

Plot: Richard, the crookback Duke of Gloucester, wades through slaughter to the throne and ultimate destruction. The Duke of Clarence, Lord Hastings, the boy king Edward V and his little brother are all dispatched remorselessly along with many others. Richard triumphs over his physical deformity and evil reputation when he woos and wins Lady Anne, the widow of the dead son of Henry VI, whom he had murdered. Finally, on his becoming king, the Duke of Buckingham, Richard's main accomplice, turns against him, but is captured and executed. Richard poisons Anne and plans to marry the sister of the murdered little princes. Richard is defeated and slain by Henry Tudor at Bosworth, after Stanley, Earl of Derby, changes sides in the middle of the battle.

Love's Labour's Lost

Plot: The King of Navarre and three lordly friends swear to forsake the company of women for three years and devote themselves to books. The Princess of France arrives with her three ladies and the young men promptly fall in love. It abounds with rich characters such as Don Armado, Holofernes, Costard and Boyet. The climax is a play within the play, an early try-out for *A Midsummer Night's Dream*, when the local villagers stage a pageant to entertain the King and his guests. This last scene of 942 lines is the longest in all Shakespeare. The mood is abruptly broken by the arrival of a messenger with news of the death of the King of France. The ladies depart; Navarre and his friends swear to live like hermits for a year to prove their love.

Romeo and Juliet

Plot: Two noble families of Verona, the Montagues and the Capulets, are engaged in an ancient feud. Old Capulet gives a party which Romeo gate-crashes with his friends Mercutio and Benvolio. Romeo meets Capulet's young daughter, Juliet, and they instantly fall in love. Later that night Romeo climbs into her garden and sees her on the balcony of her bedroom. They exchange vows, and with the connivance of Juliet's old nurse, are secretly married the next day by Friar Lawrence. In the market place Mercutio is forced into a fight by Juliet's fiery cousin, Tybalt. Romeo tries to part them but Mercutio is stabbed by Tybalt under Romeo's arm. Mercutio dies and Romeo, in his fury, kills Tybalt. He is banished by the Duke and after one secret night with his bride flees to Mantua. Meanwhile old Capulet has arranged for Juliet to marry the Duke's kinsman, Paris. To prevent this, Friar Lawrence gives Juliet a drug that brings about a death-like trance, and sends for Romeo to come and carry her off when she is in the family crypt. The Friar's message fails to arrive, and Romeo, hearing of Juliet's supposed death, comes secretly to break into her tomb. He kills Paris when he tries to prevent him, then takes poison and dies by Juliet's side. She wakes, finds dead Romeo and stabs herself. The death of the two lovers brings about the reconciliation of the two opposing families.

The Tragedy of King Richard the Second

Plot: Covers the last two years of Richard's reign from 1398 to 1400. It opens with the furious quarrel between Richard's cousin, Henry Bolingbroke, and Thomas Mowbray. Each accuses the other of treason and Richard orders them to decide the matter by single combat in the lists at Coventry. Just as they are about to commence, Richard stops the contest and banishes both. On the death of Bolingbroke's father, John of Gaunt, Richard seizes the Lancastrian estates. Richard goes to Ireland, leaving the governance to his ineffectual uncle, the Duke of York. Bolingbroke returns to claim his inheritance, and with the aid of Northumberland and his son, Harry Percy, gains control of the realm. Richard returns but is deposed and is imprisoned in Pomfret Castle where he is murdered.

A Midsummer Night's Dream

Plot: Theseus, Duke of Athens, orders entertainments for his forthcoming marriage to Hippolyta, Queen of the Amazons. Egeus comes to Theseus and begs him to invoke an ancient law. His daughter Hermia has renounced Demetrius, whom Egeus favours, for Lysander. Theseus reluctantly rules that Hermia must obey her father or choose between a convent and death. Hermia and Lysander decide to elope that night, but tell Helena, who is in love with Demetrius. Helena, in an effort to win Demetrius's affection tells him, and all four lovers venture into the forest. Meanwhile Bottom, a weaver, and his five friends, also go into the forest to rehearse a play that they hope to perform before the Duke. In the forest Oberon, King of the Fairies, and Titania, his Queen have quarrelled. Oberon orders his servant, Puck, to gather a plant and squeeze the juice of it into Titania's eyes whilst she sleeps. She will then fall in love with the first thing she sees when she awakes. Puck transforms Bottom into an ass, with whom Titania falls violently in love. Demetrius is also given an eyeful, before he wakes up and falls back in love with Helena. There is frantic chasing and misunderstanding throughout the forest, before Oberon and Puck rectify all. The four lovers are married alongside Theseus and Hippolyta, and a fully restored Bottom and his crew perform a riotous play at the wedding feast.

The Merchant of Venice

Plot: Antonio, a Venetian merchant, seeks to borrow money from Shylock, a wealthy Jew, so that his young friend, Bassanio, can voyage to Belmont and woo Portia, a wealthy heiress. Shylock lends the money on the agreement that if Antonio fails to repay the loan on time, he will forfeit a pound of flesh. Portia's hand is promised to whatever suitor makes the right choice of three caskets – the Princes of Morocco and Arragon fail, but Bassanio succeeds. His friend, Gratiano, also succeeds in wooing Portia's maid, Nerissa. As they share each other's happiness news arrives that Antonio's ventures have all failed and that Shylock, enraged by his daughter's elopement with Bassanio's friend, Lorenzo, is demanding his pound of flesh. Bassanio hurries back to Venice with gold to repay the loan, which Shylock refuses to accept. Portia, disguised as a lawyer, after consulting a learned advocate, intervenes in the trial presided over by the Duke of Venice, and saves Antonio's life. Shylock forfeits most of his fortune and is ordered to become a Christian.

The Life and Death of King John

Plot: The play covers sixteen years and mixes the historical order of events, although there is no mention of Magna Carta, the most remarkable event of John's reign. John, a devious, complex character, usurps the throne from his nephew, Arthur, who is supported by King Philip of France, his mother Constance, and the Bastard Faulconbridge, the most attractive character in the play. The Pope sends his double-talking legate, Cardinal Pandulph, to mediate but war breaks out. John eventually captures Arthur and orders Hubert de Burgh to kill him. Arthur pleads for his life and Hubert relents, but the boy is killed when he jumps from a castle wall trying to escape. The French invade and are defeated but John, the anti-hero, dies by poison. The play ends with an extremely patriotic speech by the Bastard.

The First Part of King Henry the Fourth

Plot: Covers the rebellion of the fiery Hotspur (Harry Percy). He is contrasted with Hal, the self-indulgent Prince of Wales, who seems to waste his time drinking and revelling at the Boar's Head Tavern with the dissolute fat knight, Falstaff. Hal is estranged from his father, Bolingbroke, now King Henry IV, but at the battle of Shrewsbury redeems himself by slaying Hotspur in single combat, then allows Falstaff to claim the credit.

The Second Part of King Henry the Fourth

Plot: Hotspur's father, old Northumberland, and the Archbishop of York continue the rebellion. Falstaff endeavours to play the victorious soldier in London, spends more time in the Boar's Head with Doll Tearsheet and the bombastic Pistol, before making a slow progress towards the rebels, recruiting a motley collection of soldiers from his old acquaintance, Justice Shallow. Hal's brother, Prince John, quashes the rebellion by treachery. The old king is eventually reconciled with Hal on his deathbed. Hal becomes King Henry V and rejects Falstaff.

The Life of King Henry the Fifth

Plot: Contrary to all expectations Henry is proving a just king and to prevent further rebellion follows his father's advice and 'busies giddy minds with foreign quarrels.' He reopens the war with France and claims the French crown. Falstaff, contrary to Shakespeare's promise at the end of *Henry IV Part Two*, does not accompany him but dies of a broken heart in the Boar's Head. Henry crosses to France and after a lengthy siege captures Harfleur, then begins a long march to Calais. The comic relief is now supplied by Pistol, Bardolph and the Welsh captain, Fluellen (Fluellen was the name of a Stratford citizen). Against all odds Henry wins his great victory at Agincourt, makes peace and marries the French princess, Katharine. Each act begins with a speech by the Chorus, containing much of the best poetry in the play.

The Merry Wives of Windsor

Plot: Falstaff suffering from his usual 'consumption of the purse' woos Mistresses Ford and Page, the wives of two wealthy citizens of Windsor, in the hope of extracting money from them. Doctor Caius and Slender pursue Page's daughter, Anne, for her dowry, but she is in love with Fenton, a young courtier. Mistresses Page and Ford plot to punish Falstaff and send him mock love letters which the jealous Mr Ford intercepts. Falstaff ends up humiliated after hiding in a laundry basket, being tossed in the Thames, and chased in drag by children pretending to be fairies. Ford is cured of his jealousy and Fenton marries Anne.

Much Ado About Nothing

Plot: Don Pedro, Prince of Arragon, and his companions, Benedick and Claudio, return to Messina victorious from war. They are welcomed by Leonato, Governor of the city. Don Pedro's bastard brother, Don John, plots mischief. Claudio falls in love with Leonato's daughter, Hero, and their marriage is arranged. Benedick, who has declared himself an eternal bachelor, is tricked into recognising his love for Beatrice, Leonato's niece. A similar ruse ignites Beatrice's passion for Benedick. Don John deceives Claudio into believing Hero is a whore and he denounces her at the altar. There is much ado about nothing, with comic relief from Constable Dogberry and the watch, before all is resolved in the final scene.

As You Like It

Plot: Rosalind's father, the Duke, has been usurped by his younger brother, Frederick, and taken refuge in the Forest of Arden with the cynical Jaques and other loyal companions. Rosalind sees Orlando win a wrestling match and falls in love with him. She disguises herself as a boy, calls herself Ganymede, and goes into the forest to seek her father, accompanied by her cousin, Celia (Frederick's daughter) and Touchstone, the jester. Orlando quarrels with his bad brother, Oliver, and also escapes to the forest. The exiles meet local shepherds and a happy ending is finally achieved with Rosalind marrying Orlando, Celia marrying Oliver, and the good Duke restored.

Twelfth Night; or, What You Will

Plot: Viola and her twin brother Sebastian are shipwrecked off the coast of Illyria, each believing the other to be drowned. Viola disguises herself as a boy, calls herself Cesario and becomes a page to Duke Orsino. Orsino sends Cesario to woo the lady Olivia on his behalf, but Olivia falls in love with Cesario. Olivia's rascally uncle, Sir Toby Belch, and the forlorn Sir Andrew Aguecheek, together with Maria, Olivia's waiting woman, plot against Malvolio, the bumptious steward. Sebastian arrives in Illyria; Olivia mistakes him for Cesario and marries him. Malvolio is cruelly tricked before Viola reveals herself and marries Orsino.

Julius Caesar

Plot: Caesar returns to Rome in triumph after defeating his rival, Pompey. Mark Antony publicly offers Caesar a crown, which he reluctantly refuses. Cassius persuades the high-minded Brutus to join a conspiracy to assassinate Caesar to prevent him becoming all-powerful. The conspirators kill Caesar in the Senate, then overruling Cassius's objections, Brutus not only spares Antony's life, but allows him to deliver a funeral oration. Antony, in one of Shakespeare's greatest passages, inflames the mob and Brutus and his supporters are forced to flee Rome. Antony, young Octavius, Caesar's nephew, and the ineffectual Lepidus form a triumvirate and wage war against Brutus and Cassius. The conspirators are finally defeated at Philippi where Brutus and Cassius both die by their own hands.

Hamlet, Prince of Denmark

Plot: Old Hamlet, King of Denmark, dies suddenly in his orchard. The succession is decided by election and his brother Claudius becomes king and hastily marries Gertrude, Hamlet's widow. Prince Hamlet and Horatio, his loyal friend from university, see the old king's ghost stalking the battlements of Elsinore. The ghost tells his son that he has been murdered by his brother. Hamlet swears revenge but is uncertain which course he should follow. Claudius and Gertrude are concerned by his strange behaviour. Polonius, the aged Chief Minister, believes Hamlet has become mad because of his infatuation with his daughter, Ophelia. Claudius and Polonius spy on a meeting between Ophelia and Hamlet, but Hamlet senses she is also in the plot and violently rejects her. A troupe of travelling players come to Elsinore and Hamlet has them perform a play in which a king is murdered by his brother. Claudius reveals his guilt whilst watching. Hamlet is now finally convinced and visits his mother and accuses her of betraying his father. In his anger he mistakes Polonius, eavesdropping behind a curtain, for Claudius and kills him. Claudius sends Hamlet to England, accompanied by two false friends, Rosencrantz and Guildenstern, with orders to have him killed. Polonius's son, Laertes, returns from France seeking to avenge his father's death, to find that his sister, Ophelia, has gone mad with grief. She then kills herself by drowning. Hearing that Hamlet has escaped his plans and has returned to Denmark, Claudius plots with Laertes to kill his nephew in a fencing match with an envenomed rapier and a cup of poison. Hamlet comes back to Elsinore, calmer and resigned, and after a scene with the gravediggers professes his love for the dead Ophelia. An extravagant courtier, Osric, arranges the duel before the court. Hamlet is cut by the poisoned foil then exchanges weapons. Laertes is wounded and after begging Hamlet's forgiveness dies. Gertrude drinks from the poisoned cup intended for Hamlet. Hamlet finally kills Claudius before he too dies in Horatio's arms. The play ends with Fortinbras, Prince of Norway, claiming the throne of Denmark.

Troilus and Cressida

Plot: The play begins in the seventh year of the Trojan War, which has reached stalemate. Troilus, a younger son of Priam, is in love with Cressida, the daughter of Calchas, a Trojan who has defected to the Greeks. Her lecherous uncle, Pandarus, promises to procure her for him. The Greeks are quarrelling among themselves. Achilles, their greatest warrior, stays in his tent with his friend Patroclus and refuses to fight, mocked by a deformed slave, Thersites. Ulysses tries to entice Achilles back to battle by arousing his jealousy against Ajax, who is depicted as a foolish bully. The Trojans dispute the value of continuing the war purely for the sake of Helen. Hector declares she is not worth the lives she costs, but then agrees with his brother Troilus when he argues that honour demands they fight. Hector then sends a challenge to the Greeks to single combat. He fights Ajax in a sporting contest and the opposing leaders feast together. The mood is broken when Achilles insults Hector. Troilus and Cressida have no sooner consummated their love when she is sent to join her father in exchange for a Trojan warrior. She is quickly seduced by Diomedes. Troilus, in the company of Ulysses, witnesses her faithlessness and despairs. The following day Hector, despite Cassandra's warnings, goes out to battle. He kills Patroclus and is in turn treacherously slain by Achilles and his Myrmidons. With the fall of Troy now certain, a disillusioned Troilus vows to avenge Hector and fight to the end. Pandarus is left to lament his venereal diseases.

All's Well That Ends Well

Plot: Helena, daughter of a renowned physician, lives in the house of the Countess of Rousillon. She has an unrequited love for the Countess's high-born son, Bertram. Helena cures the king of an incurable disease and is rewarded by being allowed to choose a husband from the nobility. She naturally chooses Bertram. He reluctantly marries her then goes off to war, telling her he will only truly accept her as his wife if she can obtain a ring from his finger. In Florence Bertram encounters the cowardly braggart, Parolles, and tries to seduce the fair Diana. Helena is secretly lodging in Diana's house and takes Diana's place at a midnight assignation. She obtains Bertram's ring, and he repents and accepts her.

Measure for Measure

Plot: Vincentio, the Duke of Vienna, decides to absent himself from his court and responsibilities and leaves his deputy, Angelo, to govern in his place. The Duke then explores the low life of his city, not least the activities of the bawd, Mistress Overdone, and Pompey, the tapster. Angelo, a seeming Puritan, invokes harsh laws against immorality and condemns young Claudio to death for getting his fiancée, Juliet, pregnant. Claudio's sister, the chaste Isabella, goes to Angelo to plead for her brother's life. Angelo sees Isabella and is overcome with lust. He says he will spare Claudio if she will become his mistress. Claudio begs his sister to agree but she refuses. The Duke hears what has passed and persuades Isabella to pretend to submit and then let her place at the assignation be taken by Mariana, whom Angelo had promised to marry. Angelo breaks his word and orders Claudio's execution, which is prevented by the Duke's return. Claudio marries Juliet, Angelo marries Mariana and the Duke claims the hand of Isabella.

Othello, the Moor of Venice

Plot: Othello, a Moorish general in the Venetian army, secretly marries Desdemona, daughter of a Venetian nobleman. He is sent to Cyprus with Iago and Cassio, his two lieutenants, to repel a threatened Turkish invasion. Desdemona and her maid, Emilia, who is also Iago's wife, go with them. Because he has been passed over for promotion, or thinks Othello has been with his wife, or purely out of malice, Iago plots against Othello and falsely suggests that Desdemona is unfaithful with Cassio. Othello, whose fatal flaw is jealousy, believes him with tragic results.

Macbeth

Plot: Macbeth and Banquo, having successfully repelled a Norwegian invasion, meet three witches who promise Macbeth the crown of Scotland. Macbeth informs his wife, who persuades him to murder King Duncan whilst he is a guest in their castle. Macbeth, after much soul-searching, does the deed and becomes king. Banquo, who the witches predicted would be the father of kings, is suspicious. Macbeth invites him to his banquet but has him murdered on the way, although Banquo's son, Fleance, escapes. Macbeth sees Banquo's blood-smeared ghost at his feast and is driven to distraction. He goes again to the witches to seek reassurance. They tell him that 'none of woman born' can harm him and that he will never be defeated until Birnam wood comes to his castle at Dunsinane. They also warn him to '*beware Macduff*' who has gone to England to persuade Duncan's son, Malcolm, who has sought safety there, to return to Scotland and claim the throne. Macbeth, in his fury, has Macduff's wife and children slaughtered. Lady Macbeth walks in her sleep, trying in vain to wash the imagined blood from her hands, before she commits suicide. Malcolm and Macduff, with the help of an English army, invade Scotland. The witches' prophesies are proved false, and Macbeth dies courageously in mortal combat with Macduff. Malcolm is proclaimed king.

King Lear

Plot: Lear, king of ancient Britain, foolishly decides to split his kingdom between his three daughters, promising the biggest share to the one who professes to love him best. Goneril, Duchess of Albany, and Regan, Duchess of Cornwall, make extravagant proclamations, but Cordelia, his youngest and favourite, refuses to publicly declare her love. Lear, in blind fury, disinherits her and she leaves the kingdom to marry the King of France. Lear then divides his realm between the Dukes of Albany and Cornwall, and banishes his loyal friend, Kent, when he tries to dissuade him. Kent returns in disguise, determined to still serve his old master. Lear's other old friend, Gloucester, is deceived by his bastard son, Edmund, into disinheriting his legitimate son, Edgar, who is forced to go into hiding to save his life. Lear, no longer king, quarrels in turn with both of his daughters as they disregard his wishes. Eventually, in one of the most harrowing passages in all Shakespeare, he rages out in the middle of a terrible storm accompanied only by his Fool and the disguised Kent. On a blasted heath they come across Edgar, disguised as a mad beggar. Edgar's condition awakes pity in Lear's confused mind. Gloucester seeks to help Lear but is betrayed by Edmund and blinded by the vicious Regan and her husband. In perhaps Shakespeare's greatest scene, the mad old king commiserates with the blind Gloucester. Cordelia returns with a French army to rescue her father. There is a heart-breaking reconciliation, but Cordelia is defeated by the combined powers of Goneril and Regan, who are now both besotted with the treacherous Edmund. Gloucester dies in Edgar's arms. Regan is poisoned by Goneril. Edgar kills Edmund in a duel, but is too late to prevent Cordelia being hanged. Lear carries on her body, desperately trying to bring her back to life. He recognises Kent before he dies of grief. Edgar and Albany, who has been innocent of Goneril's crimes, are left to rule the kingdom.

Timon of Athens

Plot: Timon, a wealthy citizen of Athens, is renowned for his indiscriminate generosity and reckless sociability. The cynic Apemantus disapproves. When Flavius, Timon's steward, tells him all his goods are mortgaged, Timon thinks his erstwhile friends will help. They all renounce him and Timon rails against man's cupidity, cruelty and faithlessness. He becomes a misanthrope and quits the city to live in the wilderness. Digging for roots he discovers gold and resolves to use it to destroy his native city. He gives his new-found wealth to robbers and prostitutes, and to Alcibiades, a general who is leading an army against Athens. Timon's old friends and the cynic Apemantus seek Timon's bounty once more, but he rejects them. Alcibiades takes Athens and hears of Timon's death.

Coriolanus

Plot: Caius Marcius is a proud Roman patrician, resented by the plebeian citizens. In a war against the neighbouring Volscians his bravery at the battle of Corioli wins him the title 'Coriolanus'. The patricians nominate him for consul but he must also win the 'voices' of the plebs. The tribunes stir the people against him; he turns his anger on them and is banished from the city. He joins the Volscians and his sworn enemy, Tullus Aufidius. They march on Rome together. Only the pleading of his mother, Volumnia, dissuades him from destroying his native city. He makes peace but goes back to Corioli, where he is killed by Aufidius and his followers.

Antony and Cleopatra

Plot: It zooms across the Roman Empire like the script of an epic film, in forty-two scenes, more than any other Shakespeare play. Antony, Octavius and Lepidus, continuing from *Julius Caesar,* have formed a triumvirate and jointly rule the world. Antony, besotted with Cleopatra, neglects his duties and lasciviously indulges himself in Egypt. The death of his wife and the rebellion of Pompey's son force him to return to Rome, where he attempts to resume the alliance by marrying Octavius's sister, Octavia. Cleopatra, by turns furious and heart-broken, eventually calls him back, and war breaks out between the two halves of the Roman world. Antony is defeated at the Battle of Actium after Cleopatra and her Egyptian fleet desert him. Antony's followers, including his most trusted friend Enobarbus, leave him. Cleopatra, fearing Antony's fury, sends word she is dead. Hearing this, Antony makes a botched attempt at suicide. Too late Cleopatra sends word that she is alive and Antony dies in her arms. Fearing Octavius will drag her in triumph to Rome, Cleopatra kills herself with the bite of an asp.

Pericles

Plot: You tell me.

Cymbeline

Plot: Cymbeline is king of ancient Britain. His two sons have been stolen away by the banished lord Belarius, who has brought them up as his own sons in the Welsh mountains. Cymbeline's daughter, Imogen, is married to Posthumus, but her wicked step-mother wants her to marry Cloten, her son from a previous marriage. She contrives to get Posthumus banished to Rome where he lays a wager on Imogen's chastity with the worldly Iachimo. Iachimo goes to Britain but is repulsed by Imogen. He secretly enters her bedroom in a trunk and gets intimate details of her body which convinces Posthumus of her infidelity. Posthumus sends orders to his servant Pisanio to kill Imogen, but instead he helps her escape from the court dressed as a boy. She finds refuge with her brothers in Wales, whom she does not recognise. Cloten, pursuing her, is killed by the eldest brother. The Romans invade to exact a tribute but are defeated by the valour of Belarius, the two brothers and Posthumus. Belarius is unbanished, the brothers restored, and Imogen reconciled with Posthumus.

The Winter's Tale

Plot: Leontes, King of Sicilia, watches his pregnant wife, Hermione, persuade his friend, Polixenes, King of Bohemia, to prolong his visit and becomes convinced they have committed adultery and the child is not his. He orders his trusted servant, Camillo, to poison Polixenes. Camillo tells Polixenes and they both flee to Bohemia. Leontes sends to the Delphic oracle for advice and, in his fury, confines Hermione to prison, where she gives birth to a girl. Her maid, Paulina, brings the child to Leontes but he rejects her and orders the good old lord, Antigonus, to abandon her in the wilderness. During Hermione's trial the news is brought of the death of her son, Mamillius. She collapses, apparently dead. The oracle proclaims her innocent and predicts Leontes '*will live without heir if that which is lost be not found.*' Antigonus reaches the coast of Bohemia (as noted Shakespeare's geography was not his strongest point – Bohemia is landlocked) with the child, whom he names Perdita, but following the strangest exit line in the entire canon: *Exit pursued by bear*, is duly eaten. Perdita is found by two shepherds.

Sixteen years pass and Florizel, Polixenes' son, has fallen in love with the shepherd's presumed daughter, and plans to marry her. Polixenes and Camillo go in disguise to a shepherd's feast and discover Florizel's intentions. Polixenes is furious and disowns his son. Camillo takes the young lovers back to Leontes in Sicilia where Perdita's true identity is revealed, and Paulina miraculously brings a statue of Hermione to life. As in all the later plays, all ends in reconciliation.

The Tempest

Plot: Prospero, Duke of Milan, was overthrown by his brother, Antonio, and cast upon an island with his young daughter, Miranda. He is attended by Ariel, a spirit, and Caliban, a brutish native. By magical powers Prospero raises a storm and shipwrecks Antonio on the island together with Alonso, King of Naples, his brother Sebastian and son Ferdinand. Sebastian plots with Antonio to usurp Alonso's crown. Trinculo the jester and Stephano the butler, also shipwrecked, plot with Caliban to overthrow Prospero. Ferdinand and Miranda fall in love. Prospero, aided by Ariel, prevents the plots and brings reconciliation to all. He sets Ariel free and returns to Milan as Duke.

The Famous History of the Life of King Henry the Eighth or All is True.

Plot: The play covers the events of Henry's reign from the Field of the Cloth of Gold in 1520 to the birth of Elizabeth in 1533. It begins with the downfall and execution of Buckingham, brought about by Wolsey's scheming. Katharine of Aragon is depicted as a tender-hearted Queen, pleading with Henry to revoke his tax on the impoverished weavers. Henry arrives in disguise at Wolsey's banquet and chooses to dance with Anne Bullen. Wolsey, no friend to Katharine, secures the Pope's agreement to investigate the legitimacy of her marriage, and Cardinal Campeius arrives from Rome. Katharine refuses to accept Wolsey as her judge, and after a moving speech, walks out of the court. Cranmer, the Archbishop of Canterbury, obtains the divorce and Henry marries Anne Bullen. The Lords, jealous of Wolsey's pride and humble birth, unite against him, and he is forced to give up the Great Seal. Wolsey now sick, realises how precarious it is to depend on princes' favours and repents. Anne is crowned Queen and the dying Katharine sees a vision of angels. The Lords now fear Cranmer because he is a Protestant. Henry gives Cranmer a ring as a sign of his protection. Anne gives birth to Elizabeth. At her christening Cranmer foresees her future glory.

Evenings with Shakspere

In pre-Amazon days, whenever I was on tour, I made it my duty to visit the local second-hand bookshop. I think their demise is as big a threat to our national character as the loss of the traditional English pub. So many of the books I have used in writing this were found in musty corners of little shops in such towns as Warwick, Cheltenham, Thirsk and Chester. I am not sure where I discovered *Evenings with Shakspere* but I thought it quite unique. As far as I know nobody else had attempted to lay out the parts, lines and scenes of the plays, and many other Elizabethan and Jacobean plays, in such detail. I would think they would be invaluable to any teacher, director or casting director, or any actor before he accepts a part. I have used my copy for years and it is now falling to pieces. I would hate such dedication to be lost. I therefore give you these, complete with ink stains and amendments from some long-deceased director, in memory of its author, L.M. Griffiths, and his indefatigable Victorian ladies of the Clifton Play Reading Society.

Chronological Order for Study (see pp. 18-9).	Order indicated by Split-verse Test.	Name of Play.	Total Lines.	Prose.	Verse.	Solo-verse.	Dialogue-verse.	Split-verse.	Percentage of Split-verse in Dialogue-verse.
4	1	*3 Henry VI.*	2905	3	2902	284	2618	11	.42
3	2	*2 Henry VI.*	3161	550	2611	247	2364	16	.67
2	3	*1 Henry VI.*	2678	10	2668	147	2521	18	.71
1	4	*Titus Andronicus*	2523	39	2484	137	2347	21	.89
5	5	*Comedy of Errors*	1778	237	1541	65	1476	20	1.35
8	6	*Richard II.*	2755	3	2752	79	2673	41	1.53
19	7	*Henry V.*	3380	1466	1914	343	1571	30	1.9
10	8	*Richard III.*	3618	75	3543	422	3121	60	1.92
13	9	*Taming of Shrew*	2648	561	2087	53	2034	47	2.31
17	10	*2 Henry IV.*	3446	1679	1767	89	1678	40	2.38
6	11	*Two Gentlemen of Verona*	2294	656	1638	239	1399	34	2.43
16	12	*1 Henry IV.*	3177	1496	1681	55	1626	41	2.52
12	13	*John*	2570	0	2570	116	2454	65	2.64
9	14	*Midsummer-Night's Dream*	2180	465	1715	322	1393	37	2.65
18	15	*Merry Wives of Windsor*	3019	2681	338	32	306	10	3.26
11	16	*Romeo and Juliet*	3053	455	2598	364	2234	86	3.84
20	17	*As You Like It*	2867	1682	1185	200	985	38	3.85
14	18	*Merchant of Venice*	2662	634	2028	56	1972	80	4.05
7	19	*Love's Labour's Lost*	2789	979	1810	157	1653	72	4.35
15	20	*Much Ado about Nothing*	2829	2094	735	57	678	34	5.01
21	21	*Twelfth Night*	2692	1740	952	146	806	47	5.83
22	22	*Julius Cæsar*	2480	186	2294	142	2152	126	5.85
32	23	*Troilus and Cressida*	3496	1195	2301	108	2193	132	6.01
30	24	*Pericles*	2391	454	1937	536	1401	106	7.56
23	25	*Hamlet*	3930	1174	2756	417	2339	197	8.42
26	26	*Measure for Measure*	2821	1151	1670	117	1553	147	9.46
27	27	*Lear*	3336	921	2415	244	2171	229	10.54
28	28	*Timon of Athens*	2373	680	1693	217	1476	161	10.9
25	29	*Othello*	3317	672	2645	206	2439	267	10.94
24	30	*All's Well that Ends Well*	2966	1485	1481	136	1345	154	11.44
29	31	*Macbeth*	2109	159	1950	170	1780	244	13.7
33	32	*Coriolanus*	3410	848	2562	45	2517	389	15.45
37	33	*Henry VIII.*	2822	82	2740	110	2630	408	15.51
36	34	*Tempest*	2065	461	1604	158	1446	231	15.97
35	35	*Winter's Tale*	3074	887	2187	146	2041	332	16.26
34	36	*Cymbeline*	3341	507	2834	476	2358	409	17.34
31	37	*Antony and Cleopatra*	3063	312	2751	101	2650	465	17.54

I HENRY VI.

Total Number of Lines.	CHARACTERS.	I.						II.					III.				IV.							V.				
		1	2	3	4	5	6	1	2	3	4	5	1	2	3	4	1	2	3	4	5	6	7	1	2	3	4	5
76	Bedford	46						6	10					14														
183	Gloucester	24		42									51			1	36							18				11
59	Exeter	22											15				14							6				2
96	Winchester	15		19									32				1							11			18	
43	1st Messenger	18			4				9	6									6									
7	2nd Messenger	7																										
45	3rd Messenger	45																										
133	Charles		48				22	12						5	12								11		7		16	
49	Alençon		18				2	8						1	7										2		11	
59	Reignier		21				4	4						6												20	4	
29	Bastard		13					4						5	3								4					
3	1st Warder			3																								
10	1st Serving-man			4									5										1					
1	2nd Warder			1																								
5	Woodvile			5																								
21	Mayor			11									10															
6	Officer			6																								
18	Master Gunner				18																							
15	Salisbury				15																							
406	Talbot				67	32		20	28	33				56		12	33	29			24	41	31					
2	Gargrave				2																							
1	Glansdale				1																							
4	Sergeant							4																				
4	1st Sentinel							4																				
44	Burgundy							6	12					9	12								3		2			
8	Soldier							5						3														
6	Captain								1					3						2								
1	Porter									1																		
184	Plantagenet										45	37	9				9	27								10	47	
174	Suffolk										11															103		60
64	Somerset										37		5				5		17									
72	Warwick										27		26				4										15	
29	Vernon										11					8	10											
4	Lawyer										4																	
88	Mortimer											88																
4	1st Gaoler											4																
2	2nd Serving-man												2															
10	3rd Serving-man												10															
1	"All"												1															
2	Watch													2														
8	Fastolfe													4			4											
25	Basset															10	15											
27	General																	27										
77	Lucy																		20	27			30					
47	John Talbot																				31	16						
1	Legate																							1				
5	Scout																								5			
24	Shepherd																										24	
254	Joan		50			7	3	12						30	57							16			5	34	40	
4	Boy				4																							
45	Countess								45																			
179	King												41			14	63							26				35
33	Margaret																									33		
2697		177	150	91	111	39	31	85	60	85	135	129	207	138	91	45	194	56	53	46	55	57	96	62	21	200	175	108
2678	Actual No. of Lines	177	150	91	111	39	31	82	60	82	134	129	201	137	91	45	194	56	53	46	55	57	96	62	21	195	175	108

2 HENRY VI.

Total Number of Lines.	CHARACTERS.	I.				II.				III.			IV.										V.		
		1	2	3	4	1	2	3	4	1	2	3	1	2	3	4	5	6	7	8	9	10	1	2	3
298	Suffolk	20	...	46	...	13	...	2	...	62	97	...	58	...	...	...	...	...	...	...	...	...	...	...	...
314	King	26	...	10	...	36	...	27	...	43	76	15	...	...	...	17	...	...	...	...	31	...	32	1	...
16	"All"	1	...	1	...	...	...	...	...	...	2	...	...	5	...	...	...	...	2	4	1	...	...	...	...
306	Gloucester	61	25	22	...	75	...	14	40	69	...	...	...	...	...	...	...	...	...	...	...	...	...	...	...
104	Cardinal	31	...	3	...	24	...	...	...	30	2	14	...	...	...	...	...	...	...	...	...	...	...	...	...
96	Salisbury	29	...	2	...	...	9	5	...	...	28	1	...	...	...	...	...	...	...	...	...	...	14	...	8
132	Warwick	15	...	7	...	...	17	...	...	...	64	3	...	...	...	...	...	...	...	...	...	...	8	12	6
380	York	55	...	15	31	...	58	12	...	94	...	...	...	...	...	...	...	...	...	...	...	...	90	13	12
74	Buckingham	7	...	8	8	12	...	...	...	4	...	...	...	...	...	6	...	...	...	10	3	...	16	...	...
25	Somerset	6	...	5	...	...	...	...	...	7	1	...	...	...	...	...	...	...	...	...	3	...	3	...	...
26	1st Messenger	...	3	...	...	...	...	...	...	...	...	...	...	...	...	11	...	...	4	...	8	...	...	...	...
32	Hume	...	28	...	4	...	...	...	...	...	...	...	...	...	...	...	...	...	...	...	...	...	...	...	...
10	1st Petitioner	...	...	10	...	...	...	...	...	...	...	...	...	...	...	...	...	...	...	...	...	...	...	...	...
6	2nd Petitioner	...	...	6	...	...	...	...	...	...	...	...	...	...	...	...	...	...	...	...	...	...	...	...	...
29	Peter	...	...	16	...	...	...	13	...	...	...	...	...	...	...	...	...	...	...	...	...	...	...	...	...
22	Horner	...	...	11	...	...	...	11	...	...	...	...	...	...	...	...	...	...	...	...	...	...	...	...	...
24	Bolingbroke	...	...	...	24	...	...	...	...	...	...	...	...	...	...	...	...	...	...	...	...	...	...	...	...
4	Townsman	...	...	...	...	4	...	...	...	...	...	...	...	...	...	...	...	...	...	...	...	...	...	...	...
24	Simpcox	...	...	...	...	24	...	...	...	...	...	...	...	...	...	...	...	...	...	...	...	...	...	...	...
3	Mayor	...	...	...	...	3	...	...	...	...	...	...	...	...	...	...	...	...	...	...	...	...	...	...	...
2	Beadle	...	...	...	...	2	...	...	...	...	...	...	...	...	...	...	...	...	...	...	...	...	...	...	...
3	1st Neighbour	...	...	...	...	...	...	3	...	...	...	...	...	...	...	...	...	...	...	...	...	...	...	...	...
2	2nd Neighbour	...	...	...	...	...	...	2	...	...	...	...	...	...	...	...	...	...	...	...	...	...	...	...	...
2	3rd Neighbour	...	...	...	...	...	...	2	...	...	...	...	...	...	...	...	...	...	...	...	...	...	...	...	...
2	1st Prentice	...	...	...	...	...	...	2	...	...	...	...	...	...	...	...	...	...	...	...	...	...	...	...	...
2	2nd Prentice	...	...	...	...	...	...	2	...	...	...	...	...	...	...	...	...	...	...	...	...	...	...	...	...
2	Servingman	...	...	...	...	...	...	...	2	...	...	...	...	...	...	...	...	...	...	...	...	...	...	...	...
2	Herald	...	...	...	...	...	...	...	2	...	...	...	...	...	...	...	...	...	...	...	...	...	...	...	...
4	Sheriff	...	...	...	...	...	...	...	4	...	...	...	...	...	...	...	...	...	...	...	...	...	...	...	...
7	Stanley	...	...	...	...	...	...	...	7	...	...	...	...	...	...	...	...	...	...	...	...	...	...	...	...
6	Post	...	...	...	...	...	...	...	...	6	...	...	...	...	...	...	...	...	...	...	...	...	...	...	...
5	1st Murderer	...	...	...	...	...	...	...	...	...	5	...	...	...	...	...	...	...	...	...	...	...	...	...	...
2	2nd Murderer	...	...	...	...	...	...	...	...	...	2	...	...	...	...	...	...	...	...	...	...	...	...	...	...
11	Vaux	...	...	...	...	...	...	...	...	...	11	...	...	...	...	...	...	...	...	...	...	...	...	...	...
64	Captain	...	...	...	...	...	...	...	...	...	...	...	64	...	...	...	...	...	...	...	...	...	...	...	...
7	1st Gentleman	...	...	...	...	...	...	...	...	...	...	...	7	...	...	...	...	...	...	...	...	...	...	...	...
1	Master	...	...	...	...	...	...	...	...	...	...	...	1	...	...	...	...	...	...	...	...	...	...	...	...
1	Mate	...	...	...	...	...	...	...	...	...	...	...	1	...	...	...	...	...	...	...	...	...	...	...	...
1	2nd Gentleman	...	...	...	...	...	...	...	...	...	...	...	1	...	...	...	...	...	...	...	...	...	...	...	...
18	Whitmore	...	...	...	...	...	...	...	...	...	...	...	18	...	...	...	...	...	...	...	...	...	...	...	...
18	Bevis	...	...	...	...	...	...	...	...	...	...	...	...	16	...	...	...	...	2	...	...	...	...	...	...
21	Holland	...	...	...	...	...	...	...	...	...	...	...	...	16	...	...	...	...	5	...	...	...	...	...	...
276	Cade	...	...	...	...	...	...	...	...	...	...	...	...	90	16	...	...	12	79	31	...	48	...	...	...
42	Dick	...	...	...	...	...	...	...	...	...	...	...	...	27	4	...	...	2	9	...	...	...	...	...	...
21	Smith	...	...	...	...	...	...	...	...	...	...	...	...	15	...	...	...	3	3	...	...	...	...	...	...
3	Clerk	...	...	...	...	...	...	...	...	...	...	...	...	3	...	...	...	...	...	...	...	...	...	...	...
5	Michael	...	...	...	...	...	...	...	...	...	...	...	...	5	...	...	...	...	...	...	...	...	...	...	...
16	Stafford	...	...	...	...	...	...	...	...	...	...	...	...	16	...	...	...	...	...	...	...	...	...	...	...
7	William Stafford	...	...	...	...	...	...	...	...	...	...	...	...	7	...	...	...	...	...	...	...	...	...	...	...
48	Say	...	...	...	...	...	...	...	...	...	...	...	...	...	...	7	...	...	41	...	...	...	...	...	...
5	2nd Messenger	...	...	...	...	...	...	...	...	...	...	...	...	...	...	5	...	...	...	...	...	...	...	...	...
8	Scales	...	...	...	...	...	...	...	...	...	...	...	...	...	...	...	8	...	...	...	...	...	...	...	...
5	1st Citizen	...	...	...	...	...	...	...	...	...	...	...	...	...	...	...	5	...	...	...	...	...	...	...	...
1	Soldier	...	...	...	...	...	...	...	...	...	...	...	...	...	...	...	...	1	...	...	...	...	...	...	...
56	Clifford	...	...	...	...	...	...	...	...	...	...	...	...	...	...	...	...	...	...	27	3	...	21	5	...
51	Iden	...	...	...	...	...	...	...	...	...	...	...	...	...	...	...	...	...	...	...	...	42	9	...	...
1	Edward	...	...	...	...	...	...	...	...	...	...	...	...	...	...	...	...	...	...	...	...	...	1	...	...
24	Richard	...	...	...	...	...	...	...	...	...	...	...	...	...	...	...	...	...	...	...	...	...	10	6	8
45	Young Clifford	...	...	...	...	...	...	...	...	...	...	...	...	...	...	...	...	...	...	...	...	...	3	42	...
317	Queen	9	...	57	...	10	...	12	...	68	127	...	...	...	...	14	...	...	...	...	...	...	9	11	...
119	Duchess	...	51	7	4	...	...	1	56	...	...	...	...	...	...	...	...	...	...	...	...	...	...	...	...
9	Spirit	...	...	...	9	...	...	...	...	...	...	...	...	...	...	...	...	...	...	...	...	...	...	...	...
4	Jourdain	...	...	...	4	...	...	...	...	...	...	...	...	...	...	...	...	...	...	...	...	...	...	...	...
8	Wife to Simpcox	...	...	...	...	8	...	...	...	...	...	...	...	...	...	...	...	...	...	...	...	...	...	...	...
3179		260	107	226	84	211	84	108	111	383	415	33	150	200	20	60	13	18	145	72	49	90	216	90	34
3161	... Actual Number of Lines ...	259	107	226	84	204	82	108	110	383	412	33	147	200	20	60	13	18	145	72	49	90	216	90	33

3 HENRY VI.

Total Number of Lines.	CHARACTERS.	I.				II.						III.			IV.								V.						
		1	2	3	4	1	2	3	4	5	6	1	2	3	1	2	3	4	5	6	7	8	1	2	3	4	5	6	7
436	WARWICK	45	...	...	...	80	5	17	...	...	31	...	...	91	...	28	28	...	...	22	...	22	34	33	...	...	...	...	...
173	YORK	37	37	...	99	...	...	...	...	...	...	...	...	...	...	...	...	...	...	...	...	...	...	...	...	...	...	...	...
429	EDWARD	5	9	...	...	40	38	15	...	...	23	...	57	...	63	...	11	...	8	...	43	10	28	4	16	6	23	...	30
15	MONTAGUE	5	3	...	...	...	...	...	...	...	...	...	...	...	5	...	...	...	...	...	...	1	1	...	...	...	...	...	...
390	RICHARD	6	21	...	...	65	20	13	6	...	23	...	93	...	22	...	...	...	18	...	12	3	19	...	4	...	12	44	9
3	NORFOLK	3	...	...	...	...	...	...	...	...	...	...	...	...	...	...	...	...	...	...	...	...	...	...	...	...	...	...	...
362	KING HENRY	75	...	...	...	...	23	...	...	78	...	69	...	...	...	...	...	...	...	46	...	22	...	...	...	...	...	49	...
30	NORTHUMBERLAND	13	...	...	15	...	2	...	...	...	...	...	...	...	...	...	...	...	...	...	...	...	...	...	...	...	...	...	...
140	CLIFFORD	18	...	26	13	...	46	...	7	...	30	...	...	...	...	...	...	...	...	...	...	...	...	...	...	...	...	...	...
11	WESTMORELAND	11	...	...	...	...	...	...	...	...	...	...	...	...	...	...	...	...	...	...	...	...	...	...	...	...	...	...	...
17	EXETER	12	...	...	...	...	...	...	...	3	...	...	...	...	...	...	...	...	...	...	...	2	...	...	...	...	...	...	...
37	1ST MESSENGER	...	4	...	...	24	6	...	...	...	...	...	...	...	...	...	...	...	...	...	...	...	1	...	...	2	...	...	...
1	SIR JOHN MORTIMER	...	1	...	...	...	...	...	...	...	...	...	...	...	...	...	...	...	...	...	...	...	...	...	...	...	...	...	...
3	TUTOR	...	...	3	...	...	...	...	...	...	...	...	...	...	...	...	...	...	...	...	...	...	...	...	...	...	...	...	...
105	GEORGE	...	...	...	...	...	7	11	...	...	3	...	8	...	24	1	...	...	...	9	...	3	22	...	4	...	7	...	6
22	A SON	...	...	...	...	...	...	...	...	22	...	...	...	...	...	...	...	...	...	...	...	...	...	...	...	...	...	...	...
27	A FATHER	...	...	...	...	...	...	...	...	27	...	...	...	...	...	...	...	...	...	...	...	...	...	...	...	...	...	...	...
18	1ST KEEPER	...	...	...	...	...	...	...	...	...	...	18	...	...	...	...	...	...	...	...	...	...	...	...	...	...	...	...	...
14	2ND KEEPER	...	...	...	...	...	...	...	...	...	...	14	...	...	...	...	...	...	...	...	...	...	...	...	...	...	...	...	...
2	NOBLEMAN	...	...	...	...	...	...	...	...	...	...	...	2	...	...	...	...	...	...	...	...	...	...	...	...	...	...	...	...
66	KING LEWIS	...	...	...	...	...	...	...	...	...	...	...	...	66	...	...	...	...	...	...	...	...	...	...	...	...	...	...	...
35	OXFORD	...	...	...	...	...	...	...	...	...	...	...	...	16	...	...	2	...	...	2	...	1	1	1	...	8	1	...	...
29	POST	...	...	...	...	...	...	...	...	...	...	...	...	4	18	...	...	...	...	7	...	...	...	...	...	...	...	...	...
33	SOMERSET	...	...	...	...	...	...	...	...	...	...	...	...	...	1	...	1	...	...	13	...	...	1	12	...	4	1	...	...
20	HASTINGS	...	...	...	...	...	...	...	...	...	...	...	...	...	8	...	...	...	2	...	10	...	...	...	...	...	...	...	...
3	"ALL"	...	...	...	...	...	...	...	...	...	...	...	...	...	...	1	...	...	...	...	1	1	...	...	...	...	...	...	...
8	1ST WATCHMAN	...	...	...	...	...	...	...	...	...	...	...	...	...	...	...	8	...	...	...	...	...	...	...	...	...	...	...	...
7	2ND WATCHMAN	...	...	...	...	...	...	...	...	...	...	...	...	...	...	...	7	...	...	...	...	...	...	...	...	...	...	...	...
9	3RD WATCHMAN	...	...	...	...	...	...	...	...	...	...	...	...	...	...	...	9	...	...	...	...	...	...	...	...	...	...	...	...
7	RIVERS	...	...	...	...	...	...	...	...	...	...	...	...	...	...	...	...	7	...	...	...	...	...	...	...	...	...	...	...
2	HUNTSMAN	...	...	...	...	...	...	...	...	...	...	...	...	...	...	...	...	...	2	...	...	...	...	...	...	...	...	...	...
3	LIEUTENANT	...	...	...	...	...	...	...	...	...	...	...	...	...	...	...	...	...	...	3	...	...	...	...	...	...	...	...	...
5	MAYOR	...	...	...	...	...	...	...	...	...	...	...	...	...	...	...	...	...	...	...	5	...	...	...	...	...	...	...	...
14	MONTGOMERY	...	...	...	...	...	...	...	...	...	...	...	...	...	...	...	...	...	...	...	14	...	...	...	...	...	...	...	...
3	SOLDIER	...	...	...	...	...	...	...	...	...	...	...	...	...	...	...	...	...	...	...	3	...	...	...	...	...	...	...	...
1	2ND MESSENGER	...	...	...	...	...	...	...	...	...	...	...	...	...	...	...	...	...	...	...	...	...	1	...	...	...	...	...	...
5	SOMERVILLE	...	...	...	...	...	...	...	...	...	...	...	...	...	...	...	...	...	...	...	...	...	5	...	...	...	...	...	...
279	QUEEN MARGARET	42	...	...	53	...	22	...	...	6	...	...	...	73	...	...	...	...	...	...	...	...	...	...	...	50	33	...	...
46	PRINCE	4	...	...	...	...	8	...	...	3	...	...	...	6	...	...	...	...	...	...	...	...	...	...	...	12	13	...	...
24	RUTLAND	...	...	24	...	...	...	...	...	...	...	...	...	...	...	...	...	...	...	...	...	...	...	...	...	...	...	...	...
73	LADY GREY	...	...	...	...	...	...	...	...	...	...	...	36	...	8	...	28	...	...	...	...	...	...	...	...	...	...	...	1
9	BONA	...	...	...	...	...	...	...	...	...	...	...	...	9	...	...	...	...	...	...	...	...	...	...	...	...	...	...	...
2916		276	75	53	180	209	177	56	13	139	110	101	196	268	149	30	66	35	30	102	88	65	113	50	24	82	90	93	46
2905	Actual No. of Lines	273	75	52	180	209	177	56	13	139	110	101	195	265	149	30	64	35	29	102	88	65	113	50	24	82	90	93	46

TITUS ANDRONICUS.

Total Number of Lines.	CHARACTERS.	I.	II.				III.		IV.				V.		
		1	1	2	3	4	1	2	1	2	3	4	1	2	3
209	SATURNINUS	105	...	5	35	...	...	...	...	...	...	55	...	...	9
63	BASSIANUS	48	...	1	14	...	...	...	...	...	...	...	...	...	...
303	MARCUS	74	...	3	...	47	41	10	47	...	19	...	...	1	61
6	CAPTAIN	6	...	...	...	...	...	...	...	...	...	...	...	...	...
718	TITUS	136	...	15	9	...	190	73	58	...	76	...	...	132	29
196	LUCIUS	30	...	...	...	...	46	...	...	..	...	...	41	...	79
52	CHIRON	1	20	...	10	4	...	...	...	13	...	...	...	4	..
94	DEMETRIUS	10	33	2	13	6	...	...	...	28	...	...	...	2	...
3	TRIBUNE	3	...	...	...	...	...	...	...	...	...	...	..	...	...
4	MUTIUS	4	...	..	...	...	...	...	...	...	...	...	...	...	...
28	QUINTUS	4	...	...	24	...	...	...	...	...	...	...	...	...	...
31	MARTIUS	2	...	...	29	...	...	...	...	...	...	...	...	...	...
4	"ALL"	2	...	...	...	...	...	...	...	...	...	...	...	...	2
355	AARON	...	89	...	41	...	19	...	...	110	...	...	86	...	10
7	MESSENGER	...	...	...	...	...	7	...	...	...	...	...	...	...	...
15	PUBLIUS	...	...	...	...	...	...	...	...	...	9	...	...	6	...
24	CLOWN	...	...	...	...	...	...	...	...	...	17	7	...	...	...
21	ÆMILIUS	...	...	...	...	...	...	...	...	...	...	8	6	..	7
12	1ST GOTH	...	...	...	...	...	...	...	...	...	...	...	11	...	1
21	2ND GOTH	...	...	...	...	...	...	...	...	...	...	...	21	...	...
3	3RD GOTH	...	...	...	...	...	...	...	...	...	...	...	3	...	...
257	TAMORA	66	...	...	85	...	...	...	...	...	...	43	...	61	2
58	LAVINIA	10	...	2	46	...	...	...	...	...	...	...	...	...	...
44	YOUNG LUCIUS	...	...	...	...	...	...	2	25	13	...	...	...	...	4
19	NURSE	...	...	...	...	...	...	...	...	19	...	...	...	...	...
2547		501	142	28	306	57	303	85	130	183	121	113	168	206	204
2523	Actual Number of Lines	495	135	26	306	57	301	85	129	180	121	113	165	206	204

THE TWO GENTLEMEN OF VERONA.

Total Number of Lines.	CHARACTERS.	I.			II.							III.		IV.				V.			
		1	2	3	1	2	3	4	5	6	7	1	2	1	2	3	4	1	2	3	4
393	VALENTINE	43	...	...	65	...	...	112	...	...	...	77	...	23	...	...	...	...	...	...	73
465	PROTEUS	68	...	29	...	17	...	49	...	43	...	75	42	...	57	...	30	...	15	...	40
226	SPEED	51	...	...	100	...	...	3	28	...	...	40	...	4	...	...	...	...	...	...	...
35	ANTONIO	...	...	35	...	...	...	...	...	...	...	...	...	...	...	...	...	...	...	...	...
46	PANTHINO	...	...	28	...	1	17	...	...	...	...	...	...	...	...	...	...	...	...	...	...
242	LAUNCE	...	...	...	...	...	48	...	35	...	...	104	...	...	...	...	55	...	...	...	...
56	THURIO	...	...	...	...	...	...	14	...	...	...	...	14	...	7	...	...	...	16	...	5
200	DUKE	...	...	...	...	...	...	18	...	...	...	102	42	...	...	...	...	...	18	...	20
22	1ST OUTLAW	...	...	...	...	...	...	...	...	...	...	...	...	15	...	...	...	...	...	6	1
16	2ND OUTLAW	...	...	...	...	...	...	...	...	...	...	...	...	14	...	...	...	...	...	1	1
26	3RD OUTLAW	...	...	...	...	...	...	...	...	...	...	...	...	20	...	...	...	...	...	5	1
26	HOST	...	...	...	...	...	...	...	...	...	...	...	...	...	26	...	...	...	...	...	...
29	EGLAMOUR	...	...	...	...	...	...	...	...	...	...	...	...	...	...	19	...	10	...	...	...
323	JULIA	...	91	...	...	4	...	...	...	...	72	...	...	...	27	...	99	...	10	...	20
72	LUCETTA	...	54	...	...	...	...	...	...	...	18	...	...	...	...	...	...	...	...	...	...
159	SILVIA	...	...	...	18	...	...	24	...	...	...	...	...	...	29	32	29	3	...	3	21
2336		162	145	92	183	22	65	220	63	43	90	398	98	76	146	51	213	13	59	15	182
2294	Actual No. of Lines	161	140	91	182	21	65	214	63	43	90	397	98	76	140	47	210	12	56	15	173

In II. 2, Proteus's lines should be 16, and in V. 1, Eglamour's should be 9.

THE COMEDY OF ERRORS.

Total Number of Lines.	CHARACTERS.	I.		II.		III.		IV.				V.
		1	2	1	2	1	2	1	2	3	4	1
143	Ægeon	110	...	...	...	...	...	...	...	...	...	33
91	Duke	48	...	...	...	...	...	...	...	[illegible]	...	43
1	Gaoler	1	...	...	...	...	...	...	...	[illegible]	...	...
15	1st Merchant	...	15	...	...	...	...	...	...	...	...	...
279	Antipholus of S. ...	...	55	...	84	...	86	...	...	27	5	22
248	Dromio of S.	...	2	...	67	14	62	16	25	44	7	11
161	Dromio of E.	...	33	32	...	30	...	1	...	...	44	21
212	Antipholus of E. ...	...	...	...	...	47	...	48	...	...	44	73
26	Balthazar	...	...	...	...	26	...	...	...	...	...	...
77	Angelo	...	...	...	...	2	10	34	...	...	...	31
34	2nd Merchant	...	...	...	...	...	...	11	...	...	...	23
13	Officer	...	...	...	...	...	...	3	...	...	10	...
12	Pinch	...	...	...	...	...	...	...	...	...	12	...
15	Servant	...	...	...	...	...	...	...	...	...	...	15
260	Adriana	...	...	55	63	2	...	...	34	...	31	75
96	Luciana	...	...	30	8	...	36	...	10	...	5	7
8	Luce...	...	...	...	...	8	...	...	...	...	...	...
35	Courtezan	...	...	...	...	...	...	...	...	26	6	3
73	Abbess	...	...	...	...	...	...	...	...	...	...	73
1799		159	105	117	222	129	194	113	69	97	164	430
1778	Actual Number of Lines	159	105	116	221	123	190	113	66	97	162	426

THE TAMING OF THE SHREW.

Total Number of Lines.	CHARACTERS.	Induction.		I.		II.	III.		IV.					V.	
		1	2	1	2	1	1	2	1	2	3	4	5	1	2
68	SLY	10	54	4	...	...	...	...	...	...	...	...	...	...	...
137	LORD	106	31	...	...	...	...	...	...	...	...	...	...	...	...
9	1ST HUNTSMAN	9	...	...	...	...	...	...	...	...	...	...	...	...	...
3	2ND HUNTSMAN	3	...	...	...	...	...	...	...	...	...	...	...	...	...
21	1ST SERVANT	2	14	1	...	...	3	...	1	...	...	...	...	...	...
5	PLAYER	5	...	...	...	...	...	...	...	...	...	...	...	...	...
12	2ND SERVANT	...	12	...	...	...	...	...	...	...	...	...	...	...	...
12	3RD SERVANT	...	12	...	...	...	...	...	...	...	...	...	...	...	...
2	"ALL"	...	1	...	...	...	...	...	1	...	...	...	...	...	...
8	MESSENGER	...	8	...	...	...	...	...	...	...	...	...	...	...	...
190	LUCENTIO	...	...	92	7	...	28	6	...	5	...	11	...	16	25
295	TRANIO	...	...	63	34	46	...	42	...	66	...	27	...	13	4
175	BAPTISTA	...	...	23	...	70	...	36	...	...	...	20	...	14	12
172	GREMIO	...	...	27	39	56	...	34	...	...	...	...	...	13	3
213	HORTENSIO	...	...	30	78	15	29	...	...	25	11	...	8	...	17
118	BIONDELLO	...	...	6	2	...	...	47	...	8	...	30	...	20	5
585	PETRUCHIO	...	...	...	78	162	...	62	72	...	88	...	42	18	63
187	GRUMIO	...	...	...	49	...	...	2	98	...	38	...	...	...	...
32	CURTIS	...	...	...	...	...	...	...	32	...	...	...	...	...	...
5	NATHANIEL	...	...	...	...	...	...	...	5	...	...	...	...	...	...
1	PHILIP	...	...	...	...	...	...	...	1	...	...	...	...	...	...
1	JOSEPH	...	...	...	...	...	...	...	1	...	...	...	...	...	...
1	NICHOLAS	...	...	...	...	...	...	...	1	...	...	...	...	...	...
2	PETER	...	...	...	...	...	...	...	2	...	...	...	...	...	...
54	PEDANT	...	...	...	...	...	...	...	...	15	...	21	...	18	...
1	HABERDASHER	...	...	...	...	...	...	...	...	...	1	...	...	...	...
18	TAILOR	...	...	...	...	...	...	...	...	...	18	...	...	...	...
51	VINCENTIO	...	...	...	...	...	...	...	...	...	...	...	9	40	2
5	HOSTESS	5	...	...	...	...	...	...	...	...	...	...	...	...	...
16	PAGE	...	15	1	...	...	...	...	...	...	...	...	...	...	...
220	KATHARINA	...	...	13	...	52	1	30	3	...	45	...	22	4	51
70	BIANCA	...	...	4	...	16	33	1	...	6	...	...	...	2	8
11	WIDOW	...	...	...	...	...	...	...	...	...	...	...	...	...	11
2700		140	147	264	287	417	93	260	217	125	201	109	81	158	201
2648	Actual Number of Lines	138	147	259	282	412	92	254	214	120	198	109	79	155	189

In Induction I. the Lord's lines should be 105, and in II. 1 Tranio's 47.

RICHARD III.

Total Number of Lines.	CHARACTERS	I.				II.				III.							IV.					V.				
		1	2	3	4	1	2	3	4	1	2	3	4	5	6	7	1	2	3	4	5	1	2	3	4	5
1161	GLOUCESTER	125	154	125		41	19			56			32	69		73		83	26	198				154	6	
174	CLARENCE	22			142																			10		
39	BRACKENBURY	8			25												6									
149	HASTINGS	10		5		3	1			6	70		49											5		
2	GENTLEMAN		2																							
55	RIVERS			18		4	12					17												4		
13	GREY			6								4												3		
374	BUCKINGHAM			12		12	24			58	7		12	27		156		29				27		10		
107	DERBY			8		5					13		8				11	3		17	12			21		9
15	DORSET			3		4	7										1									
62	CATESBY			2						5	16					14		2	4	8				4	7	
66	1ST MURDERER			7	59																					
69	2ND MURDERER				69																					
64	KING EDWARD					64																				
8	1ST CITIZEN							8																		
13	2ND CITIZEN							13																		
28	3RD CITIZEN							28																		
12	ARCHBISHOP								12																	
30	1ST MESSENGER								9		15									5				1		
17	MAYOR									1				11		5										
9	CARDINAL									9																
3	PURSUIVANT										3															
1	PRIEST										1															
30	RATCLIFF											3	2							10				15		
5	VAUGHAN											1												4		
7	ELY												7													
3	LOVEL												1	2												
14	SCRIVENER														14											
1	"ANOTHER"															1										
37	TYRREL																	8	29							
3	2ND MESSENGER																			3						
7	3RD MESSENGER																			7						
10	4TH MESSENGER																			10						
8	URSWICK																				8					
2	SHERIFF																					2				
136	RICHMOND																						19	85		32
2	OXFORD																						2			
1	HERBERT																						1			
8	BLUNT																						2	6		
1	SURREY																							1		
10	NORFOLK																							10		
9	GHOST OF HENRY VI.																							9		
3	"LORDS"																							3		
165	ANNE		118														39							8		
274	QUEEN ELIZABETH			50		7	21		15								32			149						
218	QUEEN MARGARET			124																94						
140	DUCHESS OF YORK						44		26								16			54						
21	BOY						21																			
9	GIRL						9																			
47	DUKE OF YORK								16	23														8		
51	PRINCE									43														8		
6	PAGE																	6								
8	GHOST OF PRINCE EDWARD																							8		
3707		165	274	360	295	140	158	49	78	201	125	25	111	109	14	249	105	131	59	555	20	29	24	377	13	41
3620	Actual Number of Lines	162	263	356	290	140	154	49	73	200	124	25	109	109	14	247	104	126	57	540	20	29	24	351	13	41

Much confusion will occur in the reading of this play if a very careful comparison of the text is not made beforehand, as the Quarto and Folio editions vary so much.

In V. 3 the lines of Clarence, Ghost of Henry VI., Ghost of Prince Edward should be respectively 8, 7, 6, and the total lines should be 3618, as the total of II. 3 should be 47.

LOVE'S LABOUR'S LOST

Total Number of Lines.	CHARACTERS.	I.		II.	III.	IV.			V.	
		1	2	1	1	1	2	3	1	2
322	King	117	...	47	...	...	...	76	...	82
70	Longaville	14	...	6	...	...	...	33	...	17
91	Dumain	8	...	2	...	...	...	44	...	37
627	Biron	128	...	18	51	...	...	237	...	193
32	Dull	9	7	...	...	...	13	...	3	...
202	Costard	44	13	...	40	26	3	4	14	58
255	Armado	...	96	...	58	...	...	...	48	53
234	Boyet	...	...	67	...	64	...	...	...	103
2	1st Lord	...	...	2	...	...	...	...	...	...
5	Forester	...	...	...	...	5	...	...	...	...
80	Nathaniel	...	...	...	...	...	45	...	13	22
200	Holofernes...	...	...	...	...	...	104	...	60	36
4	Mercade	...	...	...	...	...	...	...	...	4
168	Moth	...	70	...	60	...	...	...	24	14
18	Jaquenetta	...	6	...	...	...	8	4	...	...
289	Princess	...	...	67	...	50	...	...	...	172
42	Maria	...	...	22	...	4	...	...	...	16
46	Katharine	...	...	8	...	...	...	...	...	38
178	Rosaline	...	...	30	...	11	...	...	...	137
2865		320	192	269	209	160	173	398	162	982
2789	Actual Number of Lines	318	192	258	207	151	173	386	162	942

ROMEO AND JULIET.

Total Number of Lines.	CHARACTERS.	Prologue.	I.					Prologue.	II.						III.					IV.					V.		
			1	2	3	4	5		1	2	3	4	5	6	1	2	3	4	5	1	2	3	4	5	1	2	3
41	SAMPSON		41																								
24	GREGORY		24																								
5	ABRAHAM		5																								
161	BENVOLIO		51	20		13	1		9			14			53												
36	TYBALT		5				17								14												
6	1ST CITIZEN		2												4												
269	CAPULET		3	33			56											31	63		26		19	28			10
41	MONTAGUE		28												3												10
75	PRINCE		23												16												36
618	ROMEO		65	29		34	27		2	86	25	54		12	36		71		24						71		82
69	PARIS			4														4		23				6			32
38	1ST SERVANT			21	5		11																1				
273	MERCUTIO					73			34			95			71												
14	2ND SERVANT						7														5		2				
3	2ND CAPULET						3																				
350	FRIAR LAURENCE										72			18			87			56				25		17	75
37	PETER											7												30			
16	1ST MUSICIAN																							16			
6	2ND MUSICIAN																							6			
1	3RD MUSICIAN																							1			
32	BALTHASAR																								11		21
7	APOTHECARY																								7		
13	FRIAR JOHN																									13	
19	1ST WATCHMAN																										19
1	2ND WATCHMAN																										1
3	3RD WATCHMAN																										3
14	"PROLOGUE"	14																									
115	LADY CAPULET		1		36		1								11			2	37		3	3	3	13			5
3	LADY MONTAGUE		3																								
290	NURSE				61		15			2		63	38			31	21		25		2		4	28			
541	JULIET				8		19			114			43	7		116			105	48	12	56					13
14	"CHORUS"							14																			
9	PAGE																										9
3144		14	251	107	110	120	157	14	45	202	97	233	81	37	208	147	179	37	254	127	48	59	29	153	89	30	316
3052	Actual No. of Lines	14	244	106	106	114	147	14	42	190	94	233	80	37	202	143	175	36	241	126	47	58	27	150	86	30	310

The total lines should be 3053, as the total of IV. 4 should be 28.

RICHARD II.

Total Number of Lines.	CHARACTERS.	I.				II.				III.				IV.	V.					
		1	2	3	4	1	2	3	4	1	2	3	4	1	1	2	3	4	5	6
755	Richard	57	...	74	40	41	...	...	...	...	146	104	...	134	63	...	...	...	96	...
192	Gaunt	8	16	62	...	106	...	...	...	...	...	...	...	...	...	...	...	...	...	...
414	Bolingbroke	59	...	78	...	...	...	56	...	38	...	55	...	39	...	...	56	...	...	33
135	Mowbray	83	...	52	...	...	...	...	...	...	...	...	...	...	...	...	...	...	...	...
25	Marshal	...	...	25	...	...	...	...	...	...	...	...	...	...	...	...	...	...	...	...
85	Aumerle	...	...	5	15	...	...	...	...	...	12	3	...	26	...	11	13	...	...	...
6	1st Herald	...	...	6	...	...	...	...	...	...	...	...	...	...	...	...	...	...	...	...
7	2nd Herald	...	...	7	...	...	...	...	...	...	...	...	...	...	...	...	...	...	...	...
32	Green	...	...	...	5	...	25	...	...	2	...	...	...	...	...	...	...	...	...	...
39	Bushy	...	...	...	4	...	33	...	...	2	...	...	...	...	...	...	...	...	...	...
1	"All"	...	...	...	1	...	...	...	...	...	...	...	...	...	...	...	...	...	...	...
288	York	...	...	...	...	74	41	49	...	2	...	13	...	11	...	70	28	...	...	...
142	Northumberland	...	...	...	...	50	...	35	...	...	...	30	...	15	7	...	...	...	...	5
22	Ross	...	...	...	...	20	...	2	...	...	...	...	...	...	...	...	...	...	...	...
12	Willoughby	...	...	...	...	10	...	2	...	...	...	...	...	...	...	...	...	...	...	...
17	Servant	...	...	...	...	...	5	...	...	...	...	...	10	...	...	...	...	2	...	...
22	Bagot	...	...	...	...	...	9	...	...	...	...	...	...	13	...	...	...	...	...	...
45	Percy	...	...	...	...	...	...	21	...	...	...	8	...	5	...	...	6	...	...	5
8	Berkeley	...	...	...	...	...	...	8	...	...	...	...	...	...	...	...	...	...	...	...
15	Captain	...	...	...	...	...	...	...	15	...	...	...	...	...	...	...	...	...	...	...
20	Salisbury	...	...	...	...	...	...	...	9	...	11	...	...	...	...	...	...	...	...	...
63	Carlisle	...	...	...	...	...	...	...	...	...	14	...	...	49	...	...	...	...	...	...
37	Scroop	...	...	...	...	...	...	...	...	...	37	...	...	...	...	...	...	...	...	...
52	Gardener	...	...	...	...	...	...	...	...	...	...	...	52	...	...	...	...	...	...	...
27	Fitzwater	...	...	...	...	...	...	...	...	...	...	...	...	23	...	...	...	...	...	4
5	Lord	...	...	...	...	...	...	...	...	...	...	...	...	5	...	...	...	...	...	...
10	Surrey	...	...	...	...	...	...	...	...	...	...	...	...	10	...	...	...	...	...	...
10	Abbot	...	...	...	...	...	...	...	...	...	...	...	...	10	...	...	...	...	...	...
21	Exton	...	...	...	...	...	...	...	...	...	...	...	...	...	...	...	...	10	6	5
12	Groom	...	...	...	...	...	...	...	...	...	...	...	...	...	...	...	...	...	12	...
6	Keeper	...	...	...	...	...	...	...	...	...	...	...	...	...	...	...	...	...	6	...
58	Duchess of Gloucester	...	58	...	...	...	...	...	...	...	...	...	...	...	...	...	...	...	...	...
115	Queen	...	...	...	...	1	39	...	...	...	...	...	43	...	32	...	...	...	...	...
6	Lady	...	...	...	...	...	...	...	...	...	...	...	6	...	...	...	...	...	...	...
93	Duchess of York	...	...	...	...	...	...	...	...	...	...	...	...	...	...	45	48	...	...	...
2797		207	74	309	65	302	152	173	24	44	220	213	111	340	102	126	151	12	120	52
2756	Actual Number of Lines	205	74	309	65	299	149	171	24	44	218	209	107	334	102	117	146	12	119	52

In II. 3 Bolingbroke's lines should be 55. The total lines should be 2755, as the total of V. 4 should be 11.

A MIDSUMMER-NIGHT'S DREAM.

Total Number of Lines.	CHARACTERS.	I.		II.		III.		IV.		V.
		1	2	1	2	1	2	1	2	1
242	THESEUS	65	...	...	...	...	...	41	...	136
41	EGEUS	30	...	...	...	...	...	11	...	...
142	DEMETRIUS	2	...	23	2	...	62	25	...	28
178	LYSANDER	53	...	...	44	...	59	10	...	12
134	QUINCE	...	51	...	...	39	...	...	9	35
279	BOTTOM	...	54	...	...	94	...	51	19	61
58	FLUTE	...	5	...	...	7	...	...	12	34
14	STARVELING	...	2	...	...	3	...	...	2	7
24	SNOUT	...	2	...	...	10	...	...	...	12
16	SNUG	...	3	...	...	...	...	...	4	9
206	PUCK	...	...	37	18	11	101	3	...	36
224	OBERON	...	...	79	8	...	63	46	...	28
24	PHILOSTRATE	...	...	...	...	...	...	...	...	24
36	HIPPOLYTA	5	...	...	...	...	...	7	...	24
165	HERMIA	56	...	...	26	...	80	3	...	...
229	HELENA	43	...	34	32	...	116	4	...	...
52	FAIRY	...	...	28	24	...	...	...	...	...
143	TITANIA	...	...	72	8	34	...	25	...	4
5	PEASEBLOSSOM	...	...	...	...	4	...	1	...	...
5	COBWEB	...	...	...	...	4	...	1	...	...
3	MOTH	...	...	...	...	3	...	...	...	...
6	MUSTARDSEED	...	...	...	...	4	...	2	...	...
2226		254	117	273	162	213	481	230	46	450
2180	Actual Number of Lines	251	114	268	162	206	463	225	46	445

Contrary to the usual practice of classing Fairies with the female characters, Oberon and Puck are here put amongst the men, as the parts for the ladies are sufficiently numerous without them.

THE MERCHANT OF VENICE.

Total Number of Lines.	CHARACTERS.	I.			II.									III.					IV.		V.
		1	2	3	1	2	3	4	5	6	7	8	9	1	2	3	4	5	1	2	1
188	Antonio	46	...	39	...	...	...	...	...	6	...	...	...	...	...	19	...	...	66	...	12
109	Salarino	41	...	...	...	...	...	3	...	5	...	34	...	22	...	4	...	...	...	...	...
59	Salanio	11	...	...	...	...	...	3	...	...	...	21	...	24	...	...	...	...	...	...	...
341	Bassanio	51	...	16	...	38	...	...	...	...	...	...	...	...	144	...	...	...	50	...	42
181	Lorenzo	6	...	...	...	...	...	27	...	21	...	...	...	...	5	...	12	34	...	...	76
178	Gratiano	34	...	...	...	18	...	3	...	20	...	...	...	...	31	...	...	...	33	5	34
18	Servant	...	5	...	...	...	...	...	...	...	...	...	11	2	...	...	...	...	...	...	...
364	Shylock	...	...	134	...	...	...	...	39	...	...	...	...	72	...	16	...	...	103	...	...
103	Morocco	...	...	...	32	...	...	...	...	...	71	...	...	...	...	...	...	...	...	...	...
188	Launcelot ...	...	...	...	...	120	5	6	15	...	...	...	...	...	...	...	...	35	...	...	7
41	Old Gobbo ...	...	...	...	...	41	...	...	...	...	...	...	...	...	...	...	...	...	...	...	...
2	Leonardo	...	...	...	...	2	...	...	...	...	...	...	...	...	...	...	...	...	...	...	...
66	Arragon	...	...	...	...	...	...	...	...	...	...	...	66	...	...	...	...	...	...	...	...
16	Tubál	...	...	...	...	...	...	...	...	...	...	...	...	16	...	...	...	...	...	...	...
9	Musician	...	...	...	...	...	...	...	...	...	...	...	...	...	9	...	...	...	...	...	...
1	"All"	...	...	...	...	...	...	...	...	...	...	...	...	...	1	...	...	...	...	...	...
24	Salerio	...	...	...	...	...	...	...	...	...	...	...	...	...	20	...	...	...	4	...	...
1	Balthasar ...	...	...	...	...	...	...	...	...	...	...	...	...	...	...	...	1	...	...	...	...
57	Duke	...	...	...	...	...	...	...	...	...	...	...	...	...	...	...	...	...	57	...	...
8	Stephano	...	...	...	...	...	...	...	...	...	...	...	...	...	...	...	...	...	...	...	8
589	Portia	...	96	...	17	...	...	...	...	...	9	...	20	...	118	...	71	...	138	12	108
110	Nerissa	...	46	...	...	...	...	...	...	...	...	...	6	...	5	...	2	...	22	4	25
89	Jessica	...	...	...	...	...	16	...	4	18	...	...	...	...	7	...	1	29	...	...	14
2742		189	147	189	49	219	21	42	58	70	80	55	103	136	340	39	87	98	473	21	326
2662	Actual No. of Lines	186	147	183	46	215	21	40	57	68	79	53	101	136	330	36	84	96	458	19	307

JOHN.

Total Number of Lines.	CHARACTERS.	I.	II.	III.				IV.			V.						
		1	1	1	2	3	4	1	2	3	1	2	3	4	5	6	7
435	KING JOHN	48	104	34	3	64	...	...	119	...	27	...	8	...	...	...	28
41	CHATILLON	16	25	...	...	...	...	...	...	...	...	...	...	...	...	...	...
3	ESSEX	3	...	...	...	...	...	...	...	...	...	...	...	...	...	...	...
522	BASTARD	143	123	9	8	5	...	...	22	57	43	53	...	...	...	20	39
22	ROBERT FAULCONBRIDGE	22	...	...	...	...	...	...	...	...	...	...	...	...	...	...	...
1	GURNEY	1	...	...	...	...	...	...	...	...	...	...	...	...	...	...	...
154	LEWIS	...	28	8	...	...	18	...	...	...	...	83	...	...	17	...	...
35	AUSTRIA	...	27	8	...	...	...	...	...	...	...	...	...	...	...	...	...
193	KING PHILIP	...	119	48	...	...	26	...	...	...	...	...	...	...	...	...	...
64	1ST CITIZEN	...	64	...	...	...	...	...	...	...	...	...	...	...	...	...	...
12	FRENCH HERALD	...	12	...	...	...	...	...	...	...	...	...	...	...	...	...	...
13	ENGLISH HERALD	...	13	...	...	...	...	...	...	...	...	...	...	...	...	...	...
158	SALISBURY	...	...	6	...	...	...	...	28	53	...	32	...	19	...	...	20
165	PANDULPH	...	...	72	...	...	67	...	...	...	11	15	...	...	...	...	...
140	HUBERT	...	...	...	...	8	...	43	35	25	...	...	1	...	...	28	...
2	1ST EXECUTIONER	...	...	...	...	...	...	2	...	...	...	...	...	...	...	...	...
79	PEMBROKE	...	...	...	...	...	...	...	56	13	...	...	...	4	...	...	6
28	MESSENGER	...	...	...	...	...	...	...	14	...	...	...	8	...	6	...	...
1	PETER	...	...	...	...	...	...	...	1	...	...	...	...	...	...	...	...
9	BIGOT	...	...	...	...	...	...	...	...	9	...	...	...	...	...	...	...
39	MELUN	...	...	...	...	...	...	...	...	...	...	...	...	39	...	...	...
55	ELINOR	29	21	2	...	3	...	...	...	...	...	...	...	...	...	...	...
15	LADY FAULCONBRIDGE ...	15	...	...	...	...	...	...	...	...	...	...	...	...	...	...	...
120	ARTHUR	...	9	1	...	1	...	99	...	10	...	...	...	...	...	...	...
263	CONSTANCE	...	48	141	...	...	74	...	...	...	...	...	...	...	...	...	...
42	BLANCH	...	15	27	...	...	...	...	...	...	...	...	...	...	...	...	...
29	PRINCE HENRY	...	...	...	...	...	...	...	...	...	...	...	...	...	...	...	29
2640		277	608	356	11	81	185	144	275	167	81	183	17	62	23	48	122
2570	Actual Number of Lines	276	598	347	10	73	183	134	269	159	79	180	17	61	22	44	118

I HENRY IV.

Total Number of Lines.	CHARACTERS.	I.			II.				III.			IV.				V.				
		1	2	3	1	2	3	4	1	2	3	1	2	3	4	1	2	3	4	5
341	King	75	...	45	...	...	...	...	...	130	...	...	...	...	...	47	...	...	19	25
41	Westmoreland ...	33	...	...	...	...	...	...	...	...	...	...	7	...	...	...	...	...	1	...
688	Falstaff	...	90	...	...	63	...	248	...	...	127	...	67	...	...	22	...	27	44	...
616	Prince Henry ...	...	98	...	...	31	...	256	...	44	47	...	9	...	...	29	...	9	78	15
87	Poins	...	52	...	...	11	...	24	...	...	...	...	...	...	...	...	...	...	...	...
189	Worcester	...	...	63	...	...	...	...	16	...	...	22	...	4	...	47	34	...	...	3
26	Northumberland	...	...	26	...	...	...	...	...	...	...	...	...	...	...	...	...	...	...	...
566	Hotspur	...	...	171	...	...	72	...	109	...	...	77	...	73	...	...	39	9	16	...
41	Blunt	...	...	7	...	...	...	...	...	7	...	...	...	20	...	...	...	7	...	...
25	1st Carrier ...	...	...	...	24	...	...	1	...	...	...	...	...	...	...	...	...	...	...	...
1	Ostler	...	...	...	1	...	...	...	...	...	...	...	...	...	...	...	...	...	...	...
20	2nd Carrier ...	...	...	...	20	...	...	...	...	...	...	...	...	...	...	...	...	...	...	...
47	Gadshill	...	...	...	40	3	...	4	...	...	...	...	...	...	...	...	...	...	...	...
21	Chamberlain ...	...	...	...	21	...	...	...	...	...	...	...	...	...	...	...	...	...	...	...
31	Bardolph	...	...	...	...	3	...	12	...	...	13	...	3	...	...	...	...	...	...	...
14	Peto	...	...	...	...	1	...	13	...	...	...	...	...	...	...	...	...	...	...	...
6	1st Traveller ...	...	...	...	...	6	...	...	...	...	...	...	...	...	...	...	...	...	...	...
3	Servant	...	...	...	...	...	3	...	...	...	...	...	...	...	...	...	...	...	...	...
18	Francis	...	...	...	...	...	...	18	...	...	...	...	...	...	...	...	...	...	...	...
5	Vintner	...	...	...	...	...	...	5	...	...	...	...	...	...	...	...	...	...	...	...
8	Sheriff	...	...	...	...	...	...	8	...	...	...	...	...	...	...	...	...	...	...	...
60	Mortimer	...	...	...	...	...	...	...	60	...	...	...	...	...	...	...	...	...	...	...
80	Glendower	...	...	...	...	...	...	...	80	...	...	...	...	...	...	...	...	...	...	...
46	Douglas	...	...	...	...	...	...	...	...	...	...	13	...	4	...	...	6	15	8	...
7	1st Messenger ...	...	...	...	...	...	...	...	...	...	...	6	...	...	...	...	1	...	...	...
66	Vernon	...	...	...	...	...	...	...	...	...	...	25	...	20	...	...	21	...	...	...
34	Archbishop	...	...	...	...	...	...	...	...	...	...	...	...	...	34	...	...	...	...	...
8	Sir Michael ...	...	...	...	...	...	...	...	...	...	...	...	...	...	8	...	...	...	...	...
1	2nd Messenger ...	...	...	...	...	...	...	...	...	...	...	...	...	...	...	...	1	...	...	...
8	Lancaster	...	...	...	...	...	...	...	...	...	...	...	...	...	...	...	...	...	6	2
58	Lady Percy ...	...	...	...	...	...	47	...	11	...	...	...	...	...	...	...	...	...	...	...
57	Hostess	...	...	...	...	...	...	14	...	...	43	...	...	...	...	...	...	...	...	...
3219		108	240	312	106	118	122	603	276	181	230	143	86	121	42	145	102	67	172	45
3180	Actual No. of Lines	108	240	302	106	118	120	603	271	180	230	136	86	113	41	144	101	65	172	44

The total lines should be 3177, as the total of V. should be 169.

2 HENRY IV.

Total Number of Lines.	CHARACTERS.	Induction.	I. 1	I. 2	I. 3	II. 1	II. 2	II. 3	II. 4	III. 1	III. 2	IV. 1	IV. 2	IV. 3	IV. 4	IV. 5	V. 1	V. 2	V. 3	V. 4	V. 5	Epilogue.
86	Lord Bardolph		40		46																	
4	Porter		4																			
106	Northumberland		87					19														
16	Travers		16																			
78	Morton		78																			
719	Falstaff			185		57			122		140			108			33		36		38	
162	Lord Chief Justice			63		42												50			7	
13	Servant			13																		
149	Archbishop				33							91	25									
56	Mowbray				6							43	7									
57	Hastings				28							16	13									
10	Fang					10																
3	Snare					3																
8	Gower					8																
308	Prince Henry						93		37							81		70			27	
82	Poins						70		12													
57	Bardolph						17		11		22			1			1		5			
12	1st Drawer								12													
13	2nd Drawer								13													
81	Pistol								38										28		15	
6	Peto								6													
294	King Henry IV.									80					76	138						
77	Warwick									31					18	15		13				
223	Shallow										136						36		38		13	
47	Silence										16								31			
13	Mouldy										13											
2	Shadow										2											
2	Wart										2											
13	Feeble										13											
14	Bullcalf										14											
4	Messenger											4										
110	Westmoreland											81	17	1	11							
109	Lancaster												67	23		1		7			11	
9	Colevile													9								
17	Gloucester														9	3		5				
23	Clarence														13	6		4				
8	Harcourt														8							
39	Davy																28		11			
11	1st Beadle																			11		
3	1st Groom																				3	
1	2nd Groom																				1	
40	"Rumour"	40																				
35	Page			17			16		2													
189	Hostess					89			90											10		
5	Lady Northumberland							5														
46	Lady Percy							46														
93	Doll Tearsheet								79											14		
37	Dancer																					37
3490		40	225	278	113	209	196	70	422	111	358	235	129	142	135	244	98	149	149	35	115	37
3446	Actual Number of Lines	40	215	278	110	209	196	68	421	108	358	228	123	142	132	241	98	145	147	35	115	37

HENRY V.

Total Number of Lines.	CHARACTERS.	Prologue.	I.		Prologue.	II.				Prologue.	III.							Prologue.	IV.								Prologue.	V.		Epilogue.
			1	2		1	2	3	4		1	2	3	4	5	6	7		1	2	3	4	5	6	7	8		1	2	
223	Canterbury...	...	82	141	...	...	...	...	...	...	...	...	...	...	...	...	...	...	...	...	...	...	...	...	...	...	...	...	...	...
27	Ely	...	20	7	...	...	...	...	...	...	...	...	...	...	...	...	...	...	...	...	...	...	...	...	...	...	...	...	...	...
1063	King Henry...	...	...	120	...	...	137	...	...	...	34	...	51	...	...	45	...	...	213	...	95	...	...	12	65	58	...	...	233	...
130	Exeter	...	...	16	...	...	11	...	57	...	...	...	...	...	...	...	...	...	...	...	4	...	...	27	2	5	...	...	8	...
27	Westmoreland ...	...	...	14	...	...	3	...	...	...	...	...	...	...	...	...	...	...	...	...	7	...	...	...	...	...	...	...	3	...
17	1st Ambassador ...	...	...	17	...	...	...	...	...	...	...	...	...	...	...	...	...	...	...	...	...	...	...	...	...	...	...	...	...	...
34	Bardolph ...	...	...	...	...	26	...	6	...	...	...	2	...	...	...	...	...	...	...	...	...	...	...	...	...	...	...	...	...	...
53	Nym	...	...	...	...	42	...	5	...	...	...	6	...	...	...	...	...	...	...	...	...	...	...	...	...	...	...	...	...	...
163	Pistol ...	...	...	...	...	43	...	16	...	...	...	13	...	...	...	21	...	...	17	...	...	30	...	...	...	...	...	23	...	...
7	Bedford ...	...	...	...	...	...	3	...	...	...	...	...	...	...	...	...	...	...	...	...	...	...	...	...	...	...	...	...	...	...
13	Scroop ...	...	...	...	...	...	13	...	...	...	...	...	...	...	...	...	...	...	...	...	...	...	...	...	...	...	...	...	...	...
15	Cambridge ...	...	...	...	...	...	15	...	...	...	...	...	...	...	...	...	...	...	...	...	...	...	...	...	...	...	...	...	...	...
13	Grey	...	...	...	...	...	13	...	...	...	...	...	...	...	...	...	...	...	...	...	...	...	...	...	...	...	...	...	...	...
96	French King	...	...	...	...	...	...	...	42	...	...	...	...	...	28	...	...	...	...	...	...	...	...	...	...	...	...	...	26	...
121	Dauphin... ...	...	...	...	...	...	...	...	38	...	...	...	...	...	11	...	56	...	...	10	...	...	6	...	...	...	...	...	...	...
126	Constable ...	...	...	...	...	...	...	...	12	...	...	...	...	...	21	...	66	...	...	29	...	...	4	...	...	...	...	...	...	...
6	Messenger ...	...	...	...	...	...	...	...	2	...	...	...	...	...	...	...	3	...	...	1	...	...	...	...	...	...	...	...	...	...
310	Fluellen ...	...	...	...	...	...	...	...	...	...	...	48	...	...	...	66	...	...	17	...	...	...	...	...	83	43	...	53	...	...
75	Gower	...	...	...	...	...	...	...	...	...	...	14	...	...	...	23	...	...	4	...	...	...	...	...	15	1	...	18	...	...
12	Jamy	...	...	...	...	...	...	...	...	...	...	12	...	...	...	...	...	...	...	...	...	...	...	...	...	...	...	...	...	...
24	Macmorris ...	...	...	...	...	...	...	...	...	...	...	24	...	...	...	...	...	...	...	...	...	...	...	...	...	...	...	...	...	...
7	Governor ...	...	...	...	...	...	...	...	...	...	...	...	7	...	...	...	...	...	...	...	...	...	...	...	...	...	...	...	...	...
18	Bourbon ...	...	...	...	...	...	...	...	...	...	...	...	...	...	9	...	...	...	...	...	...	...	9	...	...	...	...	...	...	...
54	Montjoy ...	...	...	...	...	...	...	...	...	...	...	...	...	...	...	25	...	...	...	...	13	...	...	...	16	...	...	...	...	...
5	Gloucester	...	...	...	...	...	...	...	...	...	...	...	...	...	...	1	...	...	2	...	1	...	...	...	1	...	...	...	...	...
49	Orleans ...	...	...	...	...	...	...	...	...	...	...	...	...	...	...	...	41	...	...	3	...	...	5	...	...	...	...	...	...	...
11	Rambures ...	...	...	...	...	...	...	...	...	...	...	...	...	...	...	...	9	...	...	2	...	...	...	...	...	...	...	...	...	...
7	Erpingham ...	...	...	...	...	...	...	...	...	...	...	...	...	...	...	...	...	...	7	...	...	...	...	...	...	...	...	...	...	...
2	Court ...	...	...	...	...	...	...	...	...	...	...	...	...	...	...	...	...	...	2	...	...	...	...	...	...	...	...	...	...	...
21	Bates ...	...	...	...	...	...	...	...	...	...	...	...	...	...	...	...	...	...	21	...	...	...	...	...	...	...	...	...	...	...
81	Williams ...	...	...	...	...	...	...	...	...	...	...	...	...	...	...	...	...	...	46	...	...	...	...	...	12	23	...	...	...	...
18	Grandpré ...	...	...	...	...	...	...	...	...	...	...	...	...	...	...	...	...	...	...	18	...	...	...	...	...	...	...	...	...	...
9	Salisbury ...	...	...	...	...	...	...	...	...	...	...	...	...	...	...	...	...	...	...	...	9	...	...	...	...	...	...	...	...	...
2	York ...	...	...	...	...	...	...	...	...	...	...	...	...	...	...	...	...	...	...	...	2	...	...	...	...	...	...	...	...	...
20	French Soldier	...	...	...	...	...	...	...	...	...	...	...	...	...	...	...	...	...	...	...	...	20	...	...	...	...	...	...	...	...
1	Warwick ...	...	...	...	...	...	...	...	...	...	...	...	...	...	...	...	...	...	...	...	...	...	...	...	...	1	...	...	...	...
1	English Herald	...	...	...	...	...	...	...	...	...	...	...	...	...	...	...	...	...	...	...	...	...	...	...	...	1	...	...	...	...
68	Burgundy ...	...	...	...	...	...	...	...	...	...	...	...	...	...	...	...	...	...	...	...	...	...	...	...	...	...	...	...	68	...
2	"All" ...	...	...	...	...	...	...	...	...	...	...	...	...	...	...	...	...	...	...	...	...	...	...	...	...	...	...	...	2	...
223	"Chorus" ...	34	...	...	42	...	...	...	...	35	...	...	...	...	...	...	...	53	...	...	...	...	...	...	...	...	45	...	...	14
47	Hostess ...	...	...	...	...	17	...	30	...	...	...	...	...	...	...	...	...	...	...	...	...	...	...	...	...	...	...	...	...	...
80	Boy ...	...	...	...	...	5	...	9	...	...	...	34	...	...	...	...	...	...	...	...	...	32	...	...	...	...	...	...	...	...
73	Katharine ...	...	...	...	...	...	...	...	...	...	...	...	...	42	...	...	...	...	...	...	...	...	...	...	...	...	...	...	31	...
33	Alice ...	...	...	...	...	...	...	...	...	...	...	...	...	24	...	...	...	...	...	...	...	...	...	...	...	...	...	...	9	...
24	Isabel ...	...	...	...	...	...	...	...	...	...	...	...	...	...	...	...	...	...	...	...	...	...	...	...	...	...	...	...	24	...
3411		34	102	315	42	133	195	66	151	35	34	153	58	66	69	181	169	53	329	63	135	82	24	39	194	132	45	94	404	14
3380	Actual No. of Lines	34	98	310	42	133	193	66	146	35	34	153	58	66	68	181	169	53	326	63	132	82	23	38	191	131	45	94	402	14

THE MERRY WIVES OF WINDSOR.

Total Number of Lines.	CHARACTERS.	I.				II.			III.					IV.						V.				
		1	2	3	4	1	2	3	1	2	3	4	5	1	2	3	4	5	6	1	2	3	4	5
137	SHALLOW	55	...	...	...	20	...	20	14	7	...	13	...	...	4	...	...	...	...	...	4	...	...	...
163	SLENDER	107	...	...	...	...	...	3	3	4	...	23	...	...	...	...	...	...	...	...	5	...	...	18
265	EVANS	85	12	...	...	...	...	...	57	..	15	...	...	39	11	..	12	9	...	...	...	...	4	21
174	PAGE	26	...	...	...	29	...	8	16	12	13	8	...	...	8	...	22	...	...	...	7	...	...	25
488	FALSTAFF	19	...	52	...	...	120	...	...	...	40	...	105	...	15	...	...	44	...	28	...	...	...	65
29	BARDOLPH	6	...	2	...	...	5	...	...	...	...	...	5	...	...	5	...	6	...	...	...	...	...	...
61	PISTOL	6	...	28	...	13	7	...	...	...	...	...	...	...	...	...	...	...	...	...	...	...	...	7
37	NYM	6	...	21	...	10	...	...	...	...	...	...	...	...	...	...	...	...	...	...	...	...	...	...
51	SIMPLE	3	1	...	15	...	...	...	8	...	...	...	...	...	...	...	...	24	...	...	...	...	...	...
131	HOST	...	...	11	...	12	...	35	18	7	...	...	...	...	..	9	...	32	7	...	...	...	...	...
11	RUGBY	...	...	...	4	...	...	7	...	...	...	...	...	...	...	...	...	...	..	...	...	...	...	...
114	CAIUS	...	...	...	44	...	...	33	13	3	8	...	...	...	...	...	...	6	...	...	...	1	...	6
100	FENTON	...	...	...	14	...	...	...	...	...	...	27	...	...	...	...	...	...	48	...	...	...	...	11
339	FORD	...	...	...	...	34	115	...	..	39	30	...	29	..	50	...	12	...	...	2	...	...	...	28
1	"ALL"	...	...	...	...	...	...	...	...	1	...	..	...	...	...	...	...	...	...	...	...	...	...	...
4	1ST SERVANT	...	...	...	...	...	...	...	...	...	1	...	...	...	3	...	...	...	...	...	...	...	...	...
2	2ND SERVANT	...	...	...	...	...	...	...	...	...	...	...	...	...	2	...	...	...	...	...	...	...	...	...
76	ANNE PAGE	13	...	..	...	..	...	...	...	...	...	18	...	...	...	...	...	...	...	...	...	...	...	45
254	MISTRESS QUICKLY	...	...	...	103	2	81	...	...	...	...	21	16	18	...	...	...	11	...	2	...	...	...	...
361	MISTRESS PAGE ...	...	...	...	...	83	...	...	...	18	67	8	...	17	80	...	43	...	...	...	...	19	...	26
209	MISTRESS FORD ...	...	...	...	...	45	...	...	...	...	75	...	...	...	67	...	7	...	...	...	...	5	...	10
15	ROBIN	...	...	...	...	...	1	...	...	3	11	...	...	...	...	...	...	...	...	...	...	...	...	...
13	WILLIAM PAGE ...	...	...	...	...	...	...	...	...	...	...	...	...	13	...	...	...	...	...	...	...	...	...	...
3035		326	13	114	180	248	329	106	129	94	260	118	155	87	240	14	96	132	55	32	16	25	4	262
3019	Actual No. of Lines	326	13	114	180	248	329	102	129	93	260	115	155	87	240	14	91	132	55	32	16	25	4	259

The 'Globe' gives the part of the Queen of the Fairies in V. 5 to Mistress Quickly. It should be taken by Anne Page (see IV. vi. 20).

MUCH ADO ABOUT NOTHING.

Total Number of Lines.	CHARACTERS.	I.			II.			III.					IV.		V.			
		1	2	3	1	2	3	1	2	3	4	5	1	2	1	2	3	4
357	Leonato	35	14	...	39	...	46	...	4	...	...	17	69	...	108	...	...	25
34	Messenger	30	...	...	...	...	...	...	...	...	...	2	...	...	...	...	...	2
356	Don Pedro	66	...	...	71	...	71	...	51	...	...	...	12	...	71	...	7	7
474	Benedick...	99	...	...	85	...	88	...	9	...	...	...	52	...	25	66	...	50
125	Don John	2	...	46	12	19	...	...	38	...	...	...	8	...	...	...	...	...
293	Claudio	40	...	...	28	...	37	...	35	...	...	...	59	...	58	...	15	21
57	Antonio	...	15	...	7	...	...	...	...	...	...	...	...	...	32	...	...	3
41	Conrade	...	...	15	...	...	...	...	...	20	...	...	...	6	...	...	...	...
140	Borachio...	...	...	16	4	39	...	...	...	53	...	...	...	4	24	...	...	...
32	Balthasar	...	...	...	6	...	26	...	...	...	...	...	...	...	...	...	...	...
198	Dogberry	...	...	...	...	...	...	...	...	72	...	41	...	50	35	...	...	...
30	Verges	...	...	...	...	...	...	...	...	14	...	9	...	5	2	...	...	...
32	1st Watch	...	...	...	...	...	...	...	...	26	...	...	...	6	...	...	...	...
11	2nd Watch	...	...	...	...	...	...	...	...	8	..	...	...	3	...	...	...	...
84	Friar	...	...	..	...	...	...	...	...	...	...	...	75	...	...	...	...	9
17	Sexton	...	...	...	...	...	...	...	...	...	...	...	...	17	...	...	...	...
11	Lord	...	...	...	...	...	...	...	...	...	...	...	...	...	...	...	11	...
309	Beatrice	57	...	...	124	...	8	10	...	...	18	...	57	...	...	24	...	11
135	Hero	2	...	...	11	...	...	78	...	...	18	...	18	...	...	...	...	8
75	Margaret	...	...	...	6	...	...	1	...	...	58	...	...	...	...	10	...	...
51	Ursula	...	...	...	11	...	...	29	...	...	5	...	...	...	...	6	...	...
2	Boy	...	...	...	...	...	2	...	...	...	...	...	...	...	...	...	...	...
2864		331	29	77	404	58	278	118	137	193	99	69	350	91	355	106	33	136
2826	Actual No. of Lines	330	29	77	404	58	273	116	137	193	99	69	340	90	341	106	33	131

The actual number of lines should be 2829, as the total of II. 3 should be 276. In the 'Globe' three lines of the second verse of the song are not printed in full.

AS YOU LIKE IT.

Total Number of Lines.	CHARACTERS.	I.			II.							III.					IV.			V.			
		1	2	3	1	2	3	4	5	6	7	1	2	3	4	5	1	2	3	1	2	3	4
322	ORLANDO	68	40	...	...	...	23	...	...	16	32	...	62	...	...	...	41	...	...	...	29	...	11
66	ADAM	7	...	...	...	...	54	...	...	3	2	...	...	...	...	...	...	...	...	...	...	...	...
154	OLIVER	62	...	...	...	...	...	...	...	...	...	2	...	...	...	...	...	...	80	...	10	...	...
3	DENNIS	3	...	...	...	...	...	...	...	...	...	...	...	...	...	...	...	...	...	...	...	...	...
45	CHARLES	40	5	...	...	...	...	...	...	...	...	...	...	...	...	...	...	...	...	...	...	...	...
316	TOUCHSTONE	...	30	...	...	...	...	26	...	...	...	...	70	76	...	...	...	...	...	49	...	11	54
53	LE BEAU	...	53	...	...	...	...	...	...	...	...	...	...	...	...	...	...	...	...	...	...	...	...
69	DUKE FREDERICK	...	21	24	...	8	...	...	...	...	...	16	...	...	...	...	...	...	...	...	...	...	...
111	DUKE SENIOR	...	...	...	29	...	...	...	...	...	51	...	...	...	...	...	...	...	...	...	...	...	31
53	AMIENS	...	...	...	3	...	...	...	30	...	20	...	...	...	...	...	...	...	...	...	...	...	...
43	1ST LORD (DUKE SENIOR)	...	...	...	39	...	...	...	...	...	3	...	...	...	...	...	...	1	...	...	...	...	...
2	2ND LORD "	...	...	...	2	...	...	...	...	...	...	...	...	...	...	...	...	...	...	...	...	...	...
4	1ST LORD (DUKE FRED.)	...	...	...	...	4	...	...	...	...	...	...	...	...	...	...	...	...	...	...	...	...	...
9	2ND LORD "	...	...	...	...	9	...	...	...	...	...	...	...	...	...	...	...	...	...	...	...	...	...
75	CORIN	...	...	...	...	...	...	26	...	...	...	...	37	...	10	...	...	...	...	2	...	...	...
76	SILVIUS	...	...	...	...	...	...	19	...	...	...	...	...	...	...	29	...	...	14	...	13	...	1
235	JAQUES	...	...	...	...	...	...	...	35	...	100	...	24	16	...	...	18	8	...	...	...	...	34
5	SIR OLIVER	...	...	...	...	...	...	...	...	...	...	...	...	5	...	...	...	...	...	...	...	...	...
10	FORESTER	...	...	...	...	...	...	...	...	...	...	...	...	...	...	...	...	10	...	...	...	...	...
11	WILLIAM	...	...	...	...	...	...	...	...	...	...	...	...	...	...	...	...	...	...	11	...	...	...
24	"HYMEN"	...	...	...	...	...	...	...	...	...	...	...	...	...	...	...	...	...	...	...	...	...	24
6	"ALL" (SONG)	...	...	...	...	...	...	...	...	...	...	...	...	...	...	...	...	...	...	...	...	...	6
17	JAQUES DE BOYS	...	...	...	...	...	...	...	...	...	...	...	...	...	...	...	...	...	...	...	...	...	17
304	CELIA	...	93	66	...	...	...	7	...	...	...	...	72	...	32	...	12	...	22	...	...	...	...
749	ROSALIND	...	63	57	...	...	...	26	...	...	...	...	192	...	22	43	153	...	74	...	74	...	45
23	AUDREY	...	...	...	...	...	...	...	...	...	...	...	...	12	...	...	...	...	...	7	...	4	...
87	PHEBE	...	...	...	...	...	...	...	...	...	...	...	...	...	...	72	...	...	...	...	9	...	6
31	1ST PAGE	...	...	...	...	...	...	...	...	...	...	...	...	...	...	...	...	...	...	...	...	31	...
27	2ND PAGE	...	...	...	...	...	...	...	...	...	...	...	...	...	...	...	...	...	...	...	...	27	...
2930		180	305	147	73	21	77	104	65	19	208	18	457	109	64	144	224	19	190	69	135	73	229
2867	Actual Number of Lines	180	301	140	69	21	76	100	65	19	203	18	457	109	62	139	224	19	184	69	135	49	228

TWELFTH NIGHT.

Total Number of Lines.	CHARACTERS.	I.					II.					III.				IV.			V.
		1	2	3	4	5	1	2	3	4	5	1	2	3	4	1	2	3	1
221	Duke	31	...	...	27	...	...	...	...	69	...	...	...	...	...	...	...	...	94
7	Curio	2	...	...	...	...	...	...	...	5	...	...	...	...	...	...	...	...	...
14	Valentine	9	...	...	5	...	...	...	...	...	...	...	...	...	...	...	...	...	...
32	Captain	...	32	...	...	...	...	...	...	...	...	...	...	...	...	...	...	...	...
398	Sir Toby	...	...	67	...	7	...	...	63	...	44	7	36	...	144	10	13	...	7
183	Sir Andrew	...	...	53	...	...	...	...	51	...	15	7	12	...	18	7	...	...	20
344	Clown	...	...	...	...	66	...	...	33	29	...	42	...	...	...	20	77	...	77
306	Malvolio	...	...	...	...	35	...	14	20	...	115	...	...	...	58	...	45	...	19
107	Antonio	...	...	...	...	...	13	...	...	...	...	...	...	33	33	...	...	...	28
128	Sebastian	...	...	...	...	...	36	...	...	...	...	...	...	20	...	17	...	23	32
128	Fabian	...	...	...	...	...	...	...	...	...	33	...	25	...	40	...	...	...	30
4	Servant	...	...	...	...	...	...	...	...	...	...	...	...	...	4	...	...	...	...
12	1st Officer	...	...	...	...	...	...	...	...	...	...	...	...	...	6	...	...	...	6
4	2nd Officer	...	...	...	...	...	...	...	...	...	...	...	...	...	4	...	...	...	...
8	Priest	...	...	...	...	...	...	...	...	...	...	...	...	...	...	...	...	...	8
353	Viola	...	34	...	13	75	...	28	...	32	...	69	...	...	56	...	...	...	46
169	Maria	...	...	31	...	25	...	...	41	...	20	...	17	...	29	...	6	...	...
321	Olivia	...	...	...	...	127	...	...	...	...	...	54	...	...	45	16	...	12	67
2739		42	66	151	45	335	49	42	208	135	227	179	90	53	437	70	141	35	434
2692	Actual No. of Lines	41	64	151	42	330	49	42	208	127	227	176	90	49	433	69	141	35	418

JULIUS CÆSAR.

Total Number of Lines.	CHARACTERS.	I.			II.				III.			IV.			V.				
		1	2	3	1	2	3	4	1	2	3	1	2	3	1	2	3	4	5
26	FLAVIUS	26	...	...	...	...	...	...	...	...	...	...	...	...	...	...	...	...	...
1	1ST COMMONER	1	...	...	...	...	...	...	...	...	...	...	...	...	...	...	...	...	...
33	MARCELLUS	33	...	...	...	...	...	...	...	...	...	...	...	...	...	...	...	...	...
20	2ND COMMONER	20	...	...	...	...	...	...	...	...	...	...	...	...	...	...	...	...	...
154	CÆSAR	...	39	...	...	72	...	...	40	...	...	...	...	3	...	...	...	...	...
136	CASCA	...	67	57	10	...	...	...	2	...	...	...	...	...	...	...	...	...	...
327	ANTONY	...	6	...	...	1	...	...	98	146	...	38	...	...	22	...	...	8	8
18	SOOTHSAYER	...	3	...	...	...	...	14	1	...	...	...	...	...	...	...	...	...	...
727	BRUTUS	...	73	...	180	3	...	...	79	55	...	...	34	204	33	6	18	3	39
507	CASSIUS	...	143	95	37	...	...	...	46	...	...	...	7	98	49	...	32	...	...
9	CICERO	...	...	9	...	...	...	...	...	...	...	...	...	...	...	...	...	...	...
18	CINNA	...	...	9	4	...	...	...	5	...	...	...	...	...	...	...	...	...	...
33	LUCIUS	...	...	...	17	...	...	6	...	...	...	...	...	10	...	...	...	...	...
44	DECIUS	...	...	...	12	25	...	...	7	...	...	...	...	...	...	...	...	...	...
17	METELLUS	...	...	...	9	...	...	...	8	...	...	...	...	...	...	...	...	...	...
8	TREBONIUS	...	...	...	3	2	...	...	3	...	...	...	...	...	...	...	...	...	...
15	LIGARIUS	...	...	...	15	...	...	...	...	...	...	...	...	...	...	...	...	...	...
30	SERVANT	...	...	...	...	5	...	...	21	4	...	...	...	...	...	...	...	...	...
2	PUBLIUS	...	...	...	...	1	...	...	1	...	...	...	...	...	...	...	...	...	...
20	ARTEMIDORUS	...	...	...	...	...	16	...	4	...	...	...	...	...	...	...	...	...	...
2	POPILIUS	...	...	...	...	...	...	...	2	...	...	...	...	...	...	...	...	...	...
15	"ALL"	...	...	...	...	...	...	...	...	14	...	...	...	...	...	...	...	...	1
23	1ST CITIZEN	...	...	...	...	...	...	...	...	18	5	...	...	...	...	...	...	...	...
24	2ND CITIZEN	...	...	...	...	...	...	...	...	18	6	...	...	...	...	...	...	...	...
23	3RD CITIZEN	...	...	...	...	...	...	...	...	16	7	...	...	...	...	...	...	...	...
23	4TH CITIZEN	...	...	...	...	...	...	...	...	14	9	...	...	...	...	...	...	...	...
16	CINNA (POET)	...	...	...	...	...	...	...	...	...	16	...	...	...	...	...	...	...	...
47	OCTAVIUS	...	...	...	...	...	...	...	...	...	...	12	...	...	25	...	...	...	10
4	LEPIDUS	...	...	...	...	...	...	...	...	...	...	4	...	...	...	...	...	...	...
26	LUCILIUS	...	...	...	...	...	...	...	...	...	...	...	10	1	1	...	...	12	2
16	PINDARUS	...	...	...	...	...	...	...	...	...	...	...	3	...	...	...	13	...	...
5	1ST SOLDIER	...	...	...	...	...	...	...	...	...	...	...	1	...	...	...	...	4	...
2	2ND SOLDIER	...	...	...	...	...	...	...	...	...	...	...	1	...	...	...	...	1	...
1	3RD SOLDIER	...	...	...	...	...	...	...	...	...	...	...	1	...	...	...	...	...	...
7	POET	...	...	...	...	...	...	...	...	...	...	...	...	7	...	...	...	...	...
39	MESSALA	...	...	...	...	...	...	...	...	...	...	...	...	14	2	...	19	...	4
32	TITINIUS	...	...	...	...	...	...	...	...	...	...	...	...	1	...	...	31	...	...
6	VARRO	...	...	...	...	...	...	...	...	...	...	...	...	6	...	...	...	...	...
4	CLAUDIUS	...	...	...	...	...	...	...	...	...	...	...	...	4	...	...	...	...	...
4	MESSENGER	...	...	...	...	...	...	...	...	...	...	...	...	...	4	...	...	...	...
8	CATO	...	...	...	...	...	...	...	...	...	...	...	...	...	...	...	3	5	...
10	CLITUS	...	...	...	...	...	...	...	...	...	...	...	...	...	...	...	...	...	10
3	DARDANIUS	...	...	...	...	...	...	...	...	...	...	...	...	...	...	...	...	...	3
3	VOLUMNIUS	...	...	...	...	...	...	...	...	...	...	...	...	...	...	...	...	...	3
7	STRATO	...	...	...	...	...	...	...	...	...	...	...	...	...	...	...	...	...	7
27	CALPURNIA	...	1	...	...	26	...	...	...	...	...	...	...	...	...	...	...	...	...
92	PORTIA	...	...	...	62	...	...	30	...	...	...	...	...	...	...	...	...	...	...
2614		80	332	170	349	135	16	50	317	285	43	54	57	348	136	6	116	33	87
2480	Actual No. of Lines	80	326	164	334	129	16	46	298	276	43	51	52	309	126	6	110	32	82

The third name in the list should be Marullus.

HAMLET.

Total Number of Lines.	CHARACTERS.	I.					II.		III.				IV.							V.	
		1	2	3	4	5	1	2	1	2	3	4	1	2	3	4	5	6	7	1	2
38	BERNARDO	34	4	...	...	...	...	...	...	...	...	...	...	...	...	...	...	...	...	...	...
10	FRANCISCO	10	...	...	...	...	...	...	...	...	...	...	...	...	...	...	...	...	...	...	...
298	HORATIO	100	50	...	26	17	...	...	...	9	...	...	...	...	...	...	2	28	...	12	54
67	MARCELLUS	46	6	...	7	8	...	...	...	...	...	...	...	...	...	...	...	...	...	...	...
551	KING	...	93	...	...	...	...	39	40	7	50	...	34	...	44	...	67	...	141	9	27
1	CORNELIUS	...	1	...	...	...	...	...	...	...	...	...	...	...	...	...	...	...	...	...	...
22	VOLTIMAND	...	1	...	...	...	...	21	...	...	...	...	...	...	...	...	...	...	...	...	...
208	LAERTES	...	7	53	...	...	...	...	...	...	...	...	...	...	...	...	48	...	47	18	35
357	POLONIUS	...	4	68	...	...	87	146	23	13	9	7	...	...	...	...	...	...	...	...	...
1569	HAMLET	...	103	...	68	99	...	302	84	245	24	176	...	23	26	47	...	...	...	142	230
7	"ALL"	...	1	...	...	...	...	...	...	1	...	...	...	...	...	...	3	...	...	1	1
95	GHOST	...	...	...	...	89	...	...	...	...	...	6	...	...	...	...	...	...	...	...	...
15	REYNALDO	...	...	...	...	...	15	...	...	...	...	...	...	...	...	...	...	...	...	...	...
105	ROSENCRANTZ ..	...	...	...	...	...	...	50	12	15	14	...	...	9	4	1	...	...	...	...	...
57	GUILDENSTERN ...	...	...	...	...	...	...	21	5	24	5	...	...	2	...	...	...	...	...	...	...
51	1ST PLAYER	...	...	...	...	...	...	48	...	3	...	...	...	...	...	...	...	...	...	...	...
44	PLAYER KING ...	...	...	...	...	...	...	...	...	44	...	...	...	...	...	...	...	...	...	...	...
6	LUCIANUS	...	...	...	...	...	...	...	...	6	...	...	...	...	...	...	...	...	...	...	...
27	FORTINBRAS... ...	...	...	...	...	...	...	...	...	...	...	...	...	...	...	8	...	...	...	...	19
12	CAPTAIN	...	...	...	...	...	...	...	...	...	...	...	...	...	...	12	...	...	...	...	...
12	1ST GENTLEMAN ...	...	...	...	...	...	...	...	...	...	...	...	...	...	...	...	12	...	...	...	...
11	2ND GENTLEMAN...	...	...	...	...	...	...	...	...	...	...	...	...	...	...	...	11	...	...	...	...
1	SERVANT	...	...	...	...	...	...	...	...	...	...	...	...	...	...	...	...	1	...	...	...
5	1ST SAILOR	...	...	...	...	...	...	...	...	...	...	...	...	...	...	...	...	5	...	...	...
5	MESSENGER	...	...	...	...	...	...	...	...	...	...	...	...	...	...	...	...	...	5	...	...
107	1ST CLOWN	...	...	...	...	...	...	...	...	...	...	...	...	...	...	...	...	...	...	107	...
19	2ND CLOWN	...	...	...	...	...	...	...	...	...	...	...	...	...	...	...	...	...	...	19	...
13	1ST PRIEST	...	...	...	...	...	...	...	...	...	...	...	...	...	...	...	...	...	...	13	...
56	OSRIC	...	...	...	...	...	...	...	...	...	...	...	...	...	...	...	...	...	...	...	56
10	LORD	...	...	...	...	...	...	...	...	...	...	...	...	...	...	...	...	...	...	...	10
6	1ST AMBASSADOR...	...	...	...	...	...	...	...	...	...	...	...	...	...	...	...	...	...	...	...	6
158	QUEEN	...	10	...	...	...	...	20	9	4	...	47	12	...	...	...	16	...	21	12	7
175	OPHELIA	...	...	20	...	...	28	...	33	18	...	...	...	...	...	...	76	...	...	...	...
3	"PROLOGUE" ...	...	...	...	...	...	...	...	...	3	...	...	...	...	...	...	...	...	...	...	...
30	PLAYER QUEEN ...	...	...	...	...	...	...	...	...	30	...	...	...	...	...	...	...	...	...	...	...
4151		190	280	141	101	213	130	647	206	422	102	236	46	34	74	68	235	34	214	333	445
3930	Actual No. of Lines	175	258	136	91	191	119	633	196	417	98	217	45	33	70	66	220	34	195	322	414

TROILUS AND CRESSIDA.

Total Number of Lines.	CHARACTERS.	Prologue.	I. 1	I. 2	I. 3	II. 1	II. 2	II. 3	III. 1	III. 2	III. 3	IV. 1	IV. 2	IV. 3	IV. 4	IV. 5	V. 1	V. 2	V. 3	V. 4	V. 5	V. 6	V. 7	V. 8	V. 9	V. 10
541	TROILUS	...	74	...	...	...	85	...	...	90	...	...	21	5	92	11	1	90	32	2	...	8	...	...	...	30
453	PANDARUS	...	42	172	...	...	...	...	91	61	...	...	36	...	18	...	...	...	9	...	...	...	...	...	...	24
143	ÆNEAS	...	5	...	58	...	...	...	...	...	...	20	20	...	9	25	...	3	...	...	...	...	...	...	...	3
35	ALEXANDER	...	...	35	...	...	...	...	...	...	...	...	...	...	...	...	...	...	...	...	...	...	...	...	...	...
195	AGAMEMNON	...	...	...	66	...	...	59	...	...	14	...	...	...	...	36	4	...	...	...	11	...	...	...	5	...
158	NESTOR	...	...	...	93	...	...	20	...	...	2	...	...	...	...	28	...	...	...	...	14	...	...	...	1	...
488	ULYSSES	...	...	...	179	...	...	81	...	...	122	...	...	...	...	62	3	28	...	...	13	...	...	...	...	...
12	MENELAUS	...	...	...	1	...	...	...	...	...	1	...	...	...	...	9	1	...	...	...	...	...	...	...	...	...
89	AJAX	...	...	...	...	26	...	28	...	...	3	...	...	...	...	21	3	...	...	...	1	5	...	...	2	...
321	THERSITES	...	...	...	...	85	...	61	...	...	48	...	...	...	...	...	61	23	...	30	...	...	13	...	...	...
195	ACHILLES	...	...	...	...	28	...	11	...	...	74	...	...	...	...	25	23	...	...	...	4	6	8	16	...	...
70	PATROCLUS	...	...	...	...	3	...	19	...	...	31	...	...	...	...	7	10	...	...	...	...	...	...	...	...	...
20	PRIAM	...	...	...	...	...	12	...	...	...	...	...	...	...	...	...	...	...	8	...	...	...	...	...	...	...
212	HECTOR	...	...	...	...	...	75	...	...	...	...	...	...	...	...	79	5	...	35	3	...	10	...	5	...	...
4	HELENUS	...	...	...	...	...	4	...	...	...	...	...	...	...	...	...	...	...	...	...	...	...	...	...	...	...
103	PARIS	...	...	...	...	...	30	...	31	...	...	31	...	8	3	...	...	...	...	...	...	...	...	...	...	...
103	DIOMEDES	...	...	...	...	...	...	5	...	...	2	32	...	...	12	6	2	29	...	4	6	4	...	...	1	...
21	SERVANT	...	...	...	...	...	...	...	20	...	...	...	...	...	...	...	...	...	...	...	1	...	...	...	...	...
31	CALCHAS	...	...	...	...	...	...	...	...	...	29	...	...	...	...	...	...	2	...	...	...	...	...	...	...	...
2	DEIPHOBUS	...	...	...	...	...	...	...	...	...	...	1	...	...	1	...	...	...	...	...	...	...	...	...	...	...
3	"ALL"	...	...	...	...	...	...	...	...	...	...	...	...	...	...	1	...	...	...	...	...	...	...	...	1	1
3	MARGARELON	...	...	...	...	...	...	...	...	...	...	...	...	...	...	...	...	...	...	...	...	...	3	...	...	...
1	MYRMIDON	...	...	...	...	...	...	...	...	...	...	...	...	...	...	...	...	...	...	...	...	...	...	1	...	...
31	"PROLOGUE"	31	...	...	...	...	...	...	...	...	...	...	...	...	...	...	...	...	...	...	...	...	...	...	...	...
312	CRESSIDA	...	...	115	...	...	...	...	...	71	...	...	44	...	25	11	...	46	...	...	...	...	...	...	...	...
5	BOY	...	...	3	...	...	...	...	...	2	...	...	...	...	...	...	...	...	...	...	...	...	...	...	...	...
37	CASSANDRA	...	...	...	...	...	13	...	...	...	...	...	...	...	...	...	...	...	24	...	...	...	...	...	...	...
30	HELEN	...	...	...	...	...	...	...	30	...	...	...	...	...	...	...	...	...	...	...	...	...	...	...	...	...
15	ANDROMACHE	...	...	...	...	...	...	...	...	...	...	...	...	...	...	...	...	...	15	...	...	...	...	...	...	...
3633		31	121	325	397	142	219	284	172	224	326	84	121	13	160	321	113	221	123	39	50	33	24	22	10	58
3496	Actual No. of Lines	31	119	321	392	142	213	277	172	220	316	79	115	12	150	293	106	197	112	38	47	31	24	22	10	57

ALL'S WELL THAT ENDS WELL.

Total Number of Lines.	CHARACTERS.	I.			II.					III.							IV.					V.		
		1	2	3	1	2	3	4	5	1	2	3	4	5	6	7	1	2	3	4	5	1	2	3
289	BERTRAM	12	7	...	10	...	37	...	42	...	...	8	...	...	37	...	...	34	39	...	...	...	...	63
305	LAFEU	30	...	...	32	...	103	...	32	...	...	...	...	...	...	...	...	...	...	...	53	...	22	33
411	PAROLLES	67	...	...	24	...	71	25	10	...	...	...	...	1	19	...	44	...	111	...	...	...	19	20
385	KING	...	68	...	80	...	77	...	...	...	...	...	...	...	...	...	...	...	...	...	...	...	...	160
127	1ST LORD	...	6	...	8	...	1	...	...	6	...	...	...	...	34	...	...	...	72	...	...	...	...	...
168	2ND LORD	...	5	...	5	...	1	...	...	8	...	...	...	...	37	...	42	...	70	...	...	...	...	...
44	STEWARD	...	...	26	...	...	...	...	...	...	...	...	18	...	...	...	...	...	...	...	...	...	...	...
212	CLOWN	...	...	67	...	39	...	24	...	...	24	...	...	...	...	...	...	...	...	...	40	...	18	...
3	"ALL"	...	...	...	...	...	1	...	...	...	...	...	...	...	...	...	2	...	...	...	...	...	...	...
1	4TH LORD	...	...	...	...	...	1	...	...	...	...	...	...	...	...	...	...	...	...	...	...	...	...	...
19	DUKE	...	...	...	...	...	...	...	...	13	...	6	...	...	...	...	...	...	...	...	...	...	...	...
34	1ST GENTLEMAN	...	...	...	...	...	...	...	...	...	12	...	...	...	...	...	...	...	...	...	...	10	...	12
11	2ND GENTLEMAN	...	...	...	...	...	...	...	...	...	11	...	...	...	...	...	...	...	...	...	...	...	...	...
98	1ST SOLDIER	...	...	...	...	...	...	...	...	...	...	...	...	...	...	...	18	...	80	...	...	...	...	...
2	2ND SOLDIER	...	...	...	...	...	...	...	...	...	...	...	...	...	...	...	2	...	...	...	...	...	...	...
4	SERVANT	...	...	...	...	...	...	...	...	...	...	...	...	...	...	...	...	...	4	...	...	...	...	...
306	COUNTESS	46	...	113	...	35	...	...	...	...	51	...	26	...	...	...	...	...	...	...	19	...	...	16
479	HELENA	89	...	71	68	...	32	11	20	...	42	...	...	30	...	37	...	...	...	34	...	33	...	12
1	PAGE	1	...	...	...	...	...	...	...	...	...	...	...	...	...	...	...	...	...	...	...	...	...	...
66	WIDOW	...	...	...	...	...	...	...	...	...	...	...	...	42	...	17	...	...	...	3	...	1	...	3
139	DIANA	...	...	...	...	...	...	...	...	...	...	...	...	24	...	...	...	52	...	3	...	...	...	60
23	MARIANA	...	...	...	...	...	...	...	...	...	...	...	...	23	...	...	...	...	...	...	...	...	...	...
3127		245	86	277	227	74	324	60	104	27	140	14	44	120	127	54	108	86	376	40	112	44	59	379
2966	Actual No. of Lines	244	76	262	213	74	316	57	97	23	132	11	42	104	125	48	105	76	376	36	112	38	59	340

MEASURE FOR MEASURE.

Total Number of Lines.	CHARACTERS.	I.				II.				III.		IV.						V.
		1	2	3	4	1	2	3	4	1	2	1	2	3	4	5	6	1
880	Duke...	67	...	51	...	...	...	25	...	141	114	38	91	83	...	13	...	257
205	Escalus	11	...	...	...	109	...	...	...	...	32	...	...	...	8	...	...	45
321	Angelo	12	...	...	..	35	85	...	117	...	...	...	..	...	29	..	...	43
321	Lucio	...	54	...	63	...	15	...	..	...	101	...	...	25	...	...	...	63
27	1st Gentleman ...	...	27	...	...	...	...	...	...	...	...	...	...	...	...	...	...	...
11	2nd Gentleman ...	...	11	...	...	...	...	...	...	...	...	..	...	...	...	...	...	...
176	Pompey	...	19	...	...	83	...	...	...	...	16	...	25	33	...	...	...	...
115	Claudio	...	58	...	...	...	...	...	...	54	...	...	3	...	...	...	...	...
171	Provost	...	3	...	...	1	19	12	...	5	5	...	96	17	...	...	...	13
6	Friar Thomas ...	...	...	6	...	...	...	...	...	..	...	...	...	...	...	...	...	...
81	Elbow	...	...	...	...	62	...	...	...	...	19	...	...	...	...	...	...	...
11	Froth	...	...	...	...	11	...	...	...	...	...	...	...	...	...	...	...	...
3	Justice	...	...	...	...	3	...	...	...	..	...	...	...	...	...	...	...	...
6	Servant	...	...	...	...	...	4	...	2	...	..	...	...	...	...	...	...	...
23	Abhorson	...	...	...	...	...	...	...	...	...	...	...	12	11	...	...	...	....
5	Messenger	...	...	...	...	...	...	...	...	...	...	...	5	...	...	...	...	...
17	Barnardine	...	...	...	...	...	...	...	...	...	...	...	...	17	...	...	...	...
36	Friar Peter	...	...	...	...	...	...	...	...	...	...	...	...	...	...	1	6	29
37	Mistress Overdone	...	28	..	...	...	...	...	...	...	9	...	...	...	...	..	...	...
426	Isabella	...	...	...	27	...	94	...	78	97	...	25	...	9	...	...	9	87
9	Francisca	...	...	...	9	...	...	...	...	...	...	...	...	...	...	...	...	...
10	Juliet	...	...	...	...	...	...	10	...	...	...	...	...	...	...	...	...	...
6	Boy	...	...	...	...	...	...	...	...	...	...	6	...	...	...	...	...	...
68	Mariana	...	...	...	...	...	...	...	...	...	...	13	...	...	...	...	2	53
2971		90	200	57	99	304	217	47	197	297	296	82	232	195	37	14	17	590
2821	Actual No. of Lines	84	198	54	90	300	187	42	188	280	296	76	226	190	37	13	15	545

OTHELLO.

Total Number of Lines.	CHARACTERS.	I.			II.			III.				IV.			V.	
		1	2	3	1	2	3	1	2	3	4	1	2	3	1	2
123	Roderigo	42	1	16	9	...	8	...	...	...	...	...	36	...	11	...
1117	Iago	108	27	93	156	...	218	5	1	217	9	134	62	...	75	12
139	Brabantio	46	31	62	...	...	...	...	...	...	...	...	...	...	...	..
888	Othello	...	38	115	29	...	56	..	5	201	50	109	68	6	8	203
288	Cassio	...	16	...	51	...	91	21	...	12	37	31	...	...	15	14
5	1st Officer	..	3	2	...	...	...	...	...	...	...	...	...	...	...	...
73	Duke	...	...	73	...	...	...	...	...	...	...	...	...	...	...	...
28	1st Senator	...	...	28	...	...	...	...	...	...	...	...	...	...	...	...
5	2nd Senator	...	...	5	...	...	...	...	...	...	...	...	...	...	...	...
4	Sailor	...	...	4	...	...	...	...	...	...	...	...	...	...	...	...
9	Messenger	...	...	9	...	...	...	...	...	...	..	...	...	...	...	...
61	Montano	...	...	...	21	...	33	...	...	...	...	...	...	...	..	7
4	1st Gentleman	...	...	...	3	...	...	...	1	...	...	...	...	...	...	...
14	2nd Gentleman	...	...	...	14	...	...	...	...	...	..	...	...	...	...	...
17	3rd Gentleman	...	...	...	17	...	...	...	...	...	...	...	...	...	...	...
5	"All"	...	...	...	2	...	2	...	...	...	...	...	...	...	...	1
2	4th Gentleman	...	...	...	2	...	...	...	...	...	...	...	...	...	...	...
13	Herald	...	...	...	...	13	...	...	...	...	...	...	...	...	...	...
30	Clown	...	...	...	...	...	...	18	...	...	12	...	...	...	...	...
5	1st Musician...	...	...	...	...	...	...	5	...	...	...	...	..	...	...	...
76	Lodovico...	...	...	...	...	...	...	...	...	...	...	25	...	2	9	40
26	Gratiano	...	...	...	...	...	...	...	...	...	...	...	...	...	9	17
389	Desdemona	...	..	28	30	...	1	...	...	72	81	14	64	57	...	42
245	Emilia	...	...	...	3	...	...	13	...	28	18	...	44	49	4	86
36	Bianca	...	...	...	...	...	...	...	...	...	17	12	...	...	7	...
3602		196	116	435	337	13	409	62	7	530	224	325	274	114	138	422
3316	Actual Number of Lines	184	99	410	321	13	394	58	6	479	201	293	252	106	129	371

In III. 4 Desdemona's lines should be 80, and in V. 1 Cassio's 16. The total lines should be 3317, as the total of II. 3 should be 395.

MACBETH.

Total Number of Lines.	CHARACTERS.	I.							II.				III.						IV.			V.							
		1	2	3	4	5	6	7	1	2	3	4	1	2	3	4	5	6	1	2	3	1	2	3	4	5	6	7	8
69	Duncan	...	15	...	36	...	18	...	...	...	...	...	...	...	...	...	...	...	...	...	...	...	...	...	...	...	...	...	...
210	Malcolm	...	6	...	10	...	...	...	...	...	14	...	...	...	...	...	...	...	...	...	141	...	...	...	11	...	6	2	20
35	Sergeant	...	35	...	...	...	...	...	...	...	...	...	...	...	...	...	...	...	...	...	...	...	...	...	...	...	...	...	...
72	Lennox	...	2	...	...	...	...	...	...	...	20	...	...	...	...	5	...	32	6	...	...	...	7	...	...	...	...	...	...
134	Ross	...	18	16	...	...	...	...	...	...	...	26	...	...	...	5	...	...	...	19	41	...	...	...	...	...	...	...	9
705	Macbeth	...	...	50	16	4	...	48	45	39	33	...	114	41	...	105	...	...	75	...	...	...	...	55	...	44	...	10	26
112	Banquo	...	...	42	2	...	8	...	24	...	11	...	21	...	4	...	...	...	...	...	...	...	...	...	...	...	...	...	...
21	Angus	...	...	12	...	...	...	...	...	...	...	...	...	...	...	...	...	...	...	...	...	...	9	...	...	...	...	...	...
23	Messenger	...	...	...	...	5	...	...	...	...	...	...	...	...	...	...	...	...	...	9	...	...	...	...	...	9	...	...	...
40	Porter	...	...	...	...	...	...	...	...	...	40	...	...	...	...	...	...	...	...	...	...	...	...	...	...	...	...	...	...
179	Macduff	...	...	...	...	...	...	...	...	...	40	14	...	...	...	...	...	...	...	...	91	...	...	...	3	...	2	10	19
9	Donalbain	...	...	...	...	...	...	...	...	...	9	...	...	...	...	...	...	...	...	...	...	...	...	...	...	...	...	...	...
5	"All"	...	...	...	...	...	...	...	...	...	2	...	...	...	...	...	1	...	...	...	...	...	...	...	1	...	...	...	1
11	Old Man	...	...	...	...	...	...	...	...	...	...	11	...	...	...	...	...	...	...	...	...	...	...	...	...	...	...	...	...
1	Attendant	...	...	...	...	...	...	...	...	...	...	...	1	...	...	...	...	...	...	...	...	...	...	...	...	...	...	...	...
32	1st Murderer	...	...	...	...	...	...	...	...	...	...	...	10	...	11	7	...	...	...	4	...	...	...	...	...	...	...	...	...
17	2nd Murderer	...	...	...	...	...	...	...	...	...	...	...	8	...	9	...	...	...	...	...	...	...	...	...	...	...	...	...	...
5	Servant	...	...	...	...	...	...	...	...	...	...	...	...	2	...	...	...	...	...	...	...	...	...	3	...	...	...	...	...
8	3rd Murderer	...	...	...	...	...	...	...	...	...	...	...	...	...	8	...	...	...	...	...	...	...	...	...	...	...	...	...	...
24	Lord	...	...	...	...	...	...	...	...	...	...	...	...	...	...	3	...	21	...	...	...	...	...	...	...	...	...	...	...
2	1st Apparition	...	...	...	...	...	...	...	...	...	...	...	...	...	...	...	...	...	2	...	...	...	...	...	...	...	...	...	...
5	English Doctor	...	...	...	...	...	...	...	...	...	...	...	...	...	...	...	...	...	...	...	5	...	...	...	...	...	...	...	...
47	Scotch Doctor	...	...	...	...	...	...	...	...	...	...	...	...	...	...	...	...	...	...	...	...	38	...	9	...	...	...	...	...
12	Menteith	...	...	...	...	...	...	...	...	...	...	...	...	...	...	...	...	...	...	...	...	...	10	...	2	...	...	...	...
11	Caithness	...	...	...	...	...	...	...	...	...	...	...	...	...	...	...	...	...	...	...	...	...	11	...	...	...	...	...	...
5	Seyton	...	...	...	...	...	...	...	...	...	...	...	...	...	...	...	...	...	...	...	...	...	...	3	...	2	...	...	...
30	Old Siward	...	...	...	...	...	...	...	...	...	...	...	...	...	...	...	...	...	...	...	...	...	...	...	10	...	3	6	11
7	Young Siward	...	...	...	...	...	...	...	...	...	...	...	...	...	...	...	...	...	...	...	...	...	...	...	...	...	...	7	...
82	1st Witch	6	...	34	...	...	...	...	...	...	...	...	...	...	...	...	2	...	40	...	...	...	...	...	...	...	...	...	...
48	2nd Witch	6	...	12	...	...	...	...	...	...	...	...	...	...	...	...	...	...	30	...	...	...	...	...	...	...	...	...	...
48	3rd Witch	5	...	14	...	...	...	...	...	...	...	...	...	...	...	...	...	...	29	...	...	...	...	...	...	...	...	...	...
261	Lady Macbeth	...	...	...	...	71	11	43	...	46	6	...	3	18	...	40	...	...	...	...	...	23	...	...	...	...	...	...	...
2	Fleance	...	...	...	...	...	...	...	2	...	...	...	...	...	...	...	...	...	...	...	...	...	...	...	...	...	...	...	...
39	Hecate	...	...	...	...	...	...	...	...	...	...	...	...	...	...	...	34	...	5	...	...	...	...	...	...	...	...	...	...
4	2nd Apparition	...	...	...	...	...	...	...	...	...	...	...	...	...	...	...	...	...	4	...	...	...	...	...	...	...	...	...	...
5	3rd Apparition	...	...	...	...	...	...	...	...	...	...	...	...	...	...	...	...	...	5	...	...	...	...	...	...	...	...	...	...
42	Lady Macduff	...	...	...	...	...	...	...	...	...	...	...	...	...	...	...	...	...	...	42	...	...	...	...	...	...	...	...	...
21	Son	...	...	...	...	...	...	...	...	...	...	...	...	...	...	...	...	...	...	21	...	...	...	...	...	...	...	...	...
27	Gentlewoman	...	...	...	...	...	...	...	...	...	...	...	...	...	...	...	...	...	...	...	...	27	...	...	...	...	...	...	...
2410		17	76	180	64	80	37	91	71	85	175	51	157	61	32	165	37	53	196	95	278	88	37	70	27	55	11	35	86
2108	Actual No. of Lines	12	67	156	58	74	31	82	64	73	152	41	142	56	22	144	37	49	156	85	240	87	31	62	21	52	10	29	75

The total lines should be 2109, as 86 is the total of IV. 2, in which Lady Macduff's lines should be 43.

LEAR.

Total Number of Lines.	CHARACTERS.	I.					II.				III.							IV.							V.		
		1	2	3	4	5	1	2	3	4	1	2	3	4	5	6	7	1	2	3	4	5	6	7	1	2	3
379	KENT	44	...	...	37	2	...	104	...	32	41	17	...	18	...	15	...	...	...	29	...	...	...	16	...	...	24
344	GLOUCESTER ...	25	61	...	...	...	30	15	...	12	...	...	20	23	...	15	33	44	...	...	...	...	63	...	...	3	—
323	EDMUND	3	128	..	...	...	63	1	...	...	...	...	6	...	14	...	...	...	1	...	...	...	...	...	31	...	76
770	LEAR	122	...	...	131	22	...	..	..	161	..	43	...	68	...	31	...	...	...	...	...	...	106	32	...	...	58
156	ALBANY	1	...	..	11	...	...	...	...	...	...	...	...	...	...	...	...	...	43	...	...	...	...	...	14	...	87
109	CORNWALL	1	...	...	...	...	14	32	...	12	...	...	...	...	12	...	38	...	...	...	...	...	...	...	...	...	—
12	BURGUNDY	12	...	...	...	...	...	...	...	...	...	...	...	...	.	...	...	...	...	...	...	...	...	...	...	...	—
32	FRANCE	32	...	...	...	...	...	..	...	...	...	...	...	...	...	...	...	...	...	...	...	...	...	...	...	...	—
406	EDGAR	...	11	...	...	...	1	...	21	...	...	...	...	74	..	47	...	33	...	...	...	...	119	...	12	10	78
80	OSWALD	...	...	3	6	...	...	27	...	...	...	...	...	...	...	...	6	...	10	...	...	12	16	...	...	...	—
16	KNIGHT	...	...	...	16	...	...	...	...	...	...	...	...	...	...	...	...	...	...	...	...	...	...	...	...	...	—
252	FOOL	..	...	...	109	31	...	...	...	43	...	40	...	13	...	16	...	...	...	...	...	...	...	...	...	...	—
87	GENTLEMAN ...	...	...	...	...	1	...	...	...	5	17	...	...	...	...	...	...	...	...	34	...	...	16	9	...	...	5
11	CURAN	...	...	...	...	...	11	...	...	...	...	...	...	...	...	...	...	...	...	...	...	...	...	...	...	...	—
9	1ST SERVANT ...	...	...	...	...	...	...	...	...	...	...	...	...	...	...	...	9	...	...	...	...	...	...	...	...	...	—
5	2ND SERVANT ...	...	...	...	...	...	...	...	...	...	...	...	...	...	...	...	5	...	...	...	...	...	...	...	...	...	—
5	3RD SERVANT ...	...	...	...	...	...	...	...	...	...	...	...	...	...	...	...	5	...	...	...	...	...	...	...	...	...	...
12	OLD MAN	...	...	...	...	...	...	...	...	...	...	...	...	...	...	...	...	12	...	...	...	...	...	...	...	...	—
19	MESSENGER... ...	...	...	...	...	...	...	...	...	...	...	...	...	...	...	...	...	...	17	...	2	...	...	...	...	...	...
18	DOCTOR	...	...	...	...	...	...	...	...	...	...	...	...	...	...	...	...	...	...	...	5	...	...	13	...	...	...
6	CAPTAIN	...	...	...	...	...	...	...	...	...	...	...	...	...	...	...	...	...	...	...	...	...	...	...	...	...	6
10	HERALD	...	...	...	...	...	...	...	...	...	...	...	...	...	...	...	...	...	...	...	...	...	...	...	...	...	10
201	GONERIL	31	...	25	66	...	...	...	...	15	...	...	...	...	...	...	2	...	39	...	...	...	...	...	7	...	16
115	CORDELIA	46	...	...	...	...	...	...	...	...	...	...	...	...	...	...	...	...	..	...	24	...	...	40	...	...	5
191	REGAN	17	...	...	...	...	23	8	..	59	...	...	...	...	...	...	19	...	...	...	...	33	...	...	14	...	18
3568		334	200	28	376	56	142	187	21	339	58	100	26	196	26	124	117	89	110	63	31	45	320	110	78	13	379
3336	Actual No. of Lines	312	200	27	371	56	131	180	21	312	55	97	26	189	26	122	108	82	98	57	29	40	293	98	69	11	326

In II. 4 Lear's lines should be 162.

SCHEME FOR ARRANGING THE PARTS WITH EIGHTEEN MEN.

FOURTEEN CHARACTERS SINGLY AND FOUR GROUPS.

BURGUNDY	12	17	CURAN	11	17	OLD MAN	12	17	HERALD	10	19
3RD SERVANT	5		CAPTAIN	6		2ND SERVANT	5		1ST SERVANT	9	

SUGGESTIONS FOR DISCUSSION.

1. The Folio-text of *Lear* is Shakspere's revision of his own work.
2. Our estimate of *Lear*, as a whole, depends upon the view we take of the Fool.
3. A study of *Lear* shows that the language of poetry is more forcible than the language of painting.

LIST OF EARLIEST KNOWN EDITIONS.

Date.	*Printer.*	*Publisher.*	*Acted by*	*Present Owners.*
1608	——	Nathaniel Butter	The King's servants	British Museum. Bodleian Library. Trinity College, Cambridge. Duke of Devonshire, and eight others.
1608	——	Nathaniel Butter	The King's servants	British Museum. Bodleian Library. Trinity College, Cambridge. Duke of Devonshire.

On April 6 and 8, 1594, Henslowe notes performances of "Kinge leare" by "the Quenes men and my lord of Susex to geather."

In the Stationers' Registers are these entries. In that of 1594 Adam Islip's name was first entered and then struck out:

1594. May 14.
Edward White. Entred alsoe for his Copie vnder thandes of bothe the wardens a booke entituled *The moste famous Chronicle historye of* LEIRE *kinge of England and his Three Daughters* vj^d C.

1605. May 8.
Simon Stafford Entred for his Copie vnder thandes of the Wardens A booke called '*the Tragecall historie of kinge* LEIR *and his Three Daughters &c.*' *As it was latelie Acted* vj^d

John Wright Entred for his Copie by assignement from **Simon Stafford** and by consent of Master **Leake**, *The Tragicall history of kinge* LEIRE *and his Three Daughters* PROVIDED that **Simon Stafford** shall haue the printinge of this booke vj^d

Mr. Arber adds this note: "It is evident that *King* LEAR was printed by **S. Stafford** before the 8th May, 1605, though not entered until it was assigned on that date. See a similar case of *The merry wives of Windsor* . . . ." (But see p. 113). Of the book entered in 1594 no copy is known. There is a copy of the 1605 book in the British Museum entitled "The True Chronicle History of King Leir, and his three daughters, Gonorill, Ragan, and Cordella." It is said to have "been diuers and sundry times lately acted"; but the place of acting is not named. The play is reprinted in Hazlitt's *Shakespeare's Library*.

Shakspere's play was thus entered in the Registers:—

1607. November 26.
Nathanael Butter
John Busby Entred for their copie vnder thandes of Sir GEORGE BUCK knight and Thwardens A booke called . Master WILLIAM SHAKESPEARE *his* '*historye of Kinge* LEAR' *as yt was played before the kinges maiestie at Whitehall vppon Sainct Stephens night at Christmas Last by his maiesties servantes playinge vsually at the* '*Globe*' *on the Banksyde* vj^d

One of the editions published in the following year bears the title "M. William Shak-speare: His True Chronicle Historie of the life and death of King Lear and his three Daughters. With the vnfortunate life of Edgar, sonne and heire to the Earle of Gloster, and his sullen and assumed humor of Tom of Bedlam." The fact of the performance recorded in the entry is stated. The only variations in the title of the other edition are in the spelling of some words. The author's name is given as "Shake-speare." But in the texts of the two editions and in copies of the same edition there are many variations (see 'Cambridge' *Shakespeare* and Furness's edition of the play). A comparison of these two editions with one another and with the Folio should be made by the enquiring student (see a paper by Delius in the New Shakspere Society's *Transactions*, 1875-6, Part I.). In the Folio the play is called "The Tragedie of King Lear."

An investigation into the sources of the plot will be of much interest. The historical versions of the story, passages in Sidney's *Arcadia* (1598), many poetical forms of the incidents, the 1605 play, should all be looked at. Hazlitt and Furness supply all that is necessary. The more critically disposed searcher may trace the course of the story through writers other than English (see Mr. C. H. Herford's paper on "Some Variants of the Lear-story," in *Owens College Magazine*, June, 1883).

TIMON OF ATHENS.

Total Number of Lines.	CHARACTERS.	I.		II.		III.						IV.			V.			
		1	2	1	2	1	2	3	4	5	6	1	2	3	1	2	3	4
111	Poet	77	...	...	...	...	...	...	...	...	...	...	...	...	34	...	...	...
75	Painter	31	...	...	...	...	...	...	...	...	...	...	...	...	44	...	...	...
11	Merchant	11	...	...	...	...	...	...	...	...	...	...	...	...	...	...	...	...
12	Jeweller	12	...	...	...	...	...	...	...	...	...	...	...	...	...	...	...	...
863	Timon	69	106	...	73	...	...	...	21	...	56	41	...	378	119	...	...	...
20	Messenger	9	...	...	...	...	...	...	...	...	...	...	...	...	...	11	...	...
29	Old Athenian	29	...	...	...	...	...	...	...	...	...	...	...	...	...	...	...	...
5	Lucilius	5	...	...	...	...	...	...	...	...	...	...	...	...	...	...	...	...
264	Apemantus	59	80	...	30	...	...	...	...	...	...	...	...	95	...	...	...	...
160	Alcibiades	2	6	...	...	...	...	...	...	80	...	...	...	32	...	...	...	40
51	1st Lord	9	13	...	...	...	...	...	...	...	29	...	...	...	...	...	...	...
50	2nd Lord	12	8	...	...	...	...	...	...	...	30	...	...	...	...	...	...	...
9	Ventidius	...	9	...	...	...	...	...	...	...	...	...	...	...	...	...	...	...
7	"All"	...	1	...	...	...	...	...	...	...	2	...	...	4	...	...	...	...
15	3rd Lord	...	3	...	...	...	...	...	...	...	12	...	...	...	...	...	...	...
37	1st Servant	...	8	...	1	3	...	19	...	...	...	...	6	...	...	...	...	...
204	Flavius	...	25	...	77	...	...	...	21	...	...	...	33	37	11	...	...	...
11	2nd Servant	...	3	...	...	...	...	...	...	...	...	...	8	...	...	...	...	...
10	3rd Servant	...	4	...	...	...	...	...	...	...	...	...	6	...	...	...	...	...
122	1st Senator	...	...	35	...	...	...	...	...	31	...	...	...	...	27	3	...	26
21	Caphis	...	...	3	18	...	...	...	...	...	...	...	...	...	...	...	...	...
28	1st Varro's Servant	...	...	...	19	...	...	...	9	...	...	...	...	...	...	...	...	...
16	Isidore's Servant	...	...	...	16	...	...	...	...	...	...	...	...	...	...	...	...	...
25	Fool	...	...	...	25	...	...	...	...	...	...	...	...	...	...	...	...	...
30	Flaminius	...	...	...	1	25	...	...	4	...	...	...	...	...	...	...	...	...
38	Lucullus	...	...	...	...	38	...	...	...	...	...	...	...	...	...	...	...	...
44	Lucius	...	...	...	...	...	44	...	...	...	...	...	...	...	...	...	...	...
31	1st Stranger	...	...	...	...	...	31	...	...	...	...	...	...	...	...	...	...	...
7	2nd Stranger	...	...	...	...	...	7	...	...	...	...	...	...	...	...	...	...	...
20	Servilius	...	...	...	...	...	13	...	7	...	...	...	...	...	...	...	...	...
1	3rd Stranger	...	...	...	...	...	1	...	...	...	...	...	...	...	...	...	...	...
25	Sempronius	...	...	...	...	...	...	25	...	...	...	...	...	...	...	...	...	...
16	Titus	...	...	...	...	...	...	...	16	...	...	...	...	...	...	...	...	...
11	Hortensius	...	...	...	...	...	...	...	11	...	...	...	...	...	...	...	...	...
32	Lucius' Servant	...	...	...	...	...	...	...	32	...	...	...	...	...	...	...	...	...
6	Philotus	...	...	...	...	...	...	...	6	...	...	...	...	...	...	...	...	...
7	2nd Varro's Servant	...	...	...	...	...	...	...	7	...	...	...	...	...	...	...	...	...
63	2nd Senator	...	...	...	...	...	...	...	...	11	...	...	...	...	26	1	...	25
5	3rd Senator	...	...	...	...	...	...	...	...	1	...	...	...	...	...	4	...	...
3	4th Lord	...	...	...	...	...	...	...	...	...	3	...	...	...	...	...	...	...
14	1st Bandit	...	...	...	...	...	...	...	...	...	...	...	...	14	...	...	...	...
6	2nd Bandit	...	...	...	...	...	...	...	...	...	...	...	...	6	...	...	...	...
6	3rd Bandit	...	...	...	...	...	...	...	...	...	...	...	...	6	...	...	...	...
15	Soldier	...	...	...	...	...	...	...	...	...	...	...	...	...	...	...	10	5
6	"Cupid"	...	6	...	...	...	...	...	...	...	...	...	...	...	...	...	...	...
2	1st Lady	...	2	...	...	...	...	...	...	...	...	...	...	...	...	...	...	...
10	Page	...	...	...	10	...	...	...	...	...	...	...	...	...	...	...	...	...
5	Phrynia	...	...	...	...	...	...	...	...	...	...	...	...	5	...	...	...	...
8	Timandra	...	...	...	...	...	...	...	...	...	...	...	...	8	...	...	...	...
2567		325	274	38	270	66	96	44	134	123	132	41	53	585	261	19	10	96
2372	Actual No. of Lines	294	257	35	242	66	94	42	119	117	130	41	50	542	231	17	10	85

The total lines should be 2373, as the total of I. 2 should be 258.

ANTONY AND

Total Number of Lines.	CHARACTERS.	I.					II.							III.							
		1	2	3	4	5	1	2	3	4	5	6	7	1	2	3	4	5	6	7	8
16	PHILO	16	...	...	...	...	...	...	...	...	...	...	...	...	...	...	...	...	...	...	...
829	ANTONY	25	59	47	...	...	...	86	25	...	...	16	28	...	19	...	25	...	...	21	...
6	1ST ATTENDANT	1	1	...	...	...	...	...	...	...	1	...	...	...	...	...	...	...	...	...	...
5	DEMETRIUS	5	...	...	...	...	...	...	...	...	...	...	...	...	...	...	...	...	...	...	...
32	ALEXAS	...	11	...	...	17	...	...	...	...	...	...	...	...	...	4	...	...	...	...	...
32	SOOTHSAYER	...	13	...	...	...	...	...	19	...	...	...	...	...	...	...	...	...	...	...	...
356	ENOBARBUS	...	47	...	...	...	...	79	...	...	...	44	18	...	22	...	...	9	...	30	...
79	1ST MESSENGER	...	15	...	16	...	...	...	...	...	25	...	...	...	...	18	...	...	...	3	...
1	2ND ATTENDANT	...	1	...	...	...	...	...	...	...	...	...	...	...	...	...	...	...	...	...	...
4	2ND MESSENGER	...	4	...	...	...	...	...	...	...	...	...	...	...	...	...	...	...	...	...	...
420	CÆSAR	...	...	...	62	...	...	56	1	...	...	16	15	...	21	...	...	...	83	...	5
70	LEPIDUS	...	...	...	15	...	...	27	...	8	...	6	12	...	2	...	...	...	...	...	...
19	MARDIAN	...	...	...	...	...	...	...	...	...	...	...	...	...	...	...	...	...	...	...	...
136	POMPEY	...	...	...	...	...	42	...	...	...	...	64	30	...	...	...	...	...	...	...	...
6	MENECRATES	...	...	...	...	...	6	...	...	...	...	...	...	...	...	...	...	...	...	...	...
68	MENAS	...	...	...	...	...	8	...	...	...	...	27	33	...	...	...	...	...	...	...	...
4	VARRIUS	...	...	...	...	...	4	...	...	...	...	...	...	...	...	...	...	...	...	...	...
40	MECÆNAS	...	...	...	...	...	...	17	...	4	...	...	...	...	...	...	...	...	10	...	...
61	AGRIPPA	...	...	...	...	...	...	30	...	3	...	...	...	...	13	...	...	...	5	...	...
11	1ST SERVANT	...	...	...	...	...	...	...	...	...	...	...	11	...	...	...	...	...	...	...	...
8	2ND SERVANT	...	...	...	...	...	...	...	...	...	...	...	8	...	...	...	...	...	...	...	...
30	VENTIDIUS	...	...	...	...	...	...	...	...	...	...	...	...	30	...	...	...	...	...	...	...
11	SILIUS	...	...	...	...	...	...	...	...	...	...	...	...	11	...	...	...	...	...	...	...
49	EROS	...	...	...	...	...	...	...	...	...	...	...	...	...	...	...	...	18	...	...	...
25	CANIDIUS	...	...	...	...	...	...	...	...	...	...	...	...	...	...	...	...	...	...	16	...
63	1ST SOLDIER	...	...	...	...	...	...	...	...	...	...	...	...	...	...	...	...	...	...	13	...
1	TAURUS	...	...	...	...	...	...	...	...	...	...	...	...	...	...	...	...	...	...	...	1
40	SCARUS	...	...	...	...	...	...	...	...	...	...	...	...	...	...	...	...	...	...	...	...
12	"ALL"	...	...	...	...	...	...	...	...	...	...	...	...	...	...	...	...	...	...	...	...
48	DOLABELLA	...	...	...	...	...	...	...	...	...	...	...	...	...	...	...	...	...	...	...	...
16	EUPHRONIUS	...	...	...	...	...	...	...	...	...	...	...	...	...	...	...	...	...	...	...	...
31	THYREUS	...	...	...	...	...	...	...	...	...	...	...	...	...	...	...	...	...	...	...	...
15	2ND SOLDIER	...	...	...	...	...	...	...	...	...	...	...	...	...	...	...	...	...	...	...	...
13	3RD SOLDIER	...	...	...	...	...	...	...	...	...	...	...	...	...	...	...	...	...	...	...	...
5	4TH SOLDIER	...	...	...	...	...	...	...	...	...	...	...	...	...	...	...	...	...	...	...	...
2	CAPTAIN	...	...	...	...	...	...	...	...	...	...	...	...	...	...	...	...	...	...	...	...
23	1ST GUARD	...	...	...	...	...	...	...	...	...	...	...	...	...	...	...	...	...	...	...	...
4	2ND GUARD	...	...	...	...	...	...	...	...	...	...	...	...	...	...	...	...	...	...	...	...
1	3RD GUARD	...	...	...	...	...	...	...	...	...	...	...	...	...	...	...	...	...	...	...	...
21	DERCETAS	...	...	...	...	...	...	...	...	...	...	...	...	...	...	...	...	...	...	...	...
19	DIOMEDES	...	...	...	...	...	...	...	...	...	...	...	...	...	...	...	...	...	...	...	...
6	EGYPTIAN	...	...	...	...	...	...	...	...	...	...	...	...	...	...	...	...	...	...	...	...
32	PROCULEIUS	...	...	...	...	...	...	...	...	...	...	...	...	...	...	...	...	...	...	...	...
2	GALLUS	...	...	...	...	...	...	...	...	...	...	...	...	...	...	...	...	...	...	...	...
5	SELEUCUS	...	...	...	...	...	...	...	...	...	...	...	...	...	...	...	...	...	...	...	...
31	CLOWN	...	...	...	...	...	...	...	...	...	...	...	...	...	...	...	...	...	...	...	...
670	CLEOPATRA	21	6	70	...	60	...	...	...	...	106	...	...	...	...	34	...	...	...	15	...
109	CHARMIAN	...	43	8	...	8	...	...	...	...	10	...	...	...	...	9	...	...	...	...	...
30	IRAS	...	15	...	...	...	...	...	...	...	...	...	...	...	...	...	...	...	...	...	...
36	OCTAVIA	...	...	...	...	...	...	...	3	...	...	...	...	...	3	...	16	...	14	...	...
6	BOY	...	...	...	...	...	...	...	...	...	...	...	6	...	...	...	...	...	...	...	...
3558		68	215	125	93	91	60	295	48	15	143	173	161	41	80	65	41	27	112	98	6
3063	Actual No. of Lines	62	204	105	84	78	52	250	42	10	119	145	141	37	66	51	38	25	98	81	6

CLEOPATRA.

						IV.															V.	
	9	10	11	12	13	1	2	3	4	5	6	7	8	9	10	11	12	13	14	15	1	2
Antony	4		58		110		41		31	11		5	37		9		43		106	23		
1st Attendant					3																	
Enobarbus		15			44		11				20			17								
1st Messenger											2											
Cæsar				22		13					10					4					54	58
Mardian																			12			
Mecænas						5															4	
Agrippa											1	3									6	
Eros			8						1	2		2							18			
Canidius		9																				
1st Soldier								12	3	12	10			13								
Scarus		21										11			1		7					
"All"			1				1	3	1										2	1	1	2
Dolabella				5																	1	42
Euphronius				14	2																	
Thyreus				2	29																	
~~2nd Soldier~~								8						7								
~~3rd Soldier~~								6						7								
~~4th Soldier~~								5														
~~Captain~~									1													
1st Guard																			5			18
2nd Guard																			2			2
3rd Guard																			1			
Dercetas																			4		17	
Diomedes																			16	3		
Egyptian																					6	
Proculeius																					1	31
Gallus																						2
Seleucus																						5
Clown																						31
Cleopatra			8		46		2		9				5				1	8		68		211
Charmian			2						1									4		5		19
Iras			4																	4		7
	4	45	81	43	234	18	55	34	47	25	43	21	42	44	10	4	51	12	166	104	90	428
Actual No. of Lines	4	37	74	36	201	16	45	23	38	17	39	16	39	35	9	4	49	10	140	91	77	369

ANTONY AND CLEOPATRA.

SCHEME FOR ARRANGING THE PARTS WITH EIGHTEEN MEN.

SEVEN CHARACTERS SINGLY AND ELEVEN GROUPS.

Character	Lines	Total
VENTIDIUS	30	67
THYREUS	31	
TAURUS	1	
4TH SOLDIER	5	

Character	Lines	Total
EROS	49	67
DEMETRIUS	5	
3RD SOLDIER	13	

Character	Lines	Total
SCARUS	40	67
PHILO	16	
SILIUS	11	

Character	Lines	Total
DERCETAS	21	67
MENECRATES	6	
SOOTHSAYER	32	
2ND SERVANT	8	

Character	Lines	Total
MECÆNAS	40	67
1ST GUARD	23	
2ND MESSENGER	4	

Character	Lines	Total
AGRIPPA	61	67
SELEUCUS	5	
CAPTAIN	1	

Character	Lines	Total
GALLUS	2	67
1ST SOLDIER	63	
2ND ATTENDANT	1	
3RD GUARD	1	

Character	Lines	Total
CANIDIUS	25	67
ALEXAS	32	
EGYPTIAN	6	
2ND GUARD	4	

Character	Lines	Total
DIOMEDES	19	67
CLOWN	31	
1ST ATTENDANT	6	
1ST SERVANT	11	

Character	Lines	Total
DOLABELLA	48	67
VARRIUS	4	
2ND SOLDIER	15	

Character	Lines	Total
PROCULEIUS	32	67
EUPHRONIUS	16	
MARDIAN	19	

CORIOLANUS.

Total Number of Lines.	CHARACTERS.	I.										II.			III.			IV.							V.					
		1	2	3	4	5	6	7	8	9	10	1	2	3	1	2	3	1	2	3	4	5	6	7	1	2	3	4	5	6
96	1st Citizen	72	...	...	...	...	...	...	...	...	...	...	...	10	3	...	...	...	...	...	4	...	7	...	...	...	...	...	...	...
45	"All"	8	2	...	2	...	...	...	...	1	...	1	...	6	9	...	7	...	...	...	...	...	3	...	...	...	...	...	2	4
30	2nd Citizen	11	...	...	...	...	...	...	...	...	...	...	...	17	...	...	...	...	...	...	...	...	2	...	...	...	...	...	...	...
598	Menenius	92	...	...	...	...	...	...	...	...	...	130	39	13	88	20	14	5	5	...	...	...	56	...	40	58	...	38	...	...
886	Marcius	75	...	...	34	18	50	...	9	45	...	20	24	67	147	58	50	45	...	...	25	64	...	...	...	14	106	...	...	35
38	1st Messenger	2	...	...	2	...	9	...	...	...	...	9	...	...	...	...	...	...	...	...	...	...	11	...	...	...	...	5	...	...
62	1st Senator	7	7	...	8	...	...	...	...	...	...	...	13	...	17	3	1	...	...	...	...	...	...	...	...	...	...	...	6	...
281	Cominius	3	...	...	...	...	44	...	...	55	...	3	47	...	30	10	11	7	...	...	...	...	40	...	31	...	...	...	...	...
60	Titus Lartius	6	...	...	19	11	...	7	...	5	...	...	...	...	12	...	...	...	...	...	...	...	...	...	...	...	...	...	...	...
313	Sicinius	16	...	...	...	...	...	...	...	...	...	34	10	54	61	...	54	...	16	...	...	...	43	...	11	...	...	14	...	...
255	Brutus	19	...	...	...	...	...	...	...	...	...	61	14	56	44	...	25	...	10	...	...	...	22	...	4	...	...	...	...	...
274	Aufidius	...	30	...	...	...	...	...	10	...	32	...	...	...	...	...	...	...	...	...	...	56	...	48	...	1	9	...	...	88
13	2nd Senator	...	7	...	...	...	...	...	...	...	...	...	...	...	6	...	...	...	...	...	...	...	...	...	...	...	...	...	...	...
11	1st Soldier	...	...	...	7	...	...	...	...	...	4	...	...	...	...	...	...	...	...	...	...	...	...	...	...	...	...	...	...	...
1	2nd Soldier	...	...	...	1	...	...	...	...	...	...	...	...	...	...	...	...	...	...	...	...	...	...	...	...	...	...	...	...	...
34	1st Roman	...	...	...	...	1	...	...	...	...	...	...	...	...	...	...	...	...	...	33	...	...	...	...	...	...	...	...	...	...
1	2nd Roman	...	...	...	...	1	...	...	...	...	...	...	...	...	...	...	...	...	...	...	...	...	...	...	...	...	...	...	...	...
2	3rd Roman	...	...	...	...	2	...	...	...	...	...	...	...	...	...	...	...	...	...	...	...	...	...	...	...	...	...	...	...	...
12	Lieutenant	...	...	...	...	...	...	1	...	...	...	...	...	...	...	...	...	...	...	...	...	...	...	11	...	...	...	...	...	...
6	Herald	...	...	...	...	...	...	...	...	...	...	6	...	...	...	...	...	...	...	...	...	...	...	...	...	...	...	...	...	...
17	1st Officer	...	...	...	...	...	...	...	...	...	...	...	17	...	...	...	...	...	...	...	...	...	...	...	...	...	...	...	...	...
24	2nd Officer	...	...	...	...	...	...	...	...	...	...	...	24	...	...	...	...	...	...	...	...	...	...	...	...	...	...	...	...	...
62	3rd Citizen	...	...	...	...	...	...	...	...	...	...	...	...	57	...	...	...	...	...	...	...	...	5	...	...	...	...	...	...	...
7	4th Citizen	...	...	...	...	...	...	...	...	...	...	...	...	7	...	...	...	...	...	...	...	...	...	...	...	...	...	...	...	...
2	5th Citizen	...	...	...	...	...	...	...	...	...	...	...	...	2	...	...	...	...	...	...	...	...	...	...	...	...	...	...	...	...
2	6th Citizen	...	...	...	...	...	...	...	...	...	...	...	...	2	...	...	...	...	...	...	...	...	...	...	...	...	...	...	...	...
3	7th Citizen	...	...	...	...	...	...	...	...	...	...	...	...	3	...	...	...	...	...	...	...	...	...	...	...	...	...	...	...	...
16	Ædile	...	...	...	...	...	...	...	...	...	...	...	...	...	1	...	9	...	...	...	...	...	6	...	...	...	...	...	...	...
3	1st Patrician	...	...	...	...	...	...	...	...	...	...	...	...	...	1	2	...	...	...	...	...	...	...	...	...	...	...	...	...	...
1	2nd Patrician	...	...	...	...	...	...	...	...	...	...	...	...	...	1	...	...	...	...	...	...	...	...	...	...	...	...	...	...	...
24	Volsce	...	...	...	...	...	...	...	...	...	...	...	...	...	...	...	...	...	...	24	...	...	...	...	...	...	...	...	...	...
41	1st Servingman	...	...	...	...	...	...	...	...	...	...	...	...	...	...	...	...	...	...	...	...	41	...	...	...	...	...	...	...	...
42	2nd Servingman	...	...	...	...	...	...	...	...	...	...	...	...	...	...	...	...	...	...	...	...	42	...	...	...	...	...	...	...	...
57	3rd Servingman	...	...	...	...	...	...	...	...	...	...	...	...	...	...	...	...	...	...	...	...	57	...	...	...	...	...	...	...	...
20	2nd Messenger	...	...	...	...	...	...	...	...	...	...	...	...	...	...	...	...	...	...	...	...	...	6	...	...	...	...	14	...	...
35	1st Sentinel	...	...	...	...	...	...	...	...	...	...	...	...	...	...	...	...	...	...	...	...	...	...	...	...	35	...	...	...	...
14	2nd Sentinel	...	...	...	...	...	...	...	...	...	...	...	...	...	...	...	...	...	...	...	...	...	...	...	...	14	...	...	...	...
10	1st Conspirator	...	...	...	...	...	...	...	...	...	...	...	...	...	...	...	...	...	...	...	...	...	...	...	...	...	...	...	...	10
9	2nd Conspirator	...	...	...	...	...	...	...	...	...	...	...	...	...	...	...	...	...	...	...	...	...	...	...	...	...	...	...	...	9
14	3rd Conspirator	...	...	...	...	...	...	...	...	...	...	...	...	...	...	...	...	...	...	...	...	...	...	...	...	...	...	...	...	14
15	1st Lord	...	...	...	...	...	...	...	...	...	...	...	...	...	...	...	...	...	...	...	...	...	...	...	...	...	...	...	...	15
11	2nd Lord	...	...	...	...	...	...	...	...	...	...	...	...	...	...	...	...	...	...	...	...	...	...	...	...	...	...	...	...	11
4	3rd Lord	...	...	...	...	...	...	...	...	...	...	...	...	...	...	...	...	...	...	...	...	...	...	...	...	...	...	...	...	4
315	Volumnia	...	...	52	...	...	...	...	...	...	...	42	...	...	...	77	...	7	34	...	...	...	...	...	...	...	103	...	...	...
41	Virgilia	...	...	25	...	...	...	...	...	...	...	5	...	...	...	...	...	1	4	...	...	...	...	...	...	...	6	...	...	...
1	Gentlewoman	...	...	1	...	...	...	...	...	...	...	...	...	...	...	...	...	...	...	...	...	...	...	...	...	...	...	...	...	...
48	Valeria	...	...	46	...	...	...	...	...	...	...	2	...	...	...	...	...	...	...	...	...	...	...	...	...	...	...	...	...	...
2	Young Marcius	...	...	...	...	...	...	...	...	...	...	...	...	...	...	...	...	...	...	...	...	...	...	...	...	...	2	...	...	...
3858		311	46	124	73	33	103	8	19	106	36	313	188	294	420	170	171	65	69	57	29	260	201	59	86	122	226	71	8	190
3410	Actual No. of Lines	283	38	124	63	29	87	7	15	94	33	286	164	271	336	145	143	58	54	57	26	251	161	57	74	117	209	65	7	156

PERICLES.

Total Number of Lines.	CHARACTERS.	I.					II.						III.					IV.							V.			
		Chorus.	1	2	3	4	Chorus.	1	2	3	4	5	Chorus.	1	2	3	4	Chorus.	1	2	3	4	5	6	Chorus.	1	2	3
307	"Gower"	42					40						60					52				51			24		20	18
67	Antiochus		67																									
603	Pericles		98	94		17		79		25		33		59		28										115		55
28	Thaliard		6		22																							
1	Messenger		1																									
33	1st Lord			1		7			6		16															3		
11	2nd Lord			2					2		7																	
122	Helicanus			31	19						32															39		1
110	Cleon					74										14					22							
4	"All"					2			1		1																	
43	1st Fisherman							43																				
31	2nd Fisherman							31																				
20	3rd Fisherman							20																				
153	Simonides								28	67		58																
3	3rd Lord								2		1																	
7	1st Knight									6		1																
1	Marshal									1																		
2	Escanes										2																	
1	2nd Knight											1																
1	3rd Knight											1																
10	1st Sailor													10														
6	2nd Sailor													6														
109	Cerimon														84		8											17
3	Philemon														3													
6	Servant														6													
25	1st Gentleman														18								6			1		
18	2nd Gentleman														14								4					
23	Leonine																		23									
2	1st Pirate																		1	1								
1	2nd Pirate																		1									
2	3rd Pirate																		2									
32	Pandar																			28				4				
99	Boult																			44				55				
107	Lysimachus																							52		55		
9	Tyrian Sailor																									9		
2	Daughter		2																									
89	Dionyza					9										6			38		36							
82	Thaisa								22	22		4			2		10											22
11	Lychorida													11														
190	Marina																		46	16				61		65		2
117	Bawd																			74				43				
10	"Diana"																									10		
2501		42	174	128	41	109	40	173	61	121	59	98	60	86	127	48	18	52	111	163	58	51	10	215	24	297	20	115
2391	Actual No. of Lines	42	171	124	40	108	40	173	60	116	58	93	60	82	111	41	18	52	103	163	51	51	10	212	24	265	20	103

CYMBELINE.

Total Number of Lines.	CHARACTERS.	I. 1	I. 2	I. 3	I. 4	I. 5	I. 6	II. 1	II. 2	II. 3	II. 4	II. 5	III. 1	III. 2	III. 3	III. 4	III. 5	III. 6	III. 7	IV. 1	IV. 2	IV. 3	IV. 4	V. 1	V. 2	V. 3	V. 4	V. 5
66	1st Gentleman	66																										
13	2nd Gentleman	13																										
448	Posthumus	29			57						96	35												33		85	69	44
291	Cymbeline	20								15			30				29					21						176
217	Pisanio	10		13		3	4			1				27		86	28					16						29
52	1st Lord		15					7		7			1									15				7		
275	Cloten		10					31		72			24				88			27	23							
52	2nd Lord		18					32		1			1															
436	Iachimo				83		154		41		73														11			74
44	Philario				20						24																	
25	Frenchman				25																							
73	Cornelius					25																						48
9	Musician									9																		
4	Messenger									2																	2	
104	Lucius												19				10				43				5			27
336	Belarius														90			30			109		26		3			78
169	Guiderius														11			10			113		19		1			15
143	Arviragus														11			13			90		19		1			9
3	Attendant																3											
15	1st Senator																		15									
3	1st Tribune																		3									
1	2nd Senator																		1									
15	Captain																				11					4		
43	Soothsayer																				7							36
6	2nd Captain																									6		
1	"All"																										1	
51	1st Gaoler																										51	
1	2nd Gaoler																										1	
40	Sicilius																										40	
14	1st Brother																										14	
8	2nd Brother																										8	
21	"Jupiter"																										21	
166	Queen	33				67				10			22				34											
596	Imogen	45		33			83		10	54				59		134		57			85							36
15	Lady			2		1			2	9																		1
12	Mother																										12	
3768		216	43	48	185	96	241	70	53	180	193	35	97	86	112	220	192	110	19	27	481	52	64	33	21	102	219	573
3340	Actual No. of Lines	178	43	40	185	87	210	70	51	160	152	35	87	84	107	196	168	96	16	27	403	46	54	33	18	94	215	485

The total lines should be 3341, as the total of IV. 2 should be 404.

THE WINTER'S TALE.

Total Number of Lines.	CHARACTERS.	I.		II.			III.			IV.				V.		
		1	2	1	2	3	1	2	3	1	2	3		1	2	3
24	ARCHIDAMUS	24	...	...	...	...	...	...	...	...	...	...	...	...	...	...
305	CAMILLO	26	123	...	...	...	...	...	...	...	18	...	131	...	...	7
277	POLIXENES	...	129	...	...	...	...	...	...	...	44	...	94	...	...	10
681	LEONTES	...	210	108	...	109	...	73	...	...	...	...	...	105	...	76
63	1ST LORD...	...	...	18	...	12	...	9	...	...	...	...	...	24	...	...
110	ANTIGONUS	...	...	30	...	29	...	...	51	...	...	...	...	...	...	...
13	GAOLER	...	...	...	13	...	...	...	...	...	...	...	...	...	...	...
52	1ST SERVANT	...	...	...	...	8	...	5	...	...	...	...	39	...	...	...
2	2ND SERVANT	...	...	...	...	2	...	...	...	...	...	...	...	...	...	...
24	CLEOMENES	...	...	...	...	...	11	1	...	...	...	...	...	12	...	...
28	DION...	...	...	...	...	...	16	1	...	...	...	...	...	11	...	...
27	OFFICER	...	...	...	...	...	...	27	...	...	...	...	...	...	...	...
11	MARINER	...	...	...	...	...	...	...	11	...	...	...	...	...	...	...
144	SHEPHERD	...	...	...	...	...	...	...	47	...	...	...	89	...	8	...
209	CLOWN	...	...	...	...	...	...	...	38	...	...	48	86	...	37	...
32	"TIME"	...	...	...	...	...	...	...	...	32	...	...	...	...	...	...
319	AUTOLYCUS	...	...	...	...	...	...	...	...	...	...	87	207	...	25	...
205	FLORIZEL...	...	...	...	...	...	...	...	...	...	...	...	167	38	...	...
48	1ST GENTLEMAN	...	...	...	...	...	...	...	...	...	...	...	...	18	30	...
17	2ND GENTLEMAN	...	...	...	...	...	...	...	...	...	...	...	...	...	17	...
71	3RD GENTLEMAN	...	...	...	...	...	...	...	...	...	...	...	...	...	71	...
211	HERMIONE	...	68	46	...	...	...	89	...	...	...	...	...	...	...	8
22	MAMILLIUS	...	4	18	...	...	...	...	...	...	...	...	...	...	...	...
9	1ST LADY...	...	...	9	...	...	...	...	...	...	...	...	...	...	...	...
4	2ND LADY	...	...	4	...	...	...	...	...	...	...	...	...	...	...	...
331	PAULINA	...	...	...	44	84	...	60	...	...	...	...	...	67	...	76
20	EMILIA	...	...	...	20	...	...	...	...	...	...	...	...	...	...	...
128	PERDITA	...	...	...	...	...	...	...	...	...	...	...	118	3	...	7
13	DORCAS	...	...	...	...	...	...	...	...	...	...	...	13	...	...	...
21	MOPSA	...	...	...	...	...	...	...	...	...	...	...	21	...	...	...
3421		50	534	233	77	244	27	265	147	32	62	135	965	278	188	184
3074	Actual Number of Lines	50	465	199	66	207	22	244	143	32	62	135	873	233	188	155

THE TEMPEST.

Total Number of Lines.	CHARACTERS.	I.		II.		III.			IV.	V.	Epilogue.
		1	2	1	2	1	2	3	1	1	
4	MASTER	4	...	...	...	...	...	...	...	...	...
46	BOATSWAIN	29	...	...	...	...	...	...	...	17	...
110	ALONSO	2	...	26	...	...	...	26	...	56	..
148	ANTONIO	8	...	126	...	...	...	12	...	2	...
165	GONZALO	22	...	90	...	...	..	28	...	25	...
122	SEBASTIAN	4	...	98	..	...	...	12	...	8	...
8	"ALL"	5	3	...	...	...	...	...	...	...	...
665	PROSPERO	...	339	...	...	10	...	15	98	183	20
179	CALIBAN...	...	30	...	55	...	66	...	20	8	...
140	FERDINAND	...	45	...	...	59	...	...	23	13	...
12	ADRIAN	...	...	11	...	...	...	1	...	...	..
11	FRANCISCO	...	...	10	...	...	...	1	...	...	...
112	TRINCULO	...	...	...	58	...	33		16	5	...
174	STEPHANO	...		...	80	...	63	...	26	5	...
142	MIRANDA	...	87	...	...	45	...	...	3	7	...
190	ARIEL	...	87	11	...	...	4	30	29	29	...
41	"IRIS"	...	...	...	...	...	...	...	41	...	...
24	"CERES"	...	...	...	...	...	...	...	24	...	...
7	"JUNO"	...	...	...	...	...	...	...	7	...	...
2300		74	591	372	193	114	166	125	287	358	20
2065	Actual Number of Lines	72	500	327	193	96	163	109	267	318	20

HENRY VIII.

Total Number of Lines.	CHARACTERS.	Prologue.	I.				II.				III.		IV.		V.					Epilogue.
			1	2	3	4	1	2	3	4	1	2	1	2	1	2	3	4	5	
192	Buckingham		118				74													
211	Norfolk		105	9				39				54					4			
18	Abergavenny		18																	
436	Wolsey		5	42		42		32		48	40	227								
2	1st Secretary		2																	
14	Brandon		14																	
5	Sergeant		5																	
457	King			79		19		32		95		61			85	13	50		23	
2	"All"			1													1			
61	Surveyor			61																
150	Chamberlain				34	28		28	22			19					1	18		
48	Sands				21	27														
68	Lovell				27	4	6								31					
9	Guildford					9														
4	Servant					4														
112	1st Gentleman						67				3		41		1					
88	2nd Gentleman						44						44							
4	Vaux						4													
93	Suffolk							17				63			7		6			
53	Campeius							15		15	23									
91	Gardiner							2							42		47			
4	Scribe									4										
3	Crier									3										
59	Griffith									1				58						
8	Lincoln									8										
81	Surrey											79					2			
49	Cromwell											29					20			
57	3rd Gentleman												57							
4	Messenger													4						
11	Capucius													11						
4	Denny														4					
134	Cranmer														19	16	43		56	
7	Keeper															3	4			
9	Butts															9				
32	Chancellor																32			
36	Porter																	36		
3	"Within"																	3		
41	Man																	41		
4	Garter																		4	
32	"Prologue"	32																		
374	Queen Katharine			53						86	121			114						
58	Anne					4			54											
68	Old Lady								51						17					
18	Patience										12			6						
1	Boy														1					
14	"Epilogue"																			14
3229		32	268	244	82	137	195	165	127	260	199	532	142	193	207	41	210	98	83	14
2821	Actual No. of Lines	32	226	214	67	108	169	144	107	241	184	460	117	173	177	35	182	94	77	14

In I. 1 268 should be 267. In I. 2 the totals should be 245 and 215. The total lines should be 2822.

Shakespeare's Life up to 1590

The facts are sparse and much is based on conjecture. William Shakespeare was baptised on Wednesday 26 April 1564 in Holy Trinity Church, Stratford. Plague came to the town in July. A total of 237 citizens, nearly a tenth of the population, died. There is a local legend that his father took him to the nearby village of Clifford Chambers to escape the pestilence. His father, John Shakespeare, was a glover and whittawer, a dresser of white or light-coloured leather. It was softened with salt and alum then soaked in pots of excrement and urine before being laid out to dry. It must have stunk to heaven. William seems to have been very sensitive to smells and mentions gloves and leather throughout his works. John Shakespeare was also a trader in wool, a maker of malt and a moneylender. He was described as a 'merry-cheeked old man.' It has been conjectured he was the origin of John Falstaff. It is alleged he could read but not write. Nevertheless he rose to be Bailiff, the highest civic honour in Stratford, and his son would have been entitled to a free education at the King Edward Grammar School. There he would have studied Ovid's *Metamorphoses*, which contained the stories of Venus and Adonis, Pyramus and Thisbe, and many other sources of his plays, as well as Caesar, Seneca and Juvenal. He would also have learnt rhetoric, and acted in the plays of Plautus and Terence. At least two of his schoolmasters, Thomas Jenkins and Thomas Cottam, were Oxford graduates. A country boy at heart, he mentions 108 different plants, using such local Warwickshire names as love-in-idleness, crow-flowers and whortleberry. He loves birds and names sixty species.

The acting companies of The Queen's Men and the Earl of Worcester played in Stratford's Guild Hall in 1569, when John Shakespeare was Bailiff. The five-year-old William may well have seen them, thus getting his first taste of drama. Ten more groups would come over the next few years. William could have been taken by his father to see the mediaeval mystery plays at Coventry; they were only abandoned when he was fifteen.

He would use the concept of the Vice, the character that explains his villainy and shares his jokes with the audience, when he created such roles as Richard III, Falstaff and Iago.

In 1577 John Shakespeare resigned his civic duties and no longer attended council meetings. There is evidence to suggest he was heavily in debt. In 1581 a bill was passed fining Catholics severely if they failed to attend Protestant services. John may well have been a 'Recusant,' a secret follower of the old Faith. A Spiritual Testament, now lost, was found in the thatch of his house many years after his death. William probably finished school at the age of fifteen. Shelves of books have been written as to where he acquired his vast knowledge and his seeming familiarity with the aristocracy. The early plays show him to be a brilliant and witty young man. I tend to believe that he was employed as a tutor and actor in some aristocratic household. One possibility is Hoghton Tower in Lancashire, home of the Hoghtons, a Catholic family associated with the Earls of Derby. The Cottams were their Catholic neighbours. One of Shakespeare's Stratford schoolmasters, John Cottam, was a member of that family. Did he recommend an unusually bright student? In 1581 Alexander Hoghton, who kept his own troupe of players, wrote in his will: 'I most heartily require the said Sir Thomas Hesketh to be friendly unto my players, Foke Gyllome and William Shakeshafte now dwelling with me, and either take them into his service or else to help them to some good master, as my trust is he will.' Could 'Shakeshafte' be our man? Sir Thomas Hesketh also kept a company of actors as did Lord Ferdinando Stanley, the future fifth Earl of Derby, whose company performed two of Shakespeare's earliest plays. Actors were considered no better than thieves or vagabonds and were only allowed to operate under the patronage or protection of an aristocrat. The nobility owned teams of actors then as multi-billionaires own football teams today.

A Catholic witch-hunt in the North could have driven young William back home to Stratford, where he began an affair with Ann Hathaway, a farmer's daughter, seven years his senior. On 27 November 1582 a special licence, costing the huge sum of £40, was granted by the Bishop of Worcester, for William Shakespeare to marry Ann Hathaway after only one reading of the banns instead of the customary three. It was paid for by Fulke Sandells and John Richardson, two friends of Ann's father. The banns were issued on 30 November and the 'happy' couple were married the following day, probably at the church in Temple Grafton. Their daughter, Susanna, was baptised on 26 May 1583, followed by twins, Hamnet and Judith, in February 1585. Shakespeare uses twins in two plays: *Comedy of Errors* and *Twelfth Night.*

From 1585 to 1592 we have the so-called 'missing years' when there is no trace of him. Did he become an actor and join the Earl of Leicester's men – Kenilworth Castle was only thirteen miles away? In March 1586 Sir Philip Sydney wrote to a friend: 'I wrote you a letter by Will, my Lord of Leicester's jesting player, enclosed in a letter to my wife, and I never had the answer thereof...' In 1586-87 The Queen's Men (in scarlet liveries with the clown Richard Tarleton as their star), and the acting companies of the Earls of Essex and Leicester as well as Lord Stafford's, all visited Stratford. Or did young William work as a lawyer's clerk? Another of his ex-schoolmasters, Walter Roache, opened a lawyer's practice in Chapel Street, Stratford. That would explain the profusion of legal terms and phraseology throughout Shakespeare's works. Others say he was a sailor, as there is an abundance of shipwrecks and imagery of the sea in his writing. Some believe he was in Europe, a soldier fighting in the religious wars.

Nicholas Rowe, who wrote the first biography in 1709, expounded another theory: 'He had, by a misfortune common enough to young fellows, fallen into ill company; and amongst them, some that made a frequent practice of Deer-stealing, engaged him with them more than once in robbing a park that belong'd to Sir Thomas Lucy of Charlecote, near Stratford. For this he was prosecuted by that Gentleman, as he thought somewhat too severely; and in order to revenge that ill usage, he made a ballad upon him. And though this, probably the first essay of his poetry, be lost, yet it is said to have been so very bitter, that it redoubled the opposition against him to that degree, that he was obliged to leave his business and family in Warwickshire for some time and shelter himself in London.' But there were no deer at Charlecote at that time.

He may well have joined a touring company before he arrived in London as a trained actor; but like the vast majority of actors when he got there he found it extremely hard to get a job. Dr Johnson wrote in 1771: 'In the time of Elizabeth, coaches being yet uncommon, and hired coaches not at all in use, those who were too proud, too tender, or too idle to walk, went on horseback to the play. When Shakespeare fled to London from the terror of criminal prosecution, his first expedient was to wait at the door of the playhouse, and hold the horses of those who had no servants, that they might be ready again after the performance. In this office he became so conspicuous for his care and readiness, that in a short time every man when he alighted called for Will Shakespeare, and scarcely any other waiter was trusted with a horse while Will Shakespeare could be had.' Did our Will invent valet parking?

When did he start writing? When he was eventually taken on as a small-part actor did he begin by doctoring old plays or even penning early versions of his later masterpieces?

What was he really like?

His bust set in the wall above his grave makes him look like 'a self-satisfied pork butcher.' He wears an earring and looks dashing in the Chandos portrait, but there is no proof that it is him. The constipated face on the First Folio of 1623, seven years after his death, was engraved by a young man called Martin Droeshout, who had probably never seen him. He was considered by his contemporaries to be 'mellifluous and honey-tongued.' Ben Jonson said he had 'an open free nature.' He can see every side of the argument and demonstrates this time and again in his plays – we never know for certain where he really stands. John Aubrey, the seventeenth century gossip, heard from the family of Christopher Beeston, an actor in Shakespeare's company, that: 'he was very good company and had a very ready and pleasant smooth wit, and was a handsome well-shaped man. He was more to be admired because he was not a company keeper; lived in Shoreditch; wouldn't be debauched, and if invited to, writ he was in pain.' But Shakespeare's works contain more sexual puns and jokes than any of his contemporaries. There are more than thirteen hundred sexual references in the plays.

He was a better businessman than his father. He bought up properties and land. He speculated on corn and malt. He was even a moneylender. The followers of the Oxford heresy say these mercenary traits diminish his claim to the authorship of the works. But no man is perfect: the Earl of Oxford, vain and quarrelsome, falsely accused his friend of treason; Sir Francis Bacon was corrupt; Christopher Marlowe lived and died in the gutter.

Religion?

Warwickshire was a stronghold of the old religion and, as stated, I believe his father John Shakespeare was a Catholic. The three masters that taught at his school all had Catholic connections. Shakespeare portrays priests and nuns for the most part sympathetically. He does not like Puritans, such as Malvolio and Angelo but, as in all things, he seems largely ambivalent, although I sense he believed in God.

London Theatres

Public performances were first given in the courtyards of inns, forerunners of the pub theatres of today, namely: the Cross Keys and Bell Inn in Gracechurch Street; the Belsavage on Ludgate Hill and the Bull in Bishopsgate. Because of the fear of Plague and the Puritan-like tendencies of the authorities, purpose-built theatres, the first to be constructed in Europe since Roman times, were only allowed outside the city limits. The Red Lion was erected at Mile End in 1567 by John Brayne, a grocer, and his brother-in-law, a carpenter called James Burbage. In 1576 they built The Theatre on wasteland near Finsbury Fields. The following year The Curtain was built nearby in Shoreditch. South of the river in Southwark was The Rose by Paris Garden on Bankside, built around 1588 by Philip Henslowe, a theatrical entrepreneur and father-in-law of the actor, Edward Alleyn. A different play was performed each day – up to twenty-one new plays a season, plus old favourites. More money was spent on costumes than on playwrights or actors. Some things never change.

Rival Writers

In the years before Shakespeare arrived in London John Lely had been the most popular poet and playwright. His pastoral comedies had been acted by the boys of the Chapel Royal in a hall of the old monastery at Blackfriars. There is no doubt that Lely was a major influence on Shakespeare, but he had been superseded first by Thomas Kyd's *The Spanish Tragedy*, then by the plays of the '*University Wits*'. They were a group of hard-drinking, lascivious young writers, including George Peele, Robert Green, Thomas Nash and Christopher Marlowe. Nash wrote: 'We scoff and are jocund, when the sword is ready to go through us; on our wine benches we bid a Figo for ten thousand plagues.' Marlowe was the first to write his plays in the iambic pentameter. That is a rhythm with five beats to the line, the same rhythm as the human heart, the natural way to speak English blank verse. In 1587 his *Tamburlaine*, starring Edward Alleyn, took London by storm.

Shakespeare's advantage over the University wits was that he was an actor in residence, always available to write parts to suit the actors in the company and always available to write required changes at rehearsals. He remained an actor throughout his career, acted in nearly all of the plays, and would have watched every rehearsal, every performance. Moreover he understood his audience and knew the need for variation. No other writer of the period mixes comedy and tragedy so frequently. A contemporary wrote: 'Few of the University pen plays well, they smell too much of that writer Ovid and that writer Metamorphosis, and talk too much of Proserpina and Jupiter. Why here's our fellow Shakespeare puts them all down, aye and Ben Jonson too.'

He was constantly revising his plays; the versions in the 1623 Folio would have been strikingly different from the first drafts. He wrote certain parts with certain actors in mind, indeed, as I have previously stated, a great deal of the comic dialogue, which was mostly written in prose, may well have come from William Kempe, Robert Armin and others. They would have suggested better lines and comic business. Actors were not in thrall to the director, as they are today, the buggers didn't even exist. I remember one frozen look I got from Peter Hall when, as a young actor, I suggested what I considered a very sensible piece of business I recalled from a previous production.

Shakespeare wrote swiftly, sometimes ignoring the end of scenes – most of the stage directions were added later by editors. It is solely thanks to his fellow actors, John Hemminge and Henry Condell, the publishers of the First Folio in 1623, that thirty-six of his plays survived. Hundreds if not thousands of plays were written by other writers during this period, but most of them are lost. Thomas Heywood alone wrote more than 200, the majority of which were used to line pie dishes by the Bishop of Gloucester's illiterate cook.

Acting Shakespeare

Actors have fretted how to act Shakespeare from age to age. Hamlet gives us a few clues: *'Speak the speech, I pray you, as I pronounced it to you, trippingly on the tongue: but if you mouth it, às many of your players do, I had as lief the town-crier spoke my lines. Nor do not soar the air too much with your hand, thus; but use all gently: for in the very torrent, tempest, and, as I may say, the whirlwind of passion, you must acquire and beget a temperance that may give it smoothness. O, it offends me to the soul to hear a robustious periwig-pated fellow tear a passion to tatters, to very rags, to split the ears of the groundlings, who, for the most part, are capable of nothing but inexplicable dumb shows and noise…Be not too tame neither, but let your own discretion be your tutor: suit the action to the word, the word to the action; with this special observance, that you o'step not the modesty of nature: for any thing so overdone is from the purpose of playing, whose end, both at the first and now, was and is, to hold, as t'were, the mirror up to nature; to show virtue her own feature, scorn her own image, and the very age and body of the time his form and pressure. Now, this overdone, or come tardily off, though it make the unskilful laugh, cannot but make the judicious grieve; the censure of the which, one must, in your allowance, o'erweigh a whole theatre of others.'*

The early line of great Shakespearean actors stretches from Richard Burbage (1568-1619) via Thomas Betterton (1635-1710), James Quin (1693-1766), to David Garrick (1717-76). Richard Burbage was said 'to wholly transform himself into his part, putting off himself with his clothes, and never (not even in the Tiring-house) assumed himself again until the play was done.' Quin tended to emphasise every word and used little action beyond strutting with one leg before the other. David Garrick used natural gestures and had an unmatched expressiveness of his face. He hated singsong and rant, declaring: 'In the speaking of soliloquies the great art is to give variety. This can only be obtained by a strict regard to the pauses.'

Several ages later Bernard Shaw offered his own solution: 'In playing Shakespeare, play to the lines, through the lines, on the lines, but never between the lines. You would not stick five bars rest into a Beethoven Symphony to pick up your drumsticks; and similarly you must not stop the Shakespeare orchestra for business. Shakespeare at his highest pitch cannot be set aside by any mortal actor, however gifted.'

The esteemed critic, James Agate, wrote at the beginning of the last century: 'All I know about great acting is that it is an experience that leaves its mark for a life-time: something akin to being caught in a thunder storm in a rowing boat with only a pair of bathing drawers between you and the wrath of Heaven. An actor may even leave out the best of his (and Shakespeare's) lines and put in a few out of the wrong play for good measure, provided he's got in him the root of the matter. He may be melodramatic, blustering, brawling, and barnstorming provided he has a fire kindled from the divine spark, towering eloquence and the essential thunder to storm with.'

More recently Sir John Gielgud believed: 'Good verse-speaking, even at its best, can only be projected, so as to hold the audience, by the artificial technical means of tone, emphasis, and modulation.' Lord Olivier, naturally, had a different approach: 'Reach the truth behind the text through the verse – never ignore it, never sing it (natural speech is essential), but work in harmony with the inherent fabric, rhythm, beat, with full awareness of all the poetic values and nuances.'

Dear old Wilfred Lawson had the simplest answer: 'Learn the wordies.'

How do you learn the wordies?

Bernard Shaw again: 'Shakespeare is dead as a doornail. Your only chance of learning him without intolerable effort is to learn him by ear, for his music is unfailing. Never read your part: get someone to speak it at you, over and over again – to urge it on you, hurl it at you, until your mere imitative, echo faculty forces you to jabber it as a street piano forces you to hum a tune that you positively dislike.'

I've always found that constantly repeating the words, walking, driving a car, or even sitting in a bus, is the best way, even if you sometimes attract questioning looks from your fellow passengers. Edmund Kean said Shakespeare was 'stickable' – once you have properly learned his lines they stick. Shakespeare was an actor for more than twenty years, writing for his fellow-actors. He knew what was easy to say or remember. I can vouch for that. I can still recite entire speeches that I learned fifty years ago. But not cues – cues are always difficult. Wendy Toye, a distant cousin, once told me that as a child she played a fairy in *The Dream* at a gala matinee. The incomparable Ellen Terry was making one of her very final appearances as

Titania. Wendy had to hold her hand and squeeze it when it came to her cues.

Printing: Quartos and Folios

Quartos and Folios were simply the names of the size of paper the plays were printed on. The Good Quartos are thought to be the theatre prompt-books, the Bad Quartos are pirated editions, probably written down by a member of the audience or from memory by actors no longer with the company. There were no laws of copyright. As I mentioned previously, the First Folio was edited and published seven years after Shakespeare's death. John Hemminge and Henry Condell collected thirty-six plays – eighteen of which, including *As You Like It, Twelfth Night, Julius Caesar, Macbeth, Coriolanus* and *Antony and Cleopatra*, had never been published before. These masterpieces were saved for the world by humble grammar school-educated actors, not aristocrats or university wits.

Shakespeare's Early Plays

'Some of Shakespeare is still too genuine and beautiful and modern for the public.'
Bernard Shaw

The playwright Richard Greene died in poverty and squalor in the autumn 1592. On his deathbed he wrote, what he called, *A Groatsworth of Wit*, in which he warns his fellow university wits: 'There is an upstart crow, beautified with our feathers, that with his tiger's heart wrapt in a player's hide, supposes that he is well able to bumbast out a blank verse as the best of you: and being an absolute Johannes factotum, is in his own conceit the only Shakescene in a country.' The Duke of York's final defiant speech to Queen Margaret in *Henry VI Part 3*, as she taunts him with a handkerchief stained with his son's blood, contains the line: '*O tiger's heart wrapped in a woman's hide.*' Green thus gives us a clear link to Shakespeare and his first plays, *Henry VI Parts One, Two* and *Three.*

And where I did begin, there shall I end... *Julius Caesar Act V Scene III*

Index